"*Vam-pire!*"

Eromedeus stepped away from the hearth; and as the black dust cleared, his deep-set eyes glowed with a malevolent glare. From his mouth came a sinister hiss.

Cyrodian charged him, sword up. Eromedeus made no move to escape, and again Prince Cyrodian's sword sank into the courtier's body. As Cyrodian shoved it in, he stared into Eromedeus's brilliant eyes, and a chill rippled through him.

"*Demon!*"

He pushed his sword in hilt-deep, so that the crosspiece sank under Eromedeus's ribs; the point scraped the hot wall-stones behind.

No blood . . .

Eromedeus's eyes glowed. "Fool," he whispered, showing his teeth.

Cyrodian went white. He jerked the sword back and forth so that it might rend a gaping crater of a wound in Eromedeus's belly. Yet it was as though he had sunk his steel into an image of clay.

"You—" The giant gasped, and again an iciness bled within him as he stared into those eyes. "You . . . *must . . . die!*"

"I have lived forever and cannot die," the sorcerer whispered to him in his hollow, quiet voice. "Don't you think whole armies have tried to slay me, and failed?"

A low groan fluttered in Cyrodian's throat, then erupted as a hellish howl. Holding onto his sword he threw himself back and staggered, regained his balance, waved his arms, wiped hair out of his face and stared—

Stared . . .

"What . . . *are* you," he breathed, "that you cannot . . . *die?*"

The Fall of the First World by David C. Smith

Published by Pinnacle Books
Book I: THE MASTER OF EVIL
Book II: SORROWING VENGEANCE
Book III: THE PASSING OF THE GODS*

*Forthcoming

THE FALL of the FIRST WORLD

Sorrowing
Vengeance

David C. Smith

PINNACLE BOOKS NEW YORK

For
TERRY,
with love

The verse by Michael Fantina appears in this book through permission of its author.

This is a work of fiction. All the characters and events portrayed in this book are fictional, and any resemblance to real people or incidents is purely coincidental.

THE FALL OF THE FIRST WORLD BOOK II: SORROW-ING VENGEANCE

An original Pinnacle Books edition, published for the first time anywhere.

First printing, September 1983

ISBN: 0-523-41739-X

Can. ISBN: 0-523-43034-5

Cover illustration by Carl Lundgren

Printed in the United States of America

PINNACLE BOOKS, INC.
1430 Broadway
New York, New York 10018
9   8   7   6   5   4   3   2   1

Major Characters in *Sorrowing Vengeance*

In Athadia, the Western Empire, and its Territories:

King ELAD I

Queen SALIA

Lady ORAIN, wife of the banished Cyrodian

Prince GALVUS, son of Cyrodian and Orain

Count ADRED, a young Athadian aristocrat

Lord ABGARTHIS, an adviser to the Athadian Court

OGODIS, the Imbur of Gaegosh and father to Queen Salia

OMOS, friend to Galvus

SOTOS, the palace physician

RHIA, a Suloskai rebel in Bessara

Lord General THOMO, envoy to Salukadian-held Erusabad

Captain THYTAGORAS, commander of Athadian troops garrisoned in Erusabad

Lord SIROM, an Athadian official in Erusabad, acting as envoy to the Salukadians

Lord Colonel VARDORIAN, Acting-governor of Sulos in Kendia

Captain UVARS, of the Athadian Imperial Army, Cavalry

Lord UTHIS, Governor of Bessara

URWUS, a corporal in the First Legion Green, out of Abustad

Lord RHIN, a Councilor on the Congress of Nobility in Athad

Lord FALEN, a Councilor on the Congress of Nobility in Athad

BORS, a working man of Sulos

Governor SULEN, of Abustad

Lord ABADON, Governor of Hilum

SERAFICOS, Inquisitor of the Temple of Bithitu in Hilum

Others in the West:

THAMERON, once a priest, now a sorcerer
ASSIA, a prostitute and camp follower
ASAWAS, a wandering prophet

In Emaria:

King NUTATHARIS, of Emaria
EROMEDEUS, adviser to Nutatharis
CYRODIAN, exiled from Athadia, now a military adviser to
    Nutatharis
Sir JORS, adviser to Nutatharis

The Salukadian Ruling Family, in Erusabad:

HUAGRIM *ko-Ghen*, chief of Salukadia
AGORS, his elder son
NIHIM, his younger son
bin-SUTUS, a court *aihman* to Huagrim *ko-Ghen*

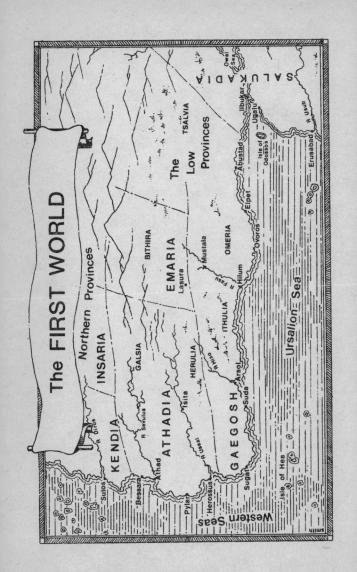

The FIRST WORLD

Northern Provinces

INSARIA

KENDIA

ATHADIA

GALSIA

BITHIRA

EMARIA
Lasura

The Low
Provinces

TSALVIA

SALUKADIA

GAEGOSH

HERULIA

ITHULIA

OMERIA

Ursalion Sea

Western Seas

Isle of Hea

R Dirus
Sulos

Besaara
Aihad

Pylar
Herosusa

Suda

Sugat

Arrol

R Usaz

R Serulus

Tsita

R Hiso

R Fasu

Mustala

Hilum

Ovoros

Elpet

Abustad

Isle of
Odoasso

Ilbukar
Ugalu

R Usub

Erusabad

Owei
Sea

smith

Es Atu

When earth was first sundered from heaven,
When God first rejoiced in the skies,
When evil announced its intention
With death to imprison all life:
      Then man was born from the clouds and rain,
      Man was born for limitless pain,
      Man was born for tears and lies,
      And made to wonder all his days,
      And made to wonder all the days.

—Opening chorus of Sossian's *Of the Lost Earth*

The Events of *The Fall of the First World*: Book I—THE MASTER OF EVIL

Part I: *A Throne of Blood*

Following the death of his father, King Evarris of Athadia, Prince Elad plots to usurp the throne from his mother, Queen Yta. He does this with the tacit approval of powerful members of the High Council and the elder of his two brothers, Prince General Cyrodian—all of whom feel that Elad will prove accommodating to their special interests once he is enthroned. Queen Yta, undecided whether or not to yield the crown to Elad, decides to query the Oracle at Mount Teplis; learning of her intention, Elad and Cyrodian, accompanied by the youngest prince, Dursoris, visit the Oracle before Yta can arrive there. When Elad fails to understand what the Oracle tells him, he forces her at swordpoint to speak more clearly. "You will rule to see everything precious destroyed," she warns him, "every hope ruined. You will rule Athadia and see the world die in anguish." Terrified by the implications of this, Elad is overcome and slays the Oracle; when he and his brothers escape from the holy mountain, Dursoris vows to bring the facts to light in court. Cyrodian therefore murders him. Yta, learning from the Oracle's spirit what has occurred, returns to the capital at Athad, orders Cyrodian imprisoned pursuant to his execution, and commands that Elad take the throne he desires so much: "No greater punishment can I offer."

Part II: *A Lamp in a Storm*

In Erusabad, a city considered holy by both the western Athadian and the eastern Salukadian empires, a young priest named Thameron runs into conflict with the bureaucracy of his temple. The Church of Bithitu is the religious foundation of the

1

Athadian Empire; but it has long ceased to embody the wisdom of its Prophet Bithitu and has, over the course of two thousand years, become a reactionary, stagnant anachronism. Thameron, believing unconditionally in the words of the Prophet, fights hypocrisy in the Church and soon finds himself expelled. Crushed and embittered, he decides to escape Erusabad and takes leave of the only true friend he has—Hapad, a fellow novitiate—and says farewell to the only woman he has ever loved—a young prostitute named Assia.

Part III: *End Without Mercy*

Elad takes the throne and kingship of the empire as his mother leaves to live out her years on Hea Isle, a religious retreat. Unknown to Elad, the angry Cyrodian has plotted with schemers loyal to him to assassinate Yta; meanwhile the Imperial Army, which holds Cyrodian in great respect as one of its own, threatens dissension unless Elad overrules the death sentence and allows his brother exile. The intimidated neophyte king orders Cyrodian removed in chains beyond Athadia's border. Conspirators loyal to Cyrodian chase down Yta's galley and murder her and her crew, then return home to plot the assassination of Elad. They are, however, discovered and executed; but when Elad orders a patrol to return the dismissed Cyrodian home to stand trial for his new crimes, he learns that his brother cannot be found.

Part IV: *The Dispossessed*

Thameron in his journeys experiences life at its most depraved and unspiritual. In despair, and still seeking enlightenment, he turns to a misanthropic sorcerer, Guburus, who promises to help guide Thameron on his mystical quest. But the impatient Thameron, dissatisfied with the lessons Guburus insists he must learn, gives up his spirit to a demonic force he scarcely comprehends. When Guburus realizes what his pupil has done, he tries to fight him, and Thameron slays the elder. Too late, Thameron realizes that he has allowed himself to become the vessel of Evil on earth—the Master of the Hell of Men.

In Athad, a humiliated but wiser Elad sincerely tries to repent for his past errors and applies himself to the task of becoming a good king. But the atmosphere of crime, death and vengeance in

2

the palace lingers. Count Adred, a friend of the slain Dursoris, offers to take Lady Orain, Cyrodian's wife (and secret lover of the good Dursoris), and her son Prince Galvus on a vacation to the uplands, to Sulos in the Province of Kendia. Mother and son readily assent; in Sulos, the three pass a pleasant month and prepare for the holiday weeks (it is the time of the Church's great celebrations) in the home of Adred's friend Count Mantho, a wealthy aristocrat. There is, however, a storm growing in Sulos— indeed, a storm is growing throughout the Athadian empire: the economy, long mismanaged by wealthy businessmen and high-seated plutocrats, has created a situation of rising unemployment, rampant inflation and increasing public anger. Attempts by the working people to change government and business policies have been met with deaf ears; riots and disturbances designed to publicize the working people's plight have been put down by force. Now, in Sulos, the first mass revolt by the workers leads to the assassination of the city governor and many aristocrts (Mantho among them) and several nights of bloodshed and violence.

Part V: *The West Is Dying*

Three generations of expansion by the eastern Salukadian peoples have brought them to the shores of the great Ursalion Sea—and to the doorstep of the wide Athadian empire. Huagrim *ko-Ghen*, Chief of the Salukads, lives in his capital at Ilbukar, where he resides in splendor. But Huagrim is old and realizes that he will die soon; therefore he decides to climax the ever-westward movement of his empire by taking complete control of the east-west shared city of Erusabad. Huagrim's elder son, Agors, supports this move, but the chief's younger son, Nihim, is against it.

Adred, who had left Sulos during the holidays but before the outbreak of violence, is in Mirukad and now hears of the rebellion. Frightened that his friends may be in danger, he tries to board any ship sailing south but learns that the harbor of Sulos is closed until further notice. King Elad, meanwhile, concluding that force must be resisted by even greater force, orders two legions north to the city, where those revolutionaries still alive are executed, their corpses beheaded and their heads piled onto a war galley. The war galley is towed to the capital, where it is displayed and burned as a warning against any further violence on the part of

3

insurrectionists within Athadia. It is a strong-willed but wrong-headed move by a king still uncertain of his crown.

Adred, at last able to get a ship to Sulos, discovers Galvus and Orain still alive and living on the docks. They tell him that Mantho was killed and that they have decided to live incognito and to help the oppressed and dispossessed as Sulos starts to rebuild. Adred, now definitely sympathetic toward the rebels, takes up their fight and sails on to the capital, where he intends to make King Elad face these matters squarely.

Part VI: *Far Paths, Other Shadows*

Cyrodian has taken refuge with King Nutatharis of Emaria, a land-locked nation situated between Athadia and the Lowlands. Nutatharis wishes to expand into the Lowlands, a breadbasket area bordering Salukadia; Huagrim agrees not to interfere with Emarian military movements while at the same time gaining guarantees from Nutatharis that should Salukadia's takeover of Erusabad lead to war with the west, Nutatharis will side with the east.

Count Adred, in the capital, engages in a hot-tempered argument with King Elad, promising him that the revolution will sweep across the empire unless Elad quickly agrees to look into matters of reform. Caught in webs of political intrigue, Elad procrastinates; meanwhile his marriage to Princess Salia, daughter of the Imbur of Gaegosh, approaches. Salia is renowned as the most beautiful woman in the world.

Adred leaves the capital and returns northward; during a stopover in Bessara, he becomes involved with the revolutionary movement there and meets Rhia, the estranged wife of Lord Solok, an aristocratic liberal and rebel sympathizer. Following a demonstration in the city, Solok and many others are arrested, but Adred and Rhia escape and go into hiding.

Part VII: *New Chains*

General Kustos of Emaria, together with his new military adviser, Cyrodian, leads the expedition into the Lowlands. The farmers and villagers of the territory fight fiercely against the sophisticated Emarians and take a heavy toll, while the invading troops are victimized by winter storms. Kustos is severely wounded during one engagement; and when it becomes apparent

4

to Nutatharis that his advance into the Lowlands has stagnated, he orders his army to hold its ground until spring and commands Kustos and Cyrodian back to the capital at Lasura. There, Nutatharis informs Cyrodian that his brother Elad has demanded Cyrodian's return to Athad; but in return for Nutatharis's refusing to submit to Elad's capias, Cyrodian binds himself to the Emarian king by a warrior's pledge—the oldest of oaths. Cyrodian hungers to become general of the Emarian army now that Kustos is dying of his wounds. When he looks in on the ill man one night, he finds the bed-ridden Kustos being harassed by one of Nutatharis's courtiers, Eromedeus. To his shock, Cyrodian learns that Eromedeus is not a man at all, but an undying creature who wishes Kustos to give up his soul for him so that Eromedeus may make his peace with the gods. Kustos dies without agreeing, and Cyrodian wrathfully stabs Eromedeus—and discovers that the man cannot be killed.

The Emarian military maneuvers in the Lowlands create apprehension in the rulers of the Athadian-controlled Province of Omeria. In response, Elad sanctions the disbursement of troops from Elpet and Abustad to guard Omeria's northern border. Among the camp followers is Assia, who left Erusabad after Thameron's departure. Ill, she had traveled with her father to Elpet, where he continued to use her as a prostitute until he was killed in a tavern brawl.

While the Emarians are attacking the Lowlands, Huagrim's soldiers occupy the northern, western-controlled section of Erusabad—an overt act of war. In Athad, members of Council demand that Elad answer this provocation with armed force; but the king, fearful of the Oracle's warning, refuses. So long as trade and pilgrimage rights for Athadian citizens are respected, Elad (who realizes that he had overreacted to the riots in Sulos) decides not to go to war with Salukadia. In Erusabad, Huagrim *ko-Ghen* orders the Temple of Bithitu to be partially dismantled and redone as an eastern pantheon.

Thameron returns to Erusabad intending to confront his mentors in the Temple and finds the city occupied by the eastern military forces. He learns that the Church elders, disgraced, had committed suicide, but finds his old friend Hapad, now living in a ghetto apartment, dying of a fever. When Hapad discovers what Thameron has done, he condemns his friend with his last breath and bemoans the fact that he did not die before learning of Thameron's everlasting damnation.

King Elad, on a winter's day, marries Lady Salia of Gaegosh. As the couple exit the state palace following the ceremony, a revolutionary disguised as one of the Khamar palace guards attacks Elad and stabs him several times before he is overpowered and slain by the king's soldiers.

PROLOGUE

The Lord of Light

When he was in his fortieth year, Omul, a farmer in the plainfields of northern Nisaria, became ill and for two weeks languished between life and death. His wife and daughters, sons and relatives all prayed worriedly for his recovery, and daily people of the farming village where Omul lived visited his hut and inquired after his health. He was a respected man and a hard worker, a good father and husband, held in esteem by all who knew him. When, late in the winter, the crisis at last passed, Omul awakened from his fever to grip his wife's shaking hand and announced to his family: "I have dreamed strange things. I have seen the Truth."

When he was able to leave his bed, Omul spent many days indoors sitting at his table in the hut or watching the village and the world as it occurred outside his windows. Before his illness, he had been a garrulous man, loud and talkative and friendly; now he was very silent. Often, as his recovery slowly progressed, Omul would lapse into short periods of sleep; and his wife was alarmed when, as her husband napped, he grunted and whispered in low, garbled words that could not be understood. When he awoke from these sleeps, his wife would ask Omul what he had dreamed. At first he could not tell her what he had seen because, as vivid as the impressions had been, it was difficult for the farmer to recall them when awake.

His sons, large men like their father, took care to maintain the house, the barn and the livestock; and whenever they were able to do so, Omul's sons-in-law helped as well. His daughters, who lived in huts close by Omul's, helped their mother in caring for their father during his recovery. Omul ate well but still lapsed into irregular short sleeps. When this happened, his wife or his daughters would lean close and try to understand what he was whispering. As the days passed, Omul's sleeping voice became stronger and clearer, and his wife and daughters became frightened by what they heard.

Perhaps a month after his illness, Omul, now well but still subject to the periods of brief sleep, was sitting on a stool outside his farmhouse whittling a length of cherry wood. He was dressed warmly against a chill, but already winter was passing and the first hints of spring were in the air. Birds chirped, green buds showed on the trees, and the gray clouds of winter had given way to blue stretches of sky that met wide empty fields at the far horizon. As Omul watched his sons go about their work in the small barn across from his hut, a village elder, Mour, accompanied by half a dozen other old men, approached Omul to ask how he was feeling.

Omul regarded Mour and, with sad eyes and a heavy voice, warned him: "I have had another dream and this one was very clear. Please—see to your wife."

Mour did not understand what Omul meant, but apprehension filled him. With the others he hurried through the village to see what might be happening; yet as he went, his oldest daughter ran sobbing toward him and met the village elder in the middle of a path to tell him that his wife had suddenly died. She had found her mother slumped against the well, an empty water bucket still in her hands.

That night Mour and the other elders of the village spoke privately with Omul. Where did his dreams come from? What had happened to him? He was a good man; did these strange dreams always betoken evil?

"Why do you think death is evil?" Omul replied to them. Gone forever was the hearty voice and the boisterous laugh. This new Omul, awakened from his fever, spoke quietly, and there was a constant light in his eyes, an interior light. "I did not warn you of this thing, Mour, so that you might become angry with me or fear me. When I awakened from my long sleep, from my illness, a new life filled me. I cannot explain it to you. But you must trust me. I see . . . many things, all things. The real things that we hold in our hands, these objects and tools—these are not actual things at all. They are only . . . symbols. They are useful, but they are not the Truth. You do not understand? I can only tell you what I feel. You see the sky? Is it the real sky? There are many other skies behind it, all around it. You see yourself reflected in a mirror or in a pool, but there are many other yous, and all are within you. It is hard to explain. . . . But I see these things, sometimes clearly, sometimes very uncertainly. I am not a wise man, Mour. I am a farmer. But I am a good man. I can only decide that God, On, has given me this gift for some purpose. Why else should this happen to me?"

Mour and the elders were bewildered. They could not punish Omul and they did not wish to. They knew stories of the traveling *ikbusa'i*—religious prophets—but Omul was not an *ikbusa*. They could only hope that this "gift" of their friend's would, in time, weaken and go away.

But it did not weaken. It grew stronger and clearer, and Omul felt himself gaining control of it. Three days after the death of Mour's wife, Omul was walking with his oldest son in a forest beyond the village. Omul stopped short and pointed to a great oak tree—the oldest in the region. "The Old Man," Omul warned his son, "will soon die."

The next day an early spring thunderstorm swept across the plains and flooded the village; a lightning bolt struck the Old Man and, shortly, the great oak tree and a whole section of forest caught fire. It burned all night until it was finally suffocated by the heavy rains in the early morning.

Omul's son told no one of his father's prediction. But only a few days after this, Omul was walking through the village and speaking with Mour and some other men when he suddenly lifted his head and seemed to sense something. "Listen. . . . Do you hear it?"

Mour and the men were perplexed. "I cannot hear anything, my friend. What is it?"

"It is the sound of . . . great breathing. As if the earth were . . . breathing . . ."

In just a few moments the animals of the village began to act strangely. Dogs barked and yelped and hid themselves beneath tables, under huts. Horses nickered and whinnied in their stalls, and from far out in the fields came the lowing of disturbed cattle. Birds, just returned for the spring warmth, took to the air in swarms and raised a deafening chorus of chirps and shrills.

But just as suddenly as the animals had begun to act absurdly, they quieted. The shivering dogs crawled out from beneath the huts and the birds, squealing, descended again to their nests.

Mour was very agitated. "Omul, Omul! What is this? What did you hear? What is happening? My friend, what did you hear?"

Omul, as though entranced, was staring up at the blue sky still seeming to listen to some distant sound. "I heard . . ." he whispered, "the earth . . . moving. The earth—it is changing. . . ."

The month of Oloros, the River, passed into Grem, the Wolf, and an early spring took hold of the land. The floods during those

9

weeks were full and sweeping, irrigating the plains for good planting, yet not inundating the village. Messengers from other villages nearby rode to Mour's to begin planning the great Spring Feast, when all the farming people in the region gathered to celebrate the passing of winter and the rebirth of a fruitful earth. As they joined to eat bread and drink wine and ceremoniously plant the first of the year's new crops, no one spoke of Omul's strange gift.

Omul and his oldest son were walking one warm afternoon in a portion of his fields when the farmer stopped and held up a hand. His son had come to know this gesture.

"What is it, Father?"

"Sem . . . toward the end of summer, when all this"—he indicated the fields—"is nearly lost in the drought, you will find water here."

"A drought?"

"It comes. Do not fear it, but prepare for it. One provides. But when the drought is nearly over and you fear that all will be lost, come here, to this place—remember it, now—and dig down until you find water. Water enough for the entire village, and more to spare for other villages." He squinted beneath the warm sun and watched Sem carefully. "Do you understand?"

"Yes, Father. . . ."

"Will you do this?"

"Yes, Father. But—won't you be here to lead me to this place again?"

Omul did not answer him but walked on alone, stepping slowly, hands behind his back.

A few days before the gathering of the villages in celebration, Omul was again alone in the fields when an overpowering lassitude gripped him. He sank to his knees. He had not slept the strange, short sleep in a long while, and he was surprised now to feel it possessing him. But he gave himself over to it and stretched out on the warm, damp soil.

The Voice came to him, and as he listened to it, Omul witnessed exceptional visions from deep in his mind.

He saw a great blazing throne drenched in blood.

He saw an Oracle woman, masked and dressed in white, beheaded by a decorated sword.

He saw plagues descending upon the land—plagues of destruction sweeping across rivers and over mountains, choking cities and ruining villages.

He saw a great war. He saw men screaming and shrieking and dying, he smelled the blood, he listened to the screams. Walls toppled, rivers rose and smashed cities with fist-like flood waters, lightning danced and ripped across the skies, fires touched the stars, and still men battled, still swords and axes chopped and struck, and blood was everywhere, screams—everywhere.

He saw an evil creature, contorted but burning brightly, hidden by skins of shadows, whispering and posturing upon a throne. But still this evil creature was destined by On, and Omul (in his dream) felt no fear toward this creature, but only sympathy and understanding.

And he saw a world draped in sunlight, he saw great rivers and oceans, he saw green forests and green fields, he saw men and women raising voices in praise of On, he saw them singing in choruses of beauty and solemnity.

When he awakened from this vision, Omul was trembling greatly. He sat up and looked at the sky, looked down at the earth. Sweat dripped from his face and forehead, as though his fever had returned. He dug his fingers into the sweet wet soil, pushed his hands down into the earth and drew them up, brown-stained. He stared at his hands, watched as innocent bits of soil dropped from his dark fingers. He imagined that they were lives, struggling to hold onto him, but falling back at last to the bruised earth. He looked up at the sky. He looked north.

It waits.

But the time was not yet.

On . . .

His was the Voice of On, the Voice of the one true god.

The evil . . .

But the evil was necessary.

Omul dropped his head upon his chest and sobbed, cried openly like a child. Tears fell from his face and struck the earth, struck his shirt and breeches. Tears, like living things, innocent bits of life struggling to hold onto him and remain part of him, but falling at last to the bruised earth.

When the day began to darken with twilight, Omul stood up, wiped dried earth from his hands, stared again to the north. Thunder boomed, very distantly, although the sky above him was bright with sunshine, unclouded. A bird flew high beyond him, wheeled and chirruped, disappeared into the north.

Omul began to walk back toward the village.

* * *

11

He had washed himself and put on a clean pair of breeches and a vest, and over these a long robe. His boots were of cowhide tied with leather thongs, crafted just this past winter. He took up in one hand his wide-brimmed hat, to protect his face from the sun. In his other hand he held a long walking staff.

When Omul stepped out from his sleeping room, his wife and his sons and daughters were waiting for him, standing around the table. Soup was cooking in a kettle on the hearth; one of his grandchildren was whining and crying; its mother picked it up from the floor and rocked it gently, bared her left breast to nurse it. The rooms were darkening and candles had been lit against the falling night. Outside, fires had been built and most of the village was sitting with visitors from other villages. There were sounds of laughter and happy voices.

Omul stepped to his wife. She stared into his eyes, while tears lined the lashes of her own eyes. Omul said to her:

"Wife, On provides. God will always provide enough for you and- for my family. You will never want for what is needed. Always eat a little less than half of what you have. Always drink a little less than half. You will live, and you will prosper with good things. Believe that On is with you. Believe that I love you always, and that I am with you."

His wife sobbed and began to cry; Omul took her in his arms and held her close to him for a long while, kissed her, held her close again.

Then he hugged his sons, each in turn, and kissed them, told them to keep their faith in On and laugh in the face of despair and to worship God when times seemed harsh. He kissed each of his daughters and hugged them, and hugged and kissed his sons-in-law and all of his grandchildren.

He kissed his wife a last time, then went out the door and did not look back. He did not carry any food with him, for he knew that On would provide. As the noises of the happy village dwindled behind him, Omul followed a path away from the people he had lived with all his years and began his long route down to the south, to larger villages, to towns, to the cities of the empire.

When, after a few days, he came to the first of these villages, the people invited him inside their homes, prepared food for him, inquired as to what news he had learned and asked him his name.

He told them, "Call me Asawas, for I am gifted with new sight, and I have come to you to foretell great things. . . ."

12

PART I

An Attack of Conscience

1.

"I—I don't like having to do this," the young woman said.

The man behind the table did not answer her, did not look up.

"I feel strange having to—do it this way. . . ."

The man at the table examined the paper before him, scribbled some figures on a spare piece of parchment to one side. He paused once to dip his reed pen in a small ink gourd, then continued scratching.

The young woman watched him with nervous intensity, then turned her head a bit to glance at the lean fellow behind the counter all the way on the other side of the tavern. He was staring at her. He was the only other person in the room. She shot a hasty look toward the front door of the place: barred and locked. She coughed slightly against a nervous tickle in her throat, turned again toward the man at the table.

He was staring at her. His round fat face was damp with perspiration, his tousled beard looked like an unkempt nest. He lifted a hand, fingered one eye sleepily, indicated the sheets before him with the end of his pen.

"I can do it for you," he told her, "but this is a rough one. It'll cost you three in short gold."

Astonished, she stared at him. "I—I haven't got—"

He interrupted her impatiently. "To forge this, I've got to get hold of some important people."

"Can't you just—"

"Change the numbers?" He grinned mirthlessly at her. "They're being more careful about these things nowadays. Everybody's poor," he told her. "Everybody's out of work. Everybody needs government money. It's tough enough when you're trying to make a real claim; they think you're lying, anyway. To forge something good enough so it'll pass . . ." He shrugged. "Half the things they send back to the capital, too. It may take you six months, may take a year, young lady, before you see anything."

13

"A *year*? I can't wait a *year*! My mother can't—" She stopped then. She knew she couldn't expect any sympathy from this man; probably he spoke to a hundred like her every day. It was a business for him. Her heart sank.

She heard a noise at the back of the tavern, and she became even more apprehensive. She had never done anything illegal before and she didn't want to do this now. She looked down a narrow hallway directly behind the fat man and saw two figures entering.

The fat man bent around, recognized them and returned to the matter at hand.

They were young men. As they came into the tavern proper, the young woman realized that she had seen the tall one several times along the docks. He was perhaps sixteen or seventeen, but he had the bearing and attitude of an aristocrat. He was handsome, light-haired and dressed in worn clothes that nevertheless had been cared for. His companion was perhaps the same age, a head shorter and of slimmer build.

They stepped up to the counter and the one with aristocratic bearing spoke in a very low voice to the housekeeper. "Did our merchandise arrive?"

A nod.

"How many crates?"

He held up five fingers.

"All right. We'll need them immediately. I want them carted over to the warehouse today. And—listen to me. I don't want Hamus taking them over there. I don't trust him. He's opening them up to 'inspect' them so he can sell a little on the side. If you use him one more time, I'll go elsewhere. You understand?" He spoke firmly, resolutely; though young, he appeared used to having authority.

"I—understand. . . . I think Hamus has sailed out, anyway."

"Whether he has or hasn't— Use that older fellow; he knows what he's doing."

"All right, I will."

Now the aristocrat flipped back his cloak and from his belt undid a heavy purse; alongside it hung a long knife, sheathed in leather. He opened the purse, counted out sixteen in long gold and twenty in silver. The housekeeper watched him carefully. When the purse was closed and returned to the belt, his lean hand stretched across the counter and covered the coins, then pulled back to drop them into his other hand.

14

The aristocrat turned and lent an eye to the young woman.

She had watched it all. He knew it, and yet it didn't seem to bother him. She stared at him for a long moment, until the fat man at the table coughed loudly enough to draw her attention. Nervous, she scrutinized him, saw that nothing had changed in those few moments and reached out for her paper.

"Three in gold," he reminded her.

"I—I can't possibly . . ."

"Pay me a little at a time."

"No." Her lips seemed to hover between a frown and a sneer. "No, thank—" She looked up again as the aristocrat and his companion stepped across the floor. The aristocrat met her eyes; then he glanced at the fat man.

"Why don't you try being a pleasant human being for a change?" he asked in a familiar, slightly contemptous tone.

"Leave me alone." The fat man faced him. "I'm a businessman, I can't—"

"Businessmen got us into this." The aristocrat picked up the paper the young woman had brought; he scanned it quickly. "What is this? Her father's work record? Name of the Prophet! Just have him start in his office five years earlier!" He looked at the woman. "You've got to present this to get your government claim, don't you?"

She nodded quickly. "It's—I'm not sure what to do. A girl I know, she told me I could come here, talk to—" She nodded. "My father died just a week before the offices would grant his claim. He worked forty years! They won't pay my mother anything at all unless we can prove that he died—"

"That he died in time," the aristocrat finished, shaking his head in disgust. "They're doing it to everyone; it's just an excuse for the government to hold onto as much money as it can." To the fat man he growled: "Three *mises* for a simple claims form! What're you charging now for land leases?"

"I told you, I'm a businessman!"

The young woman saw that he was extremely uncomfortable in the presence of this aristocratic young man. It was incredible. This coarse, middle-aged man, no more than a dockhand who was profiteering because he knew certain people in the bureaucracy—capitalizing on the misfortunes of others—upset in the presence of a boy half his age!

The aristocrat returned the woman's paper to the fat man, undid his purse and pulled out three in long gold, dropped the coins on the table. "That's twice what you're asking. Are you listening? One lousy *mis* is too much for something like this. If ten people come to you today wanting work records corrected and sealed, you do it. And you're still making out well. Ten simple forgeries for a month's wage!"

The fat man, who had been watching everything except the young man's face, now confronted him. "I don't care what you think of me," he grunted. "You seem to have enough money, but I have to make a living! You think I like being a criminal?"

"You're no criminal. We're not criminals—none of us are. You just make sure that when she comes back tomorrow morning, her business is taken care of. I know you'll do that."

The fat man moved his head, acknowledging him.

The aristocrat turned to the young woman. "You'll have more trouble with the government offices than you will with him. I'm afraid they'd prefer you to starve to death before issuing you any assistance."

She swallowed heavily, raised a trembling hand. "Thank you. . . ."

"Not at all."

"I—don't know what to say. . . ."

"If this one"—a nudge—"doesn't have your paper for you tomorrow, you talk to me about it. Ask for me on the docks. People know who I am."

"All right."

He said no more, then, but turned on his heel and quickly left the tavern, exiting down the hallway. His young companion followed him.

It took the young woman a few moments to realize that she, too, no longer had any business there. She whispered to the forger, "And—thank you. . . ."

"Uh-huh."

She shot a quick look of apprehension to the man behind the counter, then hurried down the back hallway.

Silence.

"I don't care what you say," the housekeeper sniffed, tapping his fingers on the countertop. "That young buck's somebody important."

"He certainly seems to think so."

"No . . . no . . . he's connected."

The chair squeaked as the fat man turned toward him. "If you're so interested, then why don't you ask some questions? Find out who he is."

16

"I don't know. . . ." He jangled the coins he'd been given. "I need my little extra. You need it, too."

"Gods! You'd think he was the government himself! Passing around money like that!"

"Like I said—" The lean man drummed his fingers on the wood, considered the idea, then thought it better to head into the back room to see about the five crates.

Outside, a light snow was falling. The young woman nearly slipped as she hurried. A wind was blowing in off the ocean, and the buildings were set far apart, so the streets were covered with ice.

They were just ahead of her, walking quickly despite all that. She called out—

"Please! I want to—thank you!"

They paused, turned. The young aristocrat had a tired look on his face.

"Please. . . ." She breathed clouds of steam as she came up to them. "I truly want to thank you. I don't know what I would've done if you hadn't been there!"

His eyes were deep and thoughtful, his expression one of sympathetic concern. But he was obviously very tired.

"You've thanked me already," he reminded her. "Just be certain that you're back there tomorrow. And get that started with the social assistance office immediately. They'll take their time clearing it; it may be a while before you—what? You and your mother?"

"Yes."

"Before you see anything. You'll have to get by."

"I'm sure we can now that we know something's going to be done." She was very happy.

"Just . . ." He smiled at her, glanced behind her. "People like him—we're always going to have them. Weak. If you can't work with them, work around them. It's just too bad it has to be done this way in the first place."

"I know. . . ." She pulled her thin coat more tightly about her.

"You'd better get indoors. Get warm."

"Yes." She turned, then waited a moment. "You're not . . . revolutionaries, are you?"

"In a way we are, yes."

"But you're not—I mean—"

17

"Suloskai? No. We're not reds, don't worry about that. We're just trying to help."

"I only . . ." She nodded again and hurried back down the street.

The two of them continued on, heading down toward the docks and their apartment.

"Galvus?"

"Yes."

"They always assume that, don't they?"

"What do you expect?" He wiped a hand through his hair, brushed away melted snow. "But as long as they don't know *who* I am, I can continue playing the prophet. Turning straw into honey . . ."

When they came to the apartment house, Galvus nearly fell going up the outer steps. There was no rail, and he had to lean on his friend for support. As they made their way in and up the shadowy, cold stairwell to the third floor:

"Omos, I'm exhausted. I was up all night—"

"I know."

"I'm going to get some sleep. I want to stay with mother, anyway. Can you go down to the warehouse for me? This afternoon? Just to make certain that the crates haven't been tampered with."

"Certainly, Galvus. I can do that."

"Then, tomorrow, I'll see about getting them to Dars so he can distribute everything. We did request more wool and cloth this time, didn't we?"

"Yes, a crateful of each."

"Good, good. Winter's not over yet, they'll need to make some clothes. . . ."

On the third floor they quietly opened the door to their apartment and stepped in. They removed their coats, shook the snow from them and hung them up on pegs in the wall. Galvus stepped to the fire for a moment to warm his hands. The fire was burning well, but from the broken seams around it, the wind was whistling into the room.

"Gods, this building must be two hundred years old," Galvus commented.

While Omos moved to warm some wine, Galvus crossed the floor and opened the door to his mother's room. He peeked inside and saw that she was asleep. That was good; she'd been working diligently this past week, sewing clothes for distribution on the

18

northside. And ever since she and Galvus had learned of the assassination attempt on Elad . . .

Galvus quietly closed the door. He couldn't blame her. People dealt with serious matters in extremely personal ways. For Orain, it was sleep; and perhaps when she slept, she actually was able to escape, to dream of how things once had been, or to remove private guilts or resolve conflicts within herself. . . .

While he himself worked the harder at doing what he felt he must do.

"Is she all right?" Omos asked him.

"Sleeping." Galvus sat down at the table in the middle of the room and looked at the sheets of paper on which he had scrawled all night long. Figures . . . maps of Sulos with pockets of the most needy indicated in red ink . . .

Omos poured wine from a ladle into a ceramic cup, walked the cup to Galvus and set it on the table.

Galvus, dark-eyed and slumped in his chair, gripped Omos's hand in thanks, lifted it to his lips, then kissed his friend.

"Drink your wine," Omos said, "then get some sleep. Are you expecting anyone today?"

"Mevus might stop by for some more patched clothes. She'll just have to wait."

Omos fingered the sheets on the table—not only the maps and the figurings, but the attempts at a letter. "Be careful, Galvus. Please."

"I know, I know. . . ." He sighed, yawned and sipped his wine.

Omos returned to the fire to pour for himself, and Galvus stared heavy-eyed at the several attempts he had made last night to write to Elad, to an Elad who might be dead or dying, or on his deathbed, or—The rumors that came into Sulos were unsubstantiated, as of yet.

My dear uncle, My lord, Elad—I am writing this because I want you to know why and understand why Mother and I have stayed in Sulos with the people. When we heard that an attempt had been made on your life, we were grieved, and now that we are given to understand that our king is recuperating . . . Lord Abgarthis—I write to you in confidence. . . .

His head slipped forward, Galvus closed his eyes and held his hands to his face. He nearly knocked over his wine. He was exhausted, he did not know what to say, and when tears began to creep down his cheeks, he felt that he must hide them—hide his tears from Omos, who loved him, just as he must hide his identity from the people of the streets who relied upon him so greatly for their survival. . . .

2.

"Are you going?" Adred asked Rhia.

"I'm not sure. . . ." She didn't look at him but stared at the ceiling.

"It could be dangerous," he cautioned her.

She gurgled low in her throat. "For us, everything's dangerous." She looked at him, tilting her head on the pillow. "You could still get away, if you want to."

"I know that."

"They don't know you."

"Rhia . . ."

"You've been thinking about it, haven't you?"

He didn't answer her so she suspected that she was right. After a moment Adred told her: "I don't want to throw my life away. I don't mind fighting for things, for good things. There's nothing more important than that. But if I just throw my life away, what good does that do?"

Rhia rolled over on her side, propped her head on one hand and ran her other hand over Adred's chest. She played with the hair around his nipples and said quietly: "You're very important to me, Adred. You know that. You do know that, don't you? But—out there—you're just another body in the crowd. But that's important, too. Right now we need crowds. If we're going to change— well, everything—we *need* crowds of people, streets full of people."

"So they can be slaughtered?" he grunted.

She stared at him intently. "You're worried about Elad, aren't you?"

"Yes. . . ."

"If he dies, then it means—"

"It means," he insisted, looking into her eyes, "that the country is in a civil war. That's what it means. And anything we've tried to accomplish—" His voice hardened, betraying his anxiety. "It doesn't mean that we've succeeded, it doesn't mean that the revolution has done anything. All it means is that some fool with a knife killed the king. Even if he weren't Suloskai, we'd still be blamed for it. I'm not a murderer, and neither are you. What good does that do? But we're blamed for it, we might as well be a bunch of assassins! We had plans, ideas . . . but now we're just a gang of assassins!"

"We don't know that Elad is dead."

"And if he's *not*," Adred continued, "then it's just as bad. At least before we were able to talk to him. *I* could talk to him. Even if he intended to do nothing, at least I could talk to him. We had *time*. Now we don't even have that. You think the massacre in Sulos was bad? What do you think Elad's going to do now? *If* he's alive . . . Gods!" He sat up, pulled up his knees and leaned on his arms. He glanced across the room at the closed window shutters; blue light seeped through. Adred shivered.

"You're a revolutionary," Rhia reminded him sternly.

"This isn't a . . . revolution. It's an orgy. Where are the thinking people? Where's the dialogue, the planning, the substance? Maybe Elad's right about—"

"Oh, stop it!" Rhia snapped at him angrily. "Elad's not right and you know it! The government isn't right! What's happened to you?"

Immediately he felt ashamed; he'd betrayed her, betrayed the ideals he'd fought for so ardently. What was the matter with him? Why was he so anxious, so doubtful?

"You know what your problem really is?" Rhia asked him.

"You tell me."

"You think that people are basically rational. You think that the belly in people comes to the surface only once in a while, in the middle of a crisis. But you think that even in irrational situations, most people will still act rationally. And you're wrong, Adred. I'm afraid you're wrong."

He smiled weakly. "Am I?"

"I wish you weren't, but you are. Solok felt the same way. Oh, gods!" She tried to laugh then, but it came out as a throaty sob. "They haven't even . . . executed him yet, and I'm talking about him as if he were dead!"

Adred reached out a hand and stroked her hair.

Rhia quickly kissed his hand and continued: "But people aren't rational, Adred. In our best moments, when we have full stomachs and money and when we're warm and we have our families—even then, we're not rational, not all of us. But now?

21

When we've got the kind of madness in this country that we have? Look at it! Yesterday I heard that some old woman was killed on the street by three boys. People saw it from their windows; they didn't try to help her. They just killed her. They ran away. An old woman. Probably just barely able to survive from day to day, and here come three—well, boys—and they murder her. That isn't rational. Adred . . ."

"Then why are you fighting for a revolution anyway if you're so cynical? If you think people aren't worth it?"

"I didn't say that. People are worth it." She swallowed a deep breath, looked at him, looked past him at—Shadows . . . a door . . . a table . . . "We have to believe in something," she whispered. "We have to commit ourselves to something. I do, anyway." Not saying anything more, she lay back on the bed and stared at the ceiling.

Adred slid under the covers, moved one arm across her belly. Her skin was warm; he felt her belly pulsing beneath his arm.

"Rhia," he asked her in a low voice, "do you love me?"

"Does it matter?"

He was sincere. "I don't know if it does or— Do you *love* me?"

She turned her head, studied his face, his eyes, his beard, his long hair. "No," she told him. "Does it matter?"

"I don't think so."

"You want the truth, don't you?"

"Absolutely."

"No, then. I don't love you." She grinned slyly, moved one arm under the covers, reached between his legs and held him in her hand as if he were a bag full of coins. "I like you," she reassured him. "And there are, uh, certain advantages . . . attributes. . . ." Chuckling, she lay back.

Adrid fingered her long, red hair. "It seems to me," he whispered seriously, "that now isn't the time for people to be deeply in love."

"There you go being rational again," Rhia smiled. "Sometimes people can't help it. What we need now are . . . people who *are* desperately in love. With everything."

"That's asking a lot."

"You"—she poked a finger in his chest—"wouldn't know true love if it hit you between the eyes."

"Uh-huh."

"Adred has three emotions," Rhia grinned. "He's got lust, he's got worry—"

"That's not an emotion."

"You've got that one real well. Might as well be. And you've got—"

"Lustful worrying."

She laughed out loud.

"Worrying lust?"

They studied each other's faces. Tousled hair, glossy skin, damp lips. In bed on a cold late winter morning, while crowds gathered in the streets outside.

Adred pushed closer and tightened his arms around Rhia's waist, and she snuggled against him. He lowered his mouth to hers, kissed her, moved his tongue around her open lips. Her legs tangled with his, and the feel of her legs, hidden in the warm shadows beneath the bed covers (warm shadows like secret hidden thoughts) excited Adred as much as looking into her eyes did, as much as feeling her mouth on his did.

While crowds gathered in the streets outside.

Solok was led to the executioner's block early in the afternoon, his arms chained behind his back. He was dressed only in a thin pair of cotton pants and a cotton shirt; both were bloodstained for they had been worn countless times before by other criminals taken to their deaths, and they would be used again. Solok was made to stand erect upon the stage that had been built in the center of Oru Square; behind him stood his fellow revolutionaries. All of them betrayed wounds and bruises on their faces, arms and bare feet from the beatings that had taken place in their cells.

But not one of them had betrayed fellow seditionists.

Crowds had quickly gathered in the square as soon as the execution platform was erected, and now that Solok and the thirty behind him were made to face the public, the crowds swelled into a noisy and angry mob that was held back from the stage by ropes and a cordon of mounted guards. A few rocks and old vegetables were thrown, taunts and screams rose into the air, and clouds of steam lifted like fog into the cold air.

Lord Uthis of Bessara, as he watched these crowds from the balcony of his city palace, sensed that their displays were half-hearted, insincere. Some of them were venting rage and frustration, true; but a crowd such as this should be bloodthirsty, should be nearly out of control. And they were not.

Their sentiments, Uthis realized, were almost entirely with Lord Solok and the revolutionaries.

He motioned to a soldier on the balcony and the man stepped up quickly and saluted.

"Order the executions begun immediately," Uthis told him. "Sound the horn now. I don't want that crowd turning against us."

His man saluted again and pivoted on his heel, left the balcony and entered the palace. Just inside, he gave orders to a young corporal, who followed Uthis's guard out onto the balcony; the corporal took a stance, sucked in a breath, brought his horn to his mouth and blew a strident wail.

The crowd looked up at the palace; a tidal roar of noise lifted.

Solok, gray hair and beard blowing in the breeze, refused to look at Uthis, however. He held his gaze straight before him, his eyes searching the mob. . . .

The soldiers on the platform beside him now grabbed Solok roughly and pulled him back, walked him to the executioner's block, forced him to kneel. The block was a heavy square of oak with a notch in its center to accommodate the neck. Carved into the wood was the state seal of Athadia; long ago it had become encrusted with dried blood so that now part of the lion and crown, and half the words, were completely obscured. A pair of large hands gripped Solok's shoulders and bent him down, forced his throat into the wide, shallow notch.

"If you move," a voice behind the hands promised, "we'll tie you there. Make it easy on yourself."

Solok said nothing. He knew that occasionally, when the throne decided to show leniency to a prisoner, it was customary for the executioner or an assistant to snap the prisoner's neck before lowering the axe. When done correctly, the neck was neatly broken. Sometimes, however, the neck was not broken but merely twisted; immense pain resulted, and then the prisoner prayed devoutly for the axe to fall, fall, end it. . . .

Solok was left to wait. No leniency. The sound of the crowd around him was like the ocean moving toward a shore. He kept his eyes closed, then opened them for a moment. He saw beneath him the wide wooden chest, its boards deeply grained and stained a dark brown. This was where the head dropped. . . .

How many others, Solok wondered, have stared at those designs in the grain and were wondering about them when the axe took them by surprise?

Another swell of noise rose from the mob as the axe-man took the steps to the platform. His heavy boots rocked the platform; Solok felt it trembling with his weight. From farther behind, one of the other prisoners began to sob.

24

The heavy boots came close; Solok felt the axe-man's cold shadow fall upon him.

Tension grew as the crowds became quiet.

He heard more movement behind him as Lord Uthis's appointee unrolled a scroll and read aloud: "*Kale Athadis im Porvo!* For the high crime of treason against the empire, for the felonious crimes of aiding, abetting and harboring traitors to the empire, and for the felonious crime of murdering a military officer of this state, you, Lord Solok dos Irur edos Samia of Bessara, a citizen of the Athadian Empire, are hereby condemned to death and ordered executed in the name of the throne! And may the gods have mercy on you!"

The anxious crowds whispered, breathed.

"Executioner, the throne orders you to execute the prisoner."

Heavy bootsteps.

Solok heard the sound of the axe-man's clothes as the weapon was lifted. He swallowed thickly, his throat struggling against the coarse wood, stared into the wooden box and closed his eyes. . . .

A roar exploded from the mob, loud and angry voices, followed by shrieks, more screams. Horses galloped, men and women were yelling, bodies shoving.

Solok realized that something had gone wrong. He opened his eyes, started to move his head and heard someone on the platform say that—

Rhia had gone alone to Oru Square; Adred had no desire to fight the crowds for the privilege of seeing men he respected beheaded. Rhia had taken care to rub black oil and kohol into her hair—she did this whenever she went out for her own red hair was much too conspicuous—and she had dressed as she did whenever she went into the streets. She had a long skirt that she had slit up one side, baring her right leg to the thigh; this provided her quick access to the dagger that she belted to that leg. She wore a cotton tunic and a leather vest, and over this her heavy coat. If anyone should surprise her or threaten her, Rhia could jump aside—the coat would fly open—and she could have her hand on her dagger within a heartbeat.

Adred was dressed and sitting at a table by the window. He had fired only one lamp, and this was before him. He had gone without any breakfast or lunch (he was too nervous to eat), but he was sipping a cup of hot tea and reading some revolutionary tracts.

He was surprised when Rhia came through the door only a short time after she had gone. The hood of her coat was hardly touched by the wet snow.

"What is it?" He pushed the papers aside, stood up and went to her.

She was trembling, and not from the cold. Adred helped her remove her coat.

"Rhia?"

"They—they've executed Solok. But the rest of them—they had to take them back to the prison. More of them, Adred! I didn't even get to the square! People were running down the streets everywhere! We tried to stop the executions!"

"Suloskai?"

"Yes!" Fire lit her eyes as Rhia bared her teeth in a grim smile. "They were too late to save Solok, but . . . Adred, they ran right into the square with weapons! Some of them had horses! One of them almost killed Uthis with an arrow! He was up on the balcony and the arrow flew right past him! Damn! It almost got him through the heart!"

Adred moved away from her and sat down on the bed. "Do you know what this means?"

"Yes, yes! *Yes!*" Rhia answered. "We're fighting back, Adred! We're *fighting back!*"

"We're not organized well enough to fight back," he told her. "We're fighting back, Rhia, but— It'll mean another Sulos. That's all it will mean."

"Not this time, Adred! Not now!" She walked jauntily to the fireplace, lifted the small kettle of tea from the hot brick shelf and poured herself a cupful. "We're going to win, Adred! The harder they push us—the more they fight us . . . the harder we fight back!"

He shook his head wearily; convinced, he promised her in a dull voice: "We can't reduce it to this level, Rhia. We can't. It's got to be more than this. We've got to become organized, and not just to—have the streets run with blood. . . ."

3.

And still more royal blood. Sotos, the court physician, was becoming disgusted at having his bandages habitually stained with royal blood. He undid the last of the wrappings and yanked the linen a little where it clung to the stitches in Elad's side.

The king grunted, watching him.

Sotos dropped the bandage into a box and asked his young pupil to come ahead with the water bowl. And he ordered a woman servant hovering over Elad on the other side of the bed: "Move that light nearer. The oil lamp! That's right. . . . I want to see what we have here."

Elad made a face and winced as the physician's long fingers poked and pulled around the wound.

"You're very fortunate," the old man remarked. He'd said it every time he'd checked Elad's condition and redressed his wounds, three times a day for the past three weeks. "Very fortunate. Amu, bring the bowl here."

The young fellow leaned close; Sotos dipped a fresh cloth into the warm water, dabbed along Elad's side to clean away seeping blood.

"You're going to feel this for a long time," Sotos warned his king. "Don't plan on any horseback riding until the middle of spring, at least."

"*Spring*?"

"You heard me. You've got to give these muscles time to repair. Your other two wounds will heal quickly: flesh cuts. But this . . . You're lucky he didn't get you in the heart or lung. Just missed your right lung as it is. He knew what he was doing."

"Did he?"

"Speaking from a medical perspective, of course," Sotos replied dryly. "All right." He motioned to Amu. "Put some salve on this and let's see what you've learned about wrapping. Get started." The physician stepped away and threw his hands behind his back. "Did you walk some this afternoon, Elad?"

"Yes."

"From the looks of that wound, you were trying to race ten laps around the arena! Listen to me! If you'd just stayed in this bed this week and rested, you'd be walking around now! The more strain

27

you put on this, getting up and pacing back and forth and throwing things around—I know all about your temper tantrums!—the more strain you put on this, King Elad, the longer it's going to take to mend. You stay in this bed for two complete days. When you get up to urinate, walk slowly and lean on a servant. You understand me? The more strain you put on—"

"—the longer it'll take to mend, yes, yes, yes! Tell Amu here not to wrap it so tightly. Tell him that kings have to breathe in and out like everyone else."

Sotos frowned a smile and nodded to his pupil to be more considerate. When Amu was done, he helped Elad lean forward while Sotos and the woman servant rearranged the cushions behind the king's shoulders and head.

"All right, now, lie back. That's it."

"Are you about done, now?"

"Yes, we're about done."

Amu packed up Sotos's instruments and closed the box full of used bandages. Elad ordered the servant woman to bring him a fresh decanter of wine. She carried out the old tray as she left.

"Is Abgarthis waiting outside?" Elad asked Sotos.

"Yes. Shall I ask him to step in?"

"Please."

"The . . . Imbur is waiting to see you, as well."

Elad silently mouthed an obscenity. "Ogodis can sit out there all night."

Sotos waved Amu on and followed him to the chamber door.

"Thank you, Sotos," Elad called to him from across the room.

"Certainly, certainly."

They went out, and within a moment a Khamar reopened the door to admit Lord Abgarthis. The old adviser waited until the guard had closed the door before pulling up a chair to Elad's wide bed. The servant woman returned with wine and goblets; she poured a cup for the king, but Abgarthis declined. Once she too had exited:

"So . . . what news of the day?" Elad asked.

Abgarthis informed him quietly: "Council spent the afternoon yelling at one another. Some of them want to make war upon the Salukadians; others want to make war on the rebels in the empire. This discussion"—he smiled wryly—"will be reconvened tomorrow. They intend to have some measures ready to present you when you are well enough to take the dais again."

Elad grunted noncommittally, sipped his wine.

28

"There was a mild protest at the Temple today. Some of the priests, congregants . . . a few aristocrats. They deplore your decision to give Erusabad to the easterners—"

"I didn't *give* Erusabad to anyone!"

"—and they are upset about the desecration of the Temple there."

Elad frowned. "I'm upset about that, too. I had no idea the *Ghen* intended to do that. I suppose he's still in agreement about the pilgrimage rights? As if there's anything now for pilgrims to visit."

Abgarthis answered him, "Well, the Salukadians claim to have relocated the priests and their possessions and artifacts."

"Any word from General Thomo?"

"A rider came today with a dispatch sent from Hilum; Thomo's flagship was taking on fresh water and supplies there ten nights ago. Nothing untoward has occurred."

Elad nodded, sipped more of his wine. "No word from . . . Nutatharis?"

His minister grinned sadly. "The king of Emaria seems deaf to your inquiries—or at least unable to read Athadian."

"He is protecting Cyrodian. The fool. He's got a viper in his nest." Elad sighed strongly, set aside his wine, rubbed his forehead with stiff fingers. "Anything else? No word of . . . Orain? Galvus?"

Abgarthis shook his head. "We will hear from them. I don't think they are in any danger. I don't seem to *sense* them being in any danger. Is that odd?"

"No. I feel the same thing. . . . Anything else, Abgarthis?"

"The customary tributes and greetings for you to get well from everyone in the empire. From the sound of them, you would think all of Athadia is holding its breath until you make an official appearance well and whole." The adviser did not mean this to sound cynical, only honest.

"Yes . . . well. I hardly think that all of Athadia—" He caught Abgarthis's expression. "There is something else?"

"Rather grave news."

"What has happened?" But immediately, before Abgarthis could answer: "More revolutionary trouble?"

"Yes."

"Where? Not here in the capital?"

"In Bessara."

"Tell me what happened."

"You remember the reports that Uthis was sending you a few weeks ago—before your wedding—about the surveillance he was keeping on certain suspect individuals in the city? Yes . . . He unleashed his troops upon a demonstration shortly before your marriage. Many of the rebels were wounded, and a number of them sought shelter in the apartment house of a certain Lord Solok. A rebel sympathizer—and a member of one of the oldest families in the empire."

Elad nodded. "Continue."

"The patrol surrounded the house and moved in to make arrests. There was violence. Solok himself allegedly killed a young lieutenant; he and approximately thirty others were ordered executed. The executions were to take place three days ago. Lord Solok was indeed beheaded, but before the others could be brought to the block, more rebels—these Suloskai, they're calling themselves—"

Elad winced.

"—rode into the square where the executions were being held and attacked Uthis's soldiers. Tried to assassinate him as well. Some innocent people were hurt, more rebels died, but Uthis lost a good number of soldiers. He made a great deal more arrests." Abgarthis paused; his king said nothing, and so the adviser continued: "They are learning, these rebels. Bessara has become the center of their activity, and they appear to be growing bolder."

Still Elad remained silent. He sipped a few swallows of wine, drained the goblet and handed it to Abgarthis. "Please, if you would . . ."

The minister refilled the cup and handed it back.

"I thought," he told King Elad, "that I had better alert you to this before some of your members of Council brought it to your attention."

Elad grunted and lay his head back on his pillow.

Abgarthis leaned forward. "Are you all right, my king?"

"Do you know what it is, Abgarthis, to be given the opportunity to truly look at things from a new perspective?"

His adviser seemed puzzled by this comment. "I'm not certain I understand."

Elad sat up. "I have been lying here for three weeks. Hour upon hour goes by and no one interrupts me. After the first day I became bored and restless; once I knew I would live, there was nothing to do unless I could leave this bed. I did not feel like reading—and especially I didn't feel like reading all those ridiculous documents Council litters their chamber with every day! I would drink tea to make me sleepy, then I'd just get up and flood it out. Salia came in occasionally—perhaps twice a day—but we are yet strangers to one another. It's humorous, really. Here we are, man and wife, king and queen, and the first blood to happen upon our sheets isn't virgin's blood, is it? Blood . . . And that makes me think. So I have lain here, I have stared at these high walls, my mind and imagination have wandered . . . and I have had nightmares, Abgarthis. Sometimes I feel as if I'm suffocating; other times, in my dreams, I am free of this palace, I am out in the woods somewhere. . . ."

He stopped and looked at Abgarthis. The old man was attentive.

"Yes. So . . . Last night I was especially restless. I was having more bad dreams, and Salia was sleeping in the other room back there. The palace was all sleeping, yet I needed to talk to someone."

"You should have sent a servant to me. I would have come."

"I know you would have. But . . . I sent one of the guards over to the south wing and had him rouse Sianus. You know him."

"Chief of the Royal Library." Abgarthis was interested. "You wished to speak with him?"

"He more than anyone in this empire is most familiar with our history, our culture—wouldn't you agree?"

"Yes, it's true." Abgarthis was very intrigued by this reflective change of attitude in the young king.

"Well, it took him a while—he's as old as the mountains, you know, and it was the middle of the night—but dutifully he came and sat here—right where you're sitting. I had some wine brought in, and some bread and cheese, and we talked. We talked until dawn, Abgarthis." Elad showed him a gratified expression and eyes unclouded by pain, worry or bitterness. "We talked of—the empire. The men who have ruled it, the families who have controlled it. . . . Sianus can recite from memory some of the oldest documents of our history, did you know that? And he can sing some of these songs that are five hundred—seven hundred—years old, in their proper dialect. I'd ask him a question about some of the most obscure things, and he would answer me! All the battles, the scholars and leaders, the expansions, the laws . . . We talked of the days of the villages, Abgarthis, when this capital of Athad was nothing more than a few huts, and the whole landscape was filled with thousands of small villages and towns. Long before there was any real mercantilism, long before any bureaucracy, long before . . . kings wandered these halls of the palace looking for things to do." He smiled. "Long before we had all these aristocrats causing trouble, and rebels, and more people in our cities than we know what to do with . . ."

Abgarthis remained silent.

"And I began to wonder, to actually question, why I am king. Not that I shouldn't be; not that we shouldn't have a king, no matter what these rebels think. But . . . I believe I have had an attack of conscience. The gods test me, Abgarthis; and they test me to test the empire, they test our history, they test every great man and every shallow man who calls himself an Athadian. And I have failed the gods, haven't I? I was the man who slew the Oracle at Mount Teplis. Who was the man who did that? Was it me? That is an impossible crime! You have never upbraided me for it, Abgarthis. Why? Tell me—why?"

Abgarthis paled. "Do you truly wish to know?"

"Yes."

"You will think it a ridiculous answer."

"Tell me, please."

"I assumed it to have been the result of some accident; but when I learned the truth, I had to resolve your action by believing that it must somehow have been necessary for you to have killed her. You are not a murderer, Elad; for you to murder must portend something immense. I had always hoped that . . . Cyrodian actually did the deed."

"He did not; I slew her. And that act has haunted me . . . her words have haunted me. But as I lay here, thinking about that, it occurred to me that as our empire has passed from barbarism into sophistication—enlightenment—I, too, have passed from barbarism to enlightenment. I have killed; I have taken a life. And I ordered the executions of hundreds of my citizens last year because they broke the law in profound ways. Yet . . . people are murdered every day, and nearly every man who has ruled this nation has been at least indirectly a murderer as well. Some in war, some in contests, some—by accident. But I am no longer that man who murdered the Oracle. And if I am not the sort of man who can commit murder, but have actually done it, then what of that man who tried to assassinate me?" He faced Abgarthis boldly, with pride in his eyes.

"Yes?" his minister urged him.

"Is it not possible that he was slaying his own Oracle?"

Abgarthis smiled strangely. "Enlightenment, indeed," he spoke quietly.

"I am a good man," Elad declared, as though defending himself. "Good men can be the cause of evil—I realize that now. I have been confused, caught in webs. . . . It occurred to me . . . I questioned why I am king. Our empire has existed for so long, we are so large, we are many lands in one. And here lies one man in command of all of it. In command of this empire! Doesn't that strike you as profound?"

Abgarthis nodded silently.

"These businesses . . . this Council of aristocrats and merchants . . . Do you know what Count Adred told me, the night he and I had that long talk? He's a revolutionary, you know. Did you know that?"

"Yes."

"He's joined them. The more I considered that, the more it alarmed me—and made me wonder. I promised him that I would look into the matter of reforms. But he told me that Orain and Galvus believe in this revolution as well. What can it be, this revolution, if people like this are attracted to it? Do you know what he told me that night? He told me that he believed in the best that is in men. It sounds so simple, almost . . . ineffectual. But it isn't, Abgarthis. Can you imagine the *strength* in that, the courage? Look at us! Look at the world! Our world is a dismal, bloody, screaming place; it is clogged, it is tired, it is always angry. Men grasp and steal, they rape and plunder, they—they kill one another, yes. And here is Count Adred, as harmed in his own way as a man can ever be, and still he persists in believing in the best that is in us. And do you know what struck me as I talked to Sianus and listened to a thousand years of history? We have become what we have become because of those men and women who have believed in the best. It is true. Be there wars, be there disasters, be there generations of darkness and pain and misery— still, man aspires. Humanity aspires. Sometimes we grasp too much, but we aspire. And our nation today is an empire, not because of small men or frightened men or men who try to foist their own fears and delusions upon us, but because of the *best* that is in us. Look at my father. Examine our past. It comes about so slowly that it seems not to be happening at all. One lifetime is too short. But when we look at our history and see doors opening, ideas changing, arms reaching, voices raising themselves with

33

cries of fairness and openness . . . I actually believe in progress, Abgarthis."

"Do you?"

"Yes. You don't, do you? Ah, no. You believe that time is a wheel. Well, you are being short-sighted. There *is* progress, we *can* improve things, and we do that by understanding ourselves and working for the best that is in us. But it takes great courage, great strength. Think of it! A few hundred years ago . . . five hundred years ago—look at how primitive we were! Look—at the laws we had not so long ago. But now? Perhaps our laws are not well-enforced, but we have them, we believe in them, they are our foundation, aren't they? A hundred years is a long time, but such a short time! How many wars since we became a nation? How much blood? An oceanful? Ten oceans full? And yet—we have progressed. When we compare our sophistication, our laws, our attitudes, to what we've had in the past—well, we've progressed."

"Perhaps we have," Abgarthis admitted.

Elad finished his second goblet of wine, set it aside. "I am going to try to . . . create progress, Abgarthis."

The old man, already anticipating what Elad would say and astounded by it, stared at him. "Elad!"

"These . . . *sirots* . . . that the rebels want? We will try them. We will—"

"Elad!" Abgarthis cried. He rose to his feet and clapped his hands together, trembled with the enthusiasm of his long-lost youth. "Are you serious about this?"

"I am. I have given it much thought—"

"Elad! You do a mighty thing! You will be—"

"Abgarthis . . . Please—sit down. Yes. I am not giving up my throne, you know! But—we will try it. Treat it as we would a discovery, a new path, and follow it. With courage, and with strength. These riots and demonstrations . . . they cannot continue. I could blame the revolutionaries—I could blame myself, or Council, or the businesses—but blame is easy to place. The empire has been through such things before. Like a cork in a bottle. The pressure gets to be too much inside the bottle, the cork explodes. This way, we remove the cork before any damage is done."

Abgarthis was immensely gratified by Elad's words. "You are sincere about this?"

"Absolutely. These *sirots* will have very limited authority, of

34

course. They will be overseen by our people in the cities. But I will put Count Adred's ideas to the test." Elad smiled. "As king, I can certainly be as courageous as any insurrectionist nobleman! It simply seems to me that if things were as strong today as our Councilors insist and our businessmen claim, then we would not *have* unemployed people in the streets. But we do; so there is some weakness, our system is not as strong as it should be. Recall those discussions you and I had, Abgarthis, about power and kingship. And you asked me, 'What is a king without his country? What is a king without his people?' Well, he is no king, is he? And I am as much the king of that man who tried to kill me as I am of these privileged businessmen on our Council.

"Our Councilors are worthy men, Abgarthis, but they can make errors, and so can I. I, and they, claim to believe in the best, yet so do these rebels. Well . . . we debate issues in the Council Chamber; the king decides on an issue, but voices are heard. And that is justice. Then we shall let the people of this empire, these workers, have their voice in the *sirots*. I am trying to decide whether or not to go so far as to have them actually represented in the palace. We must be cautious; we cannot give them too much too quickly. But, they shall have their *sirots*."

Abgarthis stood up and bowed slightly; his good humor seemed to have relaxed. "I'll remind you of only one thing," he told Elad. "There is great good in diversity. It's always easier to deal with matters when everything seems uniform; I know that businessmen and commanders of war tend to think that life would be much more convenient for them if they didn't have to deal with real human beings. But you must remain above that sort of close-mindedness, that limited point of view. And the finest thing you can do, King Elad, is to be what you are, and to be that honestly. You must not be contemptuous of anyone or anything; and the joys you feel at being a man must not be denied anyone else, regardless of who is making a profit, regardless of who wields the staff of power. You say you should not move too quickly in recognizing the voice of your people; I would say to that, 'Do not move too slowly.' The best thing you could have now, in your Council Chamber, would be the clash of ideas and opinions—opposite views colliding to create something new. Do not move too slowly, my king."

Elad nodded thoughtfully to this. "You have great . . . in-sight," he allowed. He gave a wide-mouthed yawn. "Forgive me. It's getting late, isn't it?"

"Yes. I'll take my leave now." Abgarthis took one of Elad's hands in his and grasped it firmly. "I always knew that you must be your father's son. Sooner or later, the child betrays the parent in him—the strengths, as well as the weaknesses."

"Thank you, Abgarthis."

"Go to the people, my king. Have you considered that? You have been in the capital for too long a time. When you are fit again, you should travel. Visit the cities."

"You're right; I should make plans to do that."

"I believe you should."

Elad yawned again. "Tell Ogodis . . . I will see him tomorrow."

A flicker of a smile. "Of course. Rest well, Elad."

"And you the same, good Abgarthis."

When she came in, much later, Elad had turned down the wick in his lamp. He was sleeping, propped up on his cushions, the blankets disheveled and half thrown off.

He awakened groggily at the sound of her breathing, the presence of her shadow. Elad opened his eyes, reached out with one hand. "Salia?"

"Yes," in a whisper. She took his hand.

He saw her smiling at him.

"I just came in to . . . look at you. . . ."

"I was dreaming, I think. . . ."

"Not more bad dreams, Elad?"

"No . . . no. . . . Good dreams." He smiled awkwardly, still asleep. He tugged on her arm.

She hesitated, as she might have with a stranger. "I—I don't know if—"

"I'm all right. Lie beside me, Salia."

She followed the pull of his hand, climbed onto the bed, rearranged the covers and stretched out alongside him. She was naked, and her slim warmth instantly invited him to embrace her. He moved carefully, positioning himself, while Salia, allowing Elad to rest his head on her shoulder, made herself as comfortable as she could. She stroked his hair with gentle fingers.

"Go to sleep," Salia whispered. "Go back to sleep. . . ."

"It . . . doesn't hurt so much . . . now. . . ."

"Shhh. . . . Go to sleep, Elad. Have some more—good dreams. . . ."

He kept his eyes closed, yawned, held himself against her and began to breathe steadily.

Salia, for the first time since she had come to Athad, no longer felt threatened—by her father, or by this king. She felt—alone, but safe. Perhaps it was simply because her husband was severely hurt and in need of her solace; perhaps it was because he didn't seem to be a king, now, but only a warm, naked man sleeping beside her; perhaps it was only because he was asleep and she was still awake, and holding him.

She felt less a stranger to herself than she had before, and she realized that tonight, for the first time in many long weeks, she would at last sleep soundly and undisturbed, all night long. . . .

Daughter, here is a secret I have learned. I will share it with you so that as queen of Athadia you will know one small secret of being a great leader: laugh. If you can laugh at a thing, you can control it, Salia.

She bent her head to kiss Elad's forehead, she gently rubbed her fingers in his hair, and—she smiled.

4.

When the first of Lord General Thomo's scarlet-and-gold-sailed galleys made dock at Port Erusabad on the eighteenth day of the month of Grem the Wolf, Captain Commander Thytagoras, in charge of the Athadian troops garrisoned in the Holy City, and Lord Sirom, Acting Athadian Consul to the Salukadian government, met Thomo on the dock. Thomo led his contingent of imperial advisers, lawyers and businessmen onto firm ground and handed his sealed order to Lord Sirom.

"We are happy that you've reached us safely," Sirom smiled to Thomo. "Your voyage was a pleasant one?"

"It was . . . unspectacular," the general assured him. "Have you made preparations for the king's people?"

Sirom ducked his head. "We have several old government buildings on this side of the city where our officials might stay indefinitely. And we've made apartments out of the top two stories of the Central Authority." To Thomo's look of inquiry: "Governor Dusar and his officers spent most of their time in villas outside the city; we thought it better to make accommodations inside the walls."

"Judicious. Huagrim and his people are here, then?"

"They arrived less than two weeks ago, Lord General."

Thomo pursed his lips.

"They've moved right in," Thytagoras commented darkly, eyeing Thomo in hopes of finding a kindred spirit. "They've taken over. The city is theirs. Really rubbing our faces in it."

Thomo fixed him with a steady gaze. "Any deaths of Athadian citizens?"

Thytagoras took that as a direct insult, and Sirom hastily answered: "None since the afternoon their troops first took control, Lord General. There were a few incidents—but you know about those. . . ."

"Yes." Still Thomo kept his eyes on Thytagoras. "Yes . . . we've reviewed everything that happened."

"Well, then, you can understand—"

"I am not here with an armed force," Thomo reminded both Sirom and Thytagoras. "And I will not order any military action against the Salukadians unless it is by direct order of King Elad or provoked by the direst of emergencies. The verbal orders given me are to take only retaliatory action, and then with extreme prudence. You men, I'm sure, can appreciate the consequences of a declaration of war in this city."

Thytagoras said nothing; mute, he colored with subdued anger.

But Sirom affirmed: "We serve our king, Lord General Thomo. You know that."

"This is a legal argument, not a military maneuver." To Thytagoras, in a more affable tone: "No matter what you and I may think of it, Captain, we are not the government. You and I might perhaps take a different stand on the matter—but we are not the throne. Agreed?"

Thytagoras accepted the proffered hand. "Agreed, General. But still—they're rubbing our faces in it."

"And that is precisely why I have brought with me four shiploads of lawyers, diplomats and businessmen." He gestured behind him to where the last of seventy ambassadors aboard his flagship were gathering on the wharf. And behind them, the *Cloud*, the *Ordavian* and the *Evarris* were dropping anchor and throwing out lines.

"Captain Thytagoras," Lord Sirom told Thomo, "has graciously accorded us a unit of his men to help your ministers to their quarters and lend them any assistance needed."

"Thank you." Thomo nodded to the captain, glanced beyond

38

him to the Athadian infantry standing stoic and proud in the wide sunlight.

"If you'll come with me, then, I'll show you to your apartment, General."

"Yes. . . ." Thomo nodded to his two retainers, young lieutenants both, and followed Lord Sirom up the dock to where two horse-drawn landaus awaited them. Sirom and Thomo rode together, in the company of Thomo's retainers.

Thomo watched the avenue as they moved along. Expressionless faces stared at him. The crowds were swirls of color and noise, dark faces and white faces, men and women, animals, vendors. . . .

"So they have destroyed the Temple, have they?" he said.

Sirom looked at him. "Yes. Not destroyed it, actually. They are . . . renovating it. Making it into a temple of their own."

"We heard that. No violent demonstrations over this? I find it hard to believe that our citizens would stand by and let such a thing occur." He eyed Sirom critically.

"Some . . . very violent demonstrations took place, in fact. The Church leaders suicided, you heard that. I suppose religious people do that sort of thing. And for the first few days of the occupation, when the Salukadians took charge of the Temple, there was quite a bit of trouble, yes. I sent a report to King Elad. Didn't he say anything to you about it?"

"No. He has been—"

"Yes, I know. The, uh, 'incident.' But since then, very little. From what I can gather, the religious in this city have accepted it as a sign of the end of the world." Sirom said it straightforwardly, although his tone betrayed his dismay with the concept. "Their apocalyptic ideas, you understand. Prophecies."

Thomo sniffed, rubbed his beard. "Yes . . . well. So that's why they've been so pacific?"

"I believe so. It's a pervasive attitude. Most of our citizens here have tried to adjust, but the religiously inclined . . . Well, they have a stronger sense of fatalism, if you will, than there is within the empire proper."

"Doom-Soulers, eh?" Thomo smiled.

"Why, yes. Are you familiar with that sect?"

"Only from what I've heard. I am not a particularly religious man." As they came into Himu Square and approached the Central Authority: "Where are the *Ghen* and his court staying?"

"In Lord Semul's old villa, by the Vilusian Gardens. We have an audience there as soon as you wish."

The carriage rolled to a stop and Thomo's door was opened by a young soldier. The general stepped out.

Sirom followed. As he led Thomo up the stairs and into the Authority: "I have been granted only one audience with him since his arrival here. He does not seem to be in the best of health, Lord General."

"Is he dying?"

"I suspect so."

Thomo paused at the top of the stairs, looked back down into the square and glanced toward the east, where the golden dome of the Temple of Bithitu had once glowed so magnificently that its brightness rivaled the sun's. Now, where that dome once had been, Thomo saw tall wooden parapets and scaffolds and hundreds of insect-sized workmen erecting statues and hammering gold sheets onto animal-shaped sculptures.

Sirom waited a moment, then lifted an arm toward the colonnaded portico that shaded the entranceway. "If you please, Lord General."

"Yes, of course. . . ."

It seemed to him that the faithful of Athadia, the faithful in Erusabad, should have been more vociferous in their protests than Sirom had indicated.

He thought again of the Doom-Soulers. . . .

It was early in the afternoon when bin-Sutus, the oldest and most respected of the *aihman-sas* serving in Huagrim's court, entered the Vilusian Gardens to find Nihim, the *Ghen's* youngest son, sitting on a bench by himself studying one of the decorative, fountain-fed pools. Nihim did not look up immediately when bin-Sutus intruded; the courtier coughed slightly to gain the *Ghen-mu's* attention.

"Yes, bin-Sutus?"

"I have been asked to tell you that the Athadian entourage comes soon to meet with your father. Your presence is required."

"Yes, yes. I am coming."

"Agors, as well. Do you know where he is? Has he gone riding?"

Nihim nodded to his right where the brick pathway lost itself in the tangled colors of the deeper gardens. "I believe he and some companions have taken a stroll. They came by here a short while ago."

"Shall I fetch him?"

"No." Nihim rose to his feet and casually straightened his robe. "No. I know where he is. I'll get him."

"They come soon, *Ghen-mu*."

"Yes. We'll be there, bin-Sutus."

bin-Sutus made a short bow; his bald head shined in the dappled sunlight, his white beard fluttered. He turned and strode down the path heading back to the villa. Even in the Gardens the noises of working men could be heard as they transformed Lord Semul's old villa into something akin to a palace. bin-Sutus followed the sounds, and as he came out of the Gardens, he waited a moment to watch the progress.

Nihim watched bin-Sutus disappear, then threw his hands behind his back and started in the opposite direction, following the walkway where it curved around the pool and led over a small bridge into an artificial forest.

It amazed him that these Gardens could so reflect an eastern appreciation of beauty and order and simplicity, tucked away as they were in a pocket of western barbarism. Astonishing. . . . But it pleased Nihim. Thoughtful, studious and observant as he was, devout subscriber to Toshin's *Wo Ayhat*—the Way—Nihim had prepared himself for this journey to the west by deciding to search out beauty and insight wherever he might find it. It would be an intellectual challenge: that had been his intention. But he had been surprised to discover, so far, very little in Erusabad that was appreciably foreign from what he knew of life in Ilbukar. The same streets, much the same sort of architecture, dialects he could understand due to his study of the Athadian tongue.

Agors was seated at an open air marble table in the center of a wide courtyard with a trio of his soldier friends. The three looked up when Nihim approached and nodded respectfully. Agors frowned.

"If you will excuse my brother and I . . ." Nihim suggested. The three stood.

"The Athadians?" Agors asked.

Nihim nodded. "bin-Sutus just came to me; they will arrive here soon, and *Ghen-ulu* wishes us present at the audience."

Agors motioned to his companions. "Go on. I'll join you later. Our tavern in the Kinesh Square."

They agreed and walked off, one of them calling back as they left, "Don't lose your temper with them, Agors!"

Taking that as a compliment, the elder prince smiled, but the smile faded when he once more faced his younger brother. "Well, then. Shall we go back?"

But Agors did not rise, and Nihim himself did not seem to be in a particular hurry to return. He circuited the patio, appreciating the beauty all around him, aware of Agors's impatient eyes.

"Well?" Agors said, rapping his fingers irritably on the marble table.

Nihim turned and faced him. His brother was always dressed in the wool and leather of a cavalry officer; always on his belts and boots he wore daggers and knives; always his hair was trimmed, his beard neat and pointed; and always he wore his dangerous *yagu*, that two-edged curved sword, hammered and folded from the finest steel by master forges of the Ilro Mountains and proudly presented to Agors *Ghen-mu* by his father. "They do not come to us," Nihim said, eyeing his brother critically, "these Athadians, to make war upon us."

"I know this."

"Do you? It seems to me, my brother, that you are contemptuous of these men of the west, but at the same time you are very much like them."

Agors had always regarded his brother as an irritant. He judged Nihim's constant wearing of robes as a posture and an insult to manhood, and he deemed Nihim's view of the world as an organism, his deference to the nature-wisdom of *Wo Ayhat*, as woefully naive and misguided. There was the faintest tone of scorn in his voice as he replied: "I take from them whatever I can use against them. We, too, Nihim, are of the west now. Look at what we have become. It should be a thorn in your heart, even as it is in mine. We have become a nation of cities, a nation of . . . merchants and cities. A hundred years ago the men of this city would have been warriors, with destinies; now they are scribblers, and buyers and sellers." He grunted with disgust. "And because I believe that men should be men, and that we of Salukadia have a vision to fulfill, you think I mean to provoke war?"

Nihim smiled tolerantly; his brother had always complained of being born too late. "The people of the west are settled; all they wish now is to maintain what they have gained: they have no desire to gain more. They have not changed in hundreds of years.

But we, Agors, have changed. 'The young tree is supple and bends with the changing wind; the old tree will not bend, a strong wind topples it.' It is true of trees, and men, and nations. If you think too much like your enemy, Agors, you become your enemy; who then is left to make war upon?" Nihim smiled. "When you go into your taverns, my brother, you should play *usto* with these men of the west. You would learn much from them. You could be a strong general, on the *usto* board."

"I am not interested in games!"

"But you should be. To play games is the heart of these men of the west. They love all the regulations and rules they concoct; they love boundaries and laws, they love to build obstacles for themselves so that they can overcome them. You can appreciate that. They love numbers; they love systems. They create things so that they can be owned by them; they love what they can hold in their hands. Games to them are very serious."

When Agors only glared at him but made no comment, Nihim continued. "There is a move in this *usto* that some westerners refer to as 'raping the queen.' Does that sound quaint, or merely barbaric? Think of it—these westerners have only one goal, and every move they make is designed to assure their gaining that goal. They see it in terms of conquest, profit, rape—not balance. When they take their opponent's queen, they have 'raped' her."

"I have played *usto* many times," Agors reminded Nihim. "Why are you prattling—"

"Because it is possible to play the game in many different ways, but these Athadians do not see that. I see it in terms of strategy and balance; for them, strategy is only a method for defeating their opponent, and they do not respect balance. They use one set of rules, they seek only one goal. And they will sacrifice everything, if need be, to gain that goal."

"Are you trying to enlighten me, brother, into the way these westerners think?"

"Their people come to us," Nihim replied, "without weapons, to make a diplomatic peace. They have allowed us the control of this city. They have already made sacrifices—and why? We have gone so far as to desecrate a temple that is very important to their people. Why do they allow this? I tell you this: when these Athadians sit down to play *usto*, they follow one set of rules, and they will sacrifice everything to gain one goal. They are a passionate people, Agors—passion allied with strength and their own sort of dignity."

Agors stared at his brother.

"What will they do, Agors, if we push the matter further?" He remained silent.

"I know what you and your companions discuss, my brother. You are men of the sword, you should have been born when our father was born, out there in the plains. But a man must conquer himself before he can conquer others; our father is an example of that. 'Seek wisdom from the ignorant as you would wine from a stone.' You love to look at maps; I know what you see in them. You think the west is weak. You think our alliance with Emaria will open a door for you to ride through. Agors . . . Look at me, my brother."

Agors did so. His eyes were hot, his fists clenched.

"When *Ghen-ulu*'s audience with this Athadian, General Thomo, is ended, I think you should make a gesture to him. I think you should send word to General Thomo that you wish to engage him in an evening's game of *usto*."

Agors unfisted his hands, tapped the marble table, cleared his throat. "You think I should do that, do you?"

"These Athadians with whom I played . . . these opponents who always thought in terms of one goal, and who would sacrifice anything to gain that goal? . . ."

"What of them?"

"My brother—I defeated every one of those players when I sat down with them. They condemned themselves; and their way of thought, and their methods of strategy—each time I defeated them. And I did not try to emulate their ways."

5.

Where Night comes down, a shadow bridge between lives, the sorcerer awakens with life as heat awakens into flame.

The address was on Akud Street. She had never been in this street before because Akud was in a prosperous district of the city. She had tried to make herself look as sophisticated as possible because Isudi had warned her that the man she was going to meet was not one of her usual arrogant bureaucrats. He was an outlander (or so Isudi had gathered), and he was in the city only for a short time; and though he lived in a vicinity where wealthy easterners were beginning to settle, he was not an easterner himself.

It was difficult to say just what he was.

But he had specifically requested that Serela be sent to him, Isudi had told her. The gentleman had seen her dancing at one of the public fetes last week and she had drawn his interest. It would do Serela much good to cultivate the attentions of such a man.

"He paid me fifty in Athadian gold! Fifty! For just one night! Do you understand what that means? This man is as rich as a king! And he's no son of the gutter with a stolen purse either! He is quality! You'll do yourself well to—"

The hired servants set down the litter and the headman came around to pull back the drapes. Serela stepped out; the headman escorted her to the door, and there she paid him with a gold piece. He bowed several times and thanked her profusely.

Serela entered the apartment building. Isudi had told her that this lord had rented the entire top floor of the building. Entranced by the shining grandeur, she made her way slowly up the wide stairs, climbing three flights before pausing to catch her breath. On the third floor landing were plants and mirrors and exquisite bas-reliefs and wall tapestries. When she leaned for a moment over the rail of the balcony, Serela saw a wide tiled patio far below, open to the skylight above, and a group of giddy aristocrats sprawled on cushions around a monumental stone fountain. When she turned to continue up the stairs, she dizzied slightly. She was unaccustomed to such displays of wealth, and she began to wonder about this mysterious outlander who had made his home in these surroundings. She moved up the stairs nervously, a little hesitantly, but curiosity, more than fear of Isudi's possible anger, prodded her on.

When she reached the fourth floor landing, Serela saw that the stairs went no higher. There were no entrances on either side, only a tall arched opening at the end of the wide corridor that was closed off with thick hanging drapes. When she reached the drapes, Serela carefully pushed them aside and looked in. The room was quite dark. She nearly gasped aloud when a voice beckoned her from the gloomy interior:

"Serela."

She caught her breath and answered nervously: "Y—yes. . . ."

"Come in, please."

She stepped inside. Her sandals made a loud noise on the

uncarpeted floor, and Serela tried to move more slowly so that the sounds would not be displeasing. As her eyes became accustomed to the darkness, she looked around but could not find the man who had spoken to her.

As though he'd read her mind, he spoke again. "I am here."

"Lord Thameron?"

"Yes. Here."

Instantly oil lamps along all four walls of the huge room increased in brilliance, and Serela was astounded by what met her eyes. It was not a room at all—not an ordinary room. Lord Thameron (or someone) had fashioned it into the semblance of a cave. It was astonishing. The walls of the grand chamber seemed to curve from floor to ceiling as though they were of hewn stone. The floor itself resembled something roughly chiseled. The only light was gained by the oil lamps, although drawn drapes against one wall indicated a balcony outside.

All furniture had been pushed to the sides of the room. In the center of the floor was a very large circular carpet with odd symbols and signs embroidered on it. And at the opposite side of the room, propped upon a platform draped in animal skins, sat Lord Thameron.

Serela paused as she stared at him; he was not at all what she had thought he might be. He was young—very young—and quite handsome. His beard and mustache were neatly trimmed, his long hair was combed and oiled and hanging to his shoulders. He was dressed in red silk trousers and a well-fitted brocade jacket. He wore few ornaments—only two rings on each hand, a light blue *sulm* or turban on his head, a few golden necklaces. His boots were new and shiny from polishing oil.

"Come ahead," Lord Thameron invited her, his voice low and quite pleeasant.

"I'm . . . afraid to step on your rug. . . ."

"It's only a rug."

She came ahead, averting her eyes from his: she felt his gaze stark upon her, studying her movements, her body, scrutinizing her in a way somehow more intent than any other man ever had. It made her feel very uncomfortable. Yet when she came close to his dais, Serela had necessarily to look up and face him, and then Lord Thameron seemed not at all sinister, only young and handsome and possessed of deep, penetrating dark eyes.

"Sit." He lowered a hand, indicating the cushions beside his dais. "There is wine; would you care for some?"

"Yes, please. . . ."

He stood and stepped from the platform, moved to a low table.

Instantly Serela was on her feet. "Lord Thameron! Let *me* serve *you*, please!"

He turned and smiled at her. "Oh, yes . . . of course."

Odd behavior for a man who had paid fifty in long gold for attentions the night through. He continued with the wine, first pouring Serela a cup, then one for himself. He handed her a goblet, moved back to his dais, sat again in his chair and turned his gaze upon her once more. "Make yourself comfortable, Serela."

Presuming that he meant the obvious, she set aside her wine and began to undo the thin gown which she wore. She bowed her head slightly and lent Lord Thameron a sly, sensual glance.

He watched her as she removed her clothes. She wore very little—only her thin gown, her sandals, a few items of jewelry. Serela noticed how Thameron's eyes glowed as he followed her hands, followed the folds of her falling gown, watched how her body swayed as she stepped out of her robe. When she was finished, she stood proudly displaying herself (as she had done so many times before for countless bureaucrats, aristocrats and crowds of men) and then with exaggerated grace moved slowly back to the dais, sat down in the cushions and took up her wine.

Thameron smiled as he looked upon her. A small woman, slim and quite pretty, with foamy dark hair falling down her back, dark eyes and full red lips, heavy breasts that swayed and rolled, long slim legs that betrayed their muscles . . .

"This has a . . . nostalgic value for me," Thameron admitted to her.

Serela, not quite certain what that might mean, smiled and sipped her wine. She was wholly unused to this—a man hiring her for the night and yet taking no initiative. She wondered what could be the problem. Perhaps he had drugged himelf? Perhaps he had . . . difficulties? Well, Serela was experienced, and once they had shared a cup or two of wine . . .

It was as she set aside her goblet, turned to look up at Thameron and stretched her long legs that Serela noticed glints of light on the floor just around the side of the dais. She turned her head to see what the lights might be and leaned forward. Her hanging breasts brushed her knees; her dark hair fell in waves to obscure her face. She uttered a gasp.

Thameron said to her, "They are stones."

Serela glanced at him, then stood and stepped across the dais and knelt to inspect them. "Lord Thameron! They are gems!" Rubies . . . emeralds, . . . opals, . . . diamonds—the wealth of a vault, scattered upon the floor!

Thameron laughed out loud. "Inspect them carefully," he told the courtesan. "See what I have done with them?"

Greedily, excitedly, Serela picked up dozens of gems, large and small ones, and noticed that all of them had been cut precisely in half. Her brow creased, she swiveled as she crouched and stared at Thameron. "Why have you cut them? Are they taken from old jewelry?"

"No," was his low-voiced reply. "I created them. Then I broke them in half. That is easy to do. But it is impossible for me to piece any of them together again so that they are whole. It cannot be done." To her strange expression: "I am a sorcerer, Serela."

That announcement did not seem to inspire fear or anxiousness in her; such proclamations were ordinary enough in this city. "But . . . these are real gems, Lord Thameron! You *created* them?" She did not believe him, but she could not offend him.

"Keep them," he told her. He drained his cup, stood up, then stepped down to her. "Keep them. You may have them." He made to move past her to refill his cup.

Serela stood up instantly, dropping the jewels to the floor. Her eyes went wide, she shrieked with excitement, she threw open her arms and embraced Thameron, taking him compleely by surprise. She rubbed her hands along his face, she pushed her legs and breasts against him, she whispered mild obscenities to him in thanks.

Thameron dropped his cup onto the table, then wound his arms about her, pressed his hands along her hips, hugged her, held her giving, soft flesh. The aroma of her was strong and enticing; the brightness of her eyes could well have been that of diamonds.

"A sorcerer!" she grinned at him, holding him tightly. She felt in control, now, with whoever this man might be; and the merest suggestion that such wealth in this room might be for her, that even one stone might be for her, sent floods of passion and desire through her.

"Those stones," he whispered, "don't matter. . . ." He led Serela into an antechamber of the room, into his bedchamber, and there Serela undressed him.

She did as he told her, and she was astounded by how often he took her, and in such a variety of ways. He seemed tireless and inexhaustible, intense in his passion. Serela, as always, was playful, by turns conniving or childish or completely wanton. Toward dawn she took up a handful of Lord Thameron's broken jewels and, to seduce him a final time, pressed them onto her damp body. They adhered easily to her glossy skin and Serela laughed and laughed, imagining herself a walking jewel.

When she dressed at last, and kissed Lord Thameron a last time, she placed all the jewels within her small wallet but dropped a small ruby into her mouth and sucked upon it as she might a seed. Her light laughter carried easily down the corridor and down the four flights of stairs into the humid early morning streets.

Meanwhile Thameron, no more exhausted by his night of endless passion than he would have been had he spent those hours asleep, drew on his clothes and walked out onto the balcony of his apartment, threw his arms behind him and looked down into the street. He saw Serela hurrying away, walking quick-stepped and not even bothering to hire a litter or a carriage. He knew that she would not be returning to Isudi.

And he realized, too, there in the dawn, that it was time he left Erusabad.

Had this Serela been enough to sate his longing for Assia?

No. Not Serela, nor any of the young women he had turned into meals for his feasting imagination.

And he felt empty. Not dissolute, not abusive, not foul, but only dissipated and lost.

When he had first started searching for her, he had feared that Assia might have died; yet something told him that she hadn't. He had inquired of people he had known before, people who had known him as a young priest in the Temple of Bithitu, and he had gone down to the docks and spoken with the sailing men who had been companions to Assia's father. But the people he had known before had not trusted him and had treated him as though he were a stranger; and the sailing men, if they knew anything, said nothing to the deep-eyed, handsomely dressed young man who might be Athadian, might be Salukadian, but might (as well) be something else entirely.

What was most intriguing and frustrating, however, was the strength of his sorcery. For Thameron could, in truth, command shadows, understand the minds of animals, bring down storms and make flames appear on the wind; he could slumber and visit strange regions; he could make gold coins from bits of lead and gems from splinters of wood; he could appear as youthful and virile as a spring soldier or as old and sinister as some virulent disease given human form. And he could accomplish things that no man on earth had ever done before: Thameron knew this of himself.

Yet, try as he might, search as he might, inquire as he might from those shadows that clung to him like a second breath, he could not discern where Assia was now, nor gain any clue as to how he might reach her.

He wondered how this could be.

Had not demons damned him? Had he not halved the stone that had opened for him all the paths at once? Had he not been warned that he had become the Evil on earth?

Were his powerful instincts, his strengths, limited in ways he did not know?

Or was Assia so distant from him that he could not locate her, no matter what he might do? Perhaps he should travel, to sense her more clearly the nearer to her he approached?

Or might it be that, despite his endless thoughts of her, Assia no longer thought of him? Was that why he had failed, time and again?

Or perhaps—

"Do you, Assia? Truly love me?"

"So much . . . It frightens me. Come back for me, Thameron. . . ."

Perhaps, as mightily as one part of him wanted her, another part of him did not want to find her again, did not want to face her with who he was now, with what he had become.

He stood on the balcony and looked upon the people and the city of holiness that had betrayed him.

As he listened to the noises of the crowds, and as he reflected upon the lust and greed of Serela, and as he thought of the Salukadians who bowed to him, the servants who begged favors of him, the children no better than animals—the huge human tide of life and toil, sweat and endurance and suffering, cruelty that achieved more than suffering and goodness ever had—

"That jewel belonged to the early gods," Guburus had warned him. "It must be broken in half in a certain way to unravel its powers. If it is not done correctly—then the spirit is damned. It is a door which, once opened, cannot be closed."

Deep within him, as he remembered, he became angry.

You are become your destiny, O man. You are chosen, the

vessel, the being, the embodiment of the last days, O man beyond men, O Prince of Darkness—

Life, he thought, can be destroyed so easily. To sever the bond of a memory from its flesh is the simplest and easiest way, and not all men are granted such easy deaths. Far worse to die inside, to know the death of oneself while the body, a shell, still stirs and quickens and lives. . . .

He turned and entered his room again.

I am not evil, thought Thameron. *I refuse that . . . destiny. Assia would understand. Hapad did not, Guburus did not, but Assia . . .*

He felt again that tug toward the north; and Thameron, his thoughts fragmentary and uncertain, could not tell if that tug toward the north was the pull of destiny, or the ache of lost love whispering to him.

You are become your destiny, O man.

But Assia would understand.

Assia. . . .

She was sitting outside one of the tents of the First Green Legion, warming herself by the campfire. She felt cold, though she was perspiring, and the little she had eaten had not filled her; so she sought to stay warm by the fire and to ignore the chill in her bones, the rumbling in her bowels.

Around her in the dark night a thousand campfires were spread upon the sloping hills, and a thousand tents. The night was nearly quiet; only a distant occasional laugh or yell from some of the soldiers broke the stillness. The air was muggy, filled with the dampness of the swamplands, air that seemed to crouch and hover. To the north, through the thick trees that led down to the Burul-Gos Stream, she could see suggestions of orange light: the signal fires that burned atop the hastily built towers, lookouts for any Emarian troop movement on the other side.

Behind her, the door flaps of the tent opened and a number of men stepped out. Some of them were laughing, some talked lowly as they moved away. Their voices sounded hollow; they looked like dark ghosts, barely lighted by her campfire. A lean young man sporting the colors of a corporal approached the young woman and sat down beside her. He moved close, reached to hold her hand. She didn't look at him.

"We're moving out tomorrow for Abustad," he said. "They're sending up some of the reserves to relieve us."

"Are they?"

"I want you to come back with me, Assia."

Now she looked at him. "Do you?" She coughed slightly. "Why?"

"I just want you to."

Assia knew why. Urwus didn't want her staying here with the other men; he wanted her all for himself. She scratched her cheek as she dully considered it. Sometimes Urwus would sing songs to her and make up poetry; other times, when he'd been drinking, he would often strike her. But he was friendlier to her than anyone else in the camp.

"Will you come back with me?" Urwus asked her.

From a group at another campfire someone called to him: "Come on, Urwus!" One hoisted a bottle of wine, tempting him.

"Will you, Assia?" He gripped her arm insistently.

"You're hurting me. . . ."

He quickly removed his hand. "I'm sorry. Look . . . I can make all the arrangements, there's no problem with that. I just want you to—"

"Yes, all right."

"You'll come back with me, then?"

"Yes, I will."

"*Ur-wus*!" yelled a voice.

"Good!" He stood up; Assia stared at the fire. His companions called to him again, and Urwus quickly rubbed Assia's head before hurrying to join them.

"Gods!" another of them laughed, his voice carrying. "You'd think she's the only piece of cod around here!"

"Oh, leave him alone, just wish you could get your hands on—"

"Here, give me some of that or Urwus'll down it all before we even—"

Their voices subsided, became low grumbling sounds bursting occasionally with crude laughter. Assia watched her fire, wrapped her arms about herself and held her knees together to stay warm. She didn't hear Laril until the woman nearly stumbled into her; she sat down beside Assia on the warm rock.

"You're missing all the entertainment," Laril informed her. From the way she rocked back and forth, Assia could tell she'd been drinking for quite a while. Laril was a big woman with bright red hair, and her bracelets clinked and shimmered and glowed in the firelight like pieces of newly hot metal.

"Am I?"

"What's the matter with you? Don't be so—"

"I don't feel very well."

"Oh." Laril tried to decide what to do about that, then thought it best to drop a heavy arm around Assia's shoulders. "It's that damned . . . swamp," she said, burping. "That's what it is."

Assia told her: "Urwus wants me to go back to Abustad with him."

Laril chuckled hoarsely. "Well, good for you! Good for you!"

"Only I don't know if I want to."

"What? Look, Sweet, anything you can do to get out of this hole, do it. That's why you came up here, isn't it? Make a little"—she rubbed thumb and forefinger together, indicating coins sliding against one another (and people)—"and you've done good for yourself, so go on back."

"I'm not sure if I can trust him. He hits me."

"Hit him back."

"People always . . . hit me. . . ." She didn't whine, but this chill she had was beginning to make her feel self-pitying.

"Look." Laril leaned close, brought her mouth to Assia's ear. "You don't like it when you get back, you hit the stones. No one says you have to stay with him when you get back there. But at least you're in a city, not in some rotting swamp."

"I know, I know. . . ."

"You really don't feel well, do you?"

They sat there, Assia staring at the fire, Laril leaning on her and burping occasionally. Abruptly, she let out a laugh.

"Anyhow, you're missing all the fun. Fusk is over there doing his imitation of Captain Bull. 'What is this? Are you men standing on your *heads*? I want to see *faces*! I want to see every soldier trimmed and groomed and ready for anything! I don't care if we *are* in the middle of a swamp! You're going to be in the middle of more than a swamp if I catch you . . . ghuh-ghuh-ghuh!' If old Bull ever catches him, he'll strip and quarter him right there! And Osu, mincing and singing, is prancing around with two boobs under his jacket. He's so drunk. What a bend-over he is! And Imos—you know who he is, don't you?—he's over there looking at the sky and telling us which stars are which and he's trying to scare everybody."

"What he's saying?" Assia inquired absently.

"Oh, he really thinks he's something, that Imos. He's saying that—All right, look. Up there. The bright one? Look to where

53

I'm pointing. Come on, Assia, look! All right, the bright one there. That star, . . . now three over. That's Imgor, right? So he says when Imgor enters this constellation—over there, that constellation— What the hell did he call it? Come on, Assia, this is scary, now! Sath, the Dragon. Imos says when Imgor looks like it's in the sign of the dragon, then something else has to happen. . . . The dragon that eats its own tail. Anyway, it means all this terrible stuff is going to happen. War and famine and all this garbage. Scary.''

"Sounds scary.''

"As-sia! This is *funny*! It's ridiculous!" Laril reached over and felt her forehead. "You're getting a fever, girl.''

"I know.''

"You better go lay down. Damn it, it's all these swamps, makes people sick, makes you want to puke your guts out. You don't feel that sick, do you?''

"I think I'm just tired. I didn't eat much today.''

"All right, look. You get back to the tent and lie down, I'll bring you some food. They're cooking some soup over there.''

"I think I will. . . .''

Laril helped Assia stand up, walked her around the fire and headed her toward one of the tents assigned to camp followers.

"Can you make it, now?''

"Yes. I'm just tired. . . .''

From his campfire Urwus saw them, stood up and yelled: "Hey! Is she all right?''

Laril turned around. "Oh, she got a good look at your ugly face and now she has to vomit!''

"Shut up, Laril!''

"Told you! Told *you*, Urwus!''

"Yeah!" Cackle. "Shut up, you old piece of . . . *hole*!''

Laril ignored them and began walking toward Fusk's fire. Urwus's boots pounded on the ground as he ran over to her.

"Is she all right? Tell me!''

"She's just tired, Urwus. Leave her alone.''

"Maybe I'd better—''

"Just leave her alone," Laril repeated sternly. "She'll be all right." Snidely, to his troubled expression: "She's going back to Abustad with you, so you'll have her all to yourself.''

Urwus growled an obscenity and jerked one arm up as though threatening a slap.

"Just leave her alone," Laril said again. "Go on back and finish drinking. I'm getting her something to eat. Let her sleep."

Urwus stood there, rocking on his feet, and he watched Laril walk away. He glanced at the camp followers' tent, then started to move in that direction.

But his companions called him back to their fire, so Urwus grunted, turned around and went back to them.

A few fires away, a sudden chorus of screams and loud laughter erupted from Imos's crowd of listeners as every face there stared up at the cold black sky and followed pointing fingers that showed the patterns of the stars, the movements of the planets. Dragons, and famines, and wars . . .

PART II

Coals Beneath the Ashes

1.

". . . hear me, Cyrodian?"

The giant jerked his head around and stared at Nutatharis. "Did you say something?"

"I *said*, 'Did you hear me?' Obviously, you did not."

"Uh," Cyrodian grunted, then turned away. "I was . . . thinking."

"I just asked your opinion on an important matter." Nutatharis rose from his supper table, picked up his wine goblet and crossed the chamber to the window where Cyrodian was standing. "What are you staring at?" Nutatharis glanced out the window himself but saw only his twilight-shadowed garden three stories down: walkway, stone fountain, gargoyles, the long southern wing of his palace. "Is someone down there?" the king asked, annoyed.

Cyrodian fisted his hands, rapped the knuckles lightly on the window sill, then reached for the wine cup he had set on the stone. "Eromedeus," he replied coldly.

"Ah."

"He just went through that door." Still, Cyrodian stared at it.

Nutatharis returned to the table and sat down in a low-backed chair, threw out his legs and crossed them casually at the ankles. "You've been avoiding him," he observed, "ever since General Kustos's death."

Cyrodian faced him.

"Why?"

Cyrodian did not answer, but he turned his back to the open window and swallowed some of his wine.

"Are you frightened of him?" Nutatharis pursued. He regarded the giant with a bemused smile. "Not . . . frightened, perhaps. The wrong word."

"It is a personal matter, Nutatharis."

"There can be no 'personal matters' in this palace that interfere with duties of state. You are a man of office, Prince Cyrodian. I must ask you to explain yourself."

Cyrodian colored slightly but moved forward, sat down at the head of the table and leaned forward on propped elbows. "It has to do with . . . Kustos's death."

"Did Eromedeus murder him?"

Cyrodian's baleful eyes narrowed to slits. "I don't think we can say that."

"My physician tells me that Kustos's heart gave out. He did not die of his wounds gotten in the Lowlands. His heart—gave out."

Cyrodian coughed, began to reach for his cup, then let it sit where it was. "He was a superstitious man, wasn't he?"

"All men are superstitious in one way or another."

"Did you know, Nutatharis, that Kustos had religious beliefs?"

"Most of us exhibit religious impulses on our deathbeds. This strays from the issue at hand, Prince Cyrodian."

The giant swallowed a deep breath, showed the king a grim expression. "You know, don't you—you've known for a long time—that Eromedeus dabbles in . . . what shall I call it?"

"Sorcery?" Nutatharis smiled. "Perhaps that, too, is the wrong word. Chicanery, perhaps."

"Perhaps . . ."

"Are you telling me that Eromedeus, this . . . charlatan . . . somehow provoked General Kustos on his deathbed? Frightened him and caused such panic in a veteran man of arms that he suffered a seizure of the heart?"

Cyrodian showed his teeth; his broad face wrinkled. He did not look at Nutatharis but wrapped his paw-like hands around his wine cup and stared at the ornamental carvings on it. "I . . . believe that's what I'm saying, yes."

"Then why are you so apprehensive, Cyrodian? You're not a man to be—"

"Perhaps I, too," the Athadian grumbled, looking up, "have some . . . religious feelings. Superstitions."

"Indeed." Nutatharis cleared his throat noisily. "I must tell you, then, that I believe the best way for a man to deal with his fears, or his superstitions, is to face them. And when you started daydreaming over there, Prince Cyrodian, I was making the point to you that I think Eromedeus has served my court quite long enough."

"What do you mean?"

"I mean—I mean that Eromedeus has been here, in this palace, for a year. Sir Jors brought him to me because the man does sleight-of-hand. I retained him because of his astonishing memory and his keen knowledge of geography and politics. Wouldn't you keep such a man in your court were you king? He made his home here and I began to observe him. Eromedeus is not prone to spend much time with his fellowmen. I never said anything directly to him but let him find his own balance. It's best to do that, I've found: the surest way to test men is to observe them, never let them know they are being tested. Needless to say, I found Eromedeus wanting."

Cyrodian listened intently; much that he had had to piece together himself from bits of gossip and occasional remarks was now corroborated by what Nutatharis was telling him.

"And—yes, yes, I know all about these servant girls he's tortured and his midnight forays into the forests and his strange little rituals. A sorcerer? Hardly. But up here?" Nutatharis tapped his forehead with a finger. "Up here, a man is anything he believes himself to be. And I find Eromedeus to be untrustworthy."

Now the king leaned forward to face the Athadian directly. "I am about to return to the Lowlands, Prince Cyrodian. I am thinking of placing you in sole control of my army."

Cyrodian's eyes lit up; it was his strongest ambition.

"But before I do that— Well, you understand. We are both leaders of men; we both understand how allegiances must be trusted, and exercised—kept in shape like a muscle. And you and I, we've shared a very strong oath, Cyrodian. You understand, don't you, why I must ask you to do what must be done."

Cyrodian, nodding his head, swallowed thickly.

"This man has spent a year in my court. I cannot let him leave, and he is not worth my trouble to banish him into the mountains." Nutatharis leaned back, posing, strong and sure of himself. "I do not ask you to do this, my friend, to test your allegiance to me; we both know who and what we are and what we share in common. I do not ask you to do this because I think you are a brutal man, because I don't believe that of you. I merely wish you to do this thing because I can *trust* you, Cyrodian. And because you and I have sworn a powerful oath to one another, I think it only fair that your part of the bargain be dispatched quickly and efficiently. Then we will worry about it no longer."

Cyrodian stared into Nutatharis's dark eyes. "*Kill* . . . him?" His voice was guttural, almost choked when he spoke; Cyrodian immediately regretted the sound of that voice so he hurriedly coughed to camouflage its meaning and continued: "When, Nutatharis?"

58

The Emarian laughed. "Don't make it sound so venal! You don't feel any compunction about killing him, do you? The man is responsible for at least ten deaths, some of them children, and many were those of young women who could have served their nation in a much finer fashion."

Cyrodian, upon whom the remarks were not lost, did not smile; he merely nodded and stared at his wine cup.

Murder him? he thought worriedly. *Murder a man who cannot die?* . . .

The long blade had disappeared halfway into Eromedeus's body. Cyrodian had felt the mild resistance of organs against steel; yet as he withdrew it, there was no sign of any blood upon the shining metal, and upon Eromedeus's person there had been only clothing sliced and torn.

No blood.

"He cannot die!" Kustos, sobbing, had whispered from the bed. "Cyrodian! *He cannot die!* He can die only if . . . another gives up his life!"

And Eromedeus had laughed cruelly, the wind of his mockery moving the flames of the oil lamps in Kustos's death chamber.

Murder a man who cannot die? . . .

"What's the matter with you?" Nutatharis asked sharply. "Cyrodian! Why are you—"

He was cut short by the giant's sudden movement. Cyrodian kicked back his chair and rose to his full height. His great shadow, rippling like a thrown blanket, fell upon the long table.

He snarled.

Nutatharis stood up as well. Why was Cyrodian so—

"Now?" the Athadian rumbled at him.

Nutatharis laughed openly. "You know where he is, my friend. Dispatch the matter and return. We'll open more wine and discuss our new strategies for the Lowlands."

Cyrodian, breathing heavily, did not answer but only stood tall, his right hand on his sword pommel, and stared across the room.

"Cyrodian?"

His nostrils flared, his lips curled, and with an abruptness the king had seldom seen in a man of his size, Cyrodian slid around the table and lunged for the door, bootsteps thundering on the stone flags.

In a moment he was gone, the wind of his exit flickering the lit candles on the table, the doors left open and creaking gently on their rusty hinges.

Troubled by this strangeness, Nutatharis sat down again, replenished his cup and rubbed his forehead. He thought for several long minutes, then reached inside his vest and withdrew the latest missive he had received from King Elad.

Nutatharis had burned the previous two, and he had not yet answered this one. But now, in the wake of Cyrodian's odd behavior, he wondered if he didn't have two madmen in his house. The Athadian had always seemed to be in full possession of himself—perhaps too much so, Nutatharis now realized. Strong men, self-disciplined, often become bowstrings drawn too taut, too apt to snap. . . .

Elad's offer began to seem more appealing. What sort of man, after all, would indeed slay his brother, and perhaps his own mother?

Gold? More lucrative trade agreements? Weapons? Elad offered Nutatharis his choice of these or any other practical benefits (short of complete international cooperation, of course).

Nutatharis listened to the creaking door. He stared at a candle on his table and at the words King Elad had sent him. Carefully, he refolded the letter.

He did not touch it to the flame but replaced it inside his vest.

It was a human storm that burst into the room.

Eromedeus, startled, rose to his feet and dropped back.

Cyrodian paused halfway across the chamber; he swayed on powerful legs, his body bent in a posture of aggression. He smiled—cruelly, evilly.

Eromedeus sucked in a breath. "What do you—"

The giant stared at him, at the slim man dressed in a robe, weaponless, looking as ineffectual and purposeless as any middle-aged courtier. The table where the sorcerer had been sitting was littered with papers, pens and gourds of colored ink, crystal spheres used for magical things, small bowls filled with powders. But there was no one else in the room—no moaning virgins being bled dry, no screaming babies being burnt alive. . . .

Cyrodian's smile did not fade as he pulled his heavy sword from the sheath at his side. He held it out before him; catching the orange glow of the hanging oil lamps and the open hearth behind Eromedeus, it shimmered like a hot brand.

"You can die," the giant whispered coldly. "I know you can, Eromedeus. You tricked me before, didn't you?"

"Cyrodian! Don't—"

"You . . . *filth*! You killed Kustos! Are you some kind of *vampire*? Is that it? I know you can—" He coughed a laugh. "I know you can die, Eromedeus. And I'm going to kill you now."

Eromedeus's eyes lit with understanding. "Nutatharis . . . has finally learned, has he?"

"Nutatharis," Cyrodian growled, "doesn't know a thing! But you're not going to do to me what you did to Kustos! *Vampire*!"

"Cyrodian!"

But the giant charged forward. Eromedeus fell back and almost stepped into the fire in the wall behind him. The long littered table was between them; Cyrodian lurched to move around it but then, in a truculent show of strength, grasped the edge of the oak table with his left hand and lifted it. He grunted. Sweat shot from his forehead and neck; the seams of his leather vest began to rip. The table shook and trembled as the giant let out a howl of wrath—

"*Vam—piiiiire*!"

—and lifted the table completely off the floor and mightily pushed it away. It tilted precariously for a moment before tipping over and crashing to the floor with shuddering impact and a hurricane of noise and dust.

"*Vam-pire*!"

Eromedeus stepped away from the hearth; and as the black dust cleared, his deep-set eyes glowed with a malevolent glare. From his mouth came a sinister hiss.

Cyrodian charged him, sword up. Eromedeus made no move to escape, and again Prince Cyrodian's sword sank into the courtier's body. As Cyrodian shoved it in, he stared into Eromedeus's brilliant eyes, and a chill rippled through him.

"*Demon*!"

He pushed his sword in hilt-deep, so that the crosspiece sank under Eromedeus's ribs; the point scraped the hot wall-stones behind.

No blood . . .

Eromedeus's eyes glowed. "Fool," he whispered, showing his teeth.

Cyrodian went white. He jerked the sword back and forth so that it might rend a gaping crater of a wound in Eromedeus's belly. Yet it was as though he had sunk his steel into an image of clay.

"You—" The giant gasped, and again an iciness bled within him as he stared into those eyes. "You . . . *must . . . die!*"

"I have lived forever and cannot die," the sorcerer whispered

61

to him in his hollow, quiet voice. "Don't you think whole armies have tried to slay me, and failed?"

A low groan fluttered in Cyrodian's throat, then erupted as a hellish howl. Holding onto his sword, he threw himself back and staggered, regained his balance, waved his arms, wiped hair out of his face and stared—

Stared . . .

"What . . . *are* you," he breathed, "that you cannot . . . *die*?"

Eromedeus hissed at him.

Cyrodian grunted and moved forward again—slowly, this time, with his head turned partially aside, as a fearful dog will do when barking at intruders. He lifted his sword—but then dropped it to the floor.

"With my *hands*, then!" he yelled, jumping at Eromedeus.

The sorcerer jumped back, moved his arms up in a defensive stance. Cyrodian slapped them aside and gripped him by his shoulders. Sweat flew from his face.

"I'll . . . break your *back*," he grunted, "throw you . . . into the—"

"*Prince Cyrodian!*"

Eromedeus's eyes shot behind the giant; Cyrodian held the sorcerer where he was and turned to look.

"Cyrodian! *Put him down!*"

Slowly the Athadian released Eromedeus, turned and stared. King Nutatharis stood tall and angry, framed by the stone doorway. His lidded gaze moved from Cyrodian to Eromedeus.

"Did you see him?" the giant thundered.

Nutatharis nodded carefully. "I . . . saw."

"Sorcery! *Sorcery*, here in your—"

"Be quiet, Prince Cyrodian." Nutatharis, keeping his eyes on Eromedeus, came into the chamber on noiseless feet. "Keep your voice down or you'll rouse the guards."

"Rouse them, then!" Cyrodian cried out. "Get them down here! You'd *better*—"

"*Cyrodian!*" Nutatharis's voice was sudden, loud and angry. And when the Athadian, breathing heavily and sweating profusely, had restrained himself: "Please, my friend, . . . get you upstairs. Leave . . . us . . . if you would, for a moment."

"You want to stay here," Cyrodian asked, shocked, "with *him*?"

"For a moment." Nutatharis's tone was a cautious one.

"You're both—" But Cyrodian left it unsaid as he, fuming,

tromped from the chamber and left a trail of loud echoes in the corridor and up the stairwell.

Nutatharis observed Eromedeus with the keenness of an inquiring scientist.

The sorcerer stood where he was.

The king tapped his right foot lightly on the floor. "You," he said coolly, "have much to explain to me, strange one. I am prepared to listen."

Eromedeus swallowed a deep breath.

"I am prepared to listen . . . now."

2.

She had walked all the way over to Himn Avenue this morning to do her shopping; she and Adred were in need of fresh fruit, cheap paper and writing ink, as well as sealing wax, and Rhia thought it best not to be seen too often on the east side of the city. She'd taken the walkway over the Irol Viaduct and was surprised as she came into Himn Avenue to see crowds greater than usual for the middle of the week. At first she feared more riots. They had become spontaneous lately since the incident in Oru Square—demonstrations, explosions of temper and planned acts of violence by splinter groups of Suloskai, or groups calling themselves Suloskai or other names. Tension was running high in Bessara; everyone was suspect; double patrols of city guards cantered through the streets night and day, and the curfew was enforced strictly. Lord Uthis had not made a public appearance since that afternoon in Oru.

Rhia entered Himn Avenue apprehensively. Caught up in the jostling crowds, she tried to ascertain what the commotion was about, but people around her grunted only fragments of information—"the king's declaration," "the revolutionaries have only hurt themselves with this," "perhaps Elad's dead after all and they're keeping it secret." Yet no one seemed frightened. Rhia pushed her way toward the Oblut Exporting building, one wall of which was used for posting public notices. A thick crowd had gathered there. Rhia lifted her head to see what they were reading, but before she could catch a glimpse of anything, someone thrust a square of paper into her hand and moved on.

Rhia looked to see who it was and noticed several young men— low-level city service recruits—working through the throngs, distributing the handouts. She began to read the one given her—and nearly gasped out loud when she saw what it proclaimed:

‐Γ♥ΛVO ‐
ΔΑ ΟΠΟ d. Ø. ΑΟVO

ⵝΔΛ± ΔⴲΔΑΙΓ IШ ΠΟΡVO ‐

±ΛΔΑ ΟΛΛΟΓ Ợ IV ΟΑΟ : ╢ ΓΡ±Ш d.
IV ΔΡΙ +óZb : ΔШÞⴸ ΟΠΟΑΙ Øι....

SULVO
ad opo d. Ø Dovo.
Kale Athadis im Porvo.
Elad ollos *o* iv odo : 22 Grem d. iv ari 1879 : ambu opodi Øi. . . .

ANNOUNCEMENT
By Order of the Throne

Long Live the Empire!

King Elad on this day, 22 Grem of the Year 1879, hereby commands that the following procedures be implemented at once by the Governors or Appointees of Acting-governorship of all Cities, Towns or Districts within the Athadian Empire, as well as the Governors or Appointees of Acting-governorship of all Cities, Towns or Districts within all Provinces or Territories maintained by the Imperial Athadian Throne:

iru 1: Any person arrested on or after this date of 22 Grem 1879 is to be held in arrest by the authorities in whose jurisdiction the alleged perpetrator's crime or crimes were committed, while all charges of Felonious or Seditious Acts against the Empire brought against these persons are to be held in suspension pursuant to further Edicts issued by the Imperial Throne;

iru 2:   Each Governor or Appointee of Acting-governor-ship in each City, Town or District within the Athadian Empire, as well as within all Provinces or Territories maintained by the Imperial Athadian Throne, will immediately appoint not less than seven but not more than twelve individuals to sit as a Committee, which Committee will follow the Rules and Guidelines as set forth in the *Imperial Law Code Revised*, Book Fourteen, Chapter Seven, *Idri* 5–12, to submit proposals for the institution of Workers' *Sirots*, these *Sirots* or Business Advisory Committees to be—

Stunned, Rhia nearly dropped the announcement.
Sirots?

   —administered by Representatives chosen by the Masters and Supervisors of the Trade Guilds and other Public Assemblies recognized by the throne, its Officials and Sponsors—

It was true!

Slowly, as astonished as she was, Rhia rolled up the announcement, clutched it tightly and began making her way out of the throng. All around her lifted spontaneous cheers; roaring voices could be heard up and down Himn Avenue. Rhia heard the city guards calling for order, blowing their trumpets and loudly warning the collected crowds to move on once they had read the edict.

   —in accordance with the Guidelines of Imperial Advisory Statute Number Thirty-seven, *Imperial Law Code Revised*, Book Twelve—

Breaking free of the crowds, Rhia ran down the avenue, hurrying back toward the Irol Viaduct. She paused in an open area beside a fish stand to reread the notice.

It was true.

What could possibly have caused King Elad to agree to such a radical innovation?

Rhia went cold. Perhaps he was, after all, dead, and this edict was only a ruse to—

"Move along, move along!" cried one of the mounted patrol.

His horse cantered close by, and Rhia, deep in thought, looked up at him quickly and stepped out of the way. She stared straight into the eyes of the officer in the saddle.

"Is this true?" she asked him, voice trembling.

"It's true." His eyes narrowed as he regarded this dark-haired woman carefully. "It's true. . . . Now move along."

Rhia rolled up the announcement once more and hurried to the viaduct.

Behind her, the mounted guard waved a gloved hand to two other soldiers coming down Himn.

"Adred!" she exclaimed, back in their apartment. "It's got to be a trick of some kind! It must be!"

"Give me a moment, let me read this again. . . ." He lay back on the bed, knees up, scrutinizing the notice.

"We can't even be sure that this came from Elad, can we? Uthis might be trying to—"

"Shhh, Rhia. . . ."

—while all charges . . . are to be held in suspension. . . .

"It's not a trick," Adred told her, looking up. "Abgarthis assured me that Elad might make some kind of reform—or begin to make reforms. He's being so cautious with this that it seems unresolved. He's left it in the hands of the guilds . . . this isn't what we're after at all. . . ."

"I don't trust it," Rhia shook her head. "Adred—I just don't trust it. Listen to me." She walked over to the bed, sat down beside him. "I think it's time you and I left Bessara. This is some sort of trick of Uthis's. He can't expect it to—"

"Even if it is, Rhia, as soon as Elad discovers it—"

"But that's what I mean! In the meantime, Uthis can start arresting everyone in sight, cut off as many heads as—" She stopped short, the image chilling her.

But Adred disagreed. "This is official," he insisted. "Look at it. It's printed in blue ink; these marks imprinted in the paper can only come from the capital."

"I still don't—"

She was interrupted by a knock at the door. Giving a look to Adred: "Who did you tell to come by?"

"No one."

Rhia continued to stare at him.

"Rhia! It's only Them-olo or some of Mirhu's friends! They're as surprised by this announcement as we are!"

A heavy fist hammered again on the door.

Adred nodded to her; Rhia slowly stood up from the bed and crossed the room.

Rhia pulled open the door—and gasped.

Adred sat up, stared—stared directly into the eyes of a sergeant of the City Patrol.

"Stay where you are!" A big man in government colors with one gray glove resting on the sword at his hip, he moved past Rhia and walked to the center of the room. "Anyone else here?"

Two more guards stepped in, one of them urging Rhia to stay where she was.

"What do you think you're doing?" she nearly screamed. "You can't come in here—"

One of the recruits in the doorway tried to grab her arm; Rhia shook him away and hurried to Adred, who moved from the bed and got to his feet.

"Still think this is *legal*?" she yelled at him. "This is one of Uthis's—"

"*Quiet!*" the sergeant shouted.

Rhia, red-faced, gritted her teeth.

"You're under arrest," the sergeant told them, "on suspicion of seditious activity. Come along quietly or we'll be forced to—"

"You can't arrest us!" Rhia yelled at him. She reached over to the bed, picked up the public notice and waved it. "You can't—"

"Rhia!" Adred took hold of her shoulders. "They *can* arrest us! They just can't—"

"We can't execute you," the sergeant finished for him. "At least not until we receive word from the capital. Now come along. You're rebels and we can't leave you free to walk the streets like lawful citizens." To one of the recruits in the doorway: "Private . . ."

The young man stepped up to Rhia. "Lift your arms above your head, please."

"I don't have any weapons! If I did, I'd have used them by now!"

The sergeant lent Adred a stern look, a warning to him to keep his woman under control.

"Rhia, it's a formality. Don't—"

But he said no more; and Rhia, defiant but cornered, raised her arms. The young private quickly, and somewhat self-consciously, ran his hands down her body and legs. He found the knife she wore strapped to her thigh and asked her to remove it. Lowering her hands cautiously, she unsheathed it and handed it to him.

"Step this way, now," the sergeant, producing a pair of manacles from his belt, instructed her.

Grimly, Rhia walked to him and put her hands behind her back; the sergeant locked her wrists together.

Adred was weaponless; the private asked him to turn around, and he was manacled.

"You're an aristocrat, aren't you?" the sergeant asked him as he led Adred and Rhia down the stairs of the apartment house.

"Yes. . . . How could you tell?"

"I can tell. After a while . . . you can tell." He shook his head. "I don't want to see any more bloodshed and people screaming and all this. I don't understand why you people, you aristocrats, are involved in this at all. I don't understand it at all, not at all."

The master of the house and a number of his guests, who were seated at tables in the front room, nearly knocked over trays as they fought to get a look at Adred and Rhia, who were led outside to a waiting cart. It was an ordinary farm cart, its bed covered with damp old straw, its walls reinforced with metal spikes.

The young private helped Rhia inside, then climbed in after her. Jumping up awkwardly, Adred followed them. The sergeant double-checked his manacles, then told him to get toward the rear of the cart.

"What would you do," Adred asked him, as the sergeant turned toward his horse, "if your son found out that the City Patrol was rotten—thoroughly rotten—and he tried to tell you about it, and you got offended and didn't want to hear that sort of talk? But he knew the City Patrol had gone to hell, and so he started planning to get rid of it and started a new kind of city patrol. What would you say to that?"

The sergeant, humoring him, grinned and shook his head. "I don't know," he replied. "I don't know. My son wouldn't ever do anything like that. And there's nothing wrong with the City Patrol in this town, young man."

Adred frowned and watched him walk to his horse, mount it and wave the cart forward. It jostled to life, and Adred struggled toward the rear and crouched beside Rhia.

3.

Lord Colonel Vardorian was not an ambitious man. He had always believed that that person serves his country best who puts his nation's interests before his own. Vardorian was even-tempered, prudent, practical; he had risen through the ranks and gained command over the Seventh Regiment West, not through any heroism in combat nor through glory-seeking, but by patiently applying whatever tools he had available to whatever tasks there were to be done. And while the ordinary Athadian citizen had never heard of Vardorian's name, the Colonel was regarded with respect by all who knew him within the Imperial Army.

It seemed appropriate to Vardorian, then, that—given his skills and his temperament—his truest test as a leader should come, not from ordering men onto a battlefield, but in taking charge of a delicate situation where divergent, antagonistic elements needed to be brought to some sort of mutual agreement or balance. When his close friend Captain First Grade Lutouk had resigned his commission in Sulos following the Shemtu Square Rebellion, Vardorian had been Lutouk's first choice to succeed him. Flattered, Vardorian had sailed from Isita on the Ussal to meet with King Elad and the Military Tribunal of the Athadian High Council, where he was sworn into his new office as Acting-governor of Sulos in the Kendia Province. It was Vardorian who had come to Sulos to take command of the Twenty-third and Twenty-fourth Legions there and to arrange for the rebuilding of the port city. And it was Vardorian who had made the first move to calm the tempers that still ran high in Sulos: he had ordered that the martial control of the city be lifted in thirty days, as well as all bans, curfews and restrictions, if the people of Sulos would keep the public peace.

His rational political gesture had accomplished much. Where Lord Uthis in Bessara to the south had imposed an iron fist upon his city in an attempt to curb seditionist violence, Vardorian's policy had led to over two months of calm in Sulos. Vardorian had made it his business to visit the taverns and halls of Sulos to speak with the people—both the working people and the aristocrats and business gentry. "You may kill a man who has an idea," Vardorian said time and again, "but that doesn't mean you've killed the idea," a saying that became common throughout Sulos. It was an astonishingly moderate attitude for a man who owed his rank and authority to a throne which had so far shown, contrarily, little lenience and less patience.

Lord Colonel Vardorian also commenced sending letters and recommendations regularly to King Elad in Athad; and it was his voice, as much as Count Adred's and a handful of other responsible aristocrats', that led Elad to begin considering the revolutionary ideals in a more open frame of mind. The assassination attempt against the king had given Vardorian much to fear: he suspected that the angers he had tried so hard to keep in check would surface again. But while this had happened in Bessara, in the capital and in other cities, Sulos itself passed through the crisis in relative calm. And in the months that followed, it seemed as if that calm would prevail.

Lord Colonel Acting-governor Vardorian was surprised and saddened, therefore, to have a report brought to him on the morning of the first of Sath which indicated that farmers in the northeastern crop district along the swollen Dirus River had blockaded the roads leading into the vicinity and, in an altercation, had taken the lives of two young businessmen representing the House of Lodul, a food processing and distributing company based in Sulos.

"Why are they doing this?" Vardorian asked his city ministers that morning over breakfast.

"The revolutionaries," he was told, "have convinced the farmers that they're being underpaid for the grain they grow and that the great profits the Loduli make should properly be shared by their workers or distributed to help the underprivileged. The growers get three silvers a bin; Lodul packages the flour or bakes it into bread and charges three *ieds* or more a bin. It costs Lodul nowhere near that much to turn grain into bread. Therefore, the revolutionaries and the farmers claim they're being taken advantage of."

"They are," Vardorian agreed, ignoring the shocked looks he received. "But matters will hardly improve if we resort to violence. I assume that the Loduli will lose a great amount of money if crops are not planted within the next few weeks, isn't that right? Well, then. These representatives of the House of Lodul—they were insured by their employers, weren't they, against . . . accidental death?"

"I believe so, Lord Vardorian. The Loduli did business with the throne, and so naturally they were obliged to buy insurance for—"

"Yes, yes, that's right." After a moment he made a practical decision. "Tell these farmers that if they remove their blockade and do as they have agreed to do with the House of Lodul, I will begin an investigation into the matter. They will hear from me within the month. Their families, as well as others, need that grain, no matter whose business ultimately claims to own it."

"Yes, Lord Vardorian."

"But we're going to have to send a squad out there to supervise the blockade's dismantling and protect the lives of these businessmen. Send Commander Lutho to me; I'll dispatch the Eighth Squadron under his direction."

"Yes, Lord Vardorian."

"And . . . get me a scribe. We're going to have to notify the throne of this. . . ."

It was Lord Abgarthis who received the report from Acting-governor Vardorian; and in the box full of dispatches, contracts and other official documents with which Vardorian's report had been shipped (and which Abgarthis routed to different offices of the bureaucracy) was a long scroll from the offices of Lord Uthis of Bessara listing the most recent political arrests in that city.

Abgarthis, who had been scanning these lists from Bessara and other northern cities for months, found his patience rewarded at last.

> . . . 20: Helud dos Helud, public involvement with Lord so-Dulis.
> *28 Grem 1879 DP:*
> 21: Viran dos Semdasian, complicity with seditionists;
> 22: Adred dos Diran, *akod*, complicity with seditionists;
> 23: Rhia des——, companion, complicity with seditionists;
> 24: Nolos dos Avurru, threatening political assassination, threatening man of the Patrol with a weapon; public drunkenness and disorder; killing the pet monkey of . . .

Adred!

He smiled hugely to see that name. Still alive, then—thank the gods! Abgarthis had realized too late that he should never have let the young man leave the capital. He was bound to get himself into trouble; but now that he was safely tucked away in Uthis's prison . . .

Well, in a day or two Abgarthis's letter would reach him, and the royal seal in itself would be persuasive enough to induce Lord Uthis to return the radical to Athad.

Abgarthis set aside the list and began sorting through the other documents and scrolls. When he read the report from Lord Vardorian, a chill went through him. Sulos had been quiet for months; if the revolutionaries meant to—

Gods!

Abgarthis, stunned, rose from his desk, walked from his chair and paced quickly as a bold plan formed in his mind. The brilliance of it excited him; but he carefully played out each step, as he considered its possible ramifications.

He poured himself a cup of sweet wine, sat again at his desk and stared at the documents. He placed Uthis's list of political prisoners on his left, Vardorian's report of the farmers' blockade on his right. He glanced from one to the other and slowly sipped his wine. Bessara . . . to Sulos . . .

Abgarthis took down a sheet of parchment from one of the desk shelves, uncapped a reed pen and unstoppered a gourd of ink, and began to write.

Early that afternoon following the midday meal, Lord Abgarthis made his way into the palace eastern gardens, where King Elad was sitting with Queen Salia taking sun and fresh air. Lord Abgarthis was pleased to see Elad out in the open, and it gladdened his heart further to find the king and his wife, this afternoon, enjoying one another's company. Salia was holding Elad's hand and whispering things to him to make him smile.

The king made to rise as Abgarthis approached, but his minister gestured for him to remain where he was.

"I am glad to see you taking exercise, my king. Queen Salia, you compliment Nature with your beauty."

"Thank you, Lord Abgarthis."

"You're in a good mood," Elad observed. "I take it that we haven't yet had any response to my public announcement?"

"None as of yet, Lord Elad."

"Well, I'm sure every man of Council and office is plotting to undo it. To what do we owe the visit?"

"I have received some dispatches from the north, and I thought you should be alerted."

Elad frowned. "News from the north puts you in a good mood? The world has changed overnight."

"Alas, no. Actually, there is a serious dispatch from Sulos and . . . important news from Bessara. But I have the idea that much benefit could come of these events."

Elad nodded at the documents Abgarthis had brought with him. "Let me see what this is. . . ."

The minister passed them to his king. "This top one is a report from Lord Colonel Vardorian in Sulos. Next is a list of political arrests recently made in Bessara. Following that—something of my own . . ."

72

Elad was intrigued; he read the papers in the order Abgarthis had handed them to him. When he'd finished the dispatch from Vardorian, he cursed quietly.

"No, the world has not changed."

"Continue, please."

Elad read the second parchment. "So . . . our Count Adred has finally been netted. Well, they won't behead him; he can thank me for that."

"Now, please read what I have done, King Elad—this one. With your permission, I'm going to send it to Bessara this evening."

Elad read.

Abgarthis leaned on his walking stick and smiled to Queen Salia. He enjoyed the beauty of the garden and glanced down the walkway at the tall, armored Khamar who stood guard beside a fountain.

"Are you serious?" Elad asked when he'd finished. His tone sounded critical.

"Absolutely," Abgarthis replied. "I leave Adred no choice—but I do it in the most civil way possible. He will agree to this."

"Are you certain?"

Abgarthis nodded succinctly and smiled.

Elad considered the plan as Salia glanced at what the minister had written.

After a moment: "Very well," the king allowed. "Send it, with my seal. And if Adred does as you've asked him to do . . . well, I'll cancel the report of his arrest and return his bank holdings and property to him. But don't tell him that."

"It wouldn't do any good to bribe him, in any event," Abgarthis smiled. "But to convince him? That is an achievement. The man is no fool."

"And neither are you, Abgarthis. Neither are you."

"Thank you, my king; your praise is generous. If you will excuse me, now? . . ."

Three days later, Lord Uthis received a Khamar in the main office of his palace. The envoy handed Uthis orders from the king; Uthis read, and scowled.

"I am not in the habit of bending my knee to prisoners of the empire."

"I believe," replied the Khamar, "that King Elad said something in his orders about immediate action?"

Uthis scowled more deeply. He was lord in his city and as

powerful as any man might be within his own domain, but even this palace guard, a soldier, had more political strength, at this hour, than did Uthis himself. It was humiliating.

He sighed heavily and pushed back his chair, stood up from his desk. "Very well. . . ." He led the way downstairs, to the first floor of his palace and still farther down, two stories underground where the prisons were located. Winding stone stairs led through damp corridors; soldiers slapped their chests respectfully and unlocked heavy iron doors; and the Khamar followed Lord Uthis every step of the way to cell number 132 where Count Adred was housed with three other revolutionaries.

"Open it," Uthis ordered the recruit on duty.

The young soldier, in awe of both his commander and an official representative of the throne, did as requested, fumbling nervously with his key until finding the right wedge to release the lock.

As soon as the door swung back, two of the prisoners inside stood up and stepped forward. The Khamar, reacting with ingrained discipline, had his longsword out in the space of a breath. The young jailer, astonished at the fleetness, moved aside and lowered his right hand to his own sword pommel—just in case trouble developed and the Khamar needed any assistance.

"Count Adred!" Uthis bawled. "Step out here!"

The two prisoners who blocked the opening carefully stepped away as Adred moved forward and entered the corridor. His clothes were rumpled, his hair tousled, his beard flecked with straw and bits of dirt. He regarded the Khamar keenly with surprise in his eyes, then shot a look of mistrust at Lord Uthis.

"What is it?" he asked quietly.

Uthis ordered the jailer: "Close the door. Now!"

The young recruit did so; the Khamar sheathed his sword, then pulled from his belt Abgarthis's rolled message. He handed it to Adred.

"Lord Abgarthis asked me to have you read this statement the moment I met you. I'm to be your escort."

Adred accepted the scroll, squinted at Uthis. "Is this some kind of trick?"

"I wish it were, you damned red."

"I am under orders from the throne, Count Adred," the Khamar assured him.

"First they knock you down," Adred muttered, unrolling the message, "then they help you up, just so they can . . . knock you down. . . ." He fell quiet as he read Abgarthis's message.

74

"Name of the . . . gods. . . ." He glanced at the Khamar. "Do you know what this says?"

A nod. "I'm under orders to assist you in fulfilling King Elad's dictate. If you decline to do so—"

"What is it, Adred?" one of the prisoners called to him.

"Shut up, you!" growled Uthis.

"You can't hurt me!" was the angry response from the cell.

"I can't *kill* you, you damned radical, but I'll sure as hell make you *bleed*!"

The letter trembled in Adred's hands as he reread it. "He wants me to—betray my friends?" he whispered.

"The decision is yours entirely, Count Adred," the Khamar told him. "But I don't believe Lord Abgarthis means for you to betray anyone; he only wishes the best for the empire."

Uthis sneered. "*I* can tell him what's best for the empire!"

Adred swallowed a deep breath, folded the parchment and tucked it inside his vest. "I'll do it," he agreed, "on one condition."

"Count Adred, King Elad's terms are unconditional."

Turning to Uthis, Adred demanded: "I want Rhia freed as well. She goes with me."

Uthis laughed in his face. "Never! Back inside with you, 'Count' Adred!"

"I'm afraid," affirmed the Khamar, "that King Elad made reference only to yourself."

"Very well," Adred agreed. "But you'll have to return to him empty-handed, and you'll have to explain why I refuse to go along with this. Because I'm willing to do as Elad and Abgarthis ask— only I want Rhia to come with me. She's no more guilty than I am. But . . . you know Abgarthis, soldier. You tell me—wouldn't he be willing to agree to this? What do you think his reaction would be?"

The Khamar didn't answer immediately, so Uthis interposed: "I suspect his answer would be to lock you up again, my friend, so back in you go. You're a political prisoner, don't you—"

"Lord Abgarthis," broke in the Khamar, "makes it a point to work *with* people, not against them. Were the conditions of this— Rhia's—arrest," he asked Uthis, "the same as Count Adred's?"

Begrudgingly, Lord Uthis had to admit that they were.

"Then I suggest," allowed the Khamar, "that, under the circumstances, we allow Count Adred this privilege and get on with the throne's business."

"It'll be your responsibility!" Uthis fumed at him. "Your

75

responsibility! Does Elad intend to free every damned radical in his kingdom, now?"

"She's my responsibility," Adred told him in a quiet voice. The Khamar nodded.

Uthis threw his hands behind his back and rocked on his feet for a moment, ground his teeth together, then told the jailer: "Cell 127. Down there."

The recruit began fishing through his key ring as he moved on down the corridor. The others followed him. When he unlocked the cell door and pulled it open, women's voices called out in surprise.

"Rhia?" Adred asked.

"Yes? . . ." She stepped to the opening.

Adred waved her outside. "Come on. We're free."

"*What*?"

"*I'm* free," he amended, as she took his hand and stared at Uthis and the Khamar. "And I'm taking you with me."

"Adred . . . what's happened?"

"All right!" Uthis barked, nodding ahead. "Let's get out of here!"

The Khamar started down the corridor with Adred and Rhia following and Uthis behind them, while the jailer locked up the cell.

"Adred!" Rhia whispered to him, holding his hand tightly. "Will you tell me what's happened?"

"We're leaving Bessara." He looked at her: she was as dirty and pale as he was. "On orders from King Elad, I have to leave Bessara and go to Sulos. And I'm taking you with me."

She stared at him wide-eyed as they followed the Khamar up the stairs.

That evening, as the purple-and-gold-sailed royal galley made its way northward under a calm breeze and a full moon, Adred and Rhia, bathed and freshly dressed, stood at the rail and watched the gray waves rock against the dark sky. The Khamar was with them.

Rhia quietly asked Adred, "Why?"

"Hm?"

"Why bring me along?"

Adred didn't answer. The Khamar, standing next to him, made a signal that he was leaving to use the bucket and stepped down into the waist. Adred faced Rhia.

"Because . . . you don't love me, I suppose." He smiled. "But I couldn't leave you there, could I? We could probably use you in Sulos."

76

" 'We?' Who's 'we,' Adred?"

He frowned. "I phrased that the wrong way. I shouldn't have—"

"Adred, will you please tell me what's happening?"

He stepped away from the rail and put his hands on her shoulders, looked her in the eyes. She was achingly beautiful in the moonlight, her long red hair touched by the cold silver of the night, her slim face partially in shadows, lips glimmering, eyes shining. Maybe she looked particularly attractive to him tonight because of—circumstances.

"We're free," he told Rhia. "But we're free only because I've agreed to do something for Elad."

"*What* are you doing for him?" Her voice was tense.

"Nothing to jeopardize us. I may be jeopardizing a friendship, but . . . that's all I'm doing."

"Adred . . ."

"The Suloskai are revolting again in Sulos," he told her. "Elad wants me to—intervene for him. Leave it at that, all right, Rhia?"

She smirked. "Something mysterious going on and I'm supposed to—"

"It's not mysterious. I just don't want to talk about it until we reach Sulos."

The Khamar returned. As he stepped up and moved to the rail, Rhia made a sound in her throat, turned from Adred and went down the steps, heading for her berth.

As the sounds of her footsteps receded, the Khamar snorted and commented: "Women."

Adred waited until Rhia had vanished into the shadows, then turned and leaned again on the rail. "Oh, she's all right," he said quietly. "She's just headstrong. She gets into trouble because she wants to do the right thing."

"Everybody," replied the Khamar, "wants to do the right thing. But the world's still in trouble."

Adred looked at him. He had never thought of the palace guards as a particularly reflective or talkative group of men: it seemed to go against their discipline and training. They were elite. But then . . . they were men.

"Tell me," he asked this one, "what provoked King Elad to do this?"

"I couldn't say, Count Adred."

"But this is totally unlike him. He has no sympathy for the rebellion, for—reformers."

"I don't know," the Khamar, staring at the moon, answered laconically. "But the whole palace feels different now. The king

77

seems to have had a change of heart since that bastard tried to stab him."

Adred contemplated it. "That would certainly change a man," he agreed, not meaning to sound disrespectful. "Perhaps I should give him more credit. Do they know we're coming?"

"No, Count Adred."

"Just as well," he muttered. "Just as well that they don't . . ."

He looked for a flock of birds in the sky, but there was none—only the full moon, the brightly painted clouds, the quick-moving silver waves.

Only those—and the sound of his own beating heart . . .

4.

The two stood alone in the small enclosed courtyard. Lightning hissed in the sky and a strong drizzle wetted them; only a single, shielded lamp, which Nutatharis held in his left hand, gave them light. Behind Nutatharis sat two of his dogs, great black beasts with coats shiny in the rain, eyes red in the darkness. Before the king stood the wanderer, Eromedeus—a very changed Eromedeus from the man Sir Jors had brought to Lasura a year earlier.

He was now an Eromedeus without pretense, an Eromedeus in whose eyes burned a timeless flame, whose erect posture and plain expression conveyed an attitude perhaps of arrogance, but again of dignity, and certainly of great pathos. A man dressed well in garments lent him by the king—heavy cloak, woolen shirt and breeches, new leather boots. Across one arm was draped a long rough robe.

"If there is anything else you wish for or will need," Nutatharis told the wanderer, "tell me now, or leave without it. You cannot return here."

Eromedeus was silent for a moment as he regarded the king. When he spoke, it was in a voice quiet but strong-willed, knowing. "Do you know what fascinates me?" he asked Nutatharis. "It fascinates me that after all I have told you, all I have described, and all that you now know, your reaction is to cast me out. That is your impulse; that is your decision. It fascinates me, Nutatharis, but it does not astonish me. I believe you fear me, or fear the fact that you can make no threat against me which has any strength. Isn't that true? But in all my years I have never met a man of authority who treated me otherwise. I am threatening to men of authority, not because I am strange—all things are strange in their essence—but because my secret is Time, Nutatharis: Time always undermines authority."

Nutatharis's reply to this was a cold one. "You can think what you like. I do not fear you, and my threats are not empty. Perhaps I can't slay you, Eromedeus, but I could chain you in a dungeon where you would never know anyone, have no food or water, where you would rot."

Eromedeus smiled wisely. "I need no food or water, king. And I have never known anyone other than myself, for who is there like myself? Your threats are hollow, Nutatharis. I would outlive your dungeon." He studied the Emarian carefully. "But I suspect that you still do not believe that I am what I say I am. Does even this monumental truth seem false to you?"

"I believe you are a sorcerer and a charlatan, in touch with shadows, and that you are a vampire, and foul. I do not believe that you have lived as long as the gods, Eromedeus."

"The gods live forever, King Nutatharis; I will live only until the tribes of man extinguish themselves." The wanderer's eyes brightened. "I ask you again—give me the life of one slave-girl, give me one soldier—and bid them willingly give their soul to me. Then I will leave your sight freely, and you will have no need to chase me."

"You will begone now, Eromedeus. You have lived forever? And you have never found a single life to give itself to you? I think you lie."

"Would you condemn yourself to eternal death, Nutatharis, out of love for one the gods have cursed? You know only yourself; I have known all of mankind. I have approached the frailest of us, those reduced by wasting disease: they have refused me. I have trodden the battlefields after days of carnage and I have whispered to mutilated carcasses that no longer deserve to be called men: they all refused me. There is no love in the hearts of men, only jealousy and acquisitiveness, wants and needs, only posturings of the heart."

"You speak of love, monster? You have tortured babies, bled young women to make them suffer."

"I bled their flesh to free their spirits, to awaken them to greater things than this earthly maze. Yet all are deluded; the tribes of men are still young, their revolving spirits are yet too lost and young."

Eromedeus shook his head. "Love, O king, is a storm; it is not a quiet dawn, it is not placid, it is not warm flesh coupling to sate lusts. Were you ever to confront true love, it would demolish you with its power. I knew it once," the wanderer admitted in a low voice, "or felt that I knew it, and thought then that surely the gods would free me."

"You speak in riddles, and I've had enough."

"I speak in great truths. I speak of purposes, King Nutatharis—and not the challenges men give themselves disguised as purposes. I am one of the great tests the gods have given to men. You feel no great wind in my presence, do you? You feel no breath of the gods, no heavy sound of time? You were born dead to such things, and life is such a trap that you have ignored doors opened to you. Your life, King Nutatharis, . . . it is a brief thing, more brief than you suspect. You fill your days and nights and hours with thoughts and troubles, intentions and actions, yet neither you nor other men ever touch what you truly are. Where is the god in you, Nutatharis? Comes to you a man who might open the wonders of eternity to you, and you think he speaks only in words, and you think him a liar. Am I a liar? I am all that you and every man fears, Nutatharis, yet all that you desire. You think your will and your identity are the makings of eternity? Eternity laughs at you!"

Nutatharis stepped ahead and unlatched the courtyard gate; his dogs rose instantly, baring their teeth, slavering. The king nodded outside—outside the city, where the night and the rain had created a damp mist that hid the green fields and the forests and the distant mountains.

"Go, now," he commanded the undying wanderer. "If your words are true, still, they are nothing to me."

"Then perhaps these words will have meaning for you, Nutatharis. Remember what I say. The world is a battlefield, the world is at war; but it is not a war of soldiers, and there is no battlefield of blood. It is a war of hearts that we witness and are joined in, a battlefield of thoughts and great purposes, of men striving to gain a balance and hold it. You believe in false things, King Nutatharis; many men have, since the start of humanity. I did once; and it is my great curse that, aware, I have lived for millennia but have gained no wisdom, for I have never died for my soul to be reborn. The rebirth of men is the cycle of their wisdom, O king; and men die and are reborn, just as the earth dies and is reborn. And that will bring about the end of this war. You will not win, Nutatharis. Were I to live a thousand times the length of what I have already suffered, still . . . I might not witness the outcome of this war. But the outcome is known to me already."

"Begone now!" Nutatharis growled at him.

"The outcome of the earth is to be reborn with the heart of a child, Nutatharis. But you . . . you will yourself be slain by the heart of a child, and your own fear will encourage the slaying. Fear . . . and a child's heart reborn in fear, thinking it truth."

Before the wrathful Nutatharis could make answer to this, Eromedeus stepped toward the open gate, then paused and looked back as though to speak.

"A man, remember, may wish for more than he can endure. Recall that, O king, when you face your own shadows."

"Get gone, wanderer!"

Eromedeus nodded and stepped outside, turned his back to the king and began to walk away into the mists of the night, into the darkness.

Nutatharis pushed closed the gate, bolted it securely, turned quickly on his heel and by the light of his small lamp started across the courtyard for his palace. His dogs began to follow, but he commanded them: "Stay! Guard this door!" The great beasts whined but crouched where they were and stared after their master as he went.

Cyrodian awoke just a little before dawn to the sounds of a loud commotion outside. He threw himself quickly from his bed and tramped to a window, yanked up the sash; he looked out over peaked portico rooftops and a garden of small trees to see troops of soldiers collecting in one of the wide palace courtyards. They were dressed in burnished armor and moving into rigid formations.

Cyrodian growled. He had had no word from Nutatharis that the king intended any military demonstration or review. What was the purpose of this?

The giant stormed across the floor and threw open his chamber door, passed through the small entrance room and heaved open a second door. In the corridor outside, guards were spaced along the walls.

"Come here!" Cyrodian called to one of them.

The young man across from him stared at the Athadian, who was dressed only in cotton breeches, belt and side-knife.

"Come here!"

The young guard moved uncertainly across the hall as his companions watched.

"What's going on out there?" Cyrodian growled. "Where's Nutatharis?"

"What do you mean, Prince Cyrodian?"

"The soldiers! The troops! They're taking formation out there! What the hell is Nutatharis doing?"

The guard shook his head. "I do not know, Prince Cyrodian. King Nutatharis—"

The giant growled at him and turned away, slammed closed the door and returned to his sleeping chamber. He furiously pulled on his boots and a shirt, a leather vest and his sword. Then he hurried out of his room and thundered down the hallway, yelling to one of the other guards he passed:

"Where's the king?"

"At his breakfast, sir."

Cyrodian stormed into the main feasting hall, but Natatharis was not there. Stewards and serving maids, who quick-stepped through the corridors, hurried out of his way as the giant stormed toward the northern exit. When Sir Jors called to him, Cyrodian snarled at him:

"Is the king out there?"

Sir Jors, dough-faced and well-dressed in his military blues, warned several young recruits with him to quiet, then asked Cyrodian: "Nutatharis?"

"Is there another king?"

"He is in the courtyard reviewing his troops."

Cyrodian moved on, passed through the rear hallways of the palace and down a wide flight of marble stairs. Two young women, just exiting the kitchens with heavy trays, quickly disappeared again into clouds of steam to escape the oncoming giant.

He made his way outside, down a long patio and through a landscaped arbor, into the enclosed courtyard. From the cramped, closed indoors, he was thrust suddenly into blinding daylight, high blue skies, and an army of three thousand soldiers and horses stretched along the bricks. On the high walls to Cyrodian's right fluttered hundreds of pennants and flags, and officers of the army stood atop the heights to inspect the formations and call out directions. Before him, as the Athadian charged ahead, was Nutatharis on a dressed white horse flanked by dozens of retainers, squadrons of helmets and shields, shining boots, and tall spears and halberds.

Nutatharis caught the gesture of one of his men, urged his horse around and watched as Cyrodian stalked toward him. The king's eyes were half-lidded, his mouth a sneering line beneath his mustache.

"Why was I not informed?" Cyrodian bellowed, as he came up to Nutatharis.

His answer, in a cold voice: "Is there any reason why I should have informed you?"

"I'm the leader of these men!" Cyrodian bawled. "What's the meaning of this, Nutatharis?"

The king studied him from where he sat. The giant was red-faced, dripping with sweat, unwashed, trembling with rage. Nutatharis moved his eyes from Cyrodian to the soldiers standing just behind him: ten officers and thirty footmen, all in a file, awaiting the call of the horns to proceed in formation.

Nutatharis lifted his right hand from the reins; the soft leather of his glove curled and wrinkled like thick flesh in the morning light. He held the hand straight and nodded quickly to the soldiers behind Cyrodian.

Before the giant understood what was happening, he heard blades whisked from their scabbards. Heavy gloves grabbed his arms, helmets and regalia surrounded him, two sword-points sank lightly into the soft behind his knees. One of the soldiers lifted Cyrodian's sword from its sheath; someone else removed the knives from his belt.

"Nutatharis! What is—"

"You are under arrest, Athadian," the king told him, "on the charge of matricide—"

"*No!*"

"—and you will be returned imme—"

"*No!*"

"—diately to the capital of your country—"

"*No!* Nutatharis, *no!*"

"—to face the mercy and justice of your brother, King Elad."

"*Damn you, Nutatharis, don't do this!*"

"Manacle him and remove him to the prison."

"Nutatharis, you *can't*—"

As Cyrodian, bellowing and howling, was dragged away, Nutatharis kneed his horse around and, feigning deafness, continued the review of his troops.

5.

When the royal galley made dock at Sulos, it was met on the wharves by a coterie of city soldiers. Blockades were set up so that the intrigued public could be kept at a distance. Word spread quickly along the streets, however, that a palace ship had thrown anchor, and very quickly crowds of spectators assembled, shoving against the wooden barricades in attempts to see past the soldiers' human wall. Raucous chants soon lifted from all directions— protests from working people, unemployed citizens, anonymous rebels and rebel sympathizers.

Adred disembarked with Rhia and the Khamar, and he was surprised to see so volatile a temperament in the streets. As the three of them made their way onto the stone quay, the officer in charge of the troops, a young lieutenant, saluted the Khamar.

"We had no word of your coming, Commander."

The Khamar handed him a small scroll bearing the royal seal. "King Elad thought it best to keep our arrival secret. Will you escort us to Lord Vardorian immediately?"

The officer saluted, lifted to his mouth the whistle that hung on a chain around his neck and blew it; instantly twenty cavalrymen advanced, and behind them a large carriage. The carriage was dirty and torn in places, the royal seal of the governorship on it defaced and discolored.

"For your protection," the lieutenant told the three, "it would be best that you remain unseen until we get past the crowds."

The Khamar nodded. Adred, as he walked toward the carriage, held Rhia's hand and asked:

"What's happened here, Lieutenant? We heard of protests by a few farmers, but that was all."

"Food riots," was the answer. "Empty bellies, my lord, and short tempers."

"Rebels?" Rhia asked, as she stepped inside the carriage.

"They're behind it, my lady, yes."

The ride through the streets and down Uia Boulevard to the governor's mansion on Shemtu Square was bewildering and frightening. The carriage was the focus of harsh yells all along its route; hurled objects—bricks, stones, pieces of wood—could be heard striking the escort patrol, and occasionally something thrown reached the carriage itself and bounced off the wooden framework with a loud crack or pushed in the covering with the effect of a blister erupting through the skin.

But the noises of the angry crowds dwindled as they approached Shemtu Square. Adred and Rhia heard a few low blasts from horns, the clatter of boots and many horses, and the screech of metal gates being pulled open. When the carriage rumbled to a stop, the lieutenant, Revar, exited first, spoke in a low tone with another officer, then lent his hand to Rhia. Adred and the Khamar followed.

Adred was shocked by the changes that had taken place in Shemtu Square. He had not been there since the previous winter—after the riots but before the rebuilding had begun. The square was no longer an open area fed by half a dozen streets and able to accommodate busy crowds of shoppers and strollers. The great fountains were gone; the small shops opposite the governor's mansion were absent; the city library, which had stood at the southeastern corner of the square, was blocked up with wooden boards and masonry. The entrance to the mansion, once open to the square, was now protected by a tall stone wall, and admittance could be gained only through a heavy metal gate guarded by numerous soldiers.

Count Adred stared at these things in awe; his fingers tightened involuntarily as he held Rhia's hand and she complained.

"It's all changed," he told her. "They've changed—everything. . . ."

She had never been to Sulos before, but she tried to imagine what he must be feeling.

Adred stared at the library like a child befuddled by the sight of a familiar parent who has suddenly changed. "The library . . . The first thing they take away . . . ideas . . ."

When a small squad of soldiers emerged from the mansion and came down to the carriage, Lieutenant Revar asked Adred, Rhia and the Khamar to go with them. The trio was escorted through the iron gate and up a broken pathway, past burnt gardens, onto the central portico. There, the Khamar handed his letter of introduction to a leader of the guard, who led them indoors and told them to wait a moment in the wide foyer.

Their escort returned in the company of a tall, robed man, middle-aged and obviously a minister of the city Assembly. "This way, if you please." He led them down another hallway, up a flight of stairs and into a small room decorated with tapestries, carvings, fresh flowers and plants. The windows were open and a slight sea breeze fluttered the wall hangings.

"Lord Vardorian will see you presently," the minister explained. "He is in a meeting with city representatives and—others. My name is Vulus." He bowed and exited just as a servant entered with trays of drink. He poured goblets and handed them around, then excused himself.

Momentarily Lord Colonel Vardorian entered, alone. "Please. . . ." He lifted an arm, indicating the couches and chairs. "Sit. Make yourselves comfortable." And once each of them had introduced himself, Vardorian said to the Khamar: "You come on instructions from the king?"

"You'll find everything in here," the guard answered, handing Vardorian a scroll. "I apologize, my lord, for intruding upon your schedule, but King Elad insisted that this visit be kept unannounced."

"That is necessary from time to time," allowed Vardorian. "I understand." He opened the wooden holder at one end, tipped out the rolled parchment, broke the royal seal and read. Vardorian made a low sound as he finished the letter. He rolled it up again, dropped it into the carrier and set it on the table before him. He poured himself a cup of wine, then turned in his chair to face Adred. "You are a . . . very fortunate young man, aren't you, Count Adred?" Vardorian smiled.

The assumption made Adred slightly ill-at-ease. He coughed lightly.

"King Elad makes no mention in his letter, however, of the young lady."

Adred scratched his beard. "Rhia was arrested with me in Bessara. The charges against her are false, and I felt it my duty to insist upon her freedom when I heard from the capital. Excuse me, Lord Vardorian, but I'm not aware of what King Elad says, precisely, in his letter. If you could—"

"He mentions his nephew and his sister-in-law."

"I see." Adred heard Rhia take in a breath and he glanced at her.

"I've ceased to be astonished," Vardorian told him, "by things which seem astonishing. I have lived too long and seen too much. Revolutionary aristocrats, however—that takes some getting used to. But so far as I know, we have no record in our offices of Prince Galvus and Princess Orain living in Sulos."

"They are here anonymously, Lord Vardorian. Or at least, they have taken aliases."

"I see. And where are they now?"

"I . . . know the address where they were living last winter."

"Last winter? They were here during the Shemtu Rebellion?"

"Yes."

"Do you know for certain—forgive me, but I must ask—that they are still alive?"

The silence in the room was very loud as Adred answered, "They were alive last winter, after the rebellion."

Vardorian grunted thoughtfully, sipped more wine, then stood up, pulled his chair from beneath the table and moved it across the floor closer to Adred and Rhia. He sat in it, quite informally, and told them:

"I am not going to interfere with what King Elad has requested; I'm certain that you and he understand far better than I the temperaments of Prince Galvus and Princess Orain. But I must tell you that if you can gain their support for—what shall I call it?— the voice of reasonableness in this city, then we all have much to gain. It may be, Count Adred, that this happens at a very opportune time."

"Why is that?" Adred asked.

Vardorian was frank. "I was appointed Acting-governor of Sulos immediately following the uprising. I think the city was shocked by the degree of violence; everyone became aware, too late, of the devastation that had been wrought, and even the rebels saw in the outcome of it more harm than good. I look upon myself, Count Adred, as a servant of the practical; I don't make it my business to place blame. I try, instead, to solve problems, to make things . . . manageable. I agree that our society suffers from certain imbalances, but I don't think that anything unfair can be repaired overnight by acts of violence."

"I agree with you, Lord Vardorian."

"Good. Good . . . For three months after the revolt the streets were calm. Tensions seemed to have abated; promises were made to the working people that reforms would be investigated. The city was calm for the duration of the winter. I have spent every day of my office since my arrival here acting as an arbiter among conflicting factions of people in Sulos. Some still want vengeance; some want to try new things; some are willing to give our present system time. However . . .

"What you saw on the streets as you made your way here are

87

crowds of people out of work and rioting for food. Let me explain what has happened. Just about two weeks ago, planters and growers in the Diruvian Valley, just outside the city, refused to begin planting their wheat and oats as a protest against the business firm that owns those fields and purchases grain from the farmers." Quickly, then, Vardorian sketched for Adred the chain of events that had led to his being sent there.

"That dissent was the start of it. Four days ago, rebels and workingmen broke into storehouses just outside Sulos and have refused entrance to anyone. They will not allow any of the meal, grain or bread in those storehouses to be shipped into the city, and eighty percent of the bread that comes into Sulos is stored in those houses. Four businesses are involved, and representatives of all four have agreed to act as I require of them. But the rebels obviously are hoping that the people, in need of that bread, will turn against the business community unless certain demands are met."

"What are their demands?"

"They want the leases to all the grainfields in the valley renegotiated so that the growers are not at the mercy of the business houses. They want work guarantees, and they want the profit from their labor distributed in different ways. They want to be certain that no one in Sulos is without bread, for whatever reason. Bread for the people, they say, comes before business profits. There is even some talk of the workers gaining controlling interest in these business houses; as it stands now, sons inherit them from their fathers, and thousands of persons' skills and livelihoods are treated as just so much property."

Adred contemplated this. "Good for them," he smiled.

"There is more," Vardorian told him. "I have been in meetings with representatives from the four business houses, and with representatives from the valley growers. We are trying to reach a decision mutually beneficial to both sides. However—"

"King Elad," Adred interrupted, "has just issued a notice that workers' *sirots* are to be investigated; very probably they will be instituted."

"That is true. His edict, however, was announced just after this latest rebellion began. And the workers mistrust it, anyway."

Adred nodded.

"Now . . ." Vardorian rubbed his hands together, reached for his wine cup and sipped from it. "Sulos, as you know, is a shipbuilding center, a trading port, and one of the most important fisheries in the empire. There seems to be a consensus growing among the working people of every industry and trade in the city that if the grain companies do not come to terms with the growers' demands, then workers in all other areas—as a show of solidarity—will stop producing, as well. I don't have to tell you what this would mean. Though the people of Sulos would suffer, nevertheless the effects would be felt, and quickly, throughout the entire country. No new ships built, no old ones repaired, and none leaving the docks. We send raw timber and lumber all down the coast: that would cease. We produce tar for shipbuilding and for other construction trades. We produce wine, salt, lead and copper, linen and wool, wax, fish oil, apples. We have cattle, we export milk and cheese and beef, leather, and a thousand craft goods. And these are only our major businesses and industries. I suspect that the working people of Sulos would readily know how to take care of one another were they to agree to hold the business community for ransom, as it were. So far, I—and members of the business community—want to come to terms with the rebels and the working people. I do not automatically discount much of what they argue. Both sides say they want fairness; certainly we want no further bloodshed."

Adred nodded thoughtfully; he felt Rhia rest a supportive hand on one arm. He glanced at her; she showed him a strong smile.

"What it comes down to, I think," Vardorian finished, "is less the idea of profit, or even the redistribution of profit, than it is the idea of dignity. Am I wrong? The working people are not fools; I get the impression from their spokesmen and their literature that if they were allowed their dignity, and everything that that implies, then matters of profit and the distribution of goods would take care of themselves."

"That sentiment," Adred affirmed, "is at the core of the revolution. The true revolution. Not . . . mobs and assassinations, but people fighting for values, for awarenesses. A new beginning."

Vardorian stood up. "We must come to terms with this quickly," he said. "Whenever you wish to visit Prince Galvus, let me know. I will send an escort with you."

"Thank you." Adred looked at Rhia. "Thank you. . . ." And, realizing what was happening, the profundity of it, he found himself thinking of a fire nearly burnt out but with the coals still

89

glowing beneath the ashes; he imagined a breeze fanning those coals into new life. He looked at Vardorian.

"Now," Adred told him. "I'm ready to go right now."

The sky had begun to cloud by the time they reached the apartment house; the air was thick and muggy, promising rain.

Adred was the first out of the carriage, and he lent his hand to help Rhia step down. The Khamar followed. Adred told Rhia that he had best go in without her, but he asked the Khamar to accompany him. They entered the apartment house; it smelled of old refuse and stale air, sad lives. Up the stairs to the third floor, and the door Adred remembered. He knocked. Almost instantly it opened, and Adred faced a man he did not know. Tall, wide-shouldered, balding, in his middle years—a dockworker.

The man's eyes hardened as he looked from Adred to the Khamar, and back again.

"Is Galvus here?" Adred asked him.

"Who?"

"Galvus . . ."

From inside came a woman's voice. "Thios, who is it?"

Adred began to tremble; he recognized Orain's voice. "Let us in, please. It's important that I—"

Thios didn't open the door; but behind him footsteps sounded and then, just inside—

Orain. Her blonde hair dull, her eyes gray in the dim light, her face pale and thin. Orain.

Adred sucked in a breath.

She whispered his name silently.

"Please," Adred insisted. "Let us in."

The dockworker had the defensive attitude of a man guarding his possessions. But Orain said quietly, "Thios . . ." She touched his shoulder.

The door was opened. Adred entered; Orain stepped back. The Khamar remained in the hallway, tall and resolute, one hand on the sword at his side. Thios lingered on the threshold, uncertain what to do.

Adred swallowed thickly. "Is—Orain, . . . is Galvus here?"

They couldn't take their eyes off one another. It had been so long—only months, but it had seemed so long. Adred wanted to hug Orain in a rush of emotion; her eyes danced nervously, her mouth trembled.

"He's . . . here, he's—"

Adred looked beyond her. More footsteps.

"Mother, I—"

And Galvus stepped from an adjacent room, saw. His face went blank. Adred. And, just outside the door, an imperial guard.

Galvus, too, had changed. He was pale, thinner; he had grown his beard, and he was dressed in patched clothes, worn boots, no ornaments.

"What are you doing here?" he asked Adred quietly. He wasn't angry, only surprised.

Adred looked again at Orain. She, understanding his discomfort, coughed quietly, went to Thios and whispered to him.

"It's all right. He's an old friend. Maybe you'd better . . . I'll speak with you later, Thios."

"Are you sure it's all right?" he asked suspiciously, eyeing the Khamar.

"Yes, yes, it's all right. I'll explain later. . . ."

Doubtful, Thios made his way down the stairs. Orain watched him go, then turned into the apartment. She seemed relieved to have the dockworker gone.

Adred was still standing in the middle of the room. Orain walked to Galvus and held his hand.

"I was in prison," Adred began abruptly. "In Bessara."

"The revolution?" Galvus asked.

"Yes. Yes. Elad ordered me freed."

Orain let out a tense breath. "Then he *is* still alive?"

"Oh, yes," Adred answered.

"We never thought he'd actually died," Galvus explained. "Only . . . news was intermittent, and we weren't sure."

Adred threw his hands behind his back. "He ordered me set free, but only if I would . . . come here. Try to help settle what's happening . . ."

"You mean," Galvus interpreted, "the rebellion in the valley."

"Yes." Adred, still nervous and uncertain, searched for words. "I'd better come right out and say it. You see, he sent me here specifically to talk with you. Galvus—Elad needs your help."

The young man stared at him.

Adred told them everything. The Khamar escorted Rhia upstairs and she sat with Adred, Orain and Galvus as they sipped tea and talked at length. Galvus told Adred what he had been able to accomplish in the city: the buying of supplies and food staples for the poverty-stricken with money obtained through channels of

91

sympathetic friends in the capital. "I have three people in Sulos who know who I am, and they divulge nothing. I get my money from the capital whenever I need it, just as I used to when we were staying with Count Mantho. We've developed a network to distribute what is needed. You have no idea how desperate these people are." After a moment: "Well, no . . . maybe you do. But it is abhorrent to me to think of these people of means who have no social conscience whatsoever." Galvus claimed, however, that he was not actively involved in the revolution, although he knew many rebels by name.

Adred explained to him what Elad wished. Keeping in mind his discussion with Lord Vardorian, he guaranteed Galvus that the Acting-governor would help in whatever way he could to ameliorate the current problems between the working people and the business interests.

"But we must act now, Galvus. We must go out to the valley and speak with these men. We must show them that we mean to do what we say we will do—that Elad and Vardorian are sincere, that no good can come of continued violence and dissension. We must have a plan and stick to it."

Galvus nodded his head thoughtfully, tapped the ends of his fingers together.

"Today, Galvus."

In a moment of quiet, as she nervously plucked at the hem of her blouse, Orain confided to Adred: "We've been talking already, over the past few weeks, about going back to Athad. There isn't much else we can do here. Everything we've started—it can continue without us."

Adred shot a look at Rhia. Would she want to stay here? Surely she wouldn't care to go to the capital? If he and Orain and Galvus left—when they left—

Rhia read his look, and smiled, then nodded slightly.

"I want," Orain said determinedly, "to return to the palace to . . . talk with Elad—"

"He will listen," Adred assured her.

"And what," Galvus asked, "what specifically, do we tell the men in the Diruvian Valley?"

Adred said: "Tell them—No. Let them tell you. Galvus, they know who you are. At least, they know what you've been doing, what you're accomplishing. You don't have to prove anything to them."

And Galvus pondered: "I'm a man of royal blood. If I let them know that—if I'm honest with them about who I am—and then if I tell them that certain things will be done, they know they'll be done. I'll be doing more for them in Athad in the palace, as a prince, than I can do for them down here. Mother is right; I've done all I can do for them, here. We need . . . a wedge, in the palace. Something . . ."

Orain encouraged her son. "It's true, Galvus. It's just what we've been talking about."

"But what if I go back," he asked Adred, "and Elad refuses—" He gestured. "What? Whatever . . ."

"Promise these men what you know *you* can deliver. You're doing it now. You can do much more of it, from Athad."

"Yes. That's true."

"I'll go back to prison," Adred told him plainly, nodding toward the Khamar who stood by the door. "Rhia and I will both go back. Sooner or later we'll be freed. But in or out of prison, we can't accomplish anything more, here, than you already have. I've learned that. We've got to use everything at our disposal, and if that means using our birthrights—"

The young man stared into his friend's eyes, and a warm smile grew on his face. Galvus turned to his mother.

Orain's eyes were wet. "Yes," she whispered.

Galvus stood up slowly, then finished his tea. "Mother," he decided, "when Omos returns from the warehouse, tell him we expect another shipment tomorrow. The papers are on the table in my room. I've already mentioned it to him."

"Yes, Galvus."

"Tell him where we've gone. And tell him"—again, the smile—"to prepare for a journey to the capital. . . ."

Rhia rode with them, as did the Khamar, in the carriage that took Adred and Galvus out into the Diruvian Valley. The storm that had been threatening broke at last and heavy rain pelted the coach, thunder and wind slapped it.

"What mother and I have been discussing," the young man told his friend, "is that what we've done in Sulos must be done in other cities. It is completely apolitical, Adred, because I refuse to ally myself with one group or another. This isn't a contest; it's simply a matter of human decency, sowing seeds to get the kind of plants you want. We're helping people to rely upon one another. With that comes personal dignity and a greater awareness of things. It's only the first step in redistributing the wealth of the empire, creating the fairest society we can. Sowing seeds."

"You are changing things, then," Adred reminded him.

"Of course. But because things are changing, our problems come from different people and groups all trying to direct that change. It's not change that threatens them, it's the question of who will control that change. And this is where they lose sight of their common goals and become partisan, and bicker and fight."

"You're quite right," his friend agreed.

"The working people are no different from the aristocracy, in the fact that they are people. It's human nature, I mean, to want to provide for yourself and protect yourself; once you've accomplished that, it's easy to forget about everyone else, or to think that because you've managed to do it, everyone else can, too. It takes times like these, times of social grievance and crisis, to make people realize that they *are* bound to one another in a society, and that one person's actions absolutely affect everyone else, somewhere, sooner or later, and will, in turn, come back to affect him. It's that awareness that must guide our policy."

When they reached the blockade, the Suloskai and the farmers guarding the road stopped the carriage and requested that everyone identify himself. They were astonished to discover an imperial guard in the company of the young man whom all knew from his work on the docks. Galvus told them, then, who he was and why he had come there; the rebels were astounded. Some of them accompanied the coach down the road to a large farmhouse where the leaders of the revolt had homed themselves.

As he stepped out of the carriage, Galvus confided to Adred in a whisper: "I'm very nervous. . . ."

"But they want to know what you have to say. They've waited a long time to hear this, Galvus."

The prince was escorted up the steps and onto the wide wooden porch of the farmhouse where a large group of men were sitting in chairs and on benches. All were dressed in rough clothes and were heavily weaponed. Many wore armbands on their sleeves: the red cloth square with the black "S" sewn onto it. Galvus was led inside, but the Khamar, Adred and Rhia were asked to remain on the porch.

Adred, anxious, stood up and walked to one end of the porch where there were some empty chairs and tables. He sat down, his back to the rain, and breathed in the cool aroma of the newly wet fields, fresh earth, damp trees and rain. After a moment, Rhia walked the length of the porch to join him. The Khamar stayed where he was.

Rhia sat down in the chair beside Adred and for a moment seemed to listen—to the rain, or to the occasional sounds of voices, hollow and distorted, from inside the farmhouse.

Then she said quietly to Adred: "I'm going to stay here. In Sulos. Help." He looked at her. "It wouldn't do me any good to go back to the capital, would it? I don't belong there. I belong with the people."

He would never see her again: that's what this meant. But somehow that didn't seem entirely true to Adred. "That might . . . be best. Yes," he agreed.

She smiled at him—white teeth, pink lips, bright eyes framed by damp red hair. "Besides, you lead too exciting a life! I'm not used to this!"

He smiled sadly at her.

After all, they didn't love one another.

Adred cocked his ear toward the wall of the farmhouse. "He's winning them over."

"You—" Rhia stared at him. "You like her, don't you?"

"Who's that?"

"Orain. Galvus's mother. You've known her for a long time, haven't you? And you like her, don't you?"

Adred didn't know what to say. He felt somewhat foolish, but his pride was wounded for he hadn't thought his feelings for Orain were so obvious; nothing could come of them, anyway.

"Don't you?" Rhia smiled at him. She reached over and gripped his arm, shook it playfully. "Oh, you're such a boy. It'll work out much better this way, Adred. Don't always be so . . . rational!"

He looked at her, smiling blandly, as something tremendous took hold of him—an emotional flux, a mood or a profound feeling, a choice made at a crossroads, or a choice made for him at the crossroads. He looked away, then, and listened to the rain, listened to the voices inside the farmhouse, and held Rhia's hand.

PART III

The Wound and the Scar

1.

In the east, the death of a king was regarded as an omen of tremendous significance: Death, believed the many tribes and peoples of Salukadia, was but a change, and the death of a monarch presaged a transition—actual and spiritual and natural—for those who had served him.

The word of the sudden (but not wholly unexpected) demise of Huagrim *ko-Ghen* was, for the people of his cities and villages, the closing down of a night promised by a long twilight. Because few of his people had known him as a man, his death seemed the more mysterious and fateful; because few of them had ever heard his human voice, the silence of his passing seemed the greater. It was as though a giant had abruptly drawn in a breath—and Salukadians of all tribes waited anxiously for that giant to respirate again.

When he heard the news of Huagrim's death, relayed to him by messengers from the potentate's palace, Lord General Thomo immediately called to him Captain Thytagoras and Lord Sirom, to discuss with them what effects this would have upon the eastern world's relations with the west. It was difficult to say, all agreed. And so Lord Thomo took the important step of asking to see the late *Ghen*'s principal *aihman*, the elderly bin-Sutus, and he made it clear to that worthy that the death of his chief in no way would alter or obviate any of the international agreements upon which the two empires had come to terms.

bin-Sutus, an admirable man, professed himself pleased to learn this. In answer to polite inquiries from Lord General Thomo, bin-Sutus discussed the new situation as well as he was able, for he knew that the Athadian must alert his own king to this abrupt change of circumstances. The *aihman* therefore assured Thomo that the Salukadian court, resting now as it did during this interregnum upon the wise counsel of the *Ghen*'s ministers and politicians, similarly would do nothing to jeopardize relations with the west. Much of the future, however, rested upon the reading of Huagrim's official will, which was stored in Ilbukar and which had to be brought to Erusabad for its interpretation and publication. Bin-Sutus did go so far as to tell Lord General Thomo that, in keeping with a tradition as old as their culture, the empire would be portioned out to the *Ghen*'s sons. But no one as yet could determine how that might pass, or when.

For the benefit of his king, then, Lord Thomo put down in a dispatch all the facts that he knew, and all the possibilities that had been discussed, and ordered the missive delivered to Elad as soon as possible.

To my lord King Elad of Athadia on this day 14 Sath 1879 DP, in the Year of the Dragon, thus: From the City of Erusabad from your Servant, Lord General Thomo. *Kale im Porvo Athadis*. My lord, I say:

I send you word of the death of the emperor Huagrim *ko-Ghen* of the Salukads. News of this was given to me two days past, and I have been in consultation regarding its importance with our officials here in Erusabad, as well as with informants and a trustworthy minister of the Saluka-dian court, one bin-Sutus, an elder in service personally to the late *Ghen*.

Most important to our empire now is the status of our relations with the east, although bin-Sutus assures me that all policies and terms so far agreed upon between Athad and Ilbukar remain actual and unconditional. The Salukadian court is, for the present, governed by a body of tribal elders, friends of the late *Ghen* and a few religious leaders; none of these, however, by custom can assume the throne or *Ghen*-ship. That office by its nature is inherited by a son of the *Ghen*; and following a habit of succession begun by Huagrim *ko-Ghen*'s grandfather, it is reckoned by my unofficial informants that the Salukadian empire will be apportioned between the two princes of the realm. That is to say, all lands taken by the *Ghen* during his lifetime are his to bequeath unto his blood.

The *Ghen*'s sons are Agors, the elder, and Nihim, the younger. Agors is a military man, and, I am told, he prides himself upon a knowledge of warfare, tactics and arma-ments. He has studied our diverse culture and has much respect for us. However, I am certain that his temperament is that of his father, who, as we know, believed all the earth to be made for his sole ownership. It is possible that Agors will, if not immediately, and if not openly then surreptitiously, seek to continue the expansion of the eastern empire; it is possible that he may even seek to overstep the boundaries of Athadia itself. This is, however, mere speculation at this point. We know that Agors cares little for the southern lands, but he may consider them invaluable and take it as a test of his will and military prowess to challenge our frontiers. The cruel expansion of the Emarians into the Low Countries last year was done, as we know, if not at the behest of Agors (called *ghen-mu*), then certainly with his tacit approval. He has a keen mind and has carried much influence at court, especially among those who matured and came into office while his father was still a horseman and conqueror.

The younger son, Nihim, is not so belligerent or grasping. I have met him (as I have Agors) and Nihim is a religious man, following the precepts of some eastern ideologue; he is calm in temperament, rational in outlook and extremely intelligent. He tells me that he believes in "balance," and I assume this to mean that were it in his power to command the forces of all Salukadia, he still would not be disposed to affront us. That is to say, he is, so far as it concerns us, the opposite in ideals and beliefs of his brother. But Nihim, because he is more self-effacing than Agors, does not draw attention to himself, and so it may be that he is not regarded as highly in the eastern court as is his brother.

Because our relations with the Salukadian empire have, thus far, been minimal, and because there are many woeful antagonisms on each side toward the other, I inquired of bin-Sutus if it would be proper for the Athadian empire to pay respects to their late *Ghen*; I went so far as to suggest to that elder than any observances my lord deigns to express should not be taken as a genuflection, but simply as the gesture of one monarch to the shade of another.

I asked bin-Sutus how long his people would be in mourning for their *Ghen*. He replied that they would worship his memory for a moon-month—that is, twenty-eight days. I inquired of bin-Sutus as to the funeral customs of his people for their monarch. He told me that the *Ghen's* sepulcher is already built and prepared for him in Ilbukar, and that his earthly remains will be transported there for internment. I asked of bin-Sutus if his court would be receptive to a representative from the Athadian court who might, by his appearance, serve to them condolences and wishes for continued mutual amity in the future. bin-Sutus told me frankly that were my lord to dispatch a representative from the western throne, that person would be welcomed and entertained by his court with all due respect and diligence.

I therefore respectfully submit to my lord that it may be to our benefit to forward such an emissary, whose sole motive in visiting Erusabad would be, not to implement trade agreements or enter into any international policy, but simply to assure the Salukadians that our intentions in this, a period of loss and uncertainty, are purely amicable. I hope my lord will ponder this suggestion as it is one of gravity and moment and may itself do much to reduce any tensions that might arise from this interregnum in the eastern government. The suspicions of Prince Agors might by this be abated; and surely we can count upon the prudence and good will of Prince Nihim were we to accord the eastern court this generous signal.

Thus, Lord General Thomo to his lord, King Elad I. *Kale Athadis im Porvo.*

When he had finished this missive and entrusted it to a messager, with orders to sail at once for the capital and deliver the letter instantly into the king's hands only, Thomo retired from his office in the old Authority Building and made his way upstairs a flight to his sleeping chamber. There he undressed, removing his boots, his armor and all his gear, save for his sword. He poured himself wine, opened a window, sat in a cushioned chair and stared out.

The night was brilliant with starlight and the flares and fumes of many fires. Flames had been stoked all along the walls of the city. and upon many of the tallest buildings. From every direction came the low, moaning wails of distant gongs and chanting crowds.

Thomo sipped his wine and thought back to the funeral of King Evarris. He had been there, in Athad, had stood among the whispering sad crowds, had been part of the confusion and the doubt. What terrible events the death of Evarris had set in motion!

Now, Thomo wondered if the passing of Huagrim *ko-Ghen* portended evil events on this side of the world. He hoped it did not, but he feared the worst.

Thomo smiled a sly grin as he sipped his wine and listened. Somewhere, he wondered, in the land of shadows, did Huagrim *ko-Ghen* sit with King Evarris and watch with him these signs of desolation and grief? And did they wonder for their people, as their people did for them? Did death strip away all the false divisions of life? Or did it enhance them?

Or was death, as some philosophers contended, only a better life not to be feared? Was the true death, the land of torment and pain, actually what we call . . . life?

2.

The most efficient route out of Emaria was southward from the capital, where a quick march covered the five leagues to the border in only a few hours. Here the open green fields rolled lazily into the northern farmlands of Ithulia, an Athadian province. Only occasional stone obelisks marked the boundary between the two territories.

The squadron assigned to escort Prince Cyrodian from Lasura to the Ithulian river-port of Mustala on the River Fasu sang loud marching songs as they made their way briskly over the hills, a team of horses behind them pulling the strong-wheeled cage that housed the renegade prince. By noon the unit had entered the small village of Orukad, still a day's march from Mustala.

Orukad was little more than a farmer's crossroads set in the middle of the sun-brightened fields. Thirty weathered buildings comprised it—most of them storage barns and stables. There was an inn, one side of which had been converted into a tavern where a dozen awkward tables offered refuge from the heat. The hosteler, a lean man browned long ago by the climate, watched implacably as twenty of the Emarian escort, led by their commander, entered the dusty tavern and took all the unoccupied chairs. The commander, although he considered the question answered before he spoke, asked the innkeeper:

"Do you speak Emarian?"

"Yes, I do."

"My men and I are stopping only to refresh ourselves; we're

transporting a prisoner to Mustala. Would you serve us your coldest beer and whatever meat you have?''

The lean proprietor nodded, and to two young women who stared out from the storage room behind he said: "Beer. Bring out cups for the travelers."

From where they sat in a dusky corner, two old farmers stared quietly at the Emarians and absently scraped dirt from beneath their fingernails using splinters of wood.

Outside, the remaining Emarians sought whatever shelter they could from the midday heat. Six of them unhooked the four cart horses and led them, along with their commander's steed, to water troughs that sat alongside the tavern. The remaining four stood guard around Cyrodian's cage.

The giant, covered with dust that dripped like mud down his sweaty face, was crouched in the center of his cage, legs crossed, body hunched forward. Gnats and mosquitoes swarmed around him in a cloud, and Cyrodian occasionally picked up fistfuls of straw in futile attempts to swat the insects away. He heard the splash of water in the troughs behind and grunted to one of his guards:

"Get me a swallow of water!"

The soldier eyed him through half-closed lids, then moved lazily to the water cask roped to the rear of the wagon. He unfastened the metal cup tied to the cask, unplugged the wooden cork on the bottom and let the water splash freely into the container. When the cup was full, the soldier bent over and lapped some of the draining water, as though he were a dog, and rubbed the excess over his hot face. He corked the cask again, turned around and reached the cup of water through the iron bars of Cyrodian's cage.

The giant took it in two hands and, chains dangling and clanking, sipped. He kept his eye on the soldier. He had formed a plan. Cyrodian knew that because Nutatharis had already contacted Elad, the Emarian soldiers must deliver him to Athadian troops in Mustala alive and unharmed. He suspected that he could manage some means of escape; but while waiting for that potential avenue of freedom to present itself, he might remedy the boredom of his captivity by murdering one or two of these soldiers. What could the commander do about it? Kill him for it? Hurt him?

As he finished, Cyrodian stared at the water soldier and perceived that the man was so sleepy and fatigued that a moment of surprise would finish him. Cyrodian could hand him the cup and when he reached for it—grab his hand, snap the wrist and yank him forward to the bars, clutch his throat and break his neck before the other three could do anything about it.

But as he nodded to the young soldier to take back the cup, voices coming down the street caught Cyrodian's attention. He turned quickly to see who was approaching; the Emarians, moving into poses of alertness, stood straight and readied themselves.

What they saw, however, hardly unnerved them. It was a middle-aged man, a farmer, dressed in a worn robe and worn boots with a staff in one hand. He was a big man, and as he advanced slowly down the dirty street, his head bobbed above the twenty or so people who crowded around him. They were mostly women, although some farmers, young men and girls were with him—and a few stray dogs.

As he approached the Emarians, the tall man paused and eyed Cyrodian. He stared, then lifted a hand and said in a low voice to those with him: "Please, my friends . . . wait here, won't you?"

The Emarian guards, stepping into the street and shielding their eyes with their hands, faced him as he came forward. When he reached them, the robed man spoke to them in the same low tone he had used with his followers:

"Please . . . I won't interfere with you. But I wonder who your prisoner is. May I ask?"

One of the soldiers replied cautiously, "He's an Athadian. We're transporting him through this village."

"I think I know him."

"I doubt that, sir. Will you please keep back?"

The tall farmer regarded him with an honest look. "There wouldn't be any problem in my speaking with him for a moment, would there?"

"I'd rather you didn't, sir. Now will you—"

"I say to you again, I know this man."

His strange eyes were compelling, his low voice reassuring. The guard, despite regulations, decided that there could be no harm in allowing the Ithulian to speak to Cyrodian, for only a moment.

"Well . . . since you say you know him . . ."

The robed man nodded, stepped forward and approached the cage.

Cyrodian, watching him grimly, uncrossed his legs and leaned into a crouch. The long chains manacled to his wrists clanked and squeaked. "What the hell do you want?" he growled.

Tall and dignified, the robed farmer gave an impression of immense self-worth despite his worn clothes and unkempt appearance. In the same controlled tone he said: "You are a prince in your country, and you have brought desolation and hardship and mighty sorrow upon your family."

Cyrodian fought back his surprise; how could word of his humiliation have come so quickly to this end of the world? And to reach this farmer dressed in the rude apparel of a wandering priest? "Who the hell are you?" he spat.

"I am Asawas, a man of god. I know who you are, Prince Cyrodian of Athadia."

The Emarian soldiers glanced nervously at one another. One shot a look toward the tavern, indicating that it might be a good idea to fetch their commander. But none of his companions moved to do it.

"You're a priest," Cyrodian grumbled. "Where did you find out—"

"I am far more than a priest, my friend. I have sensed you for some time, now, and I came to believe that our paths would cross. You must listen to what I have to say, Prince Cyrodian. You are a warning to the world."

"Get away from me or I'll—" But he quieted himself abruptly, crooked his shaggy head to one side and regarded this stranger narrowly. "Tell me," Cyrodian whispered, "who you really are."

"I have told you."

"Athadian? What are you? A spy sent by my brother?"

Asawas smiled sadly. "Prince Cyrodian, you are a cursed man. Know this: that On, the one true god, speaks to me in dreams and visions. He sees the ways of the world and he sees into every heart that lives in the world. He knows your heart far better than you do. You were born into a house of love and with a name of consequence, and you were taught as a boy good things to respect and pursue and believe in. Why have you forsaken these things, Prince Cyrodian?"

The giant was appalled. How dare this dusty beggar address him in such a fashion? Who in the names of the hells did he think he was? "Now you listen to me," he growled at Asawas, his huge voice trembling with suppressed rage. "You turn around and you take your litter of pups back to whatever den you found them in, and you—"

"You bring pain into the world, Prince Cyrodian. I condemn no man to death, yet On has pronounced your days at an end. You move forward to justice, Prince Cyrodian, and nothing can alter that course now—not anger, not prayer. You marked the route yourself. You have turned your strength against yourself, you have allowed your passions to command your soul. You die in shame, prince of Athadia, because you condemned yourself long ago."

"You . . . *cur*! . . ." Cyrodian gasped, nearly breathless with hatred. He tried to rise up, move forward to lash out at this man. Yet he did not. More than chains held him back; more than the heat weighed down on him. What was it? The eyes? The soft manner? The power of the words? The—*ideas*? "Priest! You speak too much of—"

"I am not a priest; I am a man. It is a man who confronts you now. A man, as you are a man, Prince Cyrodian. Deep within you, where your sun meets your private night, you cannot deny what I say. The pain you suffer is the most awful a man can know: to be alone, and not to know oneself, and thus not to know god. You are alone and you will always be alone, in this life and in the next, and in your lives to come. You have shown how greatly you hate yourself, through your hatred for others."

"*Farmer!*" the giant yelled at him, as though the word were an epithet. "Damned—"

Asawas held up a hand. "I have told you that On speaks to me, and he speaks through me. You, Prince Cyrodian—you will not witness the world's destruction, although, in your own way, you have helped to make the world die. But I tell you this, so that it may comfort you or torment you: Your mother's spirit, Cyrodian, still screams out her love for you, despite all that you have done."

The giant gasped.

Asawas bowed his head to him, turned and made his way back across the road.

"*Farmer!*" Cyrodian screamed. He tried to stand, he yanked on his chains, grabbed the iron bars. "*Farrr-merrr*! Come back here, damn you! *Come back here*! You cur, you foul—You have no right to—"

One of the Emarians whipped out his sword and slapped the cage with it. "Silence, Athadian! Silence yourself!"

Cyrodian, snapping his teeth, growled at him and stared after Asawas. "Farmer! You hear me, damn you! Come back here! Damn you, damn—"

But Asawas, having said what had been necessary to say,

ignored him, entered into his small crowd of followers again and disappeared beneath the shadows of a tall wooden building.

"*Farrr-merrr*! *Damn you*! *Damn you*!"

The tavern door crashed open and the Emarian commander stepped out into the heat and dust. "What the hell is going on out here? You! What the hell is he—"

"*Come back here, damn you, damn you*! . . ."

But the prophet was nowhere in sight.

As evening came down, Asawas sat in the welcome coolness with his followers. They had walked to a small hill just outside Orukad where they could see the sunset and watch the fieldmen return in long dusty clouds of brown. The Emarian escort and its prisoner had long since vanished down the southeast road. Now, as hot faces were laved by breezes, as children played in the grass and their parents listened to the prophet, Asawas said to them:

"I cannot speak to everyone in the world, therefore you must relate to everyone you meet what I say to you. But live these words, don't just speak them. Be sure to tell them that it is On that asks you to do these things, to act in the way that is best. It is not right to say that you believe in justice and fairness and then act in an unjust or unfair way. That only prolongs the agonies humanity suffers."

A young mother took a whining baby into her arms, lifted it to her right breast to nurse it. She asked Asawas: "*Ikbusa*, you say the world is going to die. Why must we suffer? We have not led evil lives."

"You are only one part of the great soul of humanity. You have done good, others have done evil. You are not being punished for doing evil; neither have the wicked been allowed to profit by their ways, although it may seem so. To see with On's eyes is to see all lives at once, all lives that have been and all that they will become. Shall we judge? Shall we judge god only by those portions he chooses to reveal to us? And when I say the world is going to die, I do not mean that it will disappear forever. Death is only a change; it is a renewal, another kind of sleep that comes before the new awakening. When you were born, you were not as you are now; can we not say that what you were then is now dead? You are no longer a baby in form, yet that baby still is within you. So it is with the world and its death; what it was has changed, and what it is now will change."

"Why is it dying, Chosen One?"

"Because we are the earth, and we are On, and On is the earth and all things; and it is necessary for things to return sometimes to what they were, so that they may continue. Sometimes, what we think is evil is good disguised, but sometimes good is only evil disguised."

"How can we then tell the difference, Asawas?"

"See what the result is. Does it achieve a balance? Does it create harmony? Does it help life, or does it harm life? If a thing is harmful to life, then it is not a good thing. Many times you will hear some people say that what they are doing will be harmful for a little while, but ultimately it will create good. They are deceptive people."

Someone asked, by way of example, "But . . . must we not sometimes hurt the body to help it mend itself?"

"That is so. And we must punish the child so that it learns right from wrong. And we must kill an animal so that we may eat the meat of it and stay alive. But these things are part of the balance. Ask yourself next time someone wants to hurt you because he says it will ultimately produce good: 'Will it produce good only for him, or for me?' If it will help only him, then it will not create a balance. When we learn to see the wisdom of harmony, then we are more apt to lead harmonious lives."

"Our leaders make us suffer," someone said, "and they say that in time it will do us much good. They prosper, we suffer, yet they say that the time will come when we too will prosper because they prosper now."

"This is an old lie," Asawas replied, "told by men who command others but have never learned to command their own hearts. The good man cannot prosper if his neighbor does not prosper. Can one man profit by doing harm to another, or by taking advantage of another, and still believe that he has done good or is successful? Remember that men are often jealous and arrogant: they love to hurt others so that they may feel good, so that they may feel superior to others, and this happens because we allow these people to isolate themselves. Is there not enough grain to feed everyone? Then why do some starve? Is there not enough money for everyone to use in barter? Then why are there rich people and poor people? It is because we have allowed some to isolate themselves, and when they are isolated, they come to believe that they are superior to those with whom they do not live.

"Show me where any aspect of nature lives in isolation. You could not show me, my friends, because the harmony and perfection of nature is in the graceful wholeness of all its parts. Therefore I say this to you: To believe that each of us is alone and isolated is an impermanent illusion created so that we may learn our greater purpose. My flesh is not your flesh, yet my spirit belongs to On, as does yours. All men and women prosper when they live in harmony; all aspects of society must be balanced. Who possesses all skills? No one does. Who can sing all melodies, or do all the work? No one person. Yet if we take a number of us, then we can work together, or share a melody. If a man listens only to his own heart, then he will see only one color, he will face only one direction, and he may commit evil, he may not lead a good life. But if that man listens to the hearts of others as well as to his own heart, he will lead a good life, he will not commit evil, because what he does will be shared by others, what he earns will be shared by others, and what he believes will be respected by others. Only when every one of us understands how much alike we are, and what we share in common, can we appreciate the differences in color and direction in each of us."

As Asawas and his friends sat on the hillside considering these things, a man and woman walked down the road toward them. The woman was supporting the man, who could only feel his way with a long walking stick. The prophet watched them as they approached, and one of the women on the hillside told him:

"That man is blind. He has always lived in our village, and he is blind."

Asawas stood up, stepped down to the road and watched silently as the man and woman came forward, their long sundown shadows quivering on the ground before them. When they reached him, the woman bowed her head and asked:

"Are you the prophet who brings word of the one god to the people, and creates miracles?"

"I am," he replied. "I am Asawas."

On the hillside behind, the small crowd watched, hushed.

"*Ikbusa*, my husband has been blind since birth. He has never blamed god for this, but he wishes to see. What curse has been laid upon him? Or is it some sin of his parents that caused him to be born without sight?"

Asawas assured her: "Your husband has committed no sin, neither have his parents. He was born thus so that I might show to the world that I am what I say I am, and that On is the light and the true god of the people. Man, cast down your staff and step to me."

Silently, the blind man handed his stick to his wife and came forward with halting steps. He stared toward Asawas with open, blank eyes.

The prophet lifted his hands to the man's face, pressed his fingers upon the eyelids. "On wishes you to suffer no more. Believe in the power of the one true god, and see what he has done."

He lowered his hands.

The blind man flickered his eyelids, opened them a bit and screamed. "It is too bright! It is too bright, it hurts me!"

Shrieking, his wife jumped to him and hugged him strongly; tears rolled down her face. "He can see, he can see!"

Loud cheers and exclamations lifted from the hillside as the people began hurrying down into the road.

"You will learn to see," Asawas told the man, "and the world will be bright for you, as it is with sleeping men just waking to the dawn. Believe in On and you will see all things and know the truth."

The man's wife moved to Asawas and dropped to her knees, took up the hem of his dirty robe and kissed it several times, touched it to her forehead. "O Chosen One, O Prophet! Tell me what I should do to thank god for this favor! I will sell myself to his Church! I will put gold in his coffers! I will travel the earth for him in thanks!"

Asawas reached down and lifted her up. "Accept what is given," he told her, wiping the tears from her face. "The one god does not wish such things from you, as many say he does. Do not serve him as you would serve men, with money or from pride or out of fear. On requires from you no ceremonies, no rituals: celebrate this gift and celebrate On by treating a stranger as you would your friend, and your friend as you would a beloved one, and your beloved husband as though he were born of your mother. In this way will all people be as one. This is all that On asks in return for his gift. Celebrate your humanity."

As evening came down the people removed to their homes, and several families asked Asawas to join them at their table. He agreed to do so, accepting the first invitation offered, and walked down the road with the man and wife toward their home holding the hand of their young son. He chatted amicably with the boy as the youngster told Asawas all kinds of stories. The four of them made their way inside the couple's small farmhouse as the prophet's loud, honest laughter echoed, alive and good, throughout the night-quiet village.

3.

Of prophets and wanderers, lovers and kings, the low and the fallen and the searching, men and women of all kinds: of lives born in a storm and wandering in a storm.

Out from the deep winds of Time comes the Voice of a destiny. Will one dream transform the destiny and make of it another destiny? Will the words of one life or the actions of another life change the road, make of it another road directed toward another destiny? Are there many roads, or are there only many roads converging into one road of immutable destiny?

Of a Voice that is humanity's voice, of a God that is humanity's god, of events that seem to return to the pools of blood and the shadows of fire from which humanity birthed itself: the pool is deep, the shadows are old, the fire burns with flames that burn forever.

O humanity, will you never change? O humanity born in a storm and wandering in a storm, why do you turn from the future and return to your past? O lost and disbelieving, you wander in your search for belief, and you dream that there is only one sun, one road, one destiny.

Shall we pluck out our eyes so that we will not see what comes? For these things that come, they come with cause. Or shall we pluck out our eyes and exchange our eyes for the eyes of others, so that we may see with other eyes, and new?

Shall we have memories, but forget those memories that remind us of what may come?

Shall we hate war, and yet make a god of war?

Shall we hate dishonesty, and yet make lords and princes of the dishonest?

Shall we believe the only thing we hear, or believe only those things we hear?

Shall we build a tower from which to look down, yet not look above?

We are small-animal spirits, seeking and learning, ignorant of our true purpose, and caught in cages of clay, trapped on an earth of seasons and storms, manacled to a series of percussions and unguided events that seem to doom us since the hour of our birth. We are masters of ourselves only so long as we perceive our slavery to be the road to freedom: yet if we think ourselves free, then surely we trap and limit ourselves with more than metal bonds—surely then we capture ourselves with words and thoughts, with indomitable constructs which are foreign to that which we may become.

Of prophets and wanderers, lovers and kings, men and women of all kinds:

Of pride, the shadow of dignity, and voices in a storm.

O humanity, O lost, born in a storm and wandering in a storm: why do you turn from the future and return to your past, and feast on blood and flame, and not look above?

In Ugalu, where he had come, the master of the hell of men lived for some nights in a room in a small building down by the waterfront. Here the closeness and the press and ache of human life was as real as the crowding of cattle in a pen; and Thameron, witness to it all but outside it, wandered the busy, hot streets at night, studied faces, studied hands he glimpsed in crowds, studied the ways women walked as they moved away from him. Women with dark eyes tried to seduce him, men with knives tried to cheat him. Here, in the city, where ships moved in and out and a dozen different languages struggled to be heard and understood—here, where sounds in the night might be the moans of lovers, or the moans of dying troubled spirits—here, he wandered—

Assia . . .

—and found no clues.

And when at last he feared that he might be poisoned by the atmosphere of Ugalu, tempted to make himself a great lord over broken shards of humanity, Thameron left the city. He went down to the docks and paid his way aboard a ship bound for Abustad, for he presumed that if Assia were not this far north, then she must be even farther north, in the empire of the west. Perhaps she was in Ilbukar, but Thameron suspected that she had gone west.

So he took the ship and sailed west with it, spending the night in a bunk in the hold. And that night, as he slept, he had a troubled dream.

He saw a shadowy figure, old as eternity, seated in a cave. Something told him that it might be Guburus, his mentor, whom he had killed in a fit of agony and fear, with sorcery; but then again—no, it was not Guburus. It was some god or demon, and it called to him.

Called to him from the north.

Thameron heard the figure in his dream whisper to him voicelessly. He was frightened, and when he looked away from the shadowy figure in the cave and stared up at the night sky, the many stars seemed to turn slowly, to revolve in a great wheel around his head, as though the great wheel were centered over himself, as though he were the commander of all the stars and they revolved at his discretion.

Disturbed by the enormity of it, he awoke from the dream in a sweat.

But as he sat in his bunk panting, the last of the dream faded, and Thameron felt a warm glow fill him. He sensed a good presence lingering near him, and suddenly he saw a face, white and pale, hovering for a moment in the darkness of the hold.

Assia.

It was Assia's face—Assia's warmth. . . .

The following evening, when the ship docked at Abustad, Thameron made his way onto the docks and felt that warmth still with him. He entered the hurrying streets, pushed his way through soldiers and sailors, merchants and mendicants, and trusted his instincts to carry him to the woman he yet loved.

The first night out from Sulos on the royal galley.

Adred was sitting on a chair on the foredeck; Orain was in another chair beside him. They were alone in the quiet, breeze-washed night, for the Khamar had retired, as had Omos and Galvus. A few sailors were leaning against the larboard rail on the other side of the ship. Lanterns rocked with the gentle rise and fall of the deck; a few gulls, white-winged, flitted around the crow's nest; the sky was open and deep and blue, star-speckled.

Adred was thinking of things that had happened long ago. Remembrances of a night in a garden, . . . evenings over supper . . . walks in marketplaces . . . He looked up to notice Orain watching him and suddenly he felt almost alarmed, as though she had read his mind.

"I missed you," she told him in a soft voice.

He smiled faintly. "I missed you, too. I was . . . afraid."

"I know. I was afraid, too. Very afraid." She yawned, looked out across the sea. "I feel so tired and—*old*!" She turned at Adred's chuckling laughter and said: "May I ask you something?"

"Yes, certainly."

"We had so little news, when we were in Sulos. It was difficult, pretending to be the people we weren't. I did it, for Galvus's sake. He's a remarkable man. Whether I'm his mother or not . . . ."

"He is indeed."

She faced him with shadowed eyes. "Tell me," Orain spoke quietly, "what happened with you and Elad, when you left us last winter."

Adred exhaled a breath. "We . . . had our talk. I told him what I felt. Got a little excited, maybe. He's . . . such a curious mixture; it's as if he's many men in one, doesn't know who he is, or who he should be."

"Oh, I know."

"He promised that he'd look into the matter of reforms, but I was sure he never meant to do anything of the kind. That's why I was so surprised to hear about his sanctioning committees to look into the *sirots*. But he'll still make it difficult."

"The palace," Orain replied, speaking from experience, "is such a web. In some ways, Elad only has as much power as Council will allow him. The business interests run everything."

"It's true. . . ."

"There are so many powerful men, and they'll fight us if we try to take anything from them, give anything back to society. The bureaucracy. They claim that you have certain rights, but then they make it so difficult. . . . It's no wonder people become dishonest. All the hypocrisy . . ." She was silent for a moment. "Why did you become a revolutionary?" she asked him then.

Adred smiled. "You know, I never actually intended to. But I went back to Bessara after I'd spoken with Elad; I already knew some people there. There was trouble; I helped out as best I could with the wounded. A street demonstration, and Uthis ordered out his steel. I was just drawn into it. You can't turn your back on people fighting for justice. I can't, anyway. Someone's hurt, you have to help."

"Is that where you met the red-haired woman? Rhia?"

"Yes . . . that's part of what happened there." He waited to see if Orain meant to make any comment; when she didn't: "We—tried to help one another," Adred said. "It's not as if we were—well . . ."

"She's an interesting woman," Orain allowed. "I can understand." She made a sound in the darkness. "It becomes very lonely. Life, I think, is a very lonely thing."

"Who was that fellow with you, the day I came back?"

"Thios?" She waved a hand. "I know twenty like him. They're lonely, too. But it's very sad, when people don't know themselves but expect you to know them, to take care of all their emotions,

112

confusions. All these hard-working men, without homes or families—they're like little children inside, really. They're attracted to me. All my motherly instincts.''

"Well, you are very attractive, Orain. You have a good heart; you care.''

"Sometimes I wish I didn't. I seem to attract all the people with muddy boots, people who need a rug to wipe them on.''

"You don't mean that.''

She sighed heartfully. "No . . . no. I don't, I suppose. . . .''

One of the sailors on the larboard rail laughed out loud, a great singing laugh, and Adred and Orain both looked in his direction. As the echoes of it died away:

"Where did Galvus meet Omos?''

Orain shook her head. "He found him in the street. He's only a boy—little more than a boy. He was a prostitute, Adred; sailors and soldiers used him. He had to do something to eat and stay warm.''

He nodded quietly. "Does it bother you that Galvus loves him?''

"No.'' She spoke plainly. "At least he's honest about it, not like some of the hypocrites in Council. If Galvus wants to love a member of his own sex—if he can find some human comfort there—Hea bless him. I've begun to wonder if that sort of thing doesn't have its advantages, myself.'' She laughed lowly. "We've had men with worse habits on the throne of state.''

"You think he'll become king?''

"It's . . . just a feeling. A strong feeling, Adred.''

"But Elad has married. If he and Salia have a child—''

"Yes, I know. But . . . it's just a feeling I have.''

Adred was mildly disturbed by the tone of her voice, her insistence.

Orain stifled another yawn, leaned back in her chair. "This Lady Salia—Queen Salia. She's a great beauty, isn't she? I've heard that.''

"Yes. Very beautiful, I hear. But I haven't seen her.''

"That should suit Elad. If only he could appreciate all things with equal earnestness— Ah, well.''

"Yes . . . Evarris did.''

"King Evarris, I think, has been gone for a very long time.''

"It certainly seems so.''

Quiet, again, for a moment. Then Orain stood up, and Adred moved to his feet.

"I'm going to sleep," Orain told him. "I hope you don't mind."

"Of course not."

She smiled at him, looked around at the night, the sea. "Lovely," Orain said. "We haven't had many pleasant nights, have we?"

"No, I'm afraid not."

"Yes. . . . Good night, Adred."

"Good night. Do you want me to—"

"I can find my own way. Thank you."

She stepped across the deck, reached for the rail leading down into the waist, then turned as Adred called to her.

"Orain?"

"Yes, what is it?" She saw him standing alone in the darkness, partially hidden in shadows, the height of him blotting out a section of stars, the wildness of his hair lit from behind by one of the rocking lanterns. His voice seemed almost disembodied.

"Do you think— When we get back to Athad . . . would you like to go sit in the garden?" He waited a moment. "Would you like to do that?"

A great smile filled her face; she returned across the deck, stepped to him. "I was afraid," Orain whispered, "that you'd forgotten that."

"Forgotten it? No . . . No. . . ."

They stared at one another for a long moment, two warm shadows in the night, sharing a memory—friends with one another, again. Orain moved forward and kissed Adred on the cheek, quickly.

"Thank you. . . ."

He didn't understand. "For—what, Orain?"

She laughed lightly. "Just—thank you." Then she went to the steps again and made her way down into the waist.

Adred listened to her go. He was flushed, he felt young and confused and—in love? He sat again in his chair, sighed, held out his hands. They were trembling slightly.

I was afraid that you'd forgotten. . . .

Forgotten . . .

There had been so much, and he couldn't forget any of it.

It occurred to him at that moment that not once during their long talk had Orain asked about Cyrodian. Adred was intrigued by that.

Yet, maybe it wasn't so surprising, after all.

To forget . . .

Feeling as though he were a visitor in some land that did not know him, he looked out at the night, and the waves, and listened to the sounds in the night. The scent of Orain's perfume was still in the air and Adred breathed it, and thought of her voice, the light fall of her hair, the color of her eyes—

Forgotten? No . . . no. How could he ever have forgotten?

When he reached the place where he sensed she must be, he waited before entering. He stood in the alley just outside. The alley was very dark, and around him in the night all shadows seemed stronger than the feeble oil lamps that sought to dissuade them. The night was very warm, and at the sills of open windows high in the building behind him, alluring women talked loudly and shrilled with laughter. But Thameron was invisible to them. He had clothed himself in darkness, as sorcerers will sometimes do, and he was now as hidden as any shadow in that alleyway. Had the sun abruptly risen on the moment to illuminate that place, still he would have seemed a shadow, natural and unrecognizable.

Yet he was a shadow that quivered with human emotions, passionate aches. He faced the door, a stout wooden door at the rear of a tavern, and inside Thameron could hear the voices of carousing men and women. He blocked out all voices but one.

Assia's.

For she was in there. There—right beyond the door, behind that dark window. He could hear her voice, distinctly, as she argued with a man.

Suddenly the tavern door was thrust open. Gusts of warm air thick with smoky fumes and the scents of human sweat, stale beer and urine carried out as on a wind. The voices inside suddenly became very loud. And the man who had pushed open the door stalked into the alley and passed by Thameron, missing him by only a hair's width—never knowing the sorcerer was there.

Thameron watched him stumble down the alley. A drunken man, slovenly dressed in disarrayed armor. Swearing to himself, he reeled down the alley and rounded the corner.

The tavern door stood ajar, sounds and smells emanating from inside.

Thameron entered.

A few patrons who glanced at the open door did not heed the flutter of shadow-line that rippled against the wood, flowed upon the floor.

"Urwus!" someone called, and laughter followed.

Thameron, a shadow, moved toward the room directly to his right. Its door was partially open; within, it was dimly lit by one oil lamp sitting on a table in a corner. On a slovenly bed pushed against the opposite wall, lying beneath an open-shuttered window—

Assia.

Thameron, invisible, moved inside, stepped into the dark corner opposite the table, across from the bed. He breathed slightly; his heart raced. . . .

Assia sat up suddenly on the bed, swung her legs to the floor and pulled the vest she was wearing more tightly about her. She stood up, stalked across the room and leaned against the door.

"Urwus!" she called. "Damn you, Urwus, you . . . coward! Pig! Where did you go?"

Laughing voices answered her. "He left!"

"*Damn* him!" She slammed the door closed and stalked again to the bed, sat down. The wooden frame creaked; the light sound of her sobs seemed very distant in the hollow darkness.

"Assia."

Startled, she looked up.

"Assia . . ."

She looked into the corner but saw only shadows. She wiped quickly at her face, glanced around for something to grab hold of, a weapon perhaps, and started to rise. "Who's there? Urwus, is that you?"

"Assia . . ."

"Who's *there*?"

"It is Thameron, Assia."

Her eyes went wide, two white lamps in the night. "Tha— *Who*?"

"I've come back for you, Assia."

"Tha-meron? . . ."

He gestured, and his invisibility began to fall from him. He stepped forward into the room, and the darkness slipped down the length of him. The light from some star seemed strangely focused on him.

Assia fell back on the bed, her face a mask of incredulity. "Thamer— Oh . . . gods . . ."

"I've come back for you."

"Where did you—where did you come from? *Thameron*? Oh—

gods! How did you get in here? How did you *find*— Is it—it's not really you!"

"But it is."

"How did you *find* me? Oh, Thameron— Thameron, it *can't* be you, it *can't* be!"

He laughed joyfully. "But it is! It is! Assia . . . Please— touch me. Oh, Assia . . ."

"Do you, Assia? Truly love me?"

"So much . . . It frightens me. . . ."

Her head leaning to one side as she inspected him, she approached him carefully, uncertainly. "How did you ever . . ." she whispered, "find me?"

He smiled. "So much has changed. So much has . . . changed . . . for me—"

"Thameron . . ." She lifted her arms, pressed her hands to his chest, felt his face, pushed her fingers through his hair.

And instantly he felt the spirit of her—the loneliness, the heaviness and the darkness in her—the fears, and the illness, the great illness. . . . Her spirit, once full, and now desolate, empty . . .

"Assia. What has become of you?"

Tears shined like diamonds on her eyelashes, broke free and coursed down her cheeks. "Oh, gods, it's really *you*!" she sobbed. She threw herself upon him, hugged him and embraced him. "It's really you, Thameron, it's really *you*!"

He held her tightly; she was trembling violently. From outside the door came the raucous sounds of the drinkers in the tavern. And as he held her to him, pressed his hands upon her, Thameron felt a warmth grow in his palms. He felt the designs of the warmth—his old scars, his wounds, the signs of his hellish betrayal from—

The door crashed open.

"*No!*" Assia gasped, pushed away from him.

"What the hell is going on in here?"

"Urwus! Go away! *Go away!*"

Slowly, Thameron turned. The warmth in his hands grew hotter.

"Who the hell are you?" Urwus bawled. He was rocking unsteadily, drunk and very angry. He showed his teeth and without looking moved one leg to kick the door closed behind him.

The small flame in the oil lamp quivered and sent shadows hurrying.

"*Answer me!*" Urwus yelled.

Assia's voice betrayed her fear. "Urwus, leave him *alone*, he's a *friend*!"

"Not *my* friend!" the soldier grunted, coughing a crude laugh. "I know all *about* your *friends*!" Sneering, chin up, he stepped up to Thameron. "Now tell me who the hell you are! And what you think you're doing here! *Answer me*, damn you!"

His hands burned. *Burned*. In an icy voice, almost in a whisper: "Get away from here and leave us alone."

Urwus chuckled evilly. He moved his right hand behind his back and produced a long shining knife. "I'm not going anywhere, my—"

"Urwus, *no*!" Assia screamed.

Outside, the sounds in the tavern quieted, and someone pounded on the door.

"I think," Urwus sniffed, "you're the one who's going to be going away, my friend. Now I'll let you walk past me, very slowly, and I'll let you go out the—"

"Leave him *alone*!" Assia sobbed. "He's my *friend*!"

"Shut up, Assia!"

His hands *burned*, and his eyes began to brighten in the darkness.

Assia moved behind Thameron, held her hands to his shoulders. "Thameron, I won't let him hurt you. I won't. Urwus is—"

"Urwus is going to get this cockeater out of here," the soldier growled, "*now*!" Moving close, he waved the knife in front of the sorcerer's face. "Just move very slowly away from her," he ordered with beery breath, "and I'll be very—"

Thameron hissed.

There was a scruffling sound on the window ledge behind Assia. Urwus looked. Thameron glided away from him, throwing out an arm to Assia, warning her back.

The pounding thundered at the door. "Urwus! Who's in there?"

The scraping at the window grew louder.

Urwus glanced at Thameron, found that he'd moved. "What—"

The window shutters exploded as a lean black shadow leaped into the room. It flew over the bed, landed on the floor and bounded up. Urwus shrieked. The shadow lunged at him, pushed him back into the door. The knife flew from his hand and clattered in the darkness.

Assia screamed.

Urwus howled, his sobs and moans lifting torturedly above the

118

vicious grunts of the "thing." Caught in the jaws of it, Urwus was thrown back and forth against the door. Wild quick claws rent his chest and face, scratched long grooves in the door planks. Fanning showers and hissing jets of blood sprayed across the room.

"Urwus!" The pounding. "*Urwus*! Who's in—"

Assia whimpered as she hugged Thameron frantically. "How did it get in here? Oh, gods, *gods*!"

The sorcerer said nothing to her but held her behind him with one arm.

In another moment it was finished. Urwus slumped to the floor. The flickering light of the oil lamp, betraying the shadow at the door, revealed a mangled arm, a savaged chest running with sheets of red, a widening pool of blood mixed with ripped flesh that poured across the floor like a soup.

The shadow turned and faced Thameron. Its eyes were yellow; it bared long white teeth, red-wet, and growled liquidly.

Thameron hissed at it, then nodded.

The shadow—a dog?—leaned forward, then jumped onto the bed and bounded out the window, vanishing as suddenly as it had appeared.

"*Urwus!*" The continued hammering at the door, the rattling of the latch. Then—screams, as those outside discovered the blood seeping beneath the door.

Assia sobbed. Thameron turned and looked at her. His eyes still glowed in the dimness; his hands were shivering violently. Assia was breathless, her face white and drawn in fear. She stared at the sorcerer—Thameron—

"Thameron? What . . . did you do to the dog?"

"Please. Come with me."

"Thameron . . ."

"I need to tell you—"

Now they were trying to kick down the door.

She stared at him, tears moving down her face.

"Out the window," he told her.

She made a sound.

"It's gone," he promised her. But when she refused to move, or was still too frightened to move, Thameron reached over the bed, pressed a hand to the window sill, looked out into the street and said again: "Please, Assia. Whatever else has happened, . . . I've come back for you."

Quietly she moved to him, took his hand and stepped up onto the bed, kneeled on the window ledge, crawled through the window and dropped into the street below.

Behind, the door of the room was forced open, clogged though it was with Urwus's corpse. New screams.

But no one noticed the shadow that flitted through the open window.

In his dream, he saw a shadowy figure, old as eternity, with the face of a boy, dressed in darkness, hungry and full of pain. Something told him that it might be Nutatharis, returned to harass him—or any one of a thousand or a hundred thousand or a thousand thousand enemies who had pursued him down the river of time. But then again—no, not Nutatharis. It was some god or demon, and it called to him.

Called to him from the south.

Eromedeus heard the figure in his dream whisper voicelessly to him. He was frightened by it, and—frightened—he awoke from his dream perspiring.

Around him was darkness, the darkness of his cave at night. From outside he heard thunder, the storm that had been building when he had fallen asleep. Yet still, awake as he was, he felt the presence, felt it as a pulsing in the darkness. . . .

He stood up. He did not light any lights but walked forward, went to the opening of his cave and looked out. The sky was black, thunderclouds swept high above him, lightning flashed and danced against the purple. Then the rain began to fall.

"Who is there?" Eromedeus called.

Yet he knew no one was there. Only his imagination. But the *shadow*, the shadow in his dream . . .

He was still afraid. The dream was still with him, powerful, and Eromedeus stood at the mouth of his cave, looked down the slope of the mountainside, saw in the distance the wide forests, the black hills and—very far away—pinpoints of light in the middle of a sea of black. Lasura.

He realized that his dream was a portent.

He understood that his dream had been a visitation from the future, and that his wandering would soon end.

Eromedeus covered his face with his hands. Night winds blew on him, sweeping rain entered the cave and splashed him. The *shadow*. . . .

In his dream, he and the shadow, together, had stood upon this mountain and stared down upon the world of humanity—two of them, outside that world and yet associated with it, in the same

120

manner that feelings, emotions and intuitions are entities associated with the living organism. Eromedeus himself—an ancient question, soon to be resolved—and this other one—an eternal haunting spirit, returned now to test mankind, to doom mankind or tempt mankind and yet be a part of humanity's rebirth . . .

The End of Days . . .

Lightning hissed, thunder clapped and Eromedeus stumbled, pressed a wet hand to the rock of his cave opening and called out into the night: "Are you there? Where are you? Show yourself!"

Only the storm, and the silence between the explosions of the storm, and his own heartbeat, rapid and choked.

He had lived since the Dawn, and yet he was still a man, an undying man, not some animated Spirit, not some Force. He knew himself to be the fulcrum between two forces; he had wandered for thousands upon thousands of years as those forces built, as man grew and changed, he had lived as man filled cities, leveled fields and mountains—

The fulcrum.

One embodying all evil would free him, and one embodying all good would free him. That would occur at the End of Days.

When humanity died.

Eromedeus screamed.

He threw himself outside, ran into the storm. He did not want to live through the end and be reborn in the new beginning, to suffer this unlife forever. He ran in mud and pushed his way past trees that grew on the mountainside, he flailed his fists at the high storm clouds. He screamed in agony, tripped over a knotted root and fell to the ground, slid on the wet earth.

Eromedeus sobbed. Rain showered on him, lightning lit him, thunder boomed. . . . He groveled there, on the wet earth, his face dirtied with soil and mud. . . .

The world is at war, but it is not a war of soldiers. It is a war of hearts that we witness and are joined in, a battlefield of thoughts and great purposes, of man striving to gain a balance and hold it. . . .

And now it had come. The great moment, coming, the End of Days, coming, when the cycle of Heaven and Time and Purpose would coincide with the cycles of Earth and Life, when Spirit and Humanity and the Hell of inhumanity all touched, merged for a moment—Eternity's spirit fusing with human time for a moment—

All things in a balance.

And himself the fulcrum . . .

He sat up, there in the mud, on the warm wet mountainside, and Eromedeus stared down into the forest and the land and saw the distant small lights of the city.

Himself, the fulcrum between the forces of purpose—the one embodying all evil and the one embodying all good.

They were down there, somewhere in the world, following their paths and moving to meet him, moving to put humanity to its test, to place humanity in the crucible.

The End of Days . . .

Out from the deep winds of Time comes the Voice of a destiny. O humanity born in a storm and wandering in a storm, why do you turn from the future and return to your past?

O prophets and wanderers, lovers and kings, men and women of all kinds!

O humanity, O lost, born in a storm and wandering in a storm! These things that come, they come with cause.

4.

And still the flames burned atop the walls of the Holy City, still the cries of the people lifted to heaven, to the Wide Plain of Clouds, with their prayers for their dead *ghen sa ko-ghen*. The corpse of the emperor was by this time washed and cleansed, scented with oils and roots, dressed in garments of silver and gold, silk and leather; and the corpse had been placed in a bronze coffin, the bronze coffin put inside a gold sarcophagus, and the gold sarcophagus placed within a bireme in the harbor, where eight vessels guarded it.

In the renovated palace in Erusabad, all were in preparation for a departure to the capital at Ilbukar and the funeral of the *Ghen*. All that remained, in accord with custom (and to ensure that the government in Erusabad would run smoothly while its officials attended the ceremonies in Ilbukar), was the reading of Huagrim's Testament: the disposal of his earthly possessions.

Bin-Sutus was chosen by lot to read the document, which had arrived only that afternoon from the capital. In a small room of the palace, he sat at an oak table and faced Agors-*ghen-mu*, Nihim-

ghen-mu and the eleven other official *aihman-sas* and deputies of the dead king. bin-Sutus unrolled the Testament, which had been taken down by a scribe on a length of animal leather, just as had Huagrim's grandfather's own will been written on animal skin. But Huagrim's Testament had been written by a scribe schooled in one of the cities of the west so that the *Ghen's* final words were painted in quick brush strokes—odd ideographs—rather than in the cruder pictographs the people of the plains had used.

The Testament of Huagrim *ko-Ghen* of All Salukadia as he is facing the Gods of Heaven on the Wide Plain of Clouds. Let it be known to all Men that Huagrim *ko-Ghen* commands this to be done with his Empire and his Goods: To his first-born son Agors, who with his sire is a man of vision, the Empire of Salukadia; to his son Nihim, who has chosen to devote his life to things other than the Empire and the ways of his sires, who were horsemen and conquerors and leaders of generals, I leave all of Nature, which he worships; to my men of Council who have served me honestly and well, and with pride—the *aihman-sas* bin-Sutus, bin-Dusu, bin-Hasses, Utto-sengar, Doru-bin-Sahar, Abru-o-binar, Ansu-o-Kem, Wen-sa-go-Illu, abin-Urdu and each of their ministers—I leave a chest of gold and jewelry, which will be found in the treasury in Ilbukar, as well as tracts of land and houses, indicated on the maps at the bottom of this Testament, and to each a funeral house when each is called by the gods from the Light of Day to the Home of Night; and to the soldiers and horsemen of my Army, who have served me honestly and have honored my name and the shades of my sires with their services, I commend allotments of gold according to their ranks, and good clothes, boots and weapons to be given to the Officers of my Army, as indicated on the bottom of this Testament. May the Gods protect my Spirit and deliver me swiftly unto the Shades of my Sires. This done by Huagrim *ko-Ghen* of All Salukadia, on the thirteenth day of the Month of the Bull in the Fifteenth Year of his reign.

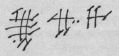

123

bin-Sutus set down the leather scroll. "That is all he has written, all that he has ordered to be done," he announced in a heavy voice. He unfurled the bottom part of the skin and showed it to the others at the table. Each man glanced at it.

Nihim, who was sitting across from bin-Sutus, stared at the old man; but bin-Sutus would not meet his gaze.

Agors, seated beside his brother, showed a wide grin to everyone in the room. But he did not gloat. That was unnecessary; anything he might say or do could only dim the words of his dead father, and the late *Ghen*'s words had said everything, succinctly and boldly. Agors was the next *Ghen*, and all these *aihman-sas* and deputies had received nothing—only jewels and houses, no power—and even his brother had received less than nothing. Salukadia was undivided, and all of it—from the Ursalion Sea to the sea-at-the-east where his great-grandfather had been born— was his.

His alone.

Several of the men at that table sucked in breaths of air; none looked at Agors.

Huagrim's eldest son pushed back his chair and stood. bin-Sutus watched him. Agors smiled coldly at the *aihman*; the old man's stare was ice.

Then Agors left the chamber, striding loudly into the outer hallway.

And one by one, the deputies and *aihman-sas*, as well, stood and bowed to bin-Sutus, bowed to Nihim-*ghen-mu*, and exited.

Until only Nihim and bin-Sutus remained, sitting opposite one another.

Silently . . .

bin-Sutus rolled up the Testament and tied it with its cords. "We must leave in the morning," he commented in a very low voice, "for Ilbukar."

Nihim shot him a deep look. "Why did he shame me, bin-Sutus?"

The old man slowly shook his head.

"He said nothing to you? Ever? Of his intention to . . . shame me, to shame his men of Council, and elevate Agors to the crown and the wolf-brand?"

"He said nothing to me. And every man here was stunned. He kept his own counsel, Nihim, I am sure of it. Every man here expected some worthy reward for his services; and every one of us expected the empire to be halved between you and Agors."

"Why would he shame me?"

"Perhaps," bin-Sutus speculated, "he does not shame you, but shames Agors." To Nihim's disgusted look: "I am sincere. He has raised Agors to become *Ghen*, but there is no land left to conquer, there are no plains left to ride, no mountains to level. Agors inherits the throne and the crown and the wolf-brand, but he can do little with them—little in the fashion that his father and foresires did. Perhaps your father did this, not to shame you—I believe he respected you, Nihim—but to remind Agors that he inherits a complete empire, not a partial one. Don't you think that if your father had halved the empire and given a portion to you, Agors sooner or later would have made war upon you, his own blood, to own all of Salukadia? Perhaps there is more wisdom than you think in your father's Testament."

"Perhaps," Nihim allowed, still hurt and his voice betraying it. "But I do not trust Agors's spirit, and he is not a reflective man. It will not speak to him, this deeper meaning in our father's decision. Don't you think, rather, bin-Sutus, that the energy Agors might have applied to winning half the empire from me he can now apply to expanding his empire by attacking the western lands?"

bin-Sutus's brow furrowed. "I think you are being alarmist. Agors has never betrayed to me any intention of making war upon the west."

Nihim pushed back his chair and stood up. "But neither did our father give you any indication of what he intended to do in his final Testament."

"I think you are worried where there is no need to be concerned, *Ghen-mu*. I have spent many hours with your brother and I don't find him eager to create war. He will challenge the west, he will play with them as—what is that game the Athadians enjoy so much?"

"*Usto*. It is a board game. It is an intellectual diversion of the aristocracy. But don't forget, bin-Sutus, that the Athadians enjoy other diversions as well. They have their arenas, you know, and their bloody sports in which men pummel one another, joust, kick and gouge." He shook his head. "These sports and games they amuse themselves with—they treat them as though they were . . . rehearsals for life's events."

Lord General Thomo was seated on his verandah behind the Authority enjoying the fragrant evening when Captain Commander Thytagoras loudly made his way past the hired servants and announced himself directly. Thomo winced as he looked across the patio; Thytagoras had just shoved aside the young man stationed at the verandah entrance and was now stalking across the bricks toward his superior. Thomo wiped his face, uncrossed his legs and tapped his fingers on the table beside him, preparing himself for the captain's display of temper.

"It's all right!" he called to the young man hovering behind Thytagoras.

The boy nodded and returned inside.

And like a whirlwind suddenly come still, Thytagoras threw himself into a chair and faced Thomo. He was perspiring heavily, panting, and he bounced one leg nervously as he sat.

"What is it?" Thomo asked him.

Thytagoras's nostrils flared; his stare was a foul one. "I feel as though I should—I should strangle you right now, where you sit," he whispered tautly.

"What are you talking about?" Thomo evinced no apprehension.

"I have just been speaking with Sirom," the captain replied coldly. "He told me about the letter you sent to King Elad."

"Did he?"

"Are you incredibly stupid, or are you just naive?" Thytagoras asked hotly. "I won't charge you with being a traitor—"

"You speak before you think, Captain," Thomo interrupted, warning him. "Watch your tongue, or I'll bring charges against you."

Thytagoras growled from low in his throat. "Why have you done this? *Why?*"

"*What* have I done, Captain?"

"You write to Elad—you tell him to send someone from the capital to witness the funeral of a—a *barbarian king*? Our *enemy*? Does the moon possess you? What could you possibly—"

"It's known as diplomacy, Captain," Thomo reminded him as levelly as he could. "And I don't look upon the Salukadian empire as our enemy."

"Our . . . antagonist, then."

"That sort of thinking leads to things that men regret. Why do you have such hatred in you, Captain? Tell me. I want to know."

The breeze was fragrant, wine was at hand, the two were alone in the evening. Thomo watched the officer and tried to understand him, tried to intuit what was happening in his mind, tried to imagine what could have shaped him.

But Thytagoras would not answer him. He stood up and took an erect, proud posture. "I'm afraid I must resign my commission," he announced gravely.

Thomo winced. "You've been drinking. Don't be foolish, Captain. You're overreacting. Sit down . . . please, sit down. Tell me why this offends you so much."

Thytagoras stared at him, threw his hands behind his back. "I simply cannot be a part of this."

"You are not an unintelligent man, Captain. Why do you insist upon hating these people? Is it the color of their skin? Is it the shape of their eyes? Some religious custom? Why do you insist on making trouble where there is none?"

"*Is* none?" Thytagoras objected, showing a shocked expression. "They moved their troops into our side of the city! They have destroyed our Temple and built some pagan monument in its place! The gods only know what they intend to do now that their old chief is being buried! And you say there is no trouble? I ask *you*, General Thomo—why do you pretend that there *is* no trouble and continue to appease these people, when I see a storm on the horizon! And it is coming at us very quickly! *Very* quickly!"

The man was sincere. Thomo gave the matter a moment's consideration before replying. "King Elad did not send me here to instigate a war, Captain. He sent me here to act as a diplomat. We can find a thousand reasons not to act amicably with the east, but that achieves nothing. Do you think these people want war with us? You know what war is. Do you think that's why they've done these things?"

Thytagoras coughed his disgust. "You're a soldier!" he countered. "Gods, man! You are a soldier! Where are your instincts? How dare you wear the armor of the imperial forces when you don't even think like a soldier!"

Thomo had had enough of that sort of slander; he rose quickly and confronted Thytagoras angrily. "My instincts as a soldier are on the battlefield—and I prefer to use those instincts on the battlefield, Captain, and not in the streets! A soldier serves his government! Damned be our nation when the government begins answering to the military! As long as my king asks me—*as a soldier!*—to do everything in my power to prevent war, then, by the gods, Thytagoras, preventing war is what I will do!"

Captain Thytagoras clenched his jaw. "I cannot be part of it."

"Then resign! Transfer to another city! I'll send you to the outbacks of the Fasu River! Tell me now! I'll draw up the papers, I'll sign all the necessary—"

Thytagoras, wholly disgusted, lifted a fist, then swung it in the air. Holding his chin high, he proclaimed: "I cannot serve my nation with honor, Commander, when my duties make me a part of dishonorableness." He reached inside his vest, withdrew a small packet and dropped it on the table. "There are my commission papers, my record of service, my badges and my formal declaration of resignation. Do whatever is necessary with them. I'll leave my uniforms in my room, and you may do with those whatever you like."

"Don't be a fool. Thytagoras." Now Thomo regretted his undiplomatic loss of temper. "When you calm down—"

"I'll strike you, Commander. I'll draw a knife on you! If that will madden you enough to kick me out of the army, I'll do it."

Thomo stared at him. Something turned cold very deep inside him. "You can't be serious," he protested quietly.

"As serious as my mother was in birthing me."

He had seldom agreed with Captain Thytagoras; they were two entirely different personalities. And yet Thomo knew the man to have served his nation honorably his entire professional life. "Thytagoras . . . I will refuse—"

"Then refuse! But I'm leaving tonight! I won't stay here and be a part of this . . . absurdity!" He looked across the verandah, stared out at the city. "They open their jaws, smiling, General— and we step into those jaws. Do you consider that diplomacy?"

"You are wrong, Thytagoras."

"And I believe you are wrong. I cannot serve you any longer, General Thomo. And—trust me—I regret that more than I can say." Failing to salute, he pivoted on a heel and crossed the patio. When he came to the arched entranceway, he turned a last time to face Thomo. "I do not *like* war, General. But for as long as men have lived, there has never *not* been war. Sometimes it is necessary; sometimes it is the needed thing. And if you understand that, then you must understand why it's important to foresee where war may happen; and if that war can't be prevented, then— by the gods!—it's important to fight that war as earnestly as you fought for your high-blessed diplomacy!"

Thomo stared at him.

"And if you do not understand now what these easterners are doing, General, then you have no right at all to be conducting our diplomacy with them."

"Good evening, Captain!"

Thytagoras saluted him fiercely, turned and went into the Authority Building.

Thomo watched him go. Then, to calm himself—

—if you do not understand what these easterners are doing—

—he reached for his wine on the table. He cursed lowly when his hand accidentally knocked aside a few strategically placed *usto* pieces.

He had been rehearsing some deceptively simple moves when Thytagoras interrupted him.

As their coach made its way down Losun Boulevard and passed beneath the great Ibar Bridge, Agors and Nihim glanced out the curtains to observe the people of their city—the crowds of them, starkly illuminated by lamps and fragrant torches set in the city walls and burning like ten thousand eyes to create a false daylight. Sailors caroused with loosely dressed women; old men walked in the company of youngsters; men and women of all ages strolled hand-in-hand; barterers and merchandisers offered fresh fish, ceramics, rice, cloth and weapons from their stalls.

When the coach reached the quay, it rumbled to a jarring halt, and the loud voices of royal guards called for the crowds and sightseers to hold back. Then the door was opened and Nihim stepped out, followed by Agors. The shadow of the great city wall behind them cast its dusk upon the quay and upon the crowds and the tall-masted ships secured along the docks. Nihim noticed the ship that held his father's sarcophagus; its sails were dressed with animal silhouettes, and hundreds of lamps glowed upon it. The rising mists of the Usub were caught in the flickering flames of the lamps and created a kind of aura about the craft.

Agors did not linger but with his military stride crossed the stone quay toward the boarding ramp. Approaching the soldiers guarding the ramp, Agors decided to loiter, while all around him moved the many throngs of people. The Salukadians among them bowed their heads and held out their hands in postures of deference when they saw Agors. Already word had reached the streets that the late *Ghen*'s eldest son was chosen by the gods to take his father's place upon the seat of the world.

"O *Ghen-mu*, grace me with your touch!" "O *Ghen-mu*, please welcome my baby into your presence!" "O Chosen of the Gods, touch me with your heart!" Such had always occurred whenever the *Ghen* himself made his rare public appearances—awed crowds bowing subserviently, collecting for a glimpse of the face or a touch of the hand.

But not all there on the quay were so devoted to the son of the gods. As Agors, beneath Nihim's critical eye, passed his hands upon numerous heads and faces, there came to him three individuals shaved bald, their heads and faces decorated with tattoos and incisions, their clothes no more than animal-skin robes painted with decorations: circles, stylized flames, letters of ancient alphabets. Agors's eyes went wide when he saw them; his hands tightened into claws.

"The grace of the Prophet on you, O *Ghen-mu* of the east," spoke the foremost of the three.

Agors sneered.

The smiling speaker did not flinch; rather, he proffered a flower, holding it out for Agors to touch or take. Behind him, shadowed by the crowds of others waiting to see the new *Ghen*, stood the other two, a man and a woman—both bald, both stained and decorated, both smiling.

Doom-Soulers . . .

"—O *Ghen-mu* . . ."

"Get away from me!" Agors whispered to him.

Nihim leaned close to his brother. "They meant no offense, Agors. You do not—"

"No offense?" He wiped the sweat from his cheeks. "For all I know, they had knives hidden in their sleeves! *No offense*?"

"I quite doubt that," Nihim spoke.

Agors growled and shook his head, moved away and started up the ramp, marching onto his barge. Nihim followed him.

On deck they stood at the rail and observed the quay below them where crowds stared up, awed, and soldiers directed the lines of workers who moved up and down the ramps with their crates and boxes.

"I am their enemy," Agors said to his brother. "Don't you think I know that? These . . . Doom-Soulers! They hold us responsible for their holy Temple!"

"We are responsible, Agors. We have despoiled it."

"They think we are . . . barbarians!"

Nihim stared down, saw where the soldiers released the three Soulers and motioned for them to get back into the city.

"Haven't you heard," he asked Agors, "that they think our desecrating their Temple is a sign of the last days?"

Agors stared at him.

But Nihim's expression was tolerant and knowing—passive.

5.

Deep into his return to her—here, now—where he knew there was no need for rooms redone to resemble caverns, no need to pay her gold for parodying herself—where he should have been honest with her and more than honest with himself—

Still—

He could not, at first, be honest with her.

"Thameron, what has happened to you? What have you—what did you do to your hands, Thameron? Thameron? . . ."

He had looked at her, shown her his eyes, and she, aware of what she herself had suffered, aware of choices she had had to make, did not comprehend everything but had sympathized with him.

"I couldn't wait. I was feeling too ill. I had to—leave. . . ."

And she had asked him, in those moments of their new togetherness, to lie to her.

"I wondered about you for so long that finally I forgot about you. People can only wonder so long. . . . So much happens . . . . I never forgot, really, but I always—I knew I'd always remember you, and I wanted to keep that—"

Eyes. Hands. New touching. Kissing, like children, new to themselves.

"I want to help you, Assia. I want to change everything for you, now."

Tell me that again, she had asked him. Tell me that again, tell me some more, and keep telling me, I want to hear you say it, I want to believe it, I want to believe it from you.

Lying there beside her, hidden away in warm shadows in some corner of the city, the humility of his congress with other human beings now past, looking into her ivory eyes, knowing that whatever had been eradicated or strangled or mutilated in her— still—some part of her remembered, and wanted him, or wanted again that one brief night, one rainy afternoon—

With the master of the hell of men.

What did you do to your hands? . . .

In love with her? Looking into her ivory eyes, in love with the aroma of her, frenzied as by any sorcery with the grunts and moans of her, the abandonment. Did it matter that it was him? Did it matter to her? Her nails in his back, drawing blood, as if it were a ceremony.

Her hair, fluttering beneath his lips. Her breasts, and sinking into the flesh of them as he might sink into the warmth of the good earth. Her nipples, like small living things, wrinkled and dark as the skin of a puckered berry.

He had sobbed, overcome, and drawn his face close, laid his head on her stomach and seen there the wide open pores of her dark tanned skin, pores from which small hairs grew: dark wheat upon a shadowed glossy field. He had moved his tongue upon her as though he were pressing soft footpads upon some clean area, the first ever to move upon such a place.

And, later, she had tried to quiet his sobbing. It was only after they had finished that she remembered him as a *priest*, the way he had been. Now he was a man, a man who had journeyed far and who knew such passions and how to create them—intricate mazes of pleasure, flowing and rolling, dipping and rising. Where had he learned such things?

With petals of flowers that he'd turned into gold he had brought her to this apartment, a vast room decorated with draperies, mosaics, statues, a small fountain and colored glass windows. She had never before been in such a place. But, being Assia, these things had been interesting only for the moment; she had been more interested in Thameron himself, and what had happened to him.

Circumventing her question, he had asked Assia about herself. And she told him everything, but told it briefly, bypassing details. Yet Thameron appreciated her gradual decline into degradation, for what else than that had happened to himself? And he'd wondered again how it was that the truly good souls are always those who are made to suffer.

It was the middle of the night, with the brilliant moon shining through the barred windows, and the flames of their lamps dancing softly. After bathing in the small fountain, Assia sipped tea and reclined upon pillows, while Thameron sat cross-legged in the *umhis* position and—

Told her everything.

"You loved me for myself . . . you were the only person who understood what I was trying to accomplish." Although they had been young then, young in experience and not yet emptied by life—still, she had been Assia then, and she was the same Assia now.

"Tell me," she whispered, her dark eyes urging him on, her hand fluttering near his feet to encourage him or simply to touch him.

He stared at her, marveling at her, remembering all the prostitutes far away, for though their bodies had been similar, and the fall of their hair—

Her long legs, shining now in the cool silver moonlight and touched by the warm tossing light of the lamps, and her slim belly, barely pushing in and out and shuddering as she breathed, and her breasts, fallen now one atop the other as she lay stretched and watching him, and her face that had become so thin and colorless from all her ills—

His wanderings. The seaports, the pleasure barges. How he had met a man named Guburus who claimed to possess great wisdom, but who had been a sorcerer, and how Guburus had allowed Thameron to be tricked into a compact with an evil entity.

"But . . . I'm not evil, Assia," he whispered to her, wanting her to believe him.

"Of course you're not, . . . of course you're not. . . ." As her hand lifted out to touch him and remind him of that.

Destruction he had caused: he had destroyed a village, taken lives; that was when he'd realized that there was a force within him, and that if he did not control it, he would succumb to it, and it would make of him a terrible thing.

"I can feel it, inside me . . . another living thing, inside me . . . pushing at me, trying to escape. . . . Sometimes it feels as if my body is a bubble, straining to burst. . . ."

His dreams of attaining enormous power, the command of nations, merely exercising this profound illumination and strength he had gained. His dreams.

"There is a man in a shadowy cave," Thameron whispered to Assia. "He calls me to him. I don't want to go, but the earth is moving beneath my feet, nights fall and days come, and every day that passes draws me closer to him. And when I meet him—kingdoms crash, I see the sky on fire and the world is buried, and I know that I am responsible for it. The stars tilt and whirl—I am making something happen. Whole crowds below me, begging me for things. And people—screaming . . . I am not *responsible* for it, and yet—I am." Now he stared at her; he saw that she was frightened by what he had said. "Such things could be," he warned her. "I have bartered with dark spirits—images and memories of ancient races, old wounds of the earth's. I never intended to, yet my questing led me to them, they chose me, and in ignorance I sought wisdom from a black fountain. Now, . . . I wish I were ignorant again. . . ." He showed her his hands. "These are signs of evil," he confessed to Assia, despair in his voice. "They are burned into my flesh, and into my soul."

He wept some more and Assia rose up and comforted him, embraced him and held him close to her. "You are not evil," she reassured him.

"But I am. I am." He grew angry with himself, then, and gently pushed Assia away. "I have been wounded, and here are the scars. All men are wounded, all men bear scars, but I have been wounded more deeply and my scars are patterned. Don't weep for me, Assia." He stood up, walked away from her and sat in a chair in the shadows. "What is good? What is evil? I have achieved my seat in a place where both are the same. Do I accomplish evil if I believe what I do is not evil? Where then is the evil?"

Assia, crouched upon her pillows, watched him and listened to him. This was another voice. Within a heartbeat, could he change so much? Was this proud and arrogant and isolated Thameron the Thameron she loved? Or was this new Thameron something more? Was he speaking truths beyond any other truths she had known? Or was this all deception?

"I could," came his voice from the shadows, "destroy all the stars with my strength. And I am led to do so by the powers that conceived me and seek refuge in me and escape through me into the human world. My own heart has been swallowed by another heart, a heart as wide as the night sky, and it is a heart as hungry as shadows are to cover all the light with their darkness. I see more in the darkness, Assia, than you can see in the light."

She trembled—with apprehension, but also with a kind of fascination. She had heard too much. Assia stood, stretching as she did so; she walked to Thameron with a feline grace, posturing herself. Had her friend changed? She too had changed. For when she knelt before him it was not in the attitude of a supplicant or a friend, but with the knowing grace, the privileged decisiveness, of a woman of talent kneeling before a man.

She looked up at him with deep eyes, moist lips, a wondrous expression. She leaned close to him, rested her hands upon his legs and stared into his shadow-guarded face.

"What happens in your mind?" Assia whispered to him in a husky voice. "What do you think? What do you know? What do you imagine? How do you make things happen?"

He touched her hair, felt her face. "You must never know. . . ."

"Do you, Assia? Truly love me?"

"So much . . . It frightens me, makes me wonder who I am, makes me wonder. . . ."

It is a door, Guburus had told him, which once opened, cannot be closed.

"Slay yourself!" the elder had demanded of him. "What have you become?"

Later, as the night approached dawn, Assia, hearing Thameron making sounds, awoke from her sleep. She sat up, wiped her face and stared at him.

He was sitting cross-legged on the other side of the room, behind the fountain. He was enclosed by a circle of burning candles, and his eyes were yellow. He was staring at her.

Wordlessly, Assia stood up and walked to him, passing through shadows, passing through moonlight streaming through the windows, passing by the tinkling sounds of the splashing fountain, coming into the warm glow of the candle flames.

Thameron lifted his hands. The candles extinguished themselves on trails of smoke.

"Kneel."

She did so, nervous and uncertain, unprepared.

Thameron leaned forward and touched her with his hands, pressed his hands to her body. His hands were warm, almost hot. Assia felt his fingers upon her breasts, felt the heat of them seeping beneath her bones, into her chest. She quickly broke out in a sweat. Thameron grunted and moved his hands, hot hands, upon her glossy breasts, now so slick with perspiration that they might have been oiled.

Assia moaned to him, "What—"

Thameron withdrew his hands, lowered his head. In a dull voice: "I thought I could—cure you, Assia. I thought I could . . . cure you. . . ."

"Oh, Thameron . . ."

"I could destroy the stars," he whispered, head still low. "But I cannot remove this disease from you. I am not—meant—to do that. . . ."

135

In the morning she dressed in clothes Thameron had purchased for her; Assia had never before worn such clothes: a skirt of silk, a blouse of soft jaconet, slippers of cloth-of-gold, a short vest of embroidered *samask*. He bought her expensive scents, perfumes extracted from rare animals and plants, a purse to wear on her belt in which to carry them and a parasol of silk with which to guard herself from the heavy sun.

And in one of the public parks in Abustad where they strolled that morning, Thameron plucked flowers for her, and Assia carried them and wore them in her hair; and other flowers he crushed in his hands, making from them more coins of gold, so much gold that they weighted Assia's purse uncomfortably.

She stared at him, lips trembling, as he dropped the last of the transformed petals into her purse. "Thameron . . ."

His eyes searched hers, an ache deep in him. "I must leave you."

"Thameron . . ."

"I cannot come back to you. Ever. I am evil, Assia. Remember me as I was before—"

"Oh, Thameron . . ."

"—please, please, . . . and use this money— There is much gold here—use it for yourself, please. Buy a house, hire servants, employ a physician, Assia. Please."

She began to weep.

"If I could make those things appear for you, create them out of the dust, I would do so, instantly . . . would have done it by now. . . ."

She began to cry openly; the colors she had carefully painted around her eyes ran down her cheeks.

Thameron wiped them away; the colors stained the marks on his palms.

"If I could . . . But for you, I can do good only by not doing evil. Assia—I still love you, but it is another kind of love, now—"

"Don't go." She clutched his arm. "Then . . . come back to me?"

"I cannot."

They stood in the soft shadows of a flowery cherry tree. The sun warmed them, but then clouds passed before the sun. Birds sang, and far away other people walked—strangers.

"I cannot come back to you. Assia—I want you to forget me,

136

now. Please. Remember . . . the Thameron who lived with you in Erusabad and was good—full of goodness and eager to serve the world. He was your friend, and he loved you. He loved you. Remember him, and believe in him, but—not in me. Assia . . . if the world should die—"

"Oh, gods, Thameron!"

He threw his arms around her and held her close, embraced her strongly, so strongly that she might never be taken from him. And she held him and sobbed and cried, begged him not to go, begged him to stay with her, because with her he could not be evil, and she would never fear life again, he would never—

"Thameron . . ."

Her wet eyes, her damp lips sparkling with her own running tears . . .

"Come . . . back?"

While in the north, a shadowy figure in a cave watched storm clouds gather and waited for the shadow in his dream to take shape—waited for the end to begin. . . .

PART IV

The Return

1.

As the royal galley reefed its sails to make dock at Port Athad Galvus was surprised to see less activity in the harbor than he ha remembered. They had only been gone from the capital for a littl over half a year; and when he and Orain and Adred had left la autumn for Kendia, it had been commonplace for trading ship barges and galleys to drop anchor half a league out from the mout of the Sevulus and wait sometimes half a day before the congeste docks were cleared enough for the next hold of goods to b unloaded. But such was not the case today. Galvus, Adred an Omos, from where they stood on the foredeck, saw only sixtee ships ahead of them making their way quickly and efficiently t the wharves and the loitering dockhands waiting to unload them

When Galvus made comment of this, the Khamar, who wa standing nearby, replied tersely: "The economy."

Even more appalling for Galvus was the sight of houseboats ill-constructed rafts and ramshackle huts that crowded not only th small outlying islets around the mouth of the Sevulus, but fille the alleys and streets behind the shipping docks for as far a Galvus could see.

"It's worse here than in Sulos!" he exclaimed.

As the galley made its way upriver toward the imperial qua below him Galvus saw hundreds of suffering faces crouched o floating hovels, living in the open sewers beneath the wharve

"They're out of work," the Khamar told him. "Can't pay re in the city, can't afford to buy food. They have to commit crime to get by, or they come down here. More of them everyday. The fish to eat, sometimes try to steal from shiploads coming in. Yo see?" He pointed.

A thin-faced, hollow-chested man poked his head around th corner of a pile and stared up blankly at the passing royal galle His left hand was missing; his arm ended in a bony stump.

"Probably some sailors caught him trying to steal something— them, or some of the patrol. So that's what he got for it."

Galvus looked away. "It wasn't this bad when I left, in Avru. That was only three months ago."

He looked at the Khamar; the guard's expression was sullen.

Lord Abgarthis interrupted Elad and Salia's after-lunch conversation to present his king with the dispatches and missives received that morning, and to alert him to the news of the day. Elad made a face when he saw the stack of letters Abgarthis carried with him; as the minister handed them to a servant, the king asked:

"What is important in all that?"

Abgarthis moved to an empty seat beside the Imbur Ogodis and poured himself some tea. "A message from Captain Mirsus, sent from Arsol three days ago. Cyrodian remains in custody and all continues without incident."

Elad nodded.

"Governor Sulen in Abustad reports that the flooding there continues. He suspects that the Emarians have been making greater advances into the Lowlands; but our northern border has not been affected, and they have actually made no sightings of either Emarian or Salukadian troop movements."

"Excellent."

"The flooding, however, has to some extent damaged the plantings of our own farmers in northeastern Omeria. Sulen may require some relief."

Chagrined, Elad shook his head. "With whom did they plead," he wondered aloud, "when they didn't have a throne to turn to?"

Ogodis grunted his approval of that comment; the Imbur of Gaegosh professed a strong belief in self-reliance and let it be known that he considered himself the embodiment of that ideal.

"Perhaps," Abgarthis commented, "to whoever might lend them aid." At a sharp look from Elad: "There is a long letter from Lord General Thomo in Erusabad. Huagrim, the *Ghen* of Salukadia, has died."

Elad lifted an eyebrow to that.

"Not entirely unexpected," Abgarthis admitted. "Thomo seems convinced that, for the moment, our policies and agreements there are not jeopardized. His letter is full of important details." He suggested that Elad read it at his earliest opportunity. "Thomo thinks it may be wise of us to send a representative to the Salukadian court, to pay our respects to the late *Ghen*'s memory."

Ogodis laughed out loud at the foolishness of such a thing, but

Elad replied simply, "I shall have to give that matter some careful thought."

Ogodis eyed him warily. "They are savages!" he complained, smiling.

Elad cautioned him: "Savages or not, our businessmen seem to think that their gold is mined the same way ours is. It may not do us any harm to strike an accord with them in this way." He held up a hand, stalling anymore of his father-in-law's opinion. "What else, Abgarthis?"

The old man smiled as he finished his tea. "Our visitors from Sulos," he announced, "have arrived."

Elad was relieved to hear it. "Orain? And Galvus?"

Abgarthis nodded deeply. "Safe and whole. Count Adred seems to have accomplished everything that we asked of him. A courier brought me the news just before I left to come here."

"Then they are on their way?"

"Probably in their coach as we speak."

"Good." Elad rapped his knuckles on the table and pushed back his chair. "Good. Good." He stood and offered his hand to Salia, who took it and gracefully moved around the table to follow him out.

"Have them taken immediately to their rooms," the king advised Abgarthis, "and as soon as they have refreshed themselves and eaten, let me know."

"It is done already, King Elad."

Abgarthis was there himself to greet them when the four, still accompanied by the ubiquitous Khamar, arrived at the palace. Galvus found more evidence of the government's stasis and public disaffection as the coach rolled to a halt in the courtyard before the wide, white steps of the southern portico: as he stepped out, the prince noticed large dark smears defacing some of the marbled walls close to the street. Dog excrement and horse dung . . .

Orain stood quiet and still, staring at the palace as if she had never lived there nor even seen it before; but when Abgarthis flew down the stairs toward her, she found herself opening her arms to embrace him. And Abgarthis hugged her with all the emotion of a father welcoming a lost daughter. He lent Adred his hand and shook his arm vigorously, stared at the young aristocrat and told him in a voice heavy with meaning: "Thank you, Count Adred. Thank you. . . ."

"Your instructions, Abgarthis, were—should I say—insistent?"

The minister laughed and turned to Galvus. Light filled his face when he saw the young man, for he had remembered him as a boy when he and his mother had left last winter. Galvus took Abgarthis's arm and, gripping him proudly, seemed to promise the elder many things with his eyes.

"You are welcome back, Prince Galvus. You are most welcome back, indeed."

"Thank you, my lord."

"And who is this young gentleman?" He turned to Omos.

Galvus introduced him. "My friend, and a friend to the empire."

"Welcome," Abgarthis greeted him, clasping Omos's hand. "Please feel that you are at your own home, here, with us."

"I thank you, Lord Abgarthis." The youth seemed happy but without a doubt intimidated by it all: the coach, the palace, the guards—the heart of the empire, here. He had wondered often if such a place actually existed; he was very far from the cold streets of Sulos.

"Now, come along inside," Abgarthis urged them all, leading the way up the steps as the coach moved off. To the Khamar: "You have your instructions to report to your commanding officer?"

"Yes, Lord Abgarthis."

"You have done well, my man. I thank you for it; and all that we promised you will be forthcoming."

"Thank you, Lord Abgarthis." The guard dipped his head, smiled at Orain and Adred and saluted them as he walked off.

Adred, wondering, stared at him for a moment before continuing up the stairs.

They were given rooms on the third floor of the east wing—an apartment for each, with sunken bathing pools, fresh clothes and servants at their disposal. As Adred trimmed his beard, he asked the man servant holding his mirror some innocent questions regarding events in the palace over the past few months. The servant seemed reticent to speak and answered the questions cursorily. Adred dressed in a new pair of trousers (a bit too long in the legs for him), a fresh cotton tunic and a plain vest. He pulled on his boots, thanked his servant for his help and went out, feeling comfortable and invigorated.

Across the hall a sitting chamber had been done over into a cenacle; hurrying servants filled a table with plates, cups and decanters. Galvus and Omos were already there, sipping wine and talking. Just as Adred came in, Abgarthis returned, leading a file of additional servants. Adred seated himself across from Galvus, while Abgarthis took a chair beneath a window.

"Please, eat," he indicated. "Fill yourselves. Whenever you're finished, we can see Elad."

"He isn't in Council?" Galvus inquired, reaching for a small loaf of bread.

Abgarthis shook his head. "Council has been suspended for two weeks; some of our ministers and lawyers are looking into preliminary plans for setting up the workers' *sirots*."

Galvus glanced at Adred—a look of bemused interest—then asked Abgarthis about all the changes he had seen in the capital: the armies of the poor living on the docks, the animal excrement flung at the palace, so few ships making dock.

Abgarthis sighed heavily. "Do you really want to hear about all that now?"

"Certainly," Galvus replied.

But explanations were held off as Orain entered, smiled to everyone and moved to sit beside Adred.

He helped her with her chair, and a little thrill went through him at the scent of her perfume, the aroma of her freshly washed hair, which fell forward in golden spirals as Orain slid her chair in place. Adred grinned at her and made some comment as he poured a cup of tea for her. Orain gently brushed his hand as she reached for her tea.

Plates of rice and vegetables, pork ribs and sausages, pheasant and duck invited them to dine in a fashion they had become unused to. Adred finished his tea and opened a decanter of wine; tasting it, he nodded his approval to Abgarthis and remarked on the excellence of it. Abgarthis, before thinking about it, told him that it was from the Diruvian vineyards and agreed that it was splendid.

Galvus cleared his throat; Adred set down the wine. Abruptly realizing what he had said, Abgarthis ventured awkwardly: "I hope that . . . knowing that . . . doesn't spoil your appreciation of it." He tried to make of it a humorous faux pas.

Neither Adred nor Galvus took offense and assured Abgarthis of that. But the comment opened the door to the prince's pursuing all that had occurred in his absence.

Abgarthis, complying, moved from his window chair to the table, poured himself a cup of the white Diruvian and sat beside Orain. Glancing from one to another of them: "Elad, of course, will tell you whatever you wish to know. But I suppose I should generally sketch in things for you." He recounted the assassination attempt, moved backwards in time to tell of Queen Salia and her father the Imbur, jumped forward to dwell on Elad's recovery and his very sincere change in attitude that accompanied his recuperation. Abgarthis briefly passed over his "retirement" from Council: "It's true that Elad and I had a falling out; both of us spoke too hastily. I refused to retract what I'd said, and his pride could not countenance such . . . insubordination. We are friends again, however, and in fact I'm sure he would reinstate me in the Chamber again if I were to request it. But things have an odd way of happening for the better. Elad seems better able to trust me simply because my voice does not become recorded in the daily reports. The two of us can speak more openly, in private. He needs that."

As empty plates were pushed aside and new decanters of wine passed around to refill cups, Galvus looked the minister in the eye and inquired politely: "And is there any word of my father?"

A heavy silence followed his question. Abgarthis looked from Galvus to Orain; Adred noticed her hands trembling on the table. She removed them and hid them in her lap.

"Again," Abgarthis was forthright, "I'm sure Elad can fill you in on all the details. But you know that Prince Cyrodian was responsible for ordering . . . Queen Yta's death? Yes. . . . He was hidden in exile at the time. We learned later that he had taken refuge with King Nutatharis of Emaria; Elad's queries to Lasura were never answered. Some in Council wanted to storm Lasura by force and capture the prince that way. But only eleven days ago, for whatever reason, Nutatharis sent a dispatch to us through our ambassadors in Lasura: he had ordered Cyrodian arrested and returned to Athad."

"He is here now?" Galvus asked.

Adred watched Orain.

"No. But we received notice today from the officer charged with returning him. They had just left Port Arsol."

Galvus smiled a strange smile. Gently he rotated the stem of his wine goblet between his fingers. Omos, concerned, wordlessly place a caring hand on Galvus's arm; Galvus nodded to him, then said to Abgarthis: "It just occurred to me—it means nothing, but it is curious—that for whatever different reasons, mother and I left here around the time father was sent away, and now we've returned just about the time he's come back. Odd . . ."

Orain coughed slightly, self-consciously; everyone glanced at her sympathetically. She shook her head. "Perhaps," she remarked, "it's as Lord Abgarthis said. That things have a way of happening for the better?"

Another prolonged silence met her observation; then Abgarthis stood, drummed his fingers on the table and advised: "Well, . . . if we're ready, I can send word to Elad. Or would you like to go out into the gardens? I believe he and Salia may still be taking their exercise in the west garden. . . ."

They made their way down one of the shaded walkways, passing a Khamar standing at guard, who nodded politely to them. And Adred, as he glanced around the lush garden, heavy with the scents of ash trees and willows, roses and chrysanthemums, noticed other imperial guards on duty at various strategic points.

Abgarthis led the way. Behind him walked Galvus and Omos, then Adred and Orain. Orain, enjoying the beauty, was walking quietly; when she noticed Adred's eyes on her, she lent him a slender smile and quietly slipped her hand into his.

The king and queen were seated in a trellised gazebo in the middle of the garden. Elad rose to his feet immediately upon seeing them and stepped down into the walkway with extended arms. "Welcome! Welcome! Galvus—thank you, please, sit down, welcome back! Orain!" They came together in the fragrant shade, Galvus introduced Omos, and Elad embraced Orain (while warning her to be careful of his tender side); then Elad faced Adred. The king took Adred's hand and shook it firmly, grinned at him heartily and, as though the past were done, thanked him in an almost confidential tone: "Welcome home, Count Adred."

"My lord . . ."

Elad ushered them up the steps into the wide, oval gazebo, where Salia stood up to greet them. But she was interrupted by two fluffy, lively dogs at her feet. She bent to admonish them and exasperatedly looped their silver chains around a leg of the table in the center of the gazebo so that they wouldn't embarrass anyone.

"The queen," Elad said, as he moved beside her.

All bowed their heads respectfully and offered their hands, as Salia expressed her joy at finally having the opportunity to meet them. Her glance lingered on Orain as though she were slightly intrigued by her.

Adred, seeing Salia for the first time, was astonished both by her beauty and her youth. Abgarthis had told him that the queen was renowned as the most beautiful woman in the world; but such exaggerations were commonplace in aristocratic circles, where the daughters of important families were regularly extolled for their wit, charm and appearance. And Adred knew that beauty was a relative thing: everyone was possessed of his or her own sort of beauty, and the tireless cataloguing of women's attributes engaged in by some men was as silly as the ponderous indexing of racehorses and athletes. And yet Salia . . .

What was it about her? Her skin? Her hair? There was something indefinable about her, something more than the simple but pronounced fall of her hair, the brightness of her eyes and curve of her lips. Adred recalled poets; it was as if the human glow of her, vulnerable but honest, shined as clearly in her features as did sunlight. And yet—was there something sad or pathetic in her eyes, in the way she lifted her arm?

Adred sat beside Orain on one of the marble benches across from Elad and Salia, and he felt his attention drawn again and again, almost impolitely, to the queen. Her presence, the aura of her—what? Fatalism? Her beauty seemed to fade before the strong sensitivity Salia exuded, as if the outward appearance was only a lure to the world, a temptation or an attraction meant to set in motion other things, other ideas or events or consequences. It was the strangest thing, looking upon a beautiful regal woman and considering such wildly implausible and contradictory thoughts. . . .

"I realize," Elad admitted, as all settled still, "that we have much to discuss. And we shall." He looked at Galvus. "But for the moment I want to emphasize that I think it important that we all engage in a mutual . . . exchange of ideas, I suppose we should call it. I think I can speak frankly, can't I? Our empire seems to be fractioning, new troubles seem to crop up every day. And it has become clear to me that our old methods of dealing with issues may not always be pertinent or appropriate in regard to these circumstances. But I think the best thing we could do now would be to set aside our passions and look at things logically and rationally."

He paused, specifically eyed Count Adred and Prince Galvus and read their expressions.

"Well . . . I wanted this brought out into the open so that you know how I feel. We have lessons to learn, but I think many good things can come of all this if we adhere to direction on the one hand and common sense on the other."

145

His eyes settled on Galvus. The young man told him plainly: "I quite agree."

Elad glanced at Count Adred; Adred, who was sitting with his arms crossed upon his chest, lowered his eyes from Queen Salia, glanced at the dogs under the table, then regarded Elad and told him: "I agree, as well, my lord. I would only stress that we keep in mind our values. We have important values in our empire, we have returned to them in times of crisis, and we've been served well by them."

"Values . . . yes," the king replied, letting his gaze linger on the young aristocrat. Then, to Galvus: "Don't you find that beard to be rather warm this time of year?"

Galvus shrugged. "One gets used to it."

"Yes, of course. . . ."

They chatted about noncommittal things, then. Salia introduced the four of them to her puppies and urged them to visit her pet garden just off the west wing; Elad was seeing to it that a habitat was constructed for her many pets and birds and other animals, for Salia confessed that she enjoyed their company at least as much as she did that of people. Adred found that intriguing. Elad casually asked Omos what he thought of the capital—that is, considering what he had seen of it—and Omos replied that it was fascinating and very big and that he didn't know if he could get used to it all.

When they adjourned, it was with Elad's insistence that they all feel free to make themselves at home that afternoon, visiting the gardens or the royal library or, if they preferred, going to see some of the games and contests at the arena. The games had become very popular; there were horse races and chariot races, boxing and wrestling matches, team sports, dramas and dances. Courses and stages had been set up in the refurbished capital *Kirgo Amax*, and admittance was free during the afternoon and only a copper in the evening. But Elad told them that he had seats for them in the imperial box.

Adred asked whether there had been any demonstrations, acts of lawlessness or violence in the capital; he mentioned again all those jobless and dispossessed outcasts on the wharves.

"They are sporadic—but there are certain areas of the city you'd be wise not to visit. There was a scene last night, apparently, at one of the arena gates." Abgarthis shook his head. "Hardly a political matter. All the seats were sold out, and a great number of people insisted on getting in." A few aristocrats had graciously given up their boxes so that several dozen spectators could be seated; but one of them was stabbed during the excitement, so that probably wouldn't happen again soon. "Count Adred, there is a strong feeling of tension—waiting—in this city. Waiting . . ."

2.

As they walked up the steps into the palace, Adred told Abgarthis that he would take the remaining hours of the afternoon to visit the capital: he was eager to see firsthand some of what was transpiring in the city (yes, he would stay clear of the troubled areas), and he wanted to give thought to matters before speaking further with King Elad that evening. Also, Adred wanted to buy himself some new clothes; the attire lent him by the palace did not quite fit him.

"Have it altered to suit you," Abgarthis urged him. "Don't go to the expense of buying everything new." And then it occurred to him: "I suppose you'll be stopping at your banking house for funds?"

"Yes, I'd planned on it."

"Before you leave, then, let me see about something first."

Adred was perplexed. "Why? What's the matter?"

Abgarthis pursed his lips. "You must remember that—well, when you were arrested in Bessara as a revolutionary, all your property and funds were immediately appropriated by the government."

He had indeed forgotten. "Of course. . . . Abgarthis, there must be—"

"Elad and I already agreed that if you succeeded in your enterprise in Sulos, all charges against you would be waived and your property returned. We took no legal action, Adred, to absorb your property; we merely posted a notice in our ledgers and informed the bank to withhold your account in the name of the throne."

Adred made a face but nodded his head.

"Give me a moment and I'll draw up an imperial forfeiture, and you can take it with you." He glanced behind the young man to where Orain was just coming. "I'll only be a moment."

Adred asked him: "Does this happen very often?"

"Very frequently, nowadays, I'm afraid. The throne is dissolving estates every day and using the funds— Oh, . . . you mean

147

to return property in this way? No . . . no. Not very often. In fact, you are . . . rather unique, Adred. But I have long suspected that."

"I'll presume to take that as a compliment, Abgarthis."

The minister laughed and walked off down the hall, as Adred turned to Orain. "You look tired," he said gently. "Didn't get much sleep on the trip here, did you?"

"I'm afraid not. And it's so warm. . . . Adred—are you going into the city now?"

"Yes."

"Would you mind if I came along? I don't want to go out alone."

Abgarthis's expression was drawn as he came up to Adred and showed him a folded document with a number scribbled on one side. "This was the amount in your account, wasn't it, Adred?"

"Yes, that's all of it."

"It's a substantial sum," the minister remarked. "This—becomes rather confusing, but I should tell you that when Elad signed his proclamation staying any executions for acts of political dissent, he faced some angry voices in Council, and to placate several of those men he agreed to an amendment that retains twenty percent of a convicted person's—"

"Twenty percent!" Adred exclaimed in shock. Hurriedly, he calculated mentally. "That's nearly thirty thousand in long gold!"

"Yes, I'm afraid it is," Abgarthis nodded. "But that twenty percent is put into a fund, an insurance fund to protect any businesses lost or any property damaged—"

"Twenty percent!" Adred complained hotly. "It's thievery! That's my family's money!"

"Adred, after all, you *were* arrested as a revolutionary, and Council felt—"

"Council felt," he interrupted bitterly, taking the document from Abgarthis, "that even if the world ended tomorrow, businessmen must still make the largest profit from it that they could! Isn't that what Council felt?"

Orain said quietly, "Please, Adred . . ."

"I wouldn't put it in exactly those words," Abgarthis temporized.

"But it's true, isn't it? Insurance fund! You and I both know—"

"The government," Abgarthis interposed, "is the most important business in this country. And businesses," he added frankly, "are seldom moral entities, or even ethical ones."

"Or even necessary ones!" Adred growled, putting the document inside his jacket. "Their gods-almighty money . . . their gods-almighty profit . . . You know, Abgarthis, I wonder sometimes where the world would be now if the gods had originally created us solely for the benefit of profit. Have you ever wondered about that?"

"I can't say that I have."

"The hell with it," Adred grunted, reaching for Orain's hand. "How the hell would the gods collect *their* twenty percent? From their priests?" He started walking away, Orain beside him; she gave Abgarthis a look of sad resignation.

"Perhaps," Abgarthis called—and Adred turned to look at him—"their investment was not specifically a monetary one. Perhaps the gods were thinking of making a spiritual profit from their enterprise?"

"Then they're bankrupt, Abgarthis. They're out of business. They're bankrupt."

By the time Adred had finished his business at his banking house, his anger had begun to subside. Even though he snarled at Orain (as he helped her into the carriage), "These banks don't perform functions for society! Society performs functions for *them!*" She refused to dwell on the unfairness of it and tried to lift Adred's spirits. At the tailor's she helped him choose his new clothes, and then they continued on to the mausoleum where his parents' urns were kept. There, he lay a white rose before each one and muttered a small prayer. When he rejoined Orain in their carriage, Adred told her:

"I've kept my father's diaries, and every letter he ever sent me. There was something he said to me once that tells me, more than anything, why he chose to live the way he did. He said to me, 'Everyone wants to change society, but no one is willing to change himself.' You see? Maybe I've fallen short of that. My father was never a revolutionary; I don't think he would have been able to comprehend just what it means to be a revolutionary—not in the way I mean it. Yet he believed in the basic goodness of people, and he always did what he could to help others; he always had time to listen to a friend, yet he seldom complained about himself. He thought the best way to change things was by example, and to give society time. Time to adjust . . . time to change . . . time to correct errors. Because he believed that eventually

149

the strongest ideas, the most human and humane ideas, and the best in men, will come forward, won't be thwarted, and that society will accept them." He wiped his face, scratched his neck. "I wonder now if it's too late for that."

On their way back to the palace Adred directed the driver to take the coach through the Pilusian Gate and follow the Ferian Road outside the city walls. Once under the Ferian Arch and past the small shops, hostels and inns that cluttered the northwest approach to the capital, the carriage entered open farmlands and vineyards. Sparse forests steadily grew denser, the hills sloped steeply upward, and occasional road markers indicated the property of aristocrats and landowners.

"Where are we going?" Orain asked.

But Adred ignored her as he pushed his head out his window to tell the driver: "The next road to your left!"

As he settled himself in his seat again, Orain tugged his sleeve. "Where are we going?"

"To . . . my father's house. I haven't been there in—well, in a few years. . . ."

"A few *years*?" Orain was astounded at how casually he admitted it.

Adred answered her in a quiet voice. "There's really nothing there any longer. I sold everything and locked up the house; everything's secured. I leased some of the land."

"You never told me about that."

Adred shrugged. "I decided I wanted to travel."

The driver steered the coach down the next road; it was marked by a spare stone marker engraved with the sign of Adred's father's seal. Very shortly the road dipped and the family mansion came into view. It sat behind a tall iron gate partially overgrown with shrubbery; and the gardens that had once surrounded the house bloomed with weeds and tall grasses. Otherwise, it seemed intact: boarded and chained.

"Look." Orain pointed, as the coach drew still before the gate.

Adred stepped out, walked around the coach and approached the gate. Suspended from an iron chain run around its hinges was a notice carved into an oak board:

PROPERTY OF THE ATHADIAN GOVERNMENT
Trespassers Will Be Prosecuted

He didn't look back at Orain but stood where he was for a few long minutes, staring past the fence at the house and its grounds. Adred kicked his right foot several times in the road, which sent up clouds of dust. Then he turned around and, with his hands thrust into the pockets of his jacket, returned to the coach and climbed in.

"They haven't taken down the sign yet," was all he said to Orain.

The driver turned the coach around and it creaked and jostled back down the road.

On their return to the capital through the northside of town, Adred and Orain witnessed more changes that had occurred during their absence. Streets that had once thronged with shoppers, sellers and travelers were now quiet; only occasional lines of the poor and unemployed passed from shadow to shadow, doorway to doorway. Closer to the center of the city, as they moved toward the urban homes and apartments of the capital's gentry, they saw signs of abandonment. Some of the homes they passed appeared to be as empty as Adred's father's estate; apparently the occupants had moved away. Other buildings had been fortified with freshly built walls and gates blockading access from the street. There were no signs of violence—only mute suggestions of tension and fear.

Waiting . . .

Adred spoke not at all; and Orain, too, was quiet, as the carriage made its way back to the palace.

Omos found Galvus sitting on the balcony outside his room when he returned, full of excitement, from the Royal Library.

"I've never seen so many books!" he exclaimed. "How large a building is that? Ten stories? And books everywhere! It must contain everything ever written!"

Galvus laughed. "Pretty much so, it does." He seemed preoccupied.

"And there were books in there that are censored everywhere else. Why do they allow that?"

Galvus shrugged. "They have to be kept somewhere for someone to keep an eye on them. But you're a guest of the palace, no one will interfere with you in there."

"They had complete sets of Radulis—every edition! The *Essays* of Oson . . . all the satires of Dimulis, . . . Evadeseth's *Liberty* . . . More poetry and philosophy than I've seen in my life! And art! That portrait of King Evarris must have taken years!"

Galvus nodded. "I seem to remember grandfather grumbling about that one."

151

As his enthusiasm died down, Omos noticed his friend's mood. "What's wrong?" he asked. "Are you all right?"

"Yes, yes . . . I'm fine."

But Omos walked to him and crouched beside Galvus's chair and took his hand. "Something's wrong. Are you just tired?"

"I suppose so." He rubbed his eyes with his free hand, settled his papers and notes in his lap. "I'm just . . . thinking." He regarded Omos keenly. "If you don't want to stay here—I mean," Galvus spoke quietly, "not right now, but eventually—if you want to go back to Sulos, it's all right."

Omos was very surprised. "What do you mean by that?"

"Just . . . homesickness, I suppose. I'm thinking about everything that's happened so far. What we're fighting. Tired of the fight even before we start it."

"Lie down for a while, Galvus. Take a nap before supper."

"I think I may do that." But he didn't get up. "I want you to know, though, that anytime you want to go back to Sulos, Omos, you can. I don't want you to think you're obliged to stay here."

"I understand," Omos answered softly. "But why would I go back? What would I go back to? Who would I go back to? There's nothing for me in Sulos."

Galvus smiled, leaned over and kissed him. "Thank you."

"It's true. I owe you everything, Galvus. And I love you very much."

"Thank you. . . ." He rubbed his eyes again.

Omos determinedly got to his feet, grabbed Galvus's hand and pulled him out of his chair. "Time for you to lie down now. I'll wake you up when your mother and Count Adred return."

"Yes, yes, all right." Then, wearily, as he set aside his papers: "I suppose, after all, that there really is nothing to go back to."

Orain and Adred were quiet during supper; Galvus noticed it and wondered what had passed between them during the afternoon. He wasn't able to inquire, however, with the Imbur Ogodis present at the table: Ogodis's garrulousness and his rude comments about the Salukadians seemed wholly out of place among the company in the Feasting Hall.

When supper was finished, Elad called for the evening's entertainment, and over wine and sweetmeats and juice-flavored ices, the company listened to singers and enjoyed brief ballets staged by the throne's subsidized repertory companies. Ogodis's ceaseless opinionatedness now focused on flaws in the perform-nces, and he made certain to stress to Elad that on his next visit to Athad, he would see to it that he brought with him some of the dance troupes from Sugat: *they* were glorious.

After about an hour's diversion, when he had finally had his fill of the Imbur's wine-induced pontifications, Elad rose and took Salia's hand, kissed it, then announced that he would retire for the remainder of the evening. He informed Galvus and Adred that he would be in one of his private chambers off the main room upstairs, and should they desire to have a word with him, or share the evening's final glass of wine with him, they could find him here.

The two waited until the king had gone, casually finished their desserts and ignored Ogodis's stares of burning intensity. Then they excused themselves, yawned and followed the main stairs up to the third floor of the palace.

3.

Adred knew that Galvus felt apprehensive about speaking openly with Elad. It was not that the young man did not trust his uncle; neither did Galvus fear that Elad would threaten him with punishment for his beliefs. The king was too sentimental regarding his nephew to do that, and Adred suspected, too, that Elad felt a responsibility toward Galvus, the only representative of a generation, born so far, from any of the three princes of the throne. Yet the young man was naturally troubled; he might, this evening, speak eloquently—his arguments might privately sway Elad the man—yet Elad the king, for whatever reasons, could dismiss Galvus's protests out of hand simply by virtue of his authority.

All this crossed Adred's mind as he and Galvus were ushered into Elad's private chamber. Adred was very surprised, therefore, when the prince immediately moved into important matters; and he was even more surprised with the clarity of judgment, the practical balance of thought, that Galvus displayed. Galvus had seen much, experienced much and learned much, and he was forthright and persuasive.

"What is most important," he began, directly upon Elad's motioning them to be seated, "is that you gain and maintain the trust of the people. Eighty percent of our people see twenty percent of the population existing upon what the eighty produce—twenty percent of the people having the benefit of eighty percent of the money and goods and utilities, and whatever remains is thrown to the masses to fight over. This we call competition; this we call enterprise; this we call business. It is rather akin to claiming that a servant in this palace is his own individual; morally he is held responsible for that, but in practice he is treated as though he were just another piece of furniture, to be used. This is a contradiction. We've now reached a point where our society is in a condition of stasis. We've developed an immense subterranean society that produces only crime and poverty and ignorance, and the wealthy seem content to close the door on that subterranean society and anyone else—the educated, the small businessmen, the entrepreneurs—who is quickly sinking into that underground. If we're going to have a society, as opposed to millions of servants living in an empire-sized palace posing as a society, then we must take the next step. We must erase all the barriers between the twenty percent on top and the eighty percent on the bottom."

"And this is the inspiration for the revolution?" Elad asked, dubious.

"This," Galvus warned him, "is the inspiration for the revolution. We have fed the fires of it ourselves—I say that as a member of the aristocracy. And that is why you, as the supreme authority in this empire, must make your commitment to gain and maintain the trust of all those people. You cannot treat them as servants. You cannot tell yourself that they are individuals if you don't give them the ability to be individuals. You cannot pretend that the business interests of the wealthy are somehow creating conditions that will eventually elevate all those servants into stations of equality. It will not happen; it could never happen. If we don't take a bold stand now, in the name of human justice, to correct this crisis created by the businesses, then the lust of a few for power and authority and privilege will destroy us.

"You see," Galvus continued, "right now we act as though the desire for money is the only incentive people have to accomplish anything for themselves. This is whorish. Don't you see that this greed has spawned a self-defeating system? It has been artificially rewarded for far too long. We have grown into a society where everything now seems to have some monetary value! Food that grows in the ground now has a certain price; love, given to us by the gods, can be had for a price; beauty . . . justice . . . all

154

these things are treated as though they can be manipulated in the marketplace. If our ideals are so valueless that they can only be had for money, they cease to be ideals. And then money becomes the only thing of value, the only thing men respect. Money is necessary—but it is not the *only* necessary thing! Business is not the *only* discipline that should be rewarded. And payment for services rendered is not the *only* incentive that makes us strive to be complete individuals. Yet if, in our society, a man does good work and accepts only barter for it, we regard him as a fool.

"Because we've allowed conditions to deteriorate so greatly—because we have literally sold ourselves into this predicament—we cannot expect to reverse the course we've taken in hopes that it will gradually return to some center of mutual benefit. We must set a new tone for our society, a tone other than one of unconscionable greed rewarded. Private enterprise should exist to benefit society; society must not exist to benefit private enterprise. And this is why you must gain and maintain the trust of the people. If you can assure the citizens of this country that what I've described is your intention, as well as their vision, they will allow you the time you need to effect it. But if they see that you're lying, or vacillating—they will consolidate their numbers and they will burn this palace to the ground. I know what I'm saying, Uncle. If they can't share in all that we have, then no one will be allowed to keep it. The best of intentions thwarted create the worst of reprisals.

"The revolution is a very real thing. Perhaps the people who swarm the streets, and attack the city guards are relatively small in numbers; but they are only the most obvious members of this revolution. Every person in this country who feels cheated by an employer, is a revolutionary; every person in this country who cannot find work, who cannot gain the education he wants, or cannot buy the bread he needs for his family, is a revolutionary. Every mother who sees her children suffering, is a revolutionary. They may not have it in them to throw stones or attack law officers, but in their hearts they are revolting, because they do not see fairness, they do not see justice.

"Your appointees have done a very thorough job in the cities of beheading, or at least imprisoning, nearly every leader of any real authority or intelligence. Those leaders spoke with voices of moderation: it was only because their voices had been silent so long that they seemed so radical when they finally spoke. The government overreacted, and now we're left with splintered factions of restive dissidents who speak for no one but themselves and in their extremism may do much harm while claiming to do good. They've lost sight of any plans or goals their leaders may have taught them; and because the people now have no leaders who treat them with dignity, they will turn against those leaders who allow them no dignity—the government and the businesses. The bridge between the two paths—those dissident voices of reasonableness—have been silenced."

"You are asking me," Elad replied, "to do a great deal in a very short space of time."

"I realize that. But you have already begun it with your notice concerning the workers' *sirots*. What," Galvus asked, "has been the response to that?"

Elad pursed his lips. "In one word, reluctancy," he said sourly. "Either the officers in my government are determined to do otherwise than I have asked, or they are indulging in every bureaucratic delay imaginable."

"You must do more," his nephew told him. "What you've proposed in your announcement, Uncle Elad, is very meager and its method of advancing reform so constrained that the people do not take it seriously. You cannot expect the working people to believe in an alternative strategy that follows the existing system, the system that is already strangling them! Don't ask for opinions from your bureaucrats. Don't go to the work bosses and the guild masters—they are as in need of reform as your Council is! You are trying to play safe; you are trying very carefully to cut through the knot that has been building for generations. Take your sword and cut through the knot! Do this, and I know for a fact that many sympathetic aristocrats will side with you."

Elad told him: "I cannot allow the people to overthrow the government on an idealistic impulse, to simply 'cut through' a hundred years' of legislation—"

"Legislation that hurts more than it helps," Glavus interrupted testily, "and—where it helps—helps only those who need it least. The people aren't asking you to overthrow our government; they're asking for their freedoms, for their own authority over their own lives. The people are demanding a redistribution of money and power and authority. They want the profits of rich men put to good use—social use. They want the control of businesses given to the people who work those businesses."

Elad stared at him. This was the same radical program that Count Adred had advocated last winter, and it was a dangerous plan. Just as Elad began to respond—

"I have already begun a method by which we can accomplish this," Galvus announced.

Both Elad and Adred showed their surprise.

"What do you mean?" the king asked him.

"When I went to the farmers in the Diruvian Valley, as you asked me to do, I went beyond asking them to cooperate with your plans for the *sirots*. That won't satisfy them: it is too little, too late. So I'm personally buying a large stretch of land in the Valley and donating it to the workers to till on their own. It will be an experiment of sorts. Ideally, the land should not have to be bought from the House of Lodul—it should be taken from them. For now, however, as a token gesture to them, and to calm tempers that are already intensified, I'm buying the land."

Adred was enormously impressed; Galvus had not given him any hint of his intention to do this.

Elad was less excited. "It is your money," he agreed, "to do with as you wish. I suppose if we look upon it as a sort of investment—"

"An investment in the people," Galvus told him. "An investment into the kind of society we're going to have in Athadia, sooner or later, no matter how many rich people refuse to believe it." He sighed heavily, wiped his nervous hands together. "We have lived too long with this childish mentality of profit for the sake of a few," he remarked. "It's time we became the mature society we consider ourselves to be."

Elad, a light in his eyes, watched him. Admiration? Indulgence?

"The only thing I ask of you now," Galvus told his uncle, "is your promise that, so far as you can control it, no one on Council will interfere with this . . . experiment. Because it is this—and quickly—or it is revolution in the streets. Anger without end, and bloodshed, and to no good purpose."

Elad chuckled. "You've thought of everything, haven't you? I will pass legislation protecting this experiment," he agreed. He stood up, walked to a table where a pot of tea was heating on a small burner, filled a cup for himself. Thoughtfully, he faced Galvus and Adred.

"I'm not going to sanction class warfare in my country. I'm the king of everyone in this nation, and I won't jeopardize the business interests already operating—and I appreciate the fact, Galvus, that you did not recommend that I do that." He shot a stern look at Adred. "Even though some of our people in the business community may be unscrupulous, they've accomplished far more good than they have evil."

"I disagree," Galvus replied. "But the fact of the matter is that we now live in a period with values entirely different from those that gave prominence to these cannibalistic businesses. And we must do all we can to encourage changes beneficial to everyone— or we will suffer even greater changes, harmful to everyone."

Elad sipped his tea and regarded Adred. "I realize that Galvus has quite adequately and thoroughly made his argument here, Count Adred. But I've known you to be quite capable of managing that exercise yourself. I don't think you've said five words since you walked in here. Surely you have something to contribute to all this?"

Adred scratched his nose, looked from Elad to Galvus, glanced at the king again. "Well," he decided, "all I really have to add is that if Galvus is opening his door for volunteers, I'd like to make myself available."

Elad grinned and shook his head. "You two are quite the pair, aren't you?"

"Oh," Adred claimed light-heartedly, "I taught him everything he knows. I just wanted to let Galvus do the talking tonight to see how well he could handle himself."

Elad laughed out loud and nearly spilled his tea: honest laughter, from an honest man.

Night in the eastern gardens of the palace. A warm night, filled with the fragrance of blossoms and trees, soft with comfortable shadows, and the lights of the many-storied palace blinking beyond the waving leaves. From where they sat, Adred and Orain could hear distant voices from open balconys, the music of flutes and mandolins, faraway laughter and the occasional echo of a passing guard's boots.

He had told her of everything that had happened during his and Galvus's meeting with Elad, and Orain was thrilled. "I'm so happy," she said. "Elad's a good man, he truly is. But I was afraid he'd simply reject Galvus . . . and Galvus wants to accomplish so much."

"He trusts you," Adred reminded her. "You're Elad's family. And that means he'll listen to you when you tell him things that must be heard." Looking at her, he moved closer toward her on the bench and held her hand.

Orain leaned her head back, smiled, closed her eyes and relaxed her hand in Adred's.

158

And he found himself letting his thoughts wander, as Orain rested against him. Family . . . his parents, . . . Adred wondered what it must be like to be married. He recalled sitting often in the company of friends and their wives and listening to the easy banter that passed between a husband and a wife—the conversation, the sly grins and the quick changes of mood and insight and understanding. The easy sympathies, the intimacies taken advantage of publicly without a misspoken word of anger. But the thing that had impressed him most was the awareness that in secure marriages there was a time and a place for everything, almost a schedule of compliances—an understanding of when to speak of trivial matters, when to discuss more important issues, of times and places appropriate to wear certain aspects of one's personality, always with the approval (and sometimes to the amusement) of one's spouse. A friendship, really—that's what the best marriages seemed to be—because there was always that undercurrent of something distinct between husband and wife that could not be shared with outsiders, could not be interfered with. That was the security of it; that was the sense of it; that was the aspect that most intrigued Adred: that bond which grew between the two. It seemed almost a permanent thing, more permanent than life itself: a spiritual, living thing, as strong as hope, as permanent as laughter—

He felt Orain draw her hand away.

An intensely human thing . . .

Adred looked at her. She was not crying, but she was wiping her face with her hands and she seemed to be momentarily breathless. He moved in the darkness; Orain sat up.

"What is it?" Adred asked.

"Nothing . . ." She shrugged. "I'm all right."

"Tell me please."

She wouldn't look at him.

"Please. . . ."

She shook her head. "I was just thinking of Cyrodian."

Adred took in a breath. "What— Are you afraid of him? Afraid of his coming back?" He remembered being there, feeling completely helpless, when Cyrodian had nearly murdered her in a fit of anger.

"Not—no, not frightened, exactly. Just—oh, I'm ashamed, that's all."

"But there's nothing to be ashamed of."

"But there is, Adred," she corrected him, her voice changing. "I'm still married to him. He's my husband."

"Do you love him?"

"Don't be ridiculous."

"Do you want him to come back so you can be everything for him that a wife is for her husband?"

"Please, Adred, don't—"

"Then he's not really your husband, is he?"

"I mean legally."

"Legally, I'm sure you can have the marriage stricken in a moment. At the very least, on grounds of estrangement; more likely for reasons of criminal behavior. Really, Orain—I'm sure Elad would nullify it for you right now. It should take all of three strokes of the pen."

She didn't say anything to that.

"Orain . . . is this what you've been living with, all this time?"

"Don't make it sound so . . . foolish."

"It's not foolish, but— Orain. Look at me." He took her by her shoulders, turned her around so that her eyes met his. "Is this why you've believed so strongly in Galvus? Is this why you turned away all those men in Sulos?"

She tried to shrug, shook her head, forced an odd smile. "I don't— Oh, I suppose so."

Adred laughed at her, pleasantly. "You've got to learn to take better care of yourself! Why would you do this to yourself?"

"It's the kind of person I am," she replied quietly. "I can't help it."

"Orain," Adred spoke lowly, "am I your friend?"

"What kind of question is that?"

"A friend always interferes when he sees the need to. That's part of the agreement. A good friend will save you from yourself, even if you don't want him to."

She smiled.

"That's more like it. Your perspective is all disorganized. If you worry this much about trivial things, what happens when a real emergency occurs? You have to learn to maintain your perspective."

He quieted, lifted a hand and pushed back some of the hair that had fallen into her eyes. "I'm your friend. Don't forget that."

"I . . . won't. I know you are."

She was staring at him. Her eyes shone in the darkness, her

face glowed, her mouth was trembling. She shivered a bit in a sudden breeze.

And Adred impulsively drew her to him and kissed her—held her to him and wound his arms about her, and kissed her again. She answered him with a tentative embrace, moved her hands to his head—

Then, abruptly, she pulled away, slumped, looked across the garden.

"This is— I feel so—" She didn't say it; nervously, she tugged at folds in her skirt.

"You feel so 'what'?" Adred whispered.

Orain regarded him steadily. "I'm thirty-five years old, Adred."

"What does that mean?"

She smiled uncertainly, turned on the bench so that her back was to him, pulled his arms around her waist and held her own hands over them. "Just . . . keep being my friend, Adred. All right?"

"Always." He kissed her hair, held her. "Always, Orain. . . ."

4.

He was sitting on a bench in one of the dusty squares near the center of town—one of the many moderate-sized towns that had grown up in the farming regions of central Omeria. He had been there all morning, attracting small children with their pets, and vagrants, to him; now, in the afternoon heat, the crowd around him dwindled. Some of the unoccupied young men mocked him or asked insulting questions; but because he answered taunts with the same honest concern as he did the attentions of small children, the troublemakers soon drifted away. Mendicants and other outcasts sat in the dust close by him, hoping that the people attracted to him would drop some spare coppers into their laps. Families who had come to barter with merchants passed a few idle moments listening to him, judging his words against the weight of their personal experiences. And still others, intrigued by his presence and heartened by his message, sat with him for hours— young women from farms or from the shops in town, travelers, occasional businessmen who no longer owned any businesses, or workers who were without work.

"No one," Asawas told his audience, "can live his life without trusting to the value of some thing. And that thing he chooses to value, it will similarly value him just as he professes to value it. What, then, should a man or woman value? Love . . . power . . . the esteem of one's fellows, . . . judiciousness, . . . tolerance . . . equality . . . wealth? Whatever you value, you will strive to strengthen that value in yourself, and, even more, you will tend to see the world as reflective of that value. And you prove this, not by your words, but by your actions: what your heart truly intends, your actions betray. If a man honors corruption because he feels that it achieves those things he wishes to achieve, even in the name of good, then he will become corrupt and deceptive, he will degrade his fellow men with his corruption and treat them with contempt—even when he professes to love them— and thus he will invite them to likewise treat him with contempt and all in the name of achievement. What, then, has he achieved? Only what was in his heart. And this will happen likewise with any other value or ideal or emotion you think you should champion to enhance yourself. Thrift becomes a means to cheat your neighbor; intolerance of some brings you the approval of others. I tell you that all values flow from the same fountain, and you should drink of that fountain moderately, believe equally in all values: do not promote one at the expense of another."

"*Ikbusa*," someone asked him, "is this why there is so much danger today? Because those who lead us do not have values?"

"Yes. They are intolerant. They do not keep their values in balance: they believe that what is right for them is right for everyone and that what they hope to achieve can be secured by falsifying their values, for they are impatient to gain. You must remember that when we are not taught to respect the world or others, then we fail to respect ourselves. A man cannot respect what he does not know; and what a man does not know frightens him because to know anything means to reach for that thing with an open mind and an open heart. Frightened men who do not understand the world make up their own world: a world of doubt and misunderstanding. And where many men are afraid and are in seats of authority, they conspire to command the world with their fears. Like the corrupt man, they degrade all those around them.

"Do you not think that the mysteries and actions of nature are difficult and severe? A drought comes and lives perish. One animal must devour another to survive. Flames destroy a forest

162

nd many creatures lose their burrows and their food. Yet if we watch nature for a long enough time, we see wisdom in how things are accomplished, we see the larger spirit of nature at work within the many small things.

"So it is with us. Evil comes from lack of knowing oneself, and to know oneself is to know others. Man endures to prevail; he does not prevail to endure. Now, you may say, this is perhaps true of one man or one woman, but what of an unjust society? We may each of us strive to be as you say, but when evil flourishes above our heads, then how can we live so simply and generously? Surely a starving man cannot live a guiltless life if those who manage his life make it necessary for him to steal bread for his family? And I say to you that this is true: I say to you that when you know the truth, you will do away with the liars, and if a man oppresses you, you must show him the true way. If he lies to you with words, show him with action the true way. But if you answer his lies with lying actions, and fail to see what it is you do, then you will yourself become a liar, and evil."

He continued to speak of these things, answering questions with insightful illustrations, sometimes posing alternative questions to his listeners so that they might solve some particular problem themselves, and then again speaking frankly of why he had come to them, why god had chosen him to do what he did.

There were questions from those who did not trust the idea of the one true god. "What does On look like?" they asked the prophet.

"He has no face; he has no form. I speak of him as a man only because I am a man. But On is neither man nor woman entirely; he is both the male and the female and all other things, because On is the All."

"What words does he speak, *ikbusa*?"

"On does not speak in words; but I, his servant, must speak in words."

"Then what does his heart sound like to you?"

"The same as the sound of your heart."

"With what eyes does he see? With your eyes?"

"He is as the wind and the air, as the stars, which are always and everywhere. On sees with all of our memories, for our memories are his memories, and our hopes his hopes."

"Why, Chosen One, is the one god called On?"

"Am I my name? Are you your name? Is On his name? Call him what you will, On is yet what he is."

163

As the numbers of the crowd shifted and moved, some goin¦
away, others pressing forward to look at and listen to this prophet
one man there, a visitor to the town and by the cut of his garment
an obviously well-to-do young man, stepped forward and stared a¦
Asawas with an intense gaze. When the *ikbusa's* audience fe¦
silent for a moment, this one spoke to the prophet in a quiet bu
powerful voice.

"I have a question for you, speaker."

Asawas turned to look upon him, at the light in his eyes, th¦
awareness in his stare. "Yes," he smiled, recognizing th¦
stranger. "I sensed you, watching me from across the square
What is your question?"

"Why was the Temple of Bithitu in Erusabad destroyed by th¦
heathens?"

Asawas's polite smile did not fade. "Because Bithitu demande¦
that no temple ever be raised in his name. Because the men ther¦
who called themselves priests did not comprehend in their heart
either On or his Prophet. And because it was a thing of the earth, ¦
symbol of the old ways that now must perish."

The stranger watched him with strong emotion in his eyes. "
was a priest in that temple."

"I know you were, my friend."

The well-dressed young man pressed his hands together intentl¦
and stared at Asawas as he felt something profound occur in hi¦
heart. "I search," he continued, "for a man whom I feel destine¦
to meet."

"There is a man of ancient shadows whom you must meet, yes
and then there is the man born of the new light," Asawas tol¦
him.

"And you are the man born of the new light."

"That is so. But our time is not yet, Thameron: it is still in th¦
future when these disguises that we wear will be discarded and a¦
humanity will wait between us. Neither you nor I are completed
yet." Asawas stood up.

The crowd in the square now drew away from him, and from
the well-dressed Thameron, as though some invisible Voice ha¦
urged them all to do so. Even the beggars who sat beside Asawa¦
sensed a power present and scrambled away in the dust.

"You come to me full of pain, afraid and grieved, Thameron. ¦
know who you are and what you are. It is a destined thing, *ro kil
su.*"

Thameron bowed his head shortly. "*Lo abu-sabith.*"

"You are terrified of the evil within you, Thameron; that is why you allow it to overpower you. Do you not understand that it is the shadow and that I am the light? The shadow hides all things; the light illuminates the All. Only good can be more terrifying than what you hold burdened in your heart. All things within the All."

"All the Paths at once," Thameron spoke slowly, as though speaking to himself, remembering some personal anguish.

Asawas shook his head. "Why did you search for the All within your heart when you had not yet opened your heart to those around you? That is the only path you need."

"But I attempted that; I strived—"

"You did not. You elevated yourself, you were not humble. When did you kiss the feet of your masters in the Temple, Thameron? When did you beg god to heap upon you the leprosy that damaged the ill man you comforted? When did you humble yourself so severely that On, in his beingness, might be one with you, and all within you? You did not do these things. You sought concourse with On's things and spirits, you sought to elevate your spirit in the belief that you were worthy. Why did you not repudiate yourself?"

"I am only a *man*!" Thameron replied boldly, becoming angry. Some in the crowd began to whisper and make noises.

"The Church I served . . . killed thousands—hundreds of thousands—and it burned books, it destroyed whole cities in the name of the Prophet . . . it mutilated children . . . encouraged soldiers to rape women . . . it sanctioned murder and greed and all sorts of foulness . . . and because I asked questions and searched for answers, they cast me out, they called me evil! And now you demand that I *humble* myself?"

"Why for, Thameron, do you question the meaning of the ever-occurring god when even your masters at the Temple, in their arrogance and pride and indulgence, never questioned it? Even they, hypocrites and brutes, poisoned by the material things of life, sad and fallen even as they sat high, not comprehending the true heart of god even though they believed that there *is* a god—even they, in their gross errors, did not question that there is the moving hand of the ever-occurring god, the all-in-All, the now and the forever. Yet you did."

"I am not—*evil*!" Thameron protested.

"You are fear," Asawas replied in a chillingly quiet tone. "Even as I speak to you with love, and am unafraid in the presence of the all-god, you are yet afraid; and so you are the

165

vessel, you are the fear we have produced in the uncertainty of our humanness. You are the doubt that does not strive but, in its arrogance, is satisfied."

Thameron said something defiant and foul.

"You know what you are, Thameron, and I know what I am. Our time is not yet. Your spirits and visions and your voices from the shadows could not warn you of me, because your powers are deep, while mine are given from on high. Yet know this: If you would now throw yourself into the dust, beg On for forgiveness, and let me place my hands upon your bruised heart, you and I may yet save mankind from itself."

Thameron stood there, shivering in the hot sun, staring at the prophet.

"Will you do this, Thameron? Or do you still fear all that humanity strives for, all that On is becoming?"

He swallowed thickly, his hands curled into fists. "Fool . . ."

Asawas slowly blinked his eyes; thin tears dripped down his cheeks. "It is destined, then, and we both understand that." But then Asawas pointed to a child sitting in the road, colored and swollen with disease. "Won't you take up this child, Thameron— even this one child—and give yourself unto it?"

Thameron looked at the child, and he felt a chill in his bowels. Its mother was sitting nearby; she showed Thameron a gaze full of dread and anguish. Her child.

"How can I," he whispered, "knowing what it is that I am?"

Asawas turned from him. "You believe this of yourself, therefore you are this. I doubt every moment that I am On, therefore I am On. Begone, Evil One. Your sadness shall bring ruination upon men like a storm of death, a plague of tears, a rage of fear upon all the lands. When next we meet, we will be voiceless; but the hearts of men will scream their understanding. Who am I to quell the fears of men? I am only the word of their god . . . just as you are the bringer of their hell."

"I do not seek to bring evil!" Thameron shouted at him.

"The storm," Asawas replied, "does not know that it floods the land, yet many perish despite the storm's ignorance. If you know or do not know, if you believe or do not believe—you are chosen *ro kil-su*. Men have hungered for your appearance for they doubt their own ability to do evil even in this hour of their growing evil. The storm comes, and you and I are the storm, Thameron. I was wrong to try to alter that."

166

"Fool!" Thameron spat at him. "I don't know you! I'm a sorcerer!"

The crowd around him gasped.

"My power is my own," he declared, "and gained through hardship and suffering!"

"God suffers more than you do, with your gaining of this power."

Angered by this presumptuous priest, Thameron stared into the crowd, spied a man leaning on a staff. In two quick strides he was beside him; he yanked the staff from the man's hand and held it aloft for Asawas and the onlookers to see.

"Am I afraid?" he yelled, his face glossy with perspiration in the sun.

What is good? What is evil? I have achieved my seat in a place where both are the same. Whatever I do I am condemned to do. Do I accomplish evil if I believe what I do is not evil? Then where is the evil? Will others condemn me for my evils? Am I to answer them, when I am myself? I have been chosen by the thing I sought to choose.

You believe this of yourself, therefore you are this. I doubt every moment that I am On, therefore I am On.

He cast the staff to the ground where, instantly, it was transformed into a thick serpent. The serpent curled and hissed, showing fangs and black unblinking eyes. Everyone in the square screamed and turned to run; mothers picked up their children; people swung hands and arms in all directions, hurting one another in their excitement and fear.

Only Asawas did not run away. Kneeling, he extended a hand toward the serpent. Hissing threateningly, it slithered toward him, its head swaying like a fist. Asawas grasped the serpent by the throat and held it up.

"I see no serpent," he announced. "I see only a staff. Am I wrong in seeing this?"

He dropped the serpent to the dust, and even as it struck the earth, it was transformed once more, becoming again the rigid staff of wood.

Thameron stared at Asawas, eyes lidded. "You are a sorcerer!" he proclaimed. "You presume to bring these people the word of god?"

"I am not a sorcerer; I am only a man who sees the Truth and can divine the truth from its false aspects."

The crowd, full of wonder, began to come forward again; some of them expressed shame in doubting the strength and insight of the prophet.

"Go from here, now," Asawas bade Thameron. "We shall meet again, soon enough, where both our paths are meant to end."

Thameron said nothing more to him but moved on, out of the square and down the street, never looking back.

As many faces stared after him, mumbling and whispering, Asawas intoned privately:

"On . . ." he whispered, "we do not cause these things, but their truth is deep within us. . . ."

As Thameron became a small distant shadow at the end of the path leading from the square, thunder rumbled in the hot skies above and a few faces turned to look up at the clouds, a few hands lifted to feel the first sprinklings of rain.

5.

Elad awoke early to the sounds of Salia playing with her puppies. He rolled over in the bed and watched her; she didn't notice him. She was naked and crouched on a wide rug in the middle of their vast sleeping chamber, where she was teasing her two puppies with one of the slim silver cords she used as a belt. Salia wriggled the cord while the puppies, heavy-footed and awkward, stepped on it, tried to catch it to gnaw on it, fell into a tumble and began wrestling with one another. Salia giggled uncontrollably.

"Shhhh!" she whispered to the puppies, holding her free hand over her mouth as she wriggled the cord. "You'll wake up Elad!" She glanced over her shoulder toward the bed and caught him looking at her. Salia smiled. "Oh, did we wake you up?"

"Yes. . . ."

Playfully, she dropped the cord over the rolling puppies, then stood up and stretched. Soft morning light moved gently over her pink body and shone in her golden hair; she closed her eyes and yawned, opened them and eyed Elad mischievously. She walked toward him slowly, lithely, but not with conscious seductiveness; her smile and her walk were the smile and walk of a young woman, almost a girl, in the guise of an alluring woman.

Elad patted the cushions and moved back as Salia slid in beside him. He watched the movements of her body as she lay back; he wrapped his arms around her and laid his head near hers. Salia playfully flicked her tongue at him and licked his nose, as one of her puppies might happily lick her, with affection.

She asked him: "Can we go out today?"

"Where did you want to go?"

"Just . . . out. I want to go riding. Let's take some horses and go riding. Wouldn't you like to do that with me?" She seemed to be almost a child, asking her parent for a favor.

"I don't know if I have the time to do that today, Salia. Your father would escort you."

She pouted, the brightness leaving her eyes. "But all he does is lecture me whenever we go riding."

"What does he lecture you about?"

"Being queen . . . being a wife. He always does that."

Elad chuckled.

"What am I going to do when he goes back home?"

Elad didn't have an answer for that.

"I don't want to stay here by myself," Salia protested.

That wounded him, although he knew that she probably hadn't meant it to. Elad realized again how young his wife was and how little she knew herself and understood things around her, and how much she relied upon others. "I'll try," he promised her, "to find time today to go riding with you."

"Don't 'try,'" she complained. "Tell me we'll do it. Can't you just take the afternoon to be with your wife? *I* want to be with *you*."

"I can understand that."

"People don't take me seriously," Salia told him. "They don't think I'm the queen, or even a woman. They think I'm just—that I'm just here."

"That's not true."

"Oh, it is and you know it. We never spend any time together. If we spent time together, people would understand me better."

"We're together now," Elad reminded her, and kissed her shoulder to coax her.

"Oh, we're always together when you want to try and . . . make puppies."

"Try and *what*?" He laughed out loud, so overcome that he slapped a hand on the cushions. "Try and make *puppies*? Is that what you said?"

Despite her frustration, Salia giggled. "You know what I mean!"

169

"Yes, my heart, I know, I know!" Elad was still laughing; he embraced her strongly.

As he held her and smelled the good smell of her and felt her golden hair on his face, Elad thought to himself that that expression was just one of the many things about Salia that so intrigued him, and even delighted him: she always referred to sexual expression in euphemisms, and sometimes in wildly childish euphemisms. Her temperament was confusing, too. It was so mercurial that, often, she would ignore Elad's amorous impatience and occupy herself with mundane things: examining herself before her mirror ("Am I really all that beautiful? Look at me. I have the same sort of nose as that old woman we saw today!"), or playing with her puppies, her birds or her kittens (Look! See him? I think our king wants us to come to bed, but we're not sleepy yet, are we? No, we want to play some more!"), or talking about some trivial matter with an exaggerated importance ("I don't think the women who do my hair are doing a very good job with it. I think I should do it myself. Abgarthis told me I could do my hair myself, if I wanted to, but father says I shouldn't, that I should let the women do it because they're supposed to."). But then at other times, when Salia's curiosity or passions were aroused, whatever time of the day that might be, she'd approach Elad for lovemaking with the same intensity and sense of importance that she'd displayed before her mirror or in her childlike rapport with her animals.

These shifts of mood in her seemed to Elad wholly without plan or intent; they were spontaneous, and only more evidence for him that Salia did not know herself, that her personality was far too reliant upon arbitrary incidents and comments and the moods about her. On one occasion she had been erotically aroused simply by watching the colors of the sunset reflected in the mirrors of their sleeping chamber; on another evening, Elad had come in to discover Salia weeping copiously because her puppies had refused to cooperate with her when she'd tried to teach them some new tricks. Nothing he could say or do would console her.

On most mornings since their marriage, then, when he and Salia were at breakfast with their ministers and courtiers, Elad had regarded Ogodis with the critical attitude of a man totally appalled by his father-in-law's methods of child-rearing. What had the Imbur done to create so inconsistent a personality in his daughter? What had he failed to do? What sort of father would raise a child who was constantly awed by her own extraordinary beauty yet did not seem vain about herself, only intrigued as one might be by someone else's appearance? What sort of father would raise a daughter who communicated better with animals and pets than she did with women of her own sex?

Once or twice, Elad had also wondered about his own motivations in wedding the most beautiful woman in the world. Was it pride that had provoked him? Had it been only an impulse? Had it been a desire in him, when he felt his own life collapsing around him, to begin a new life, one on his own terms, one he could control utterly?

The smell of her and the feel of her golden hair . . .

"Making . . . puppies!" Elad grinned, turned Salia's face toward him and kissed her. But when he sensed that she wasn't yet in the mood to answer him, he lay back, listened to the bickering puppies, and—because his mind was full of a thousand things that morning—considered a sudden, odd idea.

"I know you're the queen," he told Salia more frankly and soberly. "And I don't want you to feel like you're unwelcome here. The people will come to respect you; they'll come to love you."

Salia eyed him doubtfully.

"It's only because I was recuperating that things have become disjointed. But we'll change that. I mean it."

"I'd like to believe that. . . . I don't like spending all my time inside the palace when I know the whole world is out there, and I want to do things, Elad, and be part of everything."

"And you will, you will be. I promise you that. Salia—do you believe me?" He eyed her sincerely.

She smiled. "I'll try."

"You're still very young," Elad said to her. "But that's probably for the better, you know, because my mother was very young when she became queen, and she became a very important woman."

"I know," Salia told him. "I've seen her portraits. She was very beautiful."

"Yes, she was. . . ."

Salia eyed him cunningly, then, and while Elad was not aware of it, she quietly sneaked her hand under the covers and grabbed him between the legs.

He whooped.

Salia acted repentant. "Ohhh, . . . should I make it better for you? Do you want me to make it better for you?" She grinned and blew gently on his face, continued to hold him and lowered her head to his chest and kissed and licked him. "Poor Elad," she sighed, laying her face on his chest and looking up at him with wide eyes. "You like Salia, but you don't like Salia, and you don't know what to do. Poor Elad. I know . . ."

"That's not true," he said.

She smiled. "Oh, that's all right. I know how you feel, but that's all right." She threw back the covers and began kissing him on the chest and belly.

While a doubtful Elad watched her puppies gambol and yelp on the carpet . . .

Galvus was absent from breakfast that morning; Elad asked Omos why that was. The prince's shy friend explained:

"He didn't say anything to me, but I saw him leaving very early."

"I think," Adred interrupted from across the table, "that he might have gone riding. I saw him heading toward the stables from my window."

"Riding?" Elad wondered aloud.

Adred shrugged; the king glanced at Orain.

"He hasn't done any riding since he was here last," she told him. "Perhaps he misses it and just wanted some fresh air."

Salia knocked Elad's leg under the table, but he ignored her.

As they were finishing their breakfast, Abgarthis entered, seemingly in his usual haste to be busy with things. He had received some dispatches and requested that Elad peruse them as soon as he could.

"Let's look at them now," was the king's decision. "I have much to attend to today."

He stood up, kissed Salia on the forehead, then led Abgarthis from the dining hall.

Ogodis watched them go and commented: "He's not eager to see his brother returned, is he?"

Adred glanced at him, and Orain shot the Imbur a hurt look. Ogodis saw her and realized what he had said. He looked away, reached for his wine—"Yes . . . well"—and sipped but did not apologize.

"Captain Mirsus," Abgarthis said, placing the first of the dispatches on the table before Elad, "reports that he and his company are in Herossus. The letter is dated two days ago."

"Then we may expect Cyrodian here in two or three days."

His minister nodded. "Mirsus says that there'll be no need for them to make a stopover in Pylar, so they will sail directly here."

Elad smiled grimly. "He certainly is following my orders expressly, to get Cyrodian here in doubletime." He was silent for a moment. "Is everything that awaits his arrival in order?"

"Yes. A furnished cell has been isolated, and quite a few members of the palace guard have already applied for the extra duty."

Elad raised a finger to his lips and urged Abgarthis in a quiet voice: "Go on."

The adviser examined the next paper. "Another coalition of Church officials is calling for curtailment of trade with the Salukadians and for other measures to be taken against them. In response to their occupation of the Temple in Erusabad." Abgarthis proffered the gold-edged document, but as Elad evinced no interest in looking at it, he dropped it to the table.

"How important is their attitude in this matter, Abgarthis? I mean . . . is it possible that the Church can cause any real problems that could threaten the stability in Erusabad?" This was already the seventh or eighth appeal to Elad from Church members to promote action against the eastern empire.

But Abgarthis did not seem overly concerned. "We're a secular society," he reminded his king. "The Church is too fragmented, too splintered; it does not have great influence. Some communities, true, may decide to enforce their own trade embargoes, but I think the passions will wane as time goes on. Still . . . the Salukadian possession of the Temple was primarily a symbolic act. The structure itself had fallen into disrepair; there were a few religious leaders of consequence who lived there, but they were essentially the old guard, esteemed by the Church bureaucracy but isolated from the ordinary citizens. Keep in mind that the easterners gave them warning of what they intended to do and offered to relocate them; the Temple elders elected to take poison, but there was no real general uprising within the city. The citizens there are apathetic, not hostile. Erusabad has always shifted in its sympathies between east and west; that Temple had been overtaken before, in it history."

"I know that."

"So in terms of any real political anger toward you—no, there really is nothing of consequence developing, not from the people. And not really, in any collective sense, from the Church. But it's

173

probably well to keep in mind that the more passionate voices from any spiritual corners come from all these cults that have been springing up. I mean extreme fundamentalist doctrinaires and visionaries—Doom-Soulers and wandering prophets and *ikbusa'i.*"

Elad's expression was grim.

"They're becoming very popular," Abgarthis warned his king. "We live in troubled times, and these prophets play upon the fears of the people, urging them to give up and claiming that men cannot solve the problems they themselves have created. They argue that we are living at the end of time, and they say that people should prepare for the world's destruction. I have reports . . ."

Elad was not interested in seeing any more reports; he showed Abgarthis a solemn expression. "Sometimes," he admitted lowly, "I am troubled by such thoughts myself."

His minister was sympathetic. "Ah. The Oracle, you mean."

Elad nodded but did not pursue the matter further. "What else is there?"

"Only one more item of importance. Lords Falen and Rhin, of the Council committee investigating the institution of the *sirots,* would appreciate your presence at the arena tonight."

The king's brow furrowed. "What the hell do they want?"

"I believe they're concerned about your general sympathy toward the revolutionary movement. Perhaps they've gained some information regarding Galvus's views on this and are alarmed."

Elad chuckled.

"Shall I inform them that you agree to meet with them?"

Elad considered it. "I haven't been to the games in months. Certainly . . . let's attend. We'll make it a general event. Everyone in the palace will make an appearance."

Abgarthis nodded.

"If I have to put up with their complaints that the empire's finances are going to collapse because a handful of people intend to own a few leagues of land, I might as well do it in an enjoyable setting." He sighed. "This afternoon, Abgarthis, Salia and I are going riding, so you might attend to details here."

The elder was mildly surprised.

"I'm going to speak with her frankly about a matter of importance," Elad told the adviser. "When we return, I'd like to take an hour of your time to discuss it with you as well."

"What, exactly, is the issue?"

174

"You recall General Thomo's suggestion about sending a representative to Erusabad? To show our sympathy to the *Ghen*'s court about Huagrim's death?"

Abgarthis's eyes widened. "You mean to send the queen there?"

Elad examined the edges of his sleeves. "I want her to understand that she is an important functionary in this government, not simply an . . . ornament. I am needed here; and I'm afraid that anyone else immediately here is needed as well. Galvus would be an ideal representative, but he'd balk at the journey and the lost time. Besides, I want him in Council when we're discussing the resolution of the *sirot* issue. Our usual ambassadors have the intelligence and experience we need, but they are not of imperial rank. I'm left with the queen. She could be an important envoy. If we sent her in the company of four or five men who understand the east and have dealt with the Salukadians before, I think we could ameliorate tensions at that end of the world at least."

Abgarthis, however, was unconvinced. "But she's very young, Elad. She's had no diplomatic experience whatsoever. Her father will be appalled."

"All the better for him!" Elad laughed. "I'm not sending the butterfly into the spider's nest, Abgarthis. The travel will do her much good; she'd be required to serve a utilitarian function and win attention for us—that is all. She is a beautiful woman: surely that would not be lost upon those easterners. All the polishing and diplomatic chatter could be handled easily by our men." Still he saw that his adviser was reserved. "Well, consider the idea. There are many positive arguments for it."

Abgarthis was polite. "Perhaps . . ." he temporized, "yes . . . I think we should discuss this once you've mentioned the idea to the queen."

"She is a good woman, Abgarthis. She is intelligent, she is eager—she only lacks experience in worldly affairs, and that is her father's fault, not hers."

"I will support you," Abgarthis agreed, "in whatever you decide, assuredly."

"Thank you."

"Is that all, then?"

Elad nodded, and Abgarthis quietly made his way out.

Galvus had not gone riding—that is, not specifically for fresh air or exercise. He had taken a horse from the royal stables, but he'd stayed inside the city; and when he had returned, he hurried upstairs to his room, where a meal was brought to him. He asked Omos to locate Adred and invite him over; and while Galvus ate an early lunch, he told his friends how things had transpired.

"Our shipment of supplies into Sulos still operates smoothly," he informed them. "And," he smiled, "this may seem hard to believe, but we even have two additional men of property who've decided to help us. One of them is Count Olinthos. Did your father know him, Adred? I think he's associated with the Galsian mines."

Adred nodded slowly. "Yes . . . I've never met him, but I'm sure my father mentioned his name a few times."

"And you may know the other one, as well," Galvus told him, sipping his tea.

"Who's that?"

"Ex-Consul Captain Lutouk."

Adred tried to recall him but could not. "No . . . I don't think so."

"He was the officer in charge of executing the rebels in Sulos last winter."

Adred stared at him.

"Perhaps you don't know him," Galvus amended. "But he resigned his commission immediately after that. There was speculation that he'd committed suicide or that he'd been bribed by the revolutionaries themselves. He was apparently wholly against the action ordered. There was talk of a possible court martial, but nothing ever came of it." He poured himself a fresh cup of tea. "He's retired, now, and living in a villa out in the northwest. And he's contributing aid to the people. He may even be supplying funds secretly to the Suloskai, on his own."

Adred slowly shook his head. "Things are certainly never what they seem, are they?"

"And even less so nowadays," Galvus agreed. "And even less so now."

6.

As they returned from their ride that afternoon, Salia was quivering with excitement, utterly enthralled by Elad's suggestion that she act as the Athadian representative to the eastern court.

"I've never been farther east than Arsol!" she exclaimed to

176

him. "And my father never allowed me to actually have anything to do with the government in Sugat. Elad! This is wonderful, just wonderful! I want to do it, yes, *yes*!"

He explained to her that she would be gone only for a period of two months, perhaps a bit longer, that she would be escorted to the Holy City by a coterie of diplomats and advisory personnel, and that her function was solely that of a good-will ambassador. This was critical. "We are at an important juncture in our relations with the east," Elad explained. "Our businessmen have been trading with the Holy City for many years, but lately there's been tension. You know about that. We must maintain the best relations we can with the Salukadians. You won't be making policy, you'll simply be . . . paying them a visit."

She was proud that Elad had chosen her to accomplish this.

"You are the queen," he told her. "You'll be received as the Athadian monarch, and you'll deport yourself in that fashion. Perhaps," Elad allowed, "it *is* difficult for you to appreciate this about yourself—here, now. But I think attitudes will change once you've returned from this journey."

"I want to do all I can," Salia told Elad, "to make the Salukadians respect you as much as I do."

This caused him to lift an eyebrow, but he told her that he deeply appreciated the sentiment. And, as though he had just spontaneously remembered it: "Perhaps you should not mention this plan to your father."

"Why not, Elad?"

"Not until I've spoken to him. Please, Salia. I want to present it to him . . . in my own way."

She nodded, agreeing with him. "I'm afraid you're probably right. But I can convince him."

"Let me speak with him first. You are now," he reiterated, "first and foremost the queen of Athadia; only after that are you your father's daughter."

She gave him a wide grin, pleased with the distinction.

When they returned to the city, Elad immediately met with Abgarthis in one of the private rooms off the Council Chamber and informed his adviser that Salia was quite in agreement with his intention. Abgarthis still harbored reservations—"She is so inexperienced, Elad, that I would not make so important a task her first true imperial duty"—but as he could see no other solution, given the king's insistence on sending a representative to Erusa-

177

bad, Abgarthis consented to do all that he could to help matters along. He had already drawn up a list of suitable diplomats whose services might be solicited, and he was completely in accord with Elad's idea not to inform the Imbur until the following day.

As for the matter of the games that evening: Lords Falen and Rhin were most happy that their king had agreed to meet with them. But, Abgarthis informed Elad, no one else in the palace was really of a mind to attend.

"Prince Galvus and Count Adred claim that they are occupied preparing matters for the reconvening of Council, and young Omos, of course, won't go anywhere without Galvus. Lady Orain does not care for the spectacle. The Imbur Ogodis claims that he is coming down with a summer cold."

"The Imbur Ogodis," Elad growled, "won't be sitting in the imperial box in the king's chair—that's why he won't attend." He was not in a mood to be refused. "If you will, Abgarthis, please present my request to our royal family once again, won't you? In no uncertain terms?"

When Elad, followed by Queen Salia, her father and Abgarthis, made his appearance at the arena early that evening, the two hundred thousand spectators who were seated in the huge oval *Kirgo Amax*, the largest in the capital, stood as one and applauded wildly, raising a deafening roar of welcome. The late light of dusk, orange and purple, washed the swaying tides of humanity that shouldered the twilight with their faceless noise. The acclaim continued, uninterrupted and occasionally swelling louder, for long minutes. Salia, standing beside Elad in the imperial box, glanced at her husband and saw him beaming with pride at this spontaneous outburst. When at last he lifted his right arm in a salute of recognition, the crowd's noise rose again before gradually dwindling into suffocated pockets of sporadic applause, lingering cheers and whistles.

"I'm overwhelmed," Elad laughed, as he settled into his ornate chair. "Do my people love me so much, despite all our problems?"

Abgarthis, seated behind him, leaned forward to interpret. "This is your first public appearance, remember, since the assassination attempt, my king. And a quarter of this audience was admitted free of charge—in anticipation of your attendance."

Elad glanced back at him. "I'm certain," he answered, "that most people in the empire still feel as these good citizens do."

"Of course they do," Abgarthis affirmed, sitting back. "Of course . . ."

The program commenced with a long parade: dancers and musicians led lines of athletes, performers and animal trainers around the grounds of the arena. As they passed before the stone bulwarks, they waved at their noisy audience and received, in turns, enthusiastic yells of acclaim. Women dressed in gossamer gowns pirouetted; gymnasts stood on one another's shoulders and somersaulted; lions, bears, leopards and panthers paced and growled inside their rattling cages; athletes struck intimidating poses as they pranced and waved. Up and down the aisles, the bettors marked their lists and passed them along to the odds managers.

As the parade ended and the various performers returned to their waiting areas behind the bulwarks at the southern end of the *kirgo*, Lords Falen and Rhin, seated two rows down from the imperial box (where their view of the spectacle was nearly hidden by the protective wall), waved to Elad. The king hailed them and called for them to join him. The Councilors rose and made their way to the nearest aisle, climbed the steps and moved toward the imperial box, where Elad invited them to take the vacant seats to his left. With much graciousness they advanced to the chairs, pardoning themselves excessively as they passed before the Imbur and Queen Salia.

As dancers and mimes moved up onto the wide, festooned center stage in the middle of the arena, Elad glanced at his Councilors but found them content, for the moment, to enjoy the program in silence. The performance was of a short one-act comedy of Vodos-otos; yet while the audience laughed in carrying waves of approval, the portly Rhin and the skeleton-thin, bald-pated Falen watched in tolerant silence. As the comedy ended, and boxers and wrestlers mounted the stages to either side of the central platform, the yawning Rhin, sitting beside Elad, produced from a pocket of his coat a miniature *usto* set. Pegs on the flat bottoms of the playing pieces allowed them to be placed securely into holes drilled through the red and black squares of the board. Perhaps intolerant of the amusements on display, the two Councilors proceeded to engage one another beneath Elad's watchful stare.

As the gymnasts performed a number of hazardous exercises, Lord Rhin, staring at his board but speaking out the side of his mouth, complained to Elad: "You see? Only if one understands the rules of a game can one compete with any real degree of responsibility."

Elad leaned toward him, keeping an eye on the gymnasts. "Exactly what are you trying to say, Lord Rhin?"

"Only that competition should be left to competitors."

"You're afraid of these *sirots*, aren't you?"

Rhin bounced the warrior piece in the palm of his hand as he regarded Elad carefully. "These *sirots* we can manage," he replied in an even voice. "We were able to manage the formation of the trade guilds, and our terms with the leaders of those guilds are very specific and mutually rewarding. The same can be accomplished with these *sirots*."

"I don't intend to allow the workers to manage the government, Lord Rhin," Elad reminded him. "But I believe there should be a place for them to discuss their ideas in our halls of justice; I believe they need some context in which to argue their ideas, other than that of street violence. So what, then, are you afraid of, exactly?"

As though on cue, Lord Rhin turned from him and played his warrior, while Lord Falen glanced up and told Elad: "We're afraid that your nephew may be causing dissension in quarters where that would be inadvisable."

Elad colored. In a cold, throaty voice: "I hope I misapprehend what you say, Falen. Are you threatening him?"

The Councilor looked away. "No, King Elad."

"Are you perhaps threatening me?"

"No. King Elad . . ."

"You seem to be afraid that my nephew is involved with 'revolutionaries.' You seem to be afraid that that may allow the expression of passions which could upset the business structure of our empire. Am I correct, Lord Falen?"

Falen coughed self-consciously and returned his attention to the *usto* board.

Lord Rhin faced his monarch. "We feel it is—impolitic of you—my king, to allow these people, who are already responsible for jeopardizing the economic structure of our nation, any actual control over our destiny. They are working people; they have functions to perform; we do not actually disapprove of their earning wages to contribute to the marketplace."

Elad stared at him. "However . . ." he prodded.

"However, they are not financiers, they are not bankers or accountants, they do not truly understand business—"

180

"The rules of the game," Elad interpreted, "as we have devised them."

Rhin nodded strictly. "Competition between the competitors, yes. It's unwise to allow these workers in every trade, in every shop—millions upon millions of them—to think that their voices truly have any real effect upon the course our economy takes. Do we let children supervise their own frolics? Do we allow the uninitiated to become priests? Is every man who buys a sword therefore a swordsman? Allowing these *sirots* to federate themselves under one banner so that they can enter into our Council's economic decisions is one thing, King Elad, but to actually permit workers to organize businesses themselves outside of our general authority and with an attitude counter to the progress of the empire as a whole is to court disaster."

Elad nodded appreciatively. "You operate several very successful businesses, don't you, Lord Rhin? Ships and wagons, paper production and oils—isn't that right?"

Rhin regarded him silently.

"I understand what you're saying. I understand the benefits you and your associates have brought to the empire, and I intend to do nothing to undermine you. But put yourself in my position. You're in business to create profits, Rhin, not to employ workers. If you could produce what you're producing now with half your labor force, you'd remove half your employees tomorrow, wouldn't you?"

"That's simply business," was the answer.

"Where, then, should those workers go? Can the government, or money from the guilds, support enormous numbers of unemployed people? Or what if the number of potential workers grows so great that you and other businessmen can't employ them all? Or suppose there are only so many squares on the board, Lord Rhin, and more pieces than there are squares? What will you do then?"

Rhin did not reply.

"Drill more holes in the squares of the board, Rhin," Elad told him. "The aristocrats, the businessmen, the traders and mercantilists—those whom we really need to manage the affairs of this empire—these men sit isolated in their squares; but the workers—we place four or five or ten to a square. Do you begin to understand?"

Rhin nodded slowly.

"Believe me when I tell you that I am not actively seeking to undermine the benefits we've accrued. But if I do nothing, then those many workers out there undermine those benefits for us. Yours is the same attitude of fear that prevailed when the guilds were originally established—don't deny it. 'If the workers are allowed to create their own organizations, they will turn against us.' Wasn't that the fear? And no such thing has happened. They have not become our enemies; they have come to cooperate with us for the ultimate good of the nation. Do you know why? Human nature, Lord Rhin. And now we have workers who want to try to establish their own small economies and try to manage things differently, or separately, or by new methods. Do you know what the outcome will be of these alternative 'experiments,' Lord Rhin? Human nature. When two strong business interests collide and one cannot buy the other, what is done? Do we resort to cannibalism? They sit down, they divide up their potential markets so that neither is excluded, and the rules are followed, and the competition continues. You control your businesses in the capital; another man like you controls them in Sulos.

"These populist temper tantrums," the king concluded, "must be expected from time to time. You feel threatened by them; I see them as essentially healthy reactions. But only authority and organization can survive in the long run, and organizations have more in common with one another than their individual members do with one another. What I'm saying is this: these populist *sirots* and workers' collectives that my nephew is eager to establish will either fraction and fall apart in time, or they'll come to see the world as we know the world to be. Idealists always forget that the power they fight is the same power they themselves hunger for. Once they are successful—*if* they are successful—they will no more continue to throw their lives away on profitless dreams and unsatisfactory causes than we would."

Rhin kept his eyes on Elad for a long moment. Around them lifted a wild thunder of applause and cheers from the spectators in the *kirgo*, but neither Elad nor Rhin looked to see what had caused it. Above them, brilliant lights suddenly opened in the darkness: arena attendants were making their way around the upper stories and galleries, lighting torches and lamps against the deepening dusk.

Lord Rhin showed a provocative smile. "I just wanted to be certain," he spoke quietly, "that what I hoped to be true, and what I believed to be true, were actually the facts of the matter."

"Do you think me a fool?" Elad asked him coolly. "Do you think your king a dangerous fool? And I resent your requesting me to attend these games on the pretext of an evening's entertainment to deduce my motives."

Rhin bowed his head slightly. "Council was . . . concerned," he explained, and any apology was confined to the tone of his voice.

"Council should be busying itself creating guidelines and statutes for the establishment of the workers' *sirots*," Elad reminded him, "not worrying about their king's allegiances."

Rhin seemed consoled—his apprehensions allayed, his doubts mollified. "Well, after all," he commented, looking back to his *usto* board and glancing at Lord Falen, "it is, actually, only a game, isn't it?"

Unable to sleep, Orain slipped out of bed, pulled a loose robe about herself and lit a lamp. Her window was open; there was a cool breeze blowing in, and Orain moved to the open shutters to refresh herself and gaze out. The city was a huddle of a million lights. From far off she heard a bell tolling the sixth hour after sundown. Dawn, soon. Still, she could not sleep.

She decided she was hungry. Not wanting to disturb a servant at this hour, Orain pulled on her slippers and left her sleeping chamber. Her footsteps echoed hollowly. In the corridor outside, one of the Khamars on night duty saluted her casually and asked in a whisper:

"Can't sleep?"

"No. . . ." Orain indicated that she was going down to the kitchens to settle the growl in her stomach.

The Khamar shifted the halberd he held in his right hand to his left and leaned it against the wall behind him, then produced from a pouch at his belt a wrapped slice of brown bread coated with honey. "I get the nibbles, too," he confided to the princess, "in the middle of the night. Have some."

Orain chuckled and took half the slice, munched on it, thanked the Khamar and returned down the corridor toward her room. But as she came to her door, the open balcony farther down caught her attention. The curtains had been pulled wide and the doors propped ajar so that she felt (now that she recognized it) a mild breeze coming down the hall, fragrant with the night scents of the palace gardens. Orain continued down the corridor and stepped out onto the balcony.

She leaned upon the low wall and stared out beyond the garden to the brilliant city, then was startled when someone behind her spoke. Orain turned quickly, throwing one hand to her breast in a gesture of alarm.

"I'm sorry," Salia apologized.

"I didn't even . . . see you . . . there," Orain panted.

The queen stepped out from the shadows; Orain saw that Salia was wearing only a very thin shift, gossamer-light, which concealed none of her figure. No doubt it was cooler than the robe which Orain wore—but the immodesty of it seemed an almost premeditated affront.

Yet Salia appeared unconcerned. She leaned on the wall beside Orain, propping herself on her arms as she swallowed a deep breath of night air. Orain watched her.

"It's all mine, isn't it?" the queen said quietly. It seemed a wonder to her.

"The capital, you mean?"

"Yes. . . ."

"If . . . . you want to think of it in that way," Orain allowed, "yes, I suppose you could say that."

"Athad must be ten times the size of Sugat," Salia continued, staring out at the lights and the tall buildings shouldering the purple clouds, touched by the shimmering of all the many stars. She glanced at Orain. "I couldn't sleep. Elad's curled up like a baby"—she shrugged—"but I couldn't sleep. Restless . . . Excited . . ."

"Excited?"

"But . . . just thinking of all this . . ." The queen turned around, held herself against the wall so that she was nearly sitting on it. "I'm sorry," Salia apologized, "about my father's rude remark this morning at breakfast."

Orain needed a moment to recall it. "Oh . . . that. Don't worry about it." She dismissed it as she drew a hand through her hair.

"He tends to do that. Say something before thinking about it."

"He's king in Gaegosh, isn't he?" Orain inquired.

"Yes. 'Imbur.' It's a hereditary title, but it means the same thing as king, yes."

She said nothing more and neither did Orain, although she yawned once lightly. She watched the city, let thoughts pass randomly through her imagination.

Abruptly, Salia asked her: "You love Count Adred, don't you?"

Orain was surprised at the frankness of the question. Facing the queen, she replied: "Well . . . I suppose I do. Yes."

"You don't have to talk about it, if you don't want to. I understand that it's personal. But I can tell that you love him."

"Oh? Can you?"

"He's nice," Salia admitted. "I like him a lot. He seems to act so seriously and, yet, sometimes he's like a nervous little boy, isn't he?"

Orain laughed mildly, and Salia smiled.

"I like your son, too," she remarked. "He's very handsome." She seemed to ponder that for a moment. "Are you and Adred going to stay in Athad, now?"

"Well, for the time being, at least."

"Not going to travel anymore?"

"Oh . . . we'll probably do our share of traveling, certainly."

"He loves you, too," Salia told Orain. "I can tell."

Orain was very intrigued by the queen and her perculiar comments—mildly disturbed by this one-sided interrogation. "You can tell?"

"Oh, surely. And I think it's wonderful. Are you going to marry him?"

"Well, I don't know. That—depends . . ."

"Oh, yes. Of course."

"We've known each other," Orain said, "for some years now. But I never— We're friends. It's developed slowly, I suppose."

"Oh, of course, of course," the queen agreed. "It'll be that way with Elad and me, I'm sure."

Orain began to feel chilly, so she crossed her arms over her breasts. She shook her head thoughtfully and smiled a trifle. "It occurs to me," she remarked quietly, "that he's probably my best friend in the world, right now. Odd, isn't it?"

"I think that's very nice," Salia told her. "For you to feel that way."

Orain smiled.

"You'd probably do anything for him, wouldn't you?"

Orain wasn't sure what she meant by that.

"I mean . . . because you love him so much."

"I suppose that's true."

Salia turned around and stared at the city again. In a doubtful voice she commented darkly, "I wonder if I'll ever love anybody that much."

"Don't you think you'll come to feel that way about Elad?"

Salia didn't look at her. "I imagine so," was her reply.

"Yes . . . that's very possible. But I've never thought of myself that way. Loving someone that much. It's such a . . . personal thing. You know . . ."

Orain swallowed and looked at her: the queen, an extremely young woman, and obviously unaware of a great many things. She stifled another yawn and shivered again, rubbed her arms and said:

"I'm going to go back and try to get some sleep."

Salia didn't answer her. Orain waited a moment, then started to cross the balcony.

The queen turned around. "I'm sorry . . . I didn't hear you. Did you say something?"

"Just— I'm going back to bed."

"Oh. Good night. . . ."

"Yes, good night. . . ."

When she reached her door she glanced back and saw Salia still standing there, leaning on the balcony wall, nearly naked and alone in the cool night, staring at the city.

So alone, with herself . . .

PART V

The Prisoning Heart

1.

Tapping his foot impatiently and ignoring the plates of food that grew cold on the table before him, a pallid and very tired Nutatharis stared at the large maps covering the wall across the room. Long needles held round bits of leather to various points on the map: sixteen bits of leather, each one numbered, representing the placement of the Emarian legions.

Or their last known placement.

Four were situated in the Low Provinces at the edge of the Tsalvian Forests; a fifth, to the south, sat just across the border from Athadian-controlled Omeria. The remaining pieces of leather were dotted here and there, on both sides of the border dividing Emaria from the Provinces. A small cluster of five leather circles was pinned close to the painted crown marking Lasura.

As he stared at the map, Nutatharis imagined the Lowlands half-drowned, the encampments of his legions inundated, the surviving men picking their way through the sloppy fields and eating anything they could find—grain, roots, serpents, rats—and quite probably resorting to cannibalism. . . .

Impossible!

The king slammed his fist on the table; the strike sent his wine pitcher tottering, but Nutatharis caught it with a swift move before it spilled.

Just as he settled it in place, a loud knock at the tower door brought Nutatharis up from his brooding. He called out and watched with angry eyes as Sir Jors entered, closed the door quietly behind him and advanced to the king. The minister came before the table and poured himself a cup of wine.

"Anything?" Nutatharis asked.

"As we . . . feared, my lord."

"The Twelfth?"

Sir Jors nodded as he gulped his wine; he pulled up a chair and sat down. "A rider—a scout for the Seventh—just came in. He found what was left of their camp—there." He pointed to the map.

"Attacked?" Nutatharis inquired, disbelieving.

"From all accounts, no, not attacked. The Lowlanders seem inactive; if they're doing anything, it's just what our men are trying to do—survive the floods." He shook his head. "It's all swampland, now. The rider reported that the hillsides looked like waterfalls—torrents. It's been that way for weeks, and no one has any guess as to how long it'll continue. Apparently the Twelfth was caught in it; the stream a league north of them flash flooded and wiped them out. If anyone managed to survive, we don't know it."

"Three thousand men!" Nutatharis grunted in disgust and slapped the table again. "Three thousand men don't simply—*drown* in the middle of a forest!"

"In the Lowlands," replied Sir Jors gravely, "I'm afraid they do. We found a few locals—I mean, the Seventh did—and fed them. They swore they hadn't seen anything like this in fifty years. But—it can happen."

"All their crops—wiped out?"

Sir Jors silently ducked his head.

"And our other legions? The Third? The Eleventh?"

"No word from the Eleventh since late Grem. North," he reminded Nutathartis, "of the Twelfth. The Third is low on rations but they seem to be sufficiently able to take care of themselves. They may be breaking into storehouses in some of the villages around there, but they're managing. The First—"

Nutatharis glanced at his map.

"—is treacherously close to the swamplands right across from Omeria. The land there sits quite low; the farmers are having a rough time of it, but we haven't had any reports from our men stationed there."

The king's eyes squinted as he studied the wall hanging. "That's northeastern Omeria," he noted. "But northern Omeria—just below our border?"

"All meadowland, as you know," Sir Jors replied. "No real flooding there. It's protected by the rising terrain around it."

"But our farmers in the south aren't producing enough barley and wheat. Only half of what we had last year . . ." He lapsed into silence.

After a moment, Sir Jors coughed and suggested: "I think, my lord, that we must recall a number of our legions."

Nutatharis turned his head sharply and faced him with a glare. "We can't feed them here any more than they can feed themselves out in the Lowlands," he snapped. "Why should I recall them here? So they can starve here, and turn against me?"

Sir Jors was stunned by the remark; that was not his intention at all. He knew the army would never turn against Nutatharis. Was the king so worried over one season's inclement weather? Floods had occurred before. Not to this alarming an extent, true, but still—men who lived close to the earth reckoned on these things occasionally. Emaria's storehouses should be bursting with grain from previous crops.

"We can't feed our own in the capital," Nutatharis growled, leaning forward to pour himself a goblet of wine. "If we purchase any more bread from the Athadians or the Ithulians . . ." He sipped. "We're nearly bankrupt; I cannot repay my loans, and I will only cause more harm if I devalue our gold even more. The people on the border are bartering with the Athadians. Bartering!"

Sir Jors was greatly disturbed; he hadn't realized that Nutatharis had been this imprudent in building up his armed forces at the expense of food. He swiveled in his chair, regarded the map. A dark thought occurred to him, then—a necessary one—and the moment he considered it, he glanced at Nutatharis. In his king's eyes, he saw the same decision.

"If our soldiers," Nutatharis decided, "find it necessary to cross the Athadian border to . . . survive—they will be reprimanded, but they will not be punished. Am I understood, Sir Jors?"

His minister nodded faintly.

"I'm not going to bankrupt my treasury, and I refuse to curtail my nation's defenses simply because people are hungry. But I've never said that I will allow our troops to do what they feel is necessary. Am I further understood, Sir Jors?"

A nod.

"If any complaint is issued from the Athadians, I deny unequivocally any wrongdoing on the part of our people."

"Of course," replied Sir Jors. "Emarians would never do such a thing. We know this. We'd rather starve than voluntarily break any treaty with a neighboring state."

Nutatharis motioned to him. "As you leave, send in to me a scribe. I think it time that we made use of our agreement with the Salukadians."

Sir Jors rose to his feet, finished his wine in a gulp and saluted his king.

"Who would begin such a rumor?" Nutatharis asked. "What a vicious slander! Are the Athadians so righteous that they can accuse us of criminal activity without condemning their own first? I won't allow this sort of talk."

Sir Jors crossed the room, opened the door and turned. "When I hear anything further," he said, "I'll alert you immediately."

Nutatharis waved him gone, as Sir Jors closed the door.

As Thameron, on horseback, crossed the border into Emaria and followed a road leading toward Lasura, he came upon scenes of devastation and poverty, hunger and despair. The condition of the people he passed inspired in him neither dread nor generosity. As he was dressed, however, in rich clothes, and riding a fresh clean horse, so wanton a display was bound to arouse the tempers of many whom he passed on the road. Hollow-cheeked women holding crying babies to their flat breasts stared at him with evil eyes; men in fields so filled with water that they were no better than fens stopped to glare at Thameron as he passed by, and they called to him hotly, demanding that he share his wealth with them. One evening at twilight as he was passing through a dark copse, Thameron found himself suddenly surrounded by a dozen hungry men wielding spades and shovels. They promised to take his life if he didn't turn over to them any money he had in his pockets as well as his horse. "We'll allow you your boots," they told him, "if you don't fight us."

He might have slain them all with a gesture: Thameron knew that he could accomplish that. But what would have been the purpose? Secure in his strength, he was not alarmed at the excesses to which these hungry men resorted in their desperation. As he reached into his coat pocket, Thameron transformed the coppers he had into gold pieces and distributed them evenly to the men surrounding him. Had they become greedy at the sight of this largesse, Thameron promised himself that he would, indeed, slay them; but on the contrary, the wealth their victim produced inspired a few of the men to chuckle, and one even thanked the sorcerer and begged his pardon for the inconvenience. Thameron watched them depart as they scurried back into the shadows of the copse, then continued walking along the road to Lasura.

When he reached the capital city's walls the following morning, it occurred to the sorcerer that it might be to his benefit to seduce King Natatharis as he had the highwaymen. With this in mind, Thameron stopped at a hovel that stood in the long shadows of

Lasura's walls, and there, in return for a gold piece transformed from an appleseed, he gained from the old woman who lived in the hut a breakfast of brown bread and thin tea, plus an empty grain sack. When he took his leave of the woman, Thameron waited until he had taken a turn in the road (so that she might not witness, in her suspicion, what he was about) to pause and examine the sack. It was frayed and patched in places, and, as Thameron had expected, it had been gleaned nearly empty of all kernels of wheat. Yet a few had escaped the searching fingers of the hungry old woman. Thameron turned the sack inside out and pulled free from the coarsely woven fiber a total of five kernels. These he held in his left hand for a few moments while he concentrated; when he replaced them in the sack, they immediately caused more kernels to come into being.

Thameron carried the sack over one shoulder, and as he walked toward the southern gate of the capital city, the sack grew heavier and fuller between his shoulders until, as he strode beneath the eyes of sentries on the wall, he carried with him a full sack of fresh grain.

"Who are you and what do you here?" hailed one of the guards.

"I am a wanderer from the south," Thameron called up. "I wish to speak with your king about an urgent matter."

"What is your 'urgent matter,' traveler?"

"I come to give him grain!"

"*Grain?*" The soldier laughed derisively; two companions nearby him on the wall stepped up to the embrasures and looked down at Thameron.

Thameron hefted the sack he carried.

"Where did you steal that from?" called one of the soldiers.

The sorcerer did not reply. At this, one of the sentries came down from the wall; within a minute the great gates were pulled open. Thameron strode between their shadows.

In the courtyard, the first guard repeated his question. "Where did you steal that from?" He eyed Thameron accusingly.

"I have a secret field of my own," was the answer. "Will you escort me now to your lord?"

"It'll cost you what you carry."

"Then request this sack from your king, for I bring it to him."

Other soldiers seated before the barracks at either side of the yard now stood up and sauntered over. They asked Thameron many questions but received few answers. Finally, tiring of standing in the hot sun and thinking it best to do as the stranger requested, a number of them mounted horses and led the well-dressed young man out of the yard and down a brick street toward Lasura's palace.

Nutatharis's expression as Thameron was brought into the tower room was one of diffidence; but his attitude became one of gravity as the young sorcerer dropped the full sack of grain on the stone before the king. So much grain was there that the sack split in two places as it landed, and rivers of pouring wheat shot out in dry puddles, trickled with promises of salvation and pride restored.

King Nutatharis stood up slowly, a cold light filling his eyes. "Where did you get this grain, man?"

Thameron was unimpressed by the display of temper. He failed either to bow to Nutatharis or diminish himself in any way; he merely requested: "If we might speak alone . . ."

Nutatharis's eyes, dark beads behind slits, shot from Thameron to the soldiers behind him. The guards saluted their lord, backed out and closed the heavy door. The king's stare returned to his visitor. "Now . . . tell me."

Thameron smiled wisely and lifted his arms, shook them so that the long sleeves of his coat dropped to his elbows. He showed Nutatharis his hands, palms out.

Nutatharis paled. "A sorcerer?"

Thameron sneered as he lowered his arms. "You need grain," he told the king. "I need . . . information. Yes, I am a man of accomplishment; but that need not concern you so long as you understand that I am here, not to humble you or provoke you, but to continue upon a path I began long ago."

Nutatharis sat down again, never removing his stare from the stranger. "You ask me to bargain with you? Tell me where you got that grain."

"I created it. I have many powers, and great strength. Surely you've heard tales of sorcerers and wizards, even if you have never met one before." To Nutatharis's silence: "I request of you but one answer, and that to but one question. You are the ruler in this land, and surely nothing can occur within your borders without your being aware of it. I am pulled toward the north by an important vision, and that is the path I follow. If you consent to aid me, insofar as you can, I will not harm you in any way, but I will reward you. I will fill this tower in which we stand to its roof with

192

grain; you may feed your nation for a year. Do you consent, King Nutatharis?"

"I may not possess the answer you seek."

"If you have no answer, then let that be your answer. Only be honest with me. You are a strong man; I, too, am a strong man. Be forthright with me. Before the day is out, our business can be concluded. Do you agree?"

Nutatharis gave the matter stern thought; he wiped his beard and mustache, which had grown damp, and stared for a long while at the sorcerer. At last: "Upon the terms you have told me— agreed. What is your question?"

"I seek a man of shadows; it is he who calls me to the north. I search, King Nutatharis, for the Undying Man."

Nutatharis choked; he lost all color and bolted up from his seat. "What have you to do with him?"

Thameron was interested in the monarch's reaction to his disclosure. "What I wish from him is no concern of yours. I want you to tell me if you know where he is. If you do, tell me frankly."

Moving slowly, Nutatharis left his chair and began to pace the tower room. He stared at the sorcerer. "What foulness is it," he asked, "that draws creatures like you and—him—to me, here? What foulness is it?"

Thameron appeared to darken, as though a coverlet of shadows had been cast upon him. "No foulness, this," he told the king. "But time hurries, Nutatharis. We live in days of consequence; the incidents come more and faster: roadmarks on the path to our conclusion. Do you hear the storms at night? Don't you see it in the stars, feel it in the twilight at the end of every day? If you listen closely in the silence of the dawn, you can feel it eating away at the soul of every man and woman in this nation. The fear. The knowing. The understanding. We live at the end of time, King Nutatharis. Creatures like me and . : . the undying one . . . we have come back, returned from the Dawn to witness this great Dusk: to herald it, and begin it."

Nutatharis stared at him.

"It is the end of time that you feel, pulling at you, pressing on you. Do you really suppose that mornings now are as innocent as they were when you were a child, King Nutatharis?"

"You—" His throat was dry, his voice raspy. "You come here . . . you speak as he did. . . ."

"I am a man," Thameron assured him. "But the shadow has descended upon me, and it possesses me. On some of us falls the shadow, on others the light. I quicken with this comprehension, and I turn less and less from what I was, become more and more a power of great truth. Why do you suppose that all truth is good, Nutatharis? We live in the shadow of a mighty Wheel. You do not comprehend it; you believe that the life you live is your own. It is not. Your life is but one of many—innumerable—lives, and all of us are but fleet sparks from a great furnace, small whispers of a mighty Soul." He grinned. "I speak as he did? I speak with the voice of eternity, O Nutatharis. You would disbelieve me if I told you of the naive boy I once was—and that, not so long ago." He looked away, stared at the sack of grain and looked again into Nutatharis's disturbed eyes. "We could live a thousand years," Thameron whispered, "or ten thousand years, as men, and never feel the mystery that grows among us. But times come when that mystery must resolve itself, when many must perish so that many can be reborn. Time tests man as much as man tests time, King Nutatharis. And now we live in an age when the mysteries happen fast, visit us with cause—and so many that men don't believe what they see and feel. Do not see, then; do not feel. But the sun will die soon for all of us, and you will hear the hungry wail now; and you will see men die in numbers that battlefields have not known; and you will hear the damned scream for god as burning priests never screamed for mercy. We are destroying ourselves, Nutatharis. You are contributing to it, and so am I. My presence is only more obvious; the good contribute, as well as the evil, because they are the same. It is too late for the humble and the righteous and the good to alter the course which humanity favors; it is enough, now, that we live, so that we may die, witnessing the end."

He had spoken this in a low voice that trembled with suppressed emotion: Thameron, speaking as though another person spoke through him, as though the spirit possessing him were given its voice.

He seemed, then, to awaken from a trance; he shivered slightly, rubbed his forehead and stared at Nutatharis with wide eyes.

The king of Emaria swallowed thickly. "I—do not—" He coughed and repeated more distinctly: "I do not want your . . . grain."

"Nevertheless—"

"North of here," Nutatharis told him quickly. "Where, I do not know. But when I learned in truth what he was—*what* he was, sorcerer—I cast him out. And hoped that the gods would slay him out there . . . somewhere, far away from me."

"He cannot die," Thameron shook his head, "until the world dies." He bowed sharply, took in a breath. "I will go, then. Thank you."

"Damn you!" Nutatharis whispered hotly. "Don't *thank* me!"

Thameron laughed aloud, moved for the door and faced the king a last time. "Here is the true horror," he told Nutatharis. "Do you wish to know the true horror? Do you wish to know what eternity is? What humanity is?" His tone became grim and swollen. "Even with the end, Nutatharis, it will continue—this disease of the Spirit we call . . . humanity."

Then he went out, closing the door loudly behind him.

Nutatharis, staring at the shadowed space where Thameron had been, realized that his heart was pumping furiously, that he was perspiring, and that he was frightened.

Very frightened . . .

2.

In Abustad, where soldiers from the eastern Athadian legions came to spend a few days of civilization and comfort and where a growing number of Salukadian ships filled the wharves with trade goods bought by speculating western businessmen, the streets were filled with noise, the taverns with carousers, the shops with buyers, and the apartment houses on the lower southside with their patrons. The prostitutes and procurers had seldom before experienced such leniency from city officials; for, publicly barred from soliciting on the streets, the prostitutes had learned privately that trade of any sort was a welcome thing in Abustad. Governor Sulen, while not a corrupt man, had nevertheless allowed certain harmless diversions and vices to flourish as the influx of wealth and trade and visitors grew. For his city, like all cities within the Athadian empire, was low on funds but overcrowded with opportunities for making use of those funds. And if, because of the national economy, the throne could not provide for its own, then the people of Abustad would provide for themselves. It would have been as foolish for Sulen to disallow the entry of Salukadian ships into his harbor in this regard as it would have been for him to discourage the occasional gambling in the backrooms of taverns or the consistent need on the part of soldiers, sailors and weary travelers for an evening of feminine companionship.

A living economy needs the exchange of monies and the bartering of goods and services to sustain itself; and morality in the marketplace (if it has ever existed) was as unknown a thing as ethics in government. Sulen was not corrupt, but neither was he a hypocrite or a fool. If crime and greed and pretense had their place in the capital city, then they certainly were not out of place in Abustad. And the exchange of currencies within his port city's limits only encouraged this most practical of attitudes.

In one particular apartment house on the southside down near the docks, late in the month of Seth, sailors and travelers and businessmen made their appearances as they regularly did. But this evening a rumor had begun to spread along Podis Street, and as a crew of huskies just docked from Hilum made their way into the newly painted house, one of them grabbed a young woman by the hair, swung her about so that he could wind an arm around her and asked her:

"What's this about you shipping out?"

"By the first of the month!"

"What?" asked the fellow's companion, leaning back, as the three of them crowded down a hallway making for a spare bed. "Moving to another town? Not you, Vilis!"

She laughed garishly. "Only out to sea!" she answered. "Didn't you see them building that boat down on the water?"

The first one, who kept his arm about her waist as he steered her into the room at the end of the hall, scratched his beard and remarked, "It's *yours*?"

"No, no, no! I'm moving onto it!" was the reply. "You're going to have to swim after me if you want more of what *I* got! No more of this pissy getting arrested for winking at somebody's smelly old uncle! I'm going to be respectable!"

She leaned back on the bed and the first one fell beside her and hurriedly began undressing her as his companion closed the door.

Across the hall, a middle-aged man, dressed in clothes advertising his station in the city government, opened his door a crack and peeked out. Then he quietly closed it once more and glanced at the woman sitting against the opposite wall. He crossed the room to a low table crowded with bottles and a few cups and poured something for himself.

"I thought," he explained, "that it must be Lord Modum."

"No," the woman replied. "He'll be occupied for another hour or so." She looked at the calibrated water clock on a nearby shelf.

The city official chuckled as he sipped. "You know the habits of your clients so well?"

"Men," she told him, "have but three habits. And the only difference among them is the time involved with each. The matters we deal with here"—she smirked—"are either quickly resolved, or they're not."

The city official laughed out loud.

"Get me another glass of wine, will you?"

He set down his own cup and filled her goblet, walked it to her and took his time handing it to her so that his gaze might linger. She understood. She was a most attractive woman, dark-haired as all easterners were, and dressed in extremely fine clothes that accented the swell of her breasts and bared the shapeliness of her long legs.

"Thank you, Count Biro."

"Thank *you*." He returned to his own goblet, sipped, and seated himself in his cushioned chair. For a moment, he delighted in the intoxicating effects of his drink and the beautiful woman combined with the aroma of the curative, incense-like *minth* leaves burning in a corner stand. Then he asked: "So—you're quite serious about sailing off on this pleasure barge of yours?"

She nodded succinctly. "They should be finished renovating that old galley in a week or less. Then, we start our sail between here and Aparu. A very pleasant two weeks, Count Biro, if you can afford it."

"You're quite the businesswoman, aren't you? All your bribes paid?"

"You're the last."

He raised an eyebrow. "You *are* doing well, then, to set sail so quickly. Isn't Lady Sapima upset with you?"

"Why should she be? She has twelve women working here; I'm abducting only two of them, and paying her well. And I've two young girls and a beautiful little boy waiting for the start of the ship. It's a small boat, but it'll provide all the services required."

"But you haven't even been in Abustad two weeks!"

"Oh, I've been in Abustad before, and made Lady Sapima's acquaintance before. I was wealthy in Erusabad. I have . . . traveled."

Biro shook his head, marveling at her ingenuity, self-assurance and experience. "And . . . so young," he commented. "You're a remarkable woman, Assia."

She lifted her glass to him as though in a toast and grinned. "I agree!"

Biro sighed and leaned back in his chair, set aside his cup and sighed heavily again, then closed his eyes. He was exhausted. The day had been one long argument with his superiors, and now it had been necessary to bring Modum to this whorehouse so that the "transfers of funds" could be accommodated before the first of the month—collections from whoremasters and pimps channeled into the city coffers and mislabeled in the books as taxes or fines or other legal appropriations. There was no joy in such things; the life of a politician was the life of a frog, hopping constantly from rock to log, balancing so as not to fall into the swamp, devouring anything just to stay alive, and never certain if the next rock or log might tip to send you under. Life was a series of crises that might have become opportunities, and strokes of fortune that invariably turned into unneeded shackles.

Ah . . . but the wine this evening had been excellent, the aroma of the incense a sedative, and the company of a beautiful woman—even if only for conversation—a thing to be savored. . . .

Assia's good humor left her as she watched Biro and realized that he was falling asleep. The fool. All of them were fools. She loathed the touch of them, despised the sight of them, and wanted only to get away from them, and that as soon as possible.

And it would be soon, now. Soon . . .

There is much gold here—use it for yourself, please. Buy a house, hire servants, employ a physician to help you, Assia, please.

It had been the day after Thameron had left—when she'd realized that she would never see him again—that Assia had decided quickly, spontaneously—and bitterly—to take the gold he'd given her and transform her life. The ship . . . the bribes . . . Lady Sapima, under whose roof she had once tried to escape from her father . . .

She would never see Thameron again.

Feeling condemned because she had lost him, regained and then lost him once more, Assia had wandered Abustad's streets all night until she resolved to borrow some of Thameron's strength and not run away from herself any longer, not degrade herself any longer, but to take what he had given her and somehow do for herself what no one had done for her, ever. She had no one, and she truly had never had anyone. Was that bondage, or freedom? She had returned that night to Lady Sapima's, paid her in gold for an unsoiled bed, and lain all night, thoughtful.

198

Motifs of injustice and arbitrary cruelty had marched through her mind like an army of phantoms. Her memory became clogged with reminiscences of sitting in a muddy alley in the middle of winter . . . of watching stars at night from a campfire in an army swamp . . . of seeing her father murdered in a sharp and sudden tavern brawl. The images had nearly suffocated her. At last she had fallen asleep, dreaming herself still in love with Thameron and hearing the beating of his heart on a long-ago, rainy afternoon. And when she had awakened in the morning, it was as though she had died in her hot sleep and been reborn with the new daylight.

Now she was waiting for her pleasure barge to be completed. Biro and others had taken money from her. Taken money to allow her to do what she fully intended to do—with or without their permission? What did it matter? Money was only rose petals, and love a thing of dust—sought on an afternoon or in a shadowed alley, sated, and then forgotten, put away to fade and finally to dissolve like parchment or to dry up in a puddle left on the ground.

Emotions were vicious, and promiseless.

One's lover could be a sorcerer, or one's father, or an animal. What did it matter?

To approach life earnestly, or to take seriously its offers of justice or reward or success or achievement, was to let oneself be duped and defeated before the contest even began. All Assia wished to do now was to set sail on her whore-galley with enough children to make the venture worthwhile, and enough paying aristocrats with purses equal to their vices, so that she might recline on deck all day, listen to music and simpers and whines, and watch the waves and the sky fade into one another on a horizon she could never hope to reach.

In a small village just a few leagues north of Hilum, Asawas noticed a patrol of soldiers, bearing the city insignia of Hilum, leading among their horses a disheveled man dressed in rags, his wrists bound by manacles and a chain. When the troop paused at a roadhouse in the main street of the village to water their horses and to get a drink themselves, a small crowd collected around the guards standing by the prisoner. Asawas joined the crowd.

As the whispering and the gesticulating grew into a general noise, the prophet stepped forward and politely asked one of the soldiers: "Why is this man your prisoner?"

The officer sneered. "He's a murderer. Raped a thirteen-year-old girl who was"—he tapped his head—"and then he strangled her. Does that satisfy your curiosity?" He addressed the crowd generally. "Does that tell all of you what you want to know?"

The people mumbled, and a few of them uttered insults in low voices. But Asawas, under the sergeant's watchful stare, stepped forward until he was standing directly before the murderer.

"Why," he asked quietly, "did you do this?"

The prisoner showed him eyes full of hate. "Leave me alone, priest!"

"That's enough, now," warned the sergeant.

But Asawas continued to stare at the man so that the murderer finally had to turn his eyes away.

"Why did you do such a thing?"

The prisoner grinned foully and his eyes widened. "God told me to do it!" he spat.

Asawas shook his head. "No . . . no. God did not ask you to do this. Do you suffer so much in your heart, son of your mother, that you must make another suffer? Must you cause pain when there are so many in this world who would gladly help you relieve your own pain?"

The murderer stared at him, a hint of astonished fright in his eyes. The sergeant stepped forward, and, out of respect and not wishing to manhandle a wandering priest but feeling it necessary to intervene, said, "Please, now, that's enough."

But Asawas ignored him. He continued to stare into the prisoner's eyes as he reached out and took the murderer's raw, manacled hands into his own and held them. The prophet's hands were warm. "Are these the hands that committed this crime?" he asked, almost in a whisper. "Are these the hands that held her? That ripped the clothes from a screaming child? The hands that pushed her and struck her? That choked the life from her? Are these the hands? Look at me, man of anguish."

The prisoner could not meet Asawas's awesome gaze, but inexorably, although he tried to watch the ground, his attention was pulled back by the *ikbusa*'s power.

"Are these the eyes that watched while the hands did these things? Is that the brain, inside you, that conceived these things, that unbalanced all that you have seen and heard and learned in this world? Is this the brain that saw only one thing, that believed only one thing? Man . . . why did you do this?"

The murderer was trembling; his hands shivered inside Asawas's, his arms shook, and his eyes, fixed on the prophet's, stared deeply into the vision as though it were not possible to do otherwise. "She—wanted me—to . . . ," he whispered.

Then he fell forward and dropped to his knees as Asawas released him. The murderer lifted his chained hands to his face and sobbed heavily, beat the iron manacles against his forehead.

"I am in pain!" he howled. "I hurt inside, I hurt! She screamed at me . . . she bit me . . . she made me do it, she asked me to! . . . I hated her and she knew I hated her and she was like an animal and it made me like an animal! I was afraid! I was so afraid! I had no life! I am afraid of shadows . . . afraid of noises . . . I could hear my own heart beat, it sounded like thunder, but no one else heard! Everyone thought I was a monster! I became a monster! I could not sleep! My mind burned, my ears were clogged with sounds! God told me to hurt her! She walked by my house every day and I hurt, I was in pain, she was a stupid animal and I knew she hated me!"

On and on he railed, sobbing and moaning, until he collapsed into the dusty road and groveled there, whimpering and crying, still beating his head with the iron manacles.

The sergeant observed all this with astonishment. As his men returned from the roadhouse and hurried, incredulous, to see what had happened, the sergeant growled to Asawas: "Priest! What have you done to him? What have you done to my prisoner?" He was angry, frightened that this spectacle would prevent him from returning to Hilum with the murderer intact.

To the officer's red-suffused face, Asawas answered: "I showed him god, for god is within him, not without him, not apart from him. I showed him why he was wrong to succumb to his fears, why he should have asked help from the world, rather than try to hurt the world in his pain. Now . . . he understands. He understands that he hurt the young woman so that he could hurt himself much more—much more. . . ."

The sergeant's face screwed into a puzzled, severe expression. He comprehended none of this. Nodding quickly to several of his men nearby, he gestured, and they retrieved the sobbing prisoner, mounted their horses and began to march him down the road out of the village. The murderer's sobs carried back, above the sounds of the horses' hoofs. The sergeant's wondering gaze remained on Asawas until, at the last, he followed his men down the road in a trail of brown dust.

3.

Adred leaned forward, studied the wood grain of the table top beneath his elbows for signs of symbolic significance (a hidden number, or a hidden image of some sort), then decided impulsively that he'd dallied long enough and had best be returning to the palace.

Just as he considered it, he looked up as someone came into the tavern. It was young Omos. Adred waved and pushed back his chair as Omos came over.

"Anything wrong?"

"No . . . no. But Galvus wanted me to find you. He'd like you to come back."

"Cyrodian under lock and key?"

"Yes," Omos nodded. "Yes. They've got him in the prison."

The two drunks at the next table quieted and looked at them.

"Didn't cause any trouble, did he?"

Omos shook his head. "He didn't say a word, Adred. He didn't do—anything."

Adred thought about that as he moved to his feet. "That's very surprising. All right. Let's go back."

The two drunks were now staring at them, thoroughly intrigued.

"Hard to believe that he didn't create a commotion when they brought him in," Adred remarked again. "He's such a—"

"He's changed," Omos told him as they made their way into the street. "That's what Galvus said. He tried to speak with him but his father wouldn't answer him. But Galvus said he looked different."

"What do you mean?"

"Prince Cyrodian never had white hair, did he?"

Adred stopped and stared at Omos. "*White hair?*"

"His hair is white."

"Cyrodian's?"

Omos bobbed his head.

"What—the hell is it? Some kind of disguise?"

"No. It's—his hair. It's turned white."

It was only three blocks to the palace, but Adred nearly ran to get there.

Abgarthis was just crossing the cavernous main foyer as Adred and Omos came in. Adred called to him, and the minister turned and showed him a questioning look. "Where'd you disappear to?"

Adred shrugged. "I just thought it might be better if . . . I weren't here. I just thought—"

"Orain was asking about you.'

"Oh."

Abgarthis turned and began walking toward a stairs that led to the second floor.

"Is she up there?" Adred asked him.

"No one," Abgarthis replied, reading his mind, "is permitted to speak with Cyrodian yet. He is heavily guarded."

"And . . . Elad?"

"In session with Captains Mirsus and Uvars and representatives from the Imperial Army."

"The army isn't going to fight him on this, is it?" Adred wondered.

"That is precisely what Elad wants to ascertain."

"Abgarthis . . . you're not upset with me, are you?"

But obviously he was; or at least the elder was upset with whatever tension or drama had welcomed Cyrodian's arrival. The three of them reached the second floor landing—a loggia that looked down upon the foyer—and Abgarthis did not pause but led the way around the low wall toward another stairs leading to the third floor.

"I'm getting too old for this nonsense," he complained, pulling back his robe as he took the steps. "My knees sound like brittle wood. . . ."

Adred, behind him, asked: "What's this about Cyrodian being changed? White hair?"

"It's true," the minister panted. "Amazing, but true."

"And he won't tell anyone why?"

"He hasn't said a word to anyone yet; not one word. Perhaps—he's missing his tongue."

Adred was surprised by this remark: it was deliberately cruel and meaningful and its implication was not lost on him. Abgarthis was in a grim mood.

They reached the third floor and the elder marched down the main corridor with Adred and Omos following. Abgarthis gestured toward Orain's door. "I believe she's in there."

Adred waited as Abgarthis crossed the hall to Galvus's chamber, nodded to the Khamar on duty and entered, followed by Omos. Both the outer and inner doors had been left open; Adred caught a glimpse of Galvus in the open sitting area as he rose to greet the minister.

"Elad requests your presence," came Abgarthis's dim voice.

Galvus made no reply but followed him out into the corridor. The prince glanced briefly at Adred as he passed; there was a strong look in his eyes.

Adred watched them disappear down the stairs, then nodded to the Khamar outside Orain's chamber, entered the anteroom and knocked on her door.

While Omos went to spend the early afternoon in the library, Galvus and Abgarthis entered the Council Chamber just as Elad was speaking sternly to Captains Mirsus and Uvars and the half dozen Councilors affiliated with the Imperial Army's Military Tribune. "And we have the testimony of his co-conspirators—Lord Umothet and the others executed last winter—so there is no need to go to the pretense and expense of a prolonged trial. I want that understood."

Galvus and Abgarthis quietly moved toward empty chairs and seated themselves at a table below Elad's throne dais.

"And I further want it understood that I will brook absolutely no interference in this matter from the military. Lord Eslis . . . Lord Arego? . . ."

"Our . . . interpretation," breathed Lord Arego, a heavyset man whose bulk was barely contained by the chair that supported him, "is that the military opinion of Prince Cyrodian's—exploits—has altered substantially since the facts of the conspiracy came to light. Yes."

"Lord Eslis?" Elad eyed him.

The Councilor, a skull-faced man with close-cropped hair and many military decorations, bowed his head. "The army's attitude toward their 'brother-in-arms,' as it were, has indeed been amended, lord king. You must remember that the spontaneous outburst on the part of some of the officers and cadets when Cyrodian was originally arrested was due more to sentiment than anything else."

Elad sneered. "They threatened me with a civil conflict if I did not bow to their demands to exile Cyrodian. That, to you, is sentiment? I'd better have our vocabularies amended."

Eslis motioned with his thin fingers. "Men of weapons," he explained, "have passionate hearts."

"And quick tempers. The sword is hardly a scale of justice."

But as no one commented on this observation, Elad glanced at the others seated before him and allowed: "Are there any objections, then, to my signing the decree?"

A few coughed, several guilty pairs of eyes studied Prince Galvus—but no one rose to argue in Prince Cyrodian's behalf.

"The decree is already written. Scribe!" Elad called.

The secretary seated on the stool to the right looked up from his tablet.

"Date the decree"—Elad gave it a moment's thought—"for tomorrow. Twenty-six Sath."

The young man produced the document from the shelf beneath his seat, uncurled it and, with blue ink, scratched in the date.

"Hand me the decree." Elad held out his hand.

The scribe leaned forward and passed the scroll to his king. Elad cleared his throat, held the parchment open and read aloud to the men in the chamber, and to his nephew, his edict ordering the execution of his brother, the prince-general.

". . . by me, Elad *sollos don* Athadia, on this date, twenty-six Sath, in the Age of the Birth of Our Prophet 1879." He looked up, stared into Galvus's eyes. "If—there are no objections, then I will now sign this document and pass it to Lord Vemo"—a nod—"and order it sealed, copied and complied with."

Silence.

Elad turned his attention to his lap, studied the document a last time, then stepped down from his throne and moved to a table. He lay the scroll beside Captain Uvars, and, borrowing a blue-inked pen from his secretary, signed his name to it. Scratching sounds. The scribe melted a stick of yellow wax and dripped a circle onto the bottom of the parchment; King Elad pressed the hot wax with the heavy silver imprimatur of the Imperial Throne.

Then he straightened, rolled the parchment and handed it across the table to Lord Vemo. The king's eyes were cold.

"It is done," he whispered. "May the gods have mercy on us. . . ."

When Elad left the Council Chamber and, alone, made his way across the tiled hall to his private office—where a hundred documents sat awaiting his notice—he was in no mood for the Imbur of Gaegosh's pretentious interference into Athadian affairs of state. Ogodis, who had felt it his duty to stay on in Athad after the assassination attempt, had not returned to Sugat; but Elad knew that his father-in-law must return soon: a bureaucracy will fester like a boil unless its nominal chief lances it occasionally, and Sugat's government offices had become an unmanageable sprawl, as had Athadia's own. It was with a look of impatience that the king greeted Salia's father when he stepped through the ante-hall of his office and saw the Imbur waiting for him.

"If you have a moment, lord king."

Yet Elad could not continually dismiss him as though Ogodis were a pesky minister or bribe-tender. "Yes . . ." he sighed. "But only for a moment, Imbur. I am very occupied."

Ogodis nodded. "As I understand. May we speak in your office?"

Elad opened the doors and led the way inside; he sat down behind a wide desk while the Imbur settled himself in a chair across from it. Servants entered with trays and vanished again silently through curtained arches. Elad noticed that the room was gloomy and wished that one of them had opened his windows.

"Is the matter pressing?" he inquired. "As you can see"—he gestured to the piles of papers and the many scrolls crowding his desk top—"I have much to attend to."

"As I say, I will take but a moment. But I wish to speak with you regarding your brother."

"Cyrodian?"

"If I may be so bold."

Elad took in a breath. "I've just signed the decree for his immediate execution, Ogodis. What more is there to be said?"

The Imbur smiled. "Allow me to speak frankly," he suggested. "King Elad . . . vengeance has a way of burning like Arimu's torch—it burns clearly, but its light shows only false doors, false avenues."

Elad was astounded. This was a most unusual sentiment to come from so autocratic and unyielding a personality as the Imbur's. But he took offense. "Who spoke of vengeance?" Elad asked.

Ogodis clasped his hands in his lap. "Of course, for the crimes he has committed against Athadia, Cyrodian must be dealt with summarily. That is understood. But I wonder if there is not a scent of vengeance in it all?"

"I will become angry with you, Ogodis, if you persist. What exactly are you saying?"

"Only this. That pride is a dangerous thing. And I suspect that you feel a public execution is the only visible method by which to shame Cyrodian and cleanse yourself of his crimes in a wholly satisfactory way."

"Are you arguing that he should be reprieved? I cannot—"

"I am a soldier," Ogodis reminded Elad. "Now . . . I am that no longer, it's true, but my own father placed me in the military service when I was a boy, and I spent twelve years in the fields and in the barracks. Gaegosh, of course, has not been involved in an armed conflict in quite some time; nevertheless, our attitude of preparedness is the same as your empire's, and the military is the backbone of our country."

"Please, Ogodis, get to the point."

"Soldiers," the Imbur continued, "have a mentality of pride which can seem as duplicitous as a serpent's mentality to an outsider—to a king, if I may say it, or to a bureaucrat. Warriors serve a higher ideal than most men admit to; and most warriors feel that most men are unfortunate encumbrances to the true goal of civilization."

"Some soldiers may feel that way, Ogodis—but I believe you speak more for yourself than you do for my brother. His 'high ideals' took rather a low form."

"Nevertheless, until one has spent time with the military and learned to appreciate its values—they are as old as humanity, King Elad, and they are not false values—unless one has done this, one cannot—"

Elad was losing his temper. "I remind you again, Imbur, that I am very busy."

Ogodis nodded, got to his feet, threw his hands behind him and stalked to the opposite wall, then turned with a thoughtful eye. "Your military resented the call for Cyrodian's execution last summer, did they not?"

"What has that to do with anything?"

"Resentment in the nation's armed forces is not a good thing. You can achieve your ambition by ridding yourself of Cyrodian and recognizing the military's own code of principles, if you will allow your brother to take his own life."

Elad winced. "Impossible."

"Give the matter some thought. When a man in the military has done a disservice—less to his country than to his own code of conduct—he prefers to face death honorably, and fall upon his sword."

The king shook his head. "Cyrodian's crimes against Athadia were not accomplished within a military context. He did what he did, not by virtue of his rank or caste, but in total disregard of everything our law—and our military—holds to be valuable."

"Maybe so. But I think you ought to allow him his choice."

"I would shame the military," Elad countered, "if I were to allow Cyrodian to commit *asinmu* as though he were still an honorable member of the army."

"I do not think so," Ogodis replied. Then he held out his hands. "I only intended to take a moment of your time—to suggest this, and to explain my reasons for my feelings. I am not here to interfere with you, King Elad, but only to lend you . . . advice. From one leader with a few years of experience, to another."

"I appreciate the sentiment, Ogodis, but I cannot concur."

"Very well." He turned to make his way to the door.

Elad kept his eyes on him, then his sight fell to the scrolls on his desk top. As the Imbur opened the doors: "Ogodis . . ."

He turned. "Yes?"

"What did you mean when you made the comment about 'the true goal of civilization'? What do you believe that goal to be?"

Ogodis answered him quietly. "Peace," he replied. "Peace—and nations committed to the highest ideals men are capable of imagining."

Elad reached for one of the parchment scrolls. "And you are sincere when you tell me that you do not wish to interfere with me, but only to give me . . . advice?"

The Imbur bowed his head. "Our two great nations are now joined in a common accord," he professed. "I am very glad for it. We have become partners . . . friends. An example for the world."

Elad told him, "I'm most pleased to hear you say that, because I have no intention of compromising our friendship." He held up the scroll in one hand. "I had not intended to speak with you of this right now, but the moment seems opportune. Will you be so good as to read this?"

Ogodis stepped forward and took the scroll. "And what is it?"

"A letter to me from Lord General Thomo, my emissary to Erusabad."

Ogodis lifted an eyebrow, unfurled the parchment and read. When he had done: "An . . . intriguing proposal, isn't it?" He rolled it up.

"I must admit that I consider Thomo's suggestion a very good one, and I intend to follow through with it."

Ogodis lay the scroll on the desk top. "Indeed? And whom do you think would be best entrusted with traveling to the other end of the world, to pay our respects to the corpse of a barbarian conqueror?"

Elad suppressed a smile. "I, too," he allowed, "believe that the goal of civilization is to attain the highest ideals we can manage. But the choice of a strong candidate to deliver that message to the Salukadian empire perplexed me for some time, until the matter resolved itself splendidly right before my eyes."

Ogodis was thoughtful; his busy eyes betrayed his working mind. He lifted a jeweled finger to his bearded chin. "And what man," he inquired, "in your government has the abilities to . . . open this door but not have it slammed again in his face?"

Elad regarded the Imbur deliberately. "My choice is Queen Salia."

Ogodis's reaction to this decision was not in the least surprising.

4.

That evening, Adred was sitting on the balcony of his apartment sipping wine and enjoying a cool breeze as he went through some of the papers on which he and Galvus had been working. Daylight was fading early; Adred noticed storm clouds moving in off the ocean. He wanted to finish what he was doing before the first drops fell.

He was interrupted by footsteps in the main chamber. Thinking it to be a servant come to clean his supper tray, Adred paid no attention until the soft footfalls fell quiet directly behind him. He looked around to see that it was Omos.

"What?" Adred asked him, setting down his pen. "Anything wrong?"

"Oh, no, no . . ." Omos walked onto the balcony; Adred saw that the young man carried a small brown packet in one hand. He leaned on the rail, stretching until his shoulders popped; then he turned around, glanced at Adred and remembered what he was carrying. "This is for you. Abgarthis just gave it to me." He dropped the packet atop some of the papers on the table.

Adred smiled at him. "Thank you." He picked it up, saw that it was a letter and that the front of the packet was stamped with the seal of a commercial sailer—*Sulos*—*24 Sath 1879 D.P.*—and the scrawled signature of whoever had signed aboard parcels and deliveries.

Omos sat down in the chair opposite Adred.

"Wine?" Adred asked him. "There are some cups inside."

"No. Thank you." Omos was absently curling the corners of some papers with thumb and forefinger. "No . . . I don't feel like having any wine."

"Where's Galvus gone?" Adred asked. "Down to the cell?"

"Yes." The boy didn't look at him.

"Well—nothing's wrong, is there?"

"No . . . nothing wrong. It's just that—everything seems to be happening very quickly."

Adred smiled at him. "Yes, that's one of the problems with life, Omos. You'll find that out. Everything happens too quickly . . . Excuse me—but do you mind if I read this?"

"No, go right ahead."

Adred already suspected what it might be. He broke the packet's seal and took out the square of parchment inside, ripped the bit of wax that secured it and unfolded it.

Adred—A few lines only. I realize that it's been just a short while since you left, but somehow it seems longer. You might tell Galvus that everything here is fine, just as he left it. So he doesn't need to feel worried about that. But I think I could write this more easily than I could tell you face-to-face—especially that day out in the fields, on the farmhouse porch. It was difficult for me to say good-bye to you, even though I tried not to show it. I never meant to hurt you in anything I ever said or did—I want you to know that. Now that I'm on my own again, I find myself thinking back to that very first time we met, in Bessara, when I was talking to the people and you gave us all that money. It seems so long ago! And I find myself wondering about what it is that draws people together, whatever it is that makes people happen to one another, even for a short time. And I am glad that we knew one another and were able to spend those months together last winter. I understand now how important that was for me, and how much I depended on you. I respect you, and I admire you, and I want you to take care

210

of yourself always, because the world needs people like you. As I said, this would be difficult for me to tell you in person, because you know how I am. But I wanted you to know this. I think every person has her or his own very strong impulse, and for some people that impulse is love, and for other people it's other things. Maybe I'm wrong. But what brought you and I together for a while was an important purpose, and if we were able to make that into some kind of love for a while, I appreciate that. But I respect you, I admire you, I will always remember you and the lessons you helped me learn about myself. We must always believe in the best things we can, because that's the only way we can achieve them. Please take care of yourself, Adred, and think of me sometimes, and if or when we meet again, I hope you'll remember that you have a friend in me, and someone who believes in you. I don't know how else to say this.

Rhia

He set the letter on the table and looked out at the sky; he was very quiet. The first drops of rain began to fall. Adred felt them sting his face. He closed the letter, refolded it along its creases and slipped it inside its packet.

"Is it okay?" Omos asked him, concern in his voice.

Adred, with his emotions showing on his face, whispered to him: "Yes. It's okay." Because Omos was still watching him: "From Rhia. The woman in Sulos?"

"Yes, I remember her."

Adred nodded. "Just . . . a letter."

Omos smiled at him.

Adred began to collect the papers that were strewn on the table. He stood up as he shuffled them together and stacked them, slid them inside their folders. "We'd better get in," he remarked. "It's going to start storming."

Omos helped him carry the papers inside. Adred didn't bother closing the doors of the balcony because the fresh air and the smell of the new rain felt so good. He dropped into a chair, sipped his wine and mulled things over in his mind.

After a while, Omos excused himself and left to return to his room.

Adred took Rhia's letter from the pile of papers, opened it and reread it. Outside, thunder boomed, and curtains of driving rain

211

danced in splashes on the balcony floor, the stone table, the chairs. After he folded the letter again, Adred walked to a small bookcase and placed it in the special leather satchel he carried, placing Rhia's letter among the few books that were especially important to him, along with his father's letters and diaries.

He had nothing to say to them.

They stood, his wife and his son, just beyond his reach on the other side of the iron bars. Stood—watching him as though he were some kind of exotic or pathetic animal brought from the wilds for their sport. A vicious creature, untamed—a strange hybrid of strength and evil with a passing resemblance to a man . . .

Orain, when she had stood there last time, staring at the husband who had almost slain her in his rage, had trembled and begged him to understand. This time, she did not tremble, and she begged him for nothing. She was not fierce with him, neither was she haughty or angry. But she said to him:

"No matter what you have done—and you have slain the man I truly loved, and you were responsible for the death of a woman I truly loved—despite that, Cyrodian, I do not think you deserve death. I think it is only for the gods to decide death; and your execution will not answer the screams of those I loved, nor will it cleanse any of the blood that has already fallen."

He sneered at her—and found words to speak, at last. "Still pious, aren't you? Still protected from the world."

Orain shook her head. "It's not piety, Cyrodian. And I know all about the world. I know all about men like you, now."

"Do you?" He stared at her, moved his eyes to his son. "What about you?" he asked gruffly. "Do you know all about men like me?"

"I didn't come here to condemn you, either, Father," Galvus told him. "I didn't come down here to mock you. I came down here to talk."

"There's nothing to talk about."

"I disagree, because I'm your son, and I think sons always have many things to say to their fathers. And right now I want to tell you what I've been through, and what mother and I have been through, what we've suffered and come to believe—but it wouldn't matter to you. You wouldn't be able to understand; you'd refuse to understand. I think that's really what condemns you, too. That . . . refusal. You're the same man you've always been. Frightened."

Cyrodian glared at him.

"You're frightened of the world, Father, because it's bigger and stronger than you are, and it means more than you do, and you can't conquer it, you can't defeat it or punch it, so now you think that it's conquered you. You're full of hatred, and hatred is only weakness. You're full of fear because you refuse to try to understand anything. Not even yourself. And you won't discuss ideas, because to you ideas are useless things. You like to give orders, you like to issue commands and see things done—but you don't like to discuss ideas." Galvus told him: "I can't even pity you; there's nothing in you to pity."

Cyrodian stared at him for a very long time, black eyes burning beneath his tousled white hair. "Fear?" he asked. "And you're not afraid? Of anything?"

"Only of men like you, when you hold swords and charge at the world."

Cyrodian chuckled hollowly and leaned back on his chair, leaned back so that the shadows cast by the oil lamp in his cell covered his face. "Go away," he breathed. "I have nothing to say to you. Nothing I could say would change anything, anyway."

Orain glanced at Galvus. Galvus shook his head and nodded toward the corridor, suggesting that they leave. Orain began to move, then paused.

"We won't be back," she told her husband.

"Good."

"But if you'll tell me one thing, Cyrodian . . . I only want to know one thing."

His eyes burned at her from the shadows.

"Why?" Orain asked him. "Why did you murder Dursoris? Why did you want Queen Yta killed? Did you really think good would come of that? Did you really think you would help—this country—by doing these things?" She swallowed thickly. "Did you, Cyrodian? In your heart?"

He was silent. Staring at her. Orain thought he would not answer, and so she turned to leave.

Cyrodian's voice was hollow in the shadows. "Yes," he told her.

She watched him.

But he'd turned his head, he wasn't looking at her. "I am a strong man," Cyrodian said quietly. "And only strong men can accomplish things. And I wanted to use my strength to help my country become great again. If I failed—it's because people like

213

you . . . you failed to believe." Now he turned his stare toward her. "Yes," he told Orain a last time. "Now—leave me."

When they returned upstairs they heard the violence of the storm booming in the air, raining on the rooftops of the porticoes, breathing through the palace in long cool gusts. The downpour splashed on the window ledges of Orain's room; Galvus hurried to pull closed the sashes, then watched his mother carefully as she sat in a cushioned chair and lifted her hands to her chin.

"Are you all right?"

Orain smiled wanly. "Strangely enough, yes."

"Do you want me to order you some food, some wine?"

"No, Galvus. Thank you."

Omos came in through an annex chamber, and a moment later a knock on the door admitted Adred. In the grayness of the chamber, with the rain and the dampness, the four of them looked at one another quietly and realized that they did not have a great deal to say.

Finally, Galvus took Omos by the hand and led him out. "Let's let Mother rest a while. . . ."

But Adred did not leave. As Galvus closed the door softly behind him, Adred turned to Orain. "Anything I can do?" he asked her softly.

She shook her head, repositioned herself on the cushions, lifted one elbow to an arm of her chair and propped her cheek on her hand, contemplating. "It's so odd," she confessed.

Adred moved to sit down in the chair across from her. "What's so odd?"

"He hasn't changed, yet—he has. You remember him before. He seemed so—cruel, so one-minded. Something's happened in him, to him. . . ."

"What?"

"I can't say. He wouldn't tell us anything. Oh, he acts the way we expected him to act, but there's something about him, now. As if he's afraid. I mean it—truly afraid." She looked at Adred meaningfully.

Her comment disturbed him. "Because he realizes now that he's only mortal?"

Orain sniffled a sort of low laugh. "No . . . I don't mean that. I can't say what it is, precisely. Perhaps because he was away from Athadia, . . . away from home. Because all his plotting

214

failed. In a way, those were the only ties he had. He truly believes he was doing the right thing, Adred."

"Assassins always do; extremists always do. That revolutionary who tried to kill Elad thought the same thing. So do these churchmen who scream that everybody's wrong but them. Extremists—well, they always think that way."

Orain turned her head, looked across the room at nothing in particular. "Perhaps something happened in Emaria," she decided. "Or on the ship. His hair is . . . *white*!" Astounded by the fact, she half-smiled.

Adred continued to sit where he was, watching Orain as she sat quietly. She said little more and was apparently in no mood to chat; but she seemed to want Adred to stay with her. After about an hour, however, he decided to leave.

"I want you to lie down," he told Orain, walking over to her and taking her hands. He bent down and she kissed him. "Lie down and rest. Try to put all this out of your mind."

She made a face.

"Try," he urged her. "Don't"—smiling—"don't waste any more worrying energy over it, all right?"

She showed him a sad grin, remembering. "All right, Adred. . . ."

He kissed her hair, lifted her from the chair by her hands and walked her over to her bed, sat her down. "I'll come back later," he promised.

She nodded.

"Just clear your mind and . . . relax."

"I think I'd better. I'm starting to get a headache."

He kissed her again, lightly, on her hair and crossed the room to the door.

Lying back, Orain called to him: "Adred?"

"Yes?"

She wanted to tell him that she loved him: it was impulsive, this mood, but after looking at Cyrodian again and thinking back to Dursoris and remembering Sulos—she wanted to tell Adred that she loved him. But now, as she looked at him—what did she feel, with this hesitation? Pride? Self-consciousness? Uncertainty? "I—Nothing . . ."

Adred smiled. "Yes," he said to her. "I know. Me, too . . . Now, get some rest."

He closed her door quietly as he went out, drew the curtains in her antechamber and crossed the corridor to his room. The rain had let up, but the stone sill of the window he'd left open was dripping. Adred closed and locked the shutters, then glanced around; his eyes settled on the flask of wine on the far table. He'd ordered it brought up with supper, but he hadn't opened it yet.

He walked over to the table and picked up the bottle of wine, fought with it until he managed to open it with a small corkscrew. Then he loosened his belt, shoved the bottle halfway down his waist and pulled on a lightweight longcoat. He fit the cork loosely into the wine bottle again, fastened the coat and checked himself in his mirror before going out.

As he went through the palace, no one stopped him or hailed him or questioned him. Adred in his longcoat meant only that he was going for one of his renowned walks in the garden, or into the city for a meal and a drink in a tavern.

As he took the echoing stairs to the first floor, he met few people in the halls or on the staircases. It was getting late, and most of the palace residents or visitors were either in their rooms or at one of the intimate banquets the Councilors and ministers often hosted during the summer. As he moved toward the rear of the palace, past the kitchens and storage rooms, Adred could hear the muffled sounds of music and singers and the laughter of nobility. He took the rear stairs down a flight, went through a door and continued following the steps as they led to the lowest level of the palace— underground storerooms, ancillary weapons closets, fruit cellars and the prison.

Cyrodian wasn't sure what to make of his late-night visitor; he did not know the young Count Adred especially well, and from what he did know, he didn't particularly care for him. Immediately Cyrodian suspected that Galvus or Orain had sent Adred to him on some pretext.

But Count Adred assured Cyrodian that such was not the case. "They don't even know I'm here," he told the prisoner.

"Then why in hell *did* you come here?" Cyrodian growled, standing up and gripping the bars of his cell forcefully.

Adred stood in the flickering light of the torches. "That," he agreed, "is a very good question." He glanced down the way and saw that the door leading into the corridor had been closed. Good. He didn't suppose that the guard on duty thought his visit any more suspicious than anyone else's, but Adred wanted to remain cautious. Carefully, eyes on the barred window at the end of the hall, he opened his longcoat and pulled the wine bottle from his belt.

216

Cyrodian's eyes widened. "What's that you have there?"

"Wine." Adred undid the loosened cork and dropped it to the floor; there was no chair in the corridor, so he leaned against the wall opposite Cyrodian's cell, picked up one leg and held it to the stone, sipped the wine.

Cyrodian growled, "You son of a bitch, did you come here to—"

"Watch it!"

"—did you come here to drink wine and just *look* at me?"

Adred wiped his mouth. "No." He coughed slightly, sipped again. "No . . . I didn't."

"Then why *did* you come down here?"

Adred stepped away from the wall, approached the cell bars and held the wine bottle out to Cyrodian. "Don't drink the whole thing," he said, "but I'll drink with you."

Cyrodian eyed him suspiciously.

"All right, then . . . I *won't* drink with you. What do you think? That it's poisoned?"

Cyrodian scratched his nose, then reached a big hand through the bars; Adred let him take the wine. Cyrodian sniffed it, took a long swallow and sighed heartily as he pulled the bottle from his lips. It made a smacking sound.

Adred held out his hand. "If you don't mind . . ."

The giant returned the bottle; Adred wiped the mouth of it with the palm of one hand and sipped some more.

"So . . ." Cyrodian belched. "Why are you here, Count Adred?"

"They told me—when they came back, Orain and Galvus both said that you'd changed."

"They're lying."

"No, no—they meant it. It seemed to them that you'd changed."

Cyrodian eyed him keenly. "Do you think I've changed?"

"I don't know. I don't know you well enough. Your hair's turned white. . . ."

Cyrodian sniffed.

"How did that happen?"

"I don't know."

"You've got to admit that's a pretty remarkable thing, for a man's hair to turn snow white overnight."

"How do you know it happened overnight?"

"Well, then, within a few months."

Cyrodian, holding the bars, leaned back; shadows hid his face, but he grunted a series of low laughs. He breathed heavily, pulled himself forward again and reached through the bars. "Give me some more wine."

Adred handed him the bottle.

Cyrodian tipped it high and swallowed a great deal; he didn't give it back. "The world's going to hell. You know that, don't you?"

"I've suspected it for quite some time now."

"Oh, you have, have you?" Cyrodian sneered. "You and your . . . philosophers. What the hell good are you, Count Adred?"

"Oh, I'm probably worth my weight in gold. My bankers think so, anyway. And a few friends consider me a passable card player."

Cyrodian chuckled. "Do you know what it's like to be a real man?"

"I think so."

"Do you own a sword?"

"Yes."

"Can you use it?"

"I know how to defend myself."

"Did you ever kill anyone?"

"No," Adred admitted, "I haven't. Do you think it's essential to kill a person before you can call yourself a man?"

"It helps."

"Well, I'm disqualified, then. Could I have another sip of wine?"

"No." To assure him of that, Cyrodian nearly emptied the bottle with another long draft. When he pulled it from his mouth, he coughed and seemed a little dizzied.

Adred wondered if he'd had anything to eat all day.

Cyrodian leaned against the bars, regarded his visitor with tight eyes. "Do you know what a sorcerer is, Count Adred?"

"I've . . . heard of them."

"They're real. Yes, they are . . . I know. I met two sorcerers."

"Did you?" Adred sounded doubtful. "Is that why your hair turned—"

"One of them, . . . I cut him with my sword . . . cut him twice. He can't die."

"What do you mean, he can't die?"

"He lives in Lasura, with King Nutatharis. The cockeater can't die. You don't believe me, do you? All right . . . don't believe me. I'm telling you what I know. I stabbed him twice, right here." Cyrodian pushed the thumb of his free hand into his belly, just below the sternum; he belched slightly. "It hurts, you catch a sword there. But this one—he just looked at me. The second time, you know what I did? I moved the sword around. Stuck it in him, moved it back and forth, and—no blood." The giant laughed grimly. "He couldn't *die!*" He groaned and yawned, leaned against the bars again. "You don't believe me."

"You must admit, it's a strange story. But . . . anything's possible."

"That's right. Anything *is* possible." Cyrodian finished the wine but held onto the empty bottle; it clanked against the iron bars. "You want to know why my hair turned white?"

"Yes."

"You sure you do?"

"Yes, I'm sure."

Cyrodian looked at him, glanced down the hall, rubbed his forehead against the cell bars. Abruptly he looked up and eyed Adred tensely. "You think I'm drunk, don't you?"

"It doesn't matter. That's why I brought the wine. Everyone should get drunk once in a while. Only"—he smiled thinly—"I thought I'd get to taste more of it."

Cyrodian barked a cruel laugh. "You can always get wine. Elad won't *let* them give me any wine. If he were any kind of man himself, he'd know he should let a condemned prisoner have some wine, or a decent meal—at least his wife—before he goes to the axe."

Adred didn't say anything to that.

"You really want to know why my hair turned white? I'll tell you. It was the second sorcerer I met. You know what an *ikbusa* is?"

"They're not sorcerers, they're priests."

"This one was a sorcerer. . . . Why am I telling you all this?" Cyrodian wondered aloud.

Adred shrugged. "Because you drank all the wine, and you have to tell someone. Tell a stranger. It's the guilt."

"I don't feel guilty about anything."

"Maybe you do, maybe you don't. Maybe you only think you don't."

Cyrodian stared at him, then nodded with a heavy head; the

219

wine was indeed affecting him. "I suppose . . . that's right."
He shook his face, wiped back his hair with his free hand. He
fingered his hair, clutched it, yanked out a clump of long strands
and stared at them. "White," he murmured.

Adred stepped closer.

"They had me in a cage," Cyrodian said. "They had me in a
cage, like an animal. Had me . . . in chains. Chained. We
were—I don't know where; it doesn't matter. In Ithulia, I think. It
doesn't matter. This little village. And they had me in this cage,
and there was this priest—this *ikbusa*—in this town. Aswassa-
ahh . . . Asawas? Asawas? Awasa . . . It doesn't matter. Telling . . . stories. You know—all about god and all about this and
all . . . that. Be a good person. God loves you. All that ass shit.
Anyhow . . ."

"Go on," Adred whispered, feeling something inside him, a
remembrance of the *ikbusa* he'd heard preaching in the uplands.

"He spotted me. Saw me in the cage and—he knew who I was.
I don't know how. A sorcerer. He looks at me, he's watching me,
all these people around, and he starts talking about this and that—
I'm an evil man and I cause pain to everybody—all this ass shit.
Like I'm the only man who ever put the sword to these bastards
who deserved it in the first place. So he's telling me what a sad-
forsaken son-of-a-bitch I am . . . I spit in his eye, I remember
doing that . . . and then he starts talking about . . . I don't
know." Cyrodian, an arm's length from Adred, leaning on the
bars, stared at him, and Adred could smell the wine on his breath.
"It was his *eyes*! You know how these dogs get, so that it gets in
their *eyes*? They're not men anymore, but it's like they've been
chewing on leaves, like they're—ghosts inside? And their eyes
seem to—the eyes *glow* or—"

Adred swallowed thickly.

"—but he said to me—I can still see these *eyes*, and the heat—
it was very hot—all the dust, everywhere . . . and he's looking
at me, he's looking *through* me . . . and he's telling me what a
son-of-a-bitch I am, and then he tells me—"

Adred saw tears forming in Cyrodian's eyes.

"—he tells me . . . my mother . . . that Yta—"

He stopped abruptly. Stared at Adred. The giant colored; he
held out his free hand, pushed it between the bars and stared at it.
Wide, thick, hairy, . . . and it was shivering. Trembling. Adred
stared at the hand. The hand moved.

Adred gasped. Instantly the hand was at his collar. Cyrodian gripped him and pulled him forward; Adred was jerked as though he weighed nothing. Cyrodian spun him around and pulled him tightly against the cell bars, wrapped his huge arm around Adred's chest to pin his arms to his sides.

"What the hell do you think you're—"

There was an explosion as Cyrodian smashed the empty wine bottle upon the iron bars. With the broken neck in his left hand he threatened to cut Adred's face, or slice his throat.

"Cyrodian! What the *hell* do you—"

"Shut up, you piece of scum!" The dripping glass wavered in his hand. "Who the hell do you think you are," Cyrodian growled, "coming in here and getting me drunk, making me tell you—"

"What are you *afraid* of?" Adred gasped, not fighting Cyrodian's hold on him. He was sweating; he tried to roll his eyes around, but all he saw was the wall across from him, the torch in its sconce, and the yellow light of the torch shimmering on the rough edges of the broken wine bottle.

"Son-of-a-*bitch*!" Cyrodian grunted, his breath like a cloud on Adred's face. "Who do you think you *are*? You like to hear all this—all this *shit*? You think you're *better* than me because you never *killed* anybody, you little baby-cock?"

"No one wants to see you die, Cyrodian!" Adred said, as boldly as he could.

The giant didn't say anything, didn't move.

Adred tried to swallow, to get some air. "Why would I come down here just to look at you? Just to give you wine? Damn it, don't you think I have *demons* inside *me*, too?"

He felt Cyrodian's heavy arm relax.

Strangely, then, as he waited there, eyes on the broken bottle, trapped by Cyrodian's massive arm, Adred recalled Rhia's letter to him that afternoon. Her careful printing jumped out at him from the paper. *I am glad that we knew one another. . . . I respect you, and I admire you, and I want you to take care of yourself always, because the world needs people like you. . . .*

Cyrodian coughed. "That's—"

Adred stared at the shivering, broken bottle.

"That's true . . . I suppose . . ." Cyrodian muttered.

The broken bottle wavered . . . slowly lowered. . . .

"Gods," Cyrodian whispered. "Can't even drink wine—anymore . . ."

His great arm fell from Adred's chest. As soon as he felt it drop, Adred jumped, throwing himself against the wall opposite the cell. Wild-eyed, panting, he turned and stared at the giant.

But Cyrodian wasn't looking at him. He was sinking into a crouch on the floor, just inside the bars. "Get out of here," he muttered.

Still breathless and shaking, Adred said to him: "Not—yet . . ."

Cyrodian looked up, anger in his eyes. "I said for you to get out of here, cockeater!"

Adred shook his head and held out a trembling hand. "Give me the . . . broken bottle."

"Right between your legs," Cyrodian smiled.

"I mean it. If you stab yourself with that and bleed to death, Elad'll put *my* neck on the block."

"So?"

"Damn it, Cyrodian!" Adred nearly yelled, then glanced quickly down the hall toward the door. "Just give me the bottle!"

The giant tilted his head to one side, stared at Adred as he lifted the sharp edge directly above his pulsing throat—as though meaning to do it and daring Adred to stop him.

"*Cyrodian!*"

He didn't move.

"What do you want me to do?" Adred asked him hotly, straining to keep his voice down. "Tell you that I don't think you're a fool? That I don't think you're wrong? You want me to ask Elad not to axe you? What?"

"You're the fool," Cyrodian whispered, head still bent.

"*What*, Cyrodian?"

"I want you to tell—" At last, the giant lowered his arm and let his head fall upon his chest. "Tell—Orain . . ."

Adred breathed again. "Tell her what?"

He moved suddenly. Lifted his arm high and cast the broken bottle through the cell bars. It struck the floor on the other side of the corridor, at the base of the wall, and shattered.

Adred shot a terrified look to the door—but the latch did not lift, no guard peered through the window.

"Damn it!" he complained. "I'm as stupid as you are!"

Cyrodian chuckled, then yawned.

Adred nervously began kicking bits of the broken bottle farther down the floor, where they might be hidden in the shadows. He stopped when he came close to the cell and warily regarded

Cyrodian. But the giant said nothing to him, only stood up with a grunt and stalked to his cot; he lay down on it with a heavy noise and stretched back. Adred quickly kicked away the bits of broken glass that remained around the cell bars and just inside. Then he straightened his clothes, took a last look at Cyrodian and started to walk away.

"Count Adred."

He looked back but could not see within the shadows. "What?"

"Did you mean what you said? Did you mean . . . what you told me?"

"About what, General?"

"*General*?"

"About *what*?"

"About . . . you having your own demons inside you. Did you mean that?"

"What do *you* think?"

Silence.

Adred continued down the corridor. When he came to the door, he pulled on the handle; the door opened easily. But the noise of the latch awakened the guard sleeping just on the other side. Adred told him that the prisoner was resting, then quickly took the stairs up into the palace.

5.

In the night-dark, torchlit garden, their voices rose with anger and pride, and their footsteps sounded loud and echoed, as Salia hurried from path to path while her father, the proud Ogodis, followed her, protesting. Flying leaves burst from every bush he passed, punctuating his explosions of temper.

"I don't *mean* to hurt you!" he clarified, referring to what he had said. "I only mean that—"

Salia stopped short and turned on him, lifted her head high and protested coldly: "You don't *know* me well enough to *hurt* me, Father! You don't know me at all! What do you think I am? *Who* do you think I am? Only your daughter? Tell me!"

"Salia, listen to—"

"You've tried to make me into some . . . some other kind of *you*! And I'm not! Elad understands me better than you do!"

"Oh, in the name of the gods, Salia, don't be stupid!"

"*Stupid*?" she shot back. She would have said more—the threat of it erupted from her as a trapped squeal—but she suddenly moved on, clacking down the garden path in her slippers, heading for the torchlit wall that marked the palace entrance.

Ogodis chased after her, his voice rising with renewed humiliation and anger. "I am your *father*! You will listen with *respect* to what I'm telling you!"

"And *I* am—" She stopped again, turned once more and faced him fiercely; backlit by the torches, hair blowing in the breeze, she reminded him: "I am the *queen* of Athadia, Father!"

"Don't you dare throw that in my face!"

"Do you understand what that means?"

"You will show me resp—"

"You will show *me* respect, Father! You will—"

He slapped her. Terribly hard, so that the sound of his hand on her face carried throughout the garden.

And instantly Ogodis, stunned by what he had done, fell back a step and stared in shock at his daughter. "Why did you—make me do that? . . ."

Salia, the tears dripping from her lashes, glared at him with eyes of cold light, turned a last time and hastened down the path.

"Salia, *please*!"

But she continued running from him.

"Daughter!"

She would not listen. Ogodis came after her, not chasing her, only following her, his heart heavy, his hand still stinging. When he reached the end of the path and passed under a decorated arch that led to the palace entranceway, he heard his daughter sobbing and looked to see her clutching Elad. They stood at the top of the stairs in the shadows of the recessed door.

With hollow steps, Ogodis approached.

"In the name of the gods!" Elad whispered to him. "The whole palace could hear you!"

Abgarthis moved from his window and faced Count Adred, who was sitting at a small table nervously tightening and relaxing his hands. He asked the minister, more out of courtesy than true interest:

"Who was it?"

"The queen and her father. Arguing in the gardens. But—continue."

"That's all there is to tell," Adred sighed, leaning back in his chair. "Except to say that I was pretty stupid for doing it."

224

"Well, foolish," Abgarthis commented diplomatically. "Foolish for doing it in the way you did, but not specifically for doing it. Of course you were curious; we all are. And your assumption was right; Cyrodian did open up to you, where he refused to speak to anyone else."

Adred frowned and fingered his throat. "Yes . . ."

Abgarthis smiled and walked toward him.

"But that talk about a sorcerer—two sorcerers." Adred shook his head. "Was he lying to me, Abgarthis?"

The minister sat down across from him. "I'm tempted to say that he was deluded, but such might not be the case. I'm convinced there are such men, and that there is such a thing as magic, or sorcery."

Adred gave him a questioning look.

"Human beings," Abgarthis told him, "can do the most remarkable things; and the longer one lives, the more one tends to suspect that there is far more unknown in this world than it is possible for our mentalities to comprehend. I haven't forgotten an incident which happened in my youth. I had just come to Evarris's court, here, and he had planned a fete that lasted several days. One of the attractions was a strange man who claimed to be a prestidigitator. His name, as I recall, was Iram-adias. Very peculiar fellow. I remember that the dogs did not like him; they ran from him. He accomplished some astounding tricks, but he was most unfriendly and would not even join the nobles at their table when he'd finished his performance. Evarris rewarded him with gold and asked him to stay on for a time, but he refused. I remember hearing some of the courtiers at the time discussing the man's strange tricks. Several of them had been to the east for one reason or another and claimed that sorcerers are not uncommon there, and that a number of the illusions this Iram-adias had performed smelled to them of the same business. He certainly had a peculiar feel to him." Abgarthis remarked again, "So I suppose such things are possible. There are many strange things on earth and in the heavens. Well . . . that matter of the birds, for example—the ones you saw dive into the sea last summer."

"Yes . . ." Adred nodded slowly. "But—Cyrodian's hair turning white?"

"It seems astounding, I know, but there again I've heard of similar instances. From battlefields. Apparently when some individuals undergo a severe shock—a life-or-death incident—it can cause a whitening of the hair. Whether or not this *ikbusa* who spoke with Cyrodian was a magician—does it matter? Some of these traveling priests are very wise men, some are scoundrels; but all of them know much about human behavior. If, through insight, this one planted a few suggestions in Cyrodian's head, caught him at a weak moment—look at the condition he was in, after all—well . . . Cyrodian must have caused it to happen himself." Abgarthis smiled and shook his head. "I begin to sound like one of your philosophers. 'Are we the cause, or are we the caused?'"

Adred's chin was propped on his hand. Changing the subject, he remarked, "He *will* be executed, won't he, Abgarthis?"

"Yes, I'm afraid so."

Voices rose again from the garden, loud but obscure. Adred eyed the old minister. "Elad?"

Abgarthis sighed.

"What are they arguing about?" Adred asked. "Not Cyrodian, surely."

"No. . . . I believe Elad intends to make an announcement tomorrow morning, in Council. I'll tell you, if you promise to keep it to yourself for a while."

"Tell me what, Abgarthis?"

"You see? All this back chamber whispering and pretense, . . . after a while, life is too short; one should be straightforward. Well . . . Did you hear about the letter that General Thomo send Elad? No? You're aware that Huagrim of Salukadia is dead. Well, he has two sons, the elder is due to inherit the throne, and our relationship with the eastern empire is potentially unstable. Thomo was sent there by Elad to negotiate trade policies and so forth; now he finds himself in the middle of their change of throne. We're not sure, precisely, what that means within their government, but the proper course to take would seem to be the dispatching of a representative from our government to meet with their new *Ghen*. Thomo suggested it, and Elad has agreed to it."

"But I don't understand why that should upset the Imbur and the queen. Elad isn't going himself, is he?"

"No, no, no. He's sending a representative."

"But we really don't have anyone qualified to—" Then it dawned on him. "Not Queen Salia?"

"I'm afraid so."

Adred, at first astounded, in a moment bared an unfriendly smile. "*Salia*?"

"Now, now—be temperate." Abgarthis waved a hand. "It may not be so unusual an idea, after all."

"But Queen Salia is—"

"I know . . . we know. But we can't really spare anyone else at present, can we? Elad's sending many diplomats and so forth along with her. Salia's appearance will no doubt be purely a cosmetic one—I don't mean that to be taken the wrong way," Abgarthis smiled.

Adred let out a low whistle. "No wonder Ogodis is so upset!"

Abgarthis agreed. "Yes, she's going to be out from under his thumb, for a while. I have no doubt that Elad could have made a worse choice for a wife, but he might also have waited and made a wiser decision. He acted rather impulsively where Salia is concerned. I suppose it was reaction to what was happening at the time."

"Was he simply attracted to her beauty, do you think?"

"Oh, beauty," the minister replied, somewhat disdainfully. "Yes, she's extraordinarily attractive—but we've all bought beautiful vases that crack the moment we set them on the table. Salia is . . . I want to be fair, because she has certain strong elements in her. She's not unintelligent; she's simply—inexperienced, and unaware of so many things, and not willing to discipline herself. I'm sure it comes from the way the Imbur raised her and still treats her. Human beings are rather fragile; I suspect that our inner selves, and our hearts, are settled in us early on. You understand what I mean. The child reflecting the parent, its surroundings. We have people in the slums who are of golden character; then, we have nobles who— I shouldn't be judgmental."

Adred grinned. "Then I will be!" he said. "Ogodis . . . I don't care for him."

"Frankly, I dislike him intensely too; I dislike his values, his pride. . . . We are two entirely different sorts of men. And while I have never had any children myself—thank Mother Hea—this is clearly one instance where even an old bachelor can accuse a father of having botched his job."

"Her mother is dead?" Adred asked. "What would she have been—the Imburess?"

"Something like that, I suppose," Abgarthis yawned. "Yes. She died giving birth to Salia. And Ogodis seems to have poured every resentment and every fantasy and lost dream he held straight into his daughter during her maturing years. She hasn't traveled

227

much; she knows nothing about communicating with her own sex; she finds animals better companions than she does people. Gods! But she's a bright girl, there's no doubt about that. She's incredibly well-read, well-educated. Have you noticed that?"

"I haven't really spoken with her. Just in the garden, when we came back from Sulos."

"Oh, yes. Well, she speaks several languages and has a phenomenal memory. If the Imbur would go home so that the palace could settle down, I suppose that in ten or fifteen years Salia might mature adequately into quite a woman. I wouldn't be surprised."

Adred nodded politely.

"What bothers me most," Abgarthis went on, "is that she really doesn't know herself. You've known people like that. It's very disturbing, it truly is. She seems to need others around, needs them to—validate, perhaps—her own identity, her idea of herself. It's disturbing to see that sort of ignorance in a person. And she gets pig-headed enough to want her demands met constantly, no matter how foolish they are. She never admits it if she's wrong. She's like a bird in a cage that squawks to be let out, then once freed tries to get back inside. She's . . . frustrating!"

Abgarthis fell quiet, stared at the open window and the night and sighed heavily. Adred saw the minister's expression turn contemplative. Abgarthis said somberly, "Pride's wounds,

> too deep for hope to heal—
> The prisoning heart that suffocates love—
> The sorrowing vengeance that love cannot placate."

"That's rather grim," Adred remarked. "Your verse?"

"Oh, no . . ." Abgarthis rubbed his forhead. "Sivian. A poet from the 1600s. Too romantic for people to read these days."

"They're certainly interesting sentiments."

Abgarthis nodded. "Those lines, I believe, are from *The Crucible of Hope*." He shook his head. "The crucible of hope, indeed." Groaning a little, he stood up and rubbed his hands together. "I believe I'm getting sleepy," he announced.

Adred rose immediately to his feet. "I'm sorry. It *is* getting late. I didn't mean to desturb you."

"Not at all. I'm glad you came by." Thoughtfully, then: "I won't mention what happened—between you and Cyrodian—if you'd prefer that I don't."

"I'd appreciate that."

"Certainly. And now . . ."

"Good night, Abgarthis. Before I turn in, I think I'd better see about finding another bottle of wine. . . ."

Because the two wings of the Athadian Royal Council—the Congress of Nobility and the Congress of Common Administration—were in recess for another week, King Elad, in preparing for the first investigative hearings on the matter of the workers' *sirots*, faced a mere ten ministers in his Council Chamber on the morning of the twenty-sixth of Sath. To them he read his official proclamation that "Queen Salia, in the company of the following named ambassadors," would sail to the city of Erusabad within the Salukadian empire where she would, for a period of two months and in accordance with the guidelines "here set down, act as an emissary of good will and international trust between the Athadian and the Salukadian nations."

His pronouncement was met with awed silence.

Elad was under no compulsion to explain his decision to his Council; neither was there permitted any vote or bargaining by members of Council on such a matter. It was purely an imperial concern. It in no way affected the military, which was under the nominal control of the *Priton* Nobility, nor did it (in its literal interpretation) affect the imperially sanctioned mercantile interests, also under the control of the *Priton* Nobility. Neither did it affect the public funds or assemblies or organizations under the jurisdiction of the *Priton* Common Administration. It was solely the king's authority that prevailed in matters of ambassadorship and international relations as well as in matters affecting the Imperial Treasury.

Nevertheless, as the awareness of the King's audacious plan began to settle in the minds of those few Councilors present, one of them—a Lord Oslin—lifted his hand for permission to take the floor.

Elad, from his throne dais, regarded him critically. "Anything you have to say, Lord Oslin, cannot affect my decision."

"True, King Elad. But I should like to go on record with a statement concerning your proclamation."

Elad could not refuse him that. "You have the floor, then."

Oslin bowed his head and stood up, moved from his seat and walked around the long stone table of the Nobility, saluted his king with the gesture of respect and faced his fellow Councilors.

229

"I should like to declare, and have it so recorded by the scribe, that while I am in agreement with our king concerning the need to improve our relations with the Salukadian empire, I do not think that now is the proper time for us to do more than negotiate trade privileges—which envoys already sent to Erusabad are engaged in—nor do I consider our queen, nor any member of the royal family, whatever their other merits or abilities, suitable representatives to visit the eastern empire, at this time. I believe we should begin this process more slowly, make certain of mutual guarantees, and have our current ambssadors come to certain terms with the Salukadians before anyone from the Imperial House, for any reason whatsoever, sets foot on eastern soil." Oslin turned to face Elad. "I say this from my heart, wishing only the best for the future of our country."

Elad nodded succinctly and told him, "I respect your feelings, Lord Oslin. Thank you." He answered the Councilor's salute, then addressed his assembly. "If you gentlemen and lords will now permit me—"

"I would like to make a protest!" came a loud voice from the rear of the Nobility.

A heavy silence gripped the Chamber; as calmly as he could, Elad looked in Ogodis's direction.

"The Imbur of Gaegosh," he said tensely, "is a guest in this hall, but he has no voice in our affairs, nor any voice in this decision."

"You are sending my daughter," Ogodis yelled, rising, "into the jaws of a—"

"Sit down, Imbur!"

"—into the jaws of a dragon that will only—"

"I said, *sit down, Imbur!*"

"You are deliberately risking an international situation simply to glorify your own—"

"Guards!" Elad yelled, looking away.

"—glorify your own ambitions to—"

"*Guards!*" Elad howled, fisting one side of his throne tensely, staring at his lap and refusing to look either at Ogodis or at his Councilors.

"Why do you think that any 'good will' will mollify a dragon that obviously—"

The heavy sounds of boots filled the hall as the few Khamars positioned at the entry doors opened them and called for the services of their brothers in the outer corridor. Four from the main foyer entered and saluted King Elad.

"If you will please," he ordered with barely restrained fury, "escort the Imbur of Gaegosh from this hall?"

The Khamars moved toward him.

Ogodis held his ground, slamming his fist on the table, glaring at Elad and continuing to yell at him for the few moments left him. "You are jeopardizing my daughter's—your *wife's*!—very life by sending her into the jaws of this so-called empire, simply because of trade rights and your fears that—"

"*Peace*, Imbur!" Elad yelled at him, unable to withstand any more. "Do you recall what you said about *peace*, Imbur?"

"I *will not* have my—"

Two Khamars carefully took hold of his arms. "Your lordship . . ."

Ogodis did not fight them but continued railing as they led him from the table, his face purpling and sweating, his head turned to keep his eyes on the king. "If you think any good can come of extending an open hand to these barbarians—"

"*Will you be a man about it*?" Elad suddenly shouted, rising from his seat and shooting a wrathful look at his father-in-law. "Can't you let her out of your sight even for *one day*, Ogodis?"

"Mark me! Mark my words, Athadians! He will—"

And then he was removed outside the door and led into the corridor, while those Khamars who remained in the Chamber pulled the great doors closed.

Shaking, Elad sat down again, rubbed his aching forehead, stared at his Councilors and stared beyond them to the overcast day showing through the high, open windows. "Gentlemen," he began—but then said no more.

He turned to his scribe. "You will strike all that passed between myself and the Imbur."

"My lord, I have written nothing since Lord Oslin's statement."

Elad smiled thinly at him. "Good," he sighed. "Good. . . ."

6.

Last summer, before Yta had left on her voyage to Hea Isle, she had presented Galvus with a memento of his murdered uncle: a small gold locket that the queen had had made for Dursoris at his birth. Not intrinsically any more valuable than an ordinary, well-crafted locket, it contained inside it a small ivory cameo of Lady Orain, which Dursoris had secretly commissioned from one of the palace artisans. Galvus, aware at the moment his grandmother gave him the locket of just how important Dursoris's feelings had been for Orain, promised to keep it with him always: as a reminder both that true love could actually exist in the world and that his Uncle Dursoris, slain by his own father, had been a voice for justice and responsibility in the Imperial House.

This afternoon, as he watched the commencement of his father's execution, Galvus removed the locket from his vest and held it tightly in his right hand. A reminder . . .

A scaffold had been erected that morning in the western courtyard, just beyond the palace gardens. The three streets leading into the Fountain Square, which sat across from the courtyard, were heavily guarded by long lines of city soldiers and Khamars on horseback. Elad had allowed the public to witness the execution, but he had limited their access to the courtyard, fearing a spontaneous reaction—not necessarily because of any sentiments toward Cyrodian himself, but simply because tensions were running high. The rising joblessness, the increasing poverty and frustration, the hot, dry summer were potentially violent elements mixed in a simmering cauldron. Despite its acknowledgement that Cyrodian deserved to go to the block, the army had within it many members who still remembered whispered details concerning the events that had brought Elad to the throne; and, as well, there were many in the crowd who were eager to see the murderer of good Queen Yta meet his end with a taste of the violence the queen had suffered. Too, the public had not witnessed anything like this within the memory of anyone still living: the last of the imperial executions in Athad had taken place just after the civil wars. Banishment of royalty had superseded public bloodshed, and the post of imperial executioner had been abolished by King Darion II, Evarris's great-grandfather.

So the spectacle of Cyrodian's imperially sanctioned murder, its novelty and sense of vengeance, was not lost on the people of Athad, whose appetites had long been whetted by the tamer exhibitions of the arena. Entrepreneurs had started early, just before dawn, charging eager spectators a copper or two for the privilege of sitting atop public buildings that lent clear views of the courtyard below. By the time Elad had dismissed his brief Council meeting that morning, the crowds were swollen in the streets, and hawkers and vendors filled their purses by offering cold water and fresh fruit and skins of beer and wine.

Elad had discussed with Captains Mirsus and Uvars, and with those members of the Congress of Nobility who were on favorable terms with the military leaders, the wisdom of allowing high-ranking army officials to witness the ceremonial beheading. Assured by these intermediaries that the army would not in any way interfere with or try to delay the execution, the king had ordered a hundred or so seats made available just within the walls of the courtyard. Now, when Elad led his royal family and observers from Council onto the wide balcony overlooking the western gardens, these army officials stood as one and saluted him in a show of support, as trumpets blared to announce the king's entrance.

Elad stepped up to the balcony wall and, with a lowering of his arm, signaled the Khamars on duty to escort the prisoner from his cell. As they entered the palace, disappearing from view beneath the balcony, another Khamar, dressed in black breeches and vest, his face covered with a long hood, entered the courtyard from a garden gate and crossed the bricks to the scaffolding. As he mounted the wooden stairs, the great axe he carried in one hand bounced heavily, betraying his corded muscles. This guard's identity was unknown to anyone, even to King Elad: an extremely complex procedure had been followed wherein a dozen Khamars chose colored tiles from sealed boxes, the boxes delivered to each Khamar separately by three different palace servants. None of the Khamars knew which of them had chosen the black tile, for each was ordered to a single, separated cell in various barracks houses throughout the city, in which cell each was to remain until well after the execution. The Khamar whose lot it was to perform the execution had been instructed to follow an elaborate path through the palace and through a secret passageway to an ancillary armory where he would dress and choose a weapon; following the execution, he would return to his cell by the same secret route.

Abgarthis had devised this complex scheme, and Elad had adopted it to insure that no one involved might feel the least bit of guilt or shame. "It is the state which orders Cyrodian dead," Abgarthis had said. "Not simply the king. And it is not simply one man out of thousands who will slay him; it is every citizen in the empire."

Standing to Elad's right on the balcony was Queen Salia, and beside her the wise Abgarthis, and just behind Abgarthis, a dour Imbur Ogodis. To Elad's left stood Prince Galvus, beside him Orain, and to her left, Count Adred. Omos, not eager to witness the violence, stood behind Galvus. Stretching along the balcony on either side of the royal family, two rows deep, gathered the dozens of Councilors, ministers and necessary officials of the state.

Galvus held tightly onto Dursoris's locket.

Orain gripped Adred's hand in hers, their clasp hidden by the balcony wall.

As the throngs below swayed and murmured, yelled and laughed, Elad watched the soldiers in the courtyard, then looked out over his city, and remembered many things.

"I'm a man of my word, Elad. If he can't tell what happened, he can't take it to court. You're going to be king, and no one is going to stop that! I haven't put in a lifetime of planning to have you back down now!"

From the heavy clouds high above, a few stray raindrops fell; they splashed off the balcony wall, spattering silently.

"What? Have they named you, brother? Did they discover the blood on your sword?"

Trumpets blared again. A wave of noise flowed back through the crowds from those nearest the spectacle in the Fountain Square. In the courtyard, the military officers stood at attention.

"Oh, gods! Live, Dursoris, liiiiive! I do not want this throne!"

The Khamar escort came out of the palace bearing the bound Cyrodian, only his hair showing above the gleaming crested helmets. The officers of the army saluted the giant and called out: "Hrux! Hrux!" It had been their nickname for him in the service. "Hrux! Hrux! *Hrux!*"

And he remembered the Oracle. *"Already the future takes hold of you, Prince Elad. You will take the throne, and none other after you, and you will rule to see everything precious destroyed, every hope ruined, every man and woman wailing in torment. . . ."*

"Hrux! Hrux! *Hrux!*"

As Cyrodian was led to the steps of the stage, the trumpeter let out another strident blast.

Rain fell softly in wavering breezes upon the silent, expectant crowds.

Cyrodian did not fight as two Khamars walked him up the steps and onto the platform and stood him before the block.

Thunder boomed, high above, and heat lightning hissed far away, over the ocean.

Orain gripped Adred's hand so tightly, he almost felt pain. He glanced at her: tears threatened at the rims of her eyes, but she stared straight ahead. She stared not at Cyrodian but out over the city—out to where masts and sails were rocking in the harbor, beyond the city walls.

Another trumpet blast—and an official of the Law Court stepped up onto the stage, stood before the masked executioner, unrolled a parchment and read aloud King Elad's decree.

"For the grievous and unpardonable crimes of fratricide, the conspiracy of matricide, the conspiracy of assassination of the Queen of the Empire and a Prince of the Empire, for the conspiracy to assassinate the King of the Empire—"

Elad looked down.

Cyrodian was staring at him.

"—this throne hereby declares the prisoner, Cyrodian *dos* Evarro *edos* Yta, once Prince General Crescented of the Athadian Empire—"

Elad swallowed and looked away.

"—to be condemned to death by public execution on the twenty-sixth day of Sath of this year. By me, Elad *sollos don* Athadia, on this date, twenty-sixth Sath in the Age of the Birth of Our Prophet 1879."

The official looked up, rolled the scroll, cleared his throat and asked in as loud a voice as he could muster: "Has the prisoner any last statement to make before the decree is complied with?"

Thunder boomed high above. Thousands of eyes in the courtyard and in the streets and from the buildings all around stared at the stage. The rain fell more heavily, wetting Cyrodian's hair and face and beard, beginning to drip down his tunic and pants. He glanced up at the balcony again, stared at Elad, stared at Galvus and Orain.

Orain sobbed. Overcome, she turned to Adred, threw her arms about him and dropped her head on his shoulder.

Adred's heart stopped. He stared at Cyrodian—

—and the giant trembled. He threw back his head—

"Has the prisoner any last—"

—and laughed like a demon, laughed loudly and forcefully, his tremendous voice carrying up and out from the courtyard, booming as the thunder boomed. Laughed and laughed and laughed.

The official eyed him apprehensively. The hooded Khamar twisted the axe in nervous hands. Was the tension, prolonged and not yet expressed, at last breaking through, a dam before a flood?

Cyrodian half-turned, wriggled his shoulders with difficulty because his arms were tied so tightly behind his back. "Kill me now!" he bellowed to the executioner. "Kill me now, and be done with it! Those are my words!"

Adred glanced at Elad; he saw the king's hands curl and tighten upon the edge of the balcony wall.

Cyrodian knelt down, crashing to his knees awkwardly before the chopping block. He bent his head forward, fit his throat into the wide groove. The space was barely large enough to contain his bull neck.

"Executioner," the official declared, "the empire orders you to execute the prisoner."

Another trumpet blast sounded.

The official hurried down from the stage and hastened across the brick courtyard, hurried into the palace.

Elad leaned forward, holding the wall.

Orain muttered an incomplete sob, pressed her cheek to Adred's shoulder and stared, stared at the gray faces around her, at the balcony entranceway, at somber colors and dull shadows and things blurred because of her tears. . . .

The hooded Khamar stepped up, stood beside the kneeling Cyrodian, hefted the axe.

"Go on and do it!" the giant growled at him.

The Imbur Ogodis was perspiring.

"Name of the gods . . ." someone on the balcony whispered.

Adred, holding Orain very tightly, looked down and wondered if Cyrodian at this moment were thinking—thinking, before his earthly thoughts were ended—of whatever had happened in that cage, between him and that *ikbusa*. Thinking . . . of his mother.

The Khamar lifted the axe.

Several in the crowds below shielded their eyes from the rain with their hands.

Salia glanced at her father; he sensed her stare. Salia's eyes were cold.

Cyrodian squirmed a bit, as if fitting his throat more comfortably into the block.

The rain—

At the last moment, Galvus choked and looked away.

The sound of the strike was a hollow noise from the center of the courtyard, followed, within a heartbeat, by a second hollow noise, as Cyrodian's head dropped into the wooden box before the block.

Thunder boomed, and with it came a thousand-voiced gasp from the crowds.

The locket in his hand burned as though on fire, and Galvus gasped and dropped it to the balcony floor. He closed his eyes, did not bend to retrieve it.

From the darkness behind his eyes, he heard his mother sob in anguish.

PART VI

Stormtide

1.

"But time hurries, Nutatharis. We live in days of consequence; the incidents come more and faster: roadmarks on the path to our conclusion. Do you not hear the storms at night? Don't you see it in the stars, feel it in the twilight at the end of every day? If you listen closely, in the silence of the dawn, you can feel it eating away at the soul of every man and woman in this nation. The fear. The knowing. The understanding. We live at the end of time. . . ."

It was as though, in leaving the Isle of Odossos, in leaving Erusabad, in coming away from Abustad and in leaving behind Lasura, he had in some profound and actual way left behind civilization, and society, and the temporal things of men, and all men and all women. And he had left behind also the tremendous fears that had possessed him, the shadowed truths, the awareness. He wrestled no more with his destiny. Leaving Assia for the last time had changed him, or completed the transformation within him. Not willing to hide from it any longer, unable any more to refuse the awesomeness of it, yet still frightened of identifying himself with it—this truth, this shadow, this awesomeness—Thameron nevertheless accepted it. Accepted it in the way a man accepts the fact that a disease has taken hold of him; accepted it in the way a woman accepts the irrefutable truth of the death of her husband—not wanting it, not welcoming it but no longer denying it. Truth as unpleasant as it is insistent.

The Chosen One had completed the awareness for him. *"But our time is not yet. Thameron: it is still in the future, when these disguises which we wear will be discarded, and all humanity will wait between us. There is a man of ancient shadows whom you must meet. It is a destined thing, ro kil-su.*

"You are fear," Asawas had told him. *"You are the fear we have produced in the uncertainly of our humanness. You are the doubt that does not strive but, in its arrogance, is satisfied."*

Within three days of leaving Lasura, he had come into the mountains and begun following a trail that he only sensed but did not physically see. When night came down, he looked at the stars, and it seemed to Thameron that he could feel the earth rumble and stretch beneath him, preparing itself. In the days, as he climbed into the mountains, the sun burned him, the sweat poured down him, but he did not feel any less strong, nor any less determined.

When, on the afternoon of the fifth day, he scaled a gravelly steepness and paused, looked up and saw the open mouth of a cool cave, he understood that he had come to the end of the road he had begun in that other cave, on Odossos.

The man of shadows came out of the cave and looked down, saw him. An expression of dread filled his features, followed by perplexity. As Thameron made his way up the incline toward him, Eromedeus asked him:

"You? Are you the one I've been waiting for? You're only a boy!"

Panting from his labors, Thameron approached him proudly, wiped the sweat from his face. "I am Thameron," he announced. "I am alone in coming to you."

"Alone?" Eromedeus shook his head, gestured down the mountainside in the direction from which Thameron had come. "How can you say that you are alone, when all humanity follows you?"

That evening, as Eromedeus cooked some of the roots, herbs and fruits he lived on and mixed them into a stew with meat he had obtained from hunting, Thameron, reclining on a grass mat, asked him:

"And if I offered to give up my life for you? Would your spirit answer to that and be released?"

Eromedeus shivered his head. "No. That would not happen. Don't you understand?"

And, later, as they ate the stew and sipped cold water brought from a mountain spring: "I never intended to do evil," Thameron confessed to Eromedeus. "I never intended to become the house of evil. Isn't it odd that I can be aware of that?"

"That doesn't matter," the shadowed one answered him. "That doesn't matter. It will come. . . ."

Outside, a storm, blowing in from the west, began to build.

"The storm," Asawas had told him, *"does not know that it floods the land, yet many perish, despite the storm's ignorance. If*

239

you know or do not know, if you believe or do not believe—you are
chosen. Men have hungered for your appearance."

"I was chosen," Thameron said, "by the thing I sought to
choose."

"Most men," Eromedeus replied, "are chosen by the things
they seek to avoid."

"But do we make these things happen? Are they us? Or do they
happen despite us?"

Eromedeus told him: "Don't you realize that when men desire
things, they never fully comprehend what they desire? That is the
paradox of spirit trapped in flesh. A man can desire strength and
love the strength of brutality but not the strength of mercy or
tolerance. Humanity," he said, "ceased to ask questions long ago.
It lives now with lies—and, living with lies, humanity divides
some lies into truths and others into mistruths. It lives in darkness,
this humanity that dwells below us like a carpet; yet, not knowing
this, humanity divides some of the darkness into light and accepts
the remainder as darkness. It has busied itself for many long years
preparing for its own annihilation, Thameron. Can a father not
pass his hatreds on to his sons, and never expect all sons
everywhere to destroy one another? It demands of you, of the
spirit in you, only the least you can do, not the greatest. That is
one of the foundations of evil."

"You speak as though evil were not a mighty thing."

"Evil," Eromedeus told him, "is a very simple thing, and in its
simplicity it is mundane, and artificial, and imbalanced. Otherwise, men would not continually return to its lures. Good," he
continued, "is a very simple thing, as well, but in its simplicity it
is awesome. It demands that men forgive the most obvious in
themselves."

Outside, the storm hurried, thundering and hissing with
lightning.

Eromedeus told Thameron: "I speak to you of things you
already know. Truth—goodness—recognizes itself, and is honest.
Evil . . . evil never believes that it is evil, and wears a
thousand disguises. It is time, Thameron, that you went out into
the storm."

Thameron looked at the man of shadows, the undying one.

"Go out, Thameron, into the storm."

Thameron stood up.

Eromedeus remained sitting where he was. "I have lived for so long, I have almost forgotten how long it has been. And here I am, speaking with the one I always knew would come, instructing him as though he were the boy he appears to be, and I his tutor." He looked Thameron in the eyes. "Do you understand how completely terrified I am of you?"

"No."

Eromedeus gestured. "Go out—into the storm. . . ."

Out from the deep winds of Time comes the Voice of a destiny, a Voice that is humanity's voice, the voice that calls humanity to return to the pools of blood and the shadows of fire from which it was born: the pool is deep, the shadows are old, the fire burns with flames that burn forever. O humanity born in a storm and wandering in a storm!

Our hearts are writhing serpents' nests, the storm is what we believe ourselves to be: thunder and noise, active as though with meaning, churning as with rage, nurturing ourselves as we do ourselves damage.

O many-faced, all-voiced humanity, your enemy is astride your shoulder, it is fast-held in your mirror, it breathes with your breath, quickens with your life, dreams with your dreams.

O Time, your face is human.

O Death, your name is Man.

O humanity, reducing strong elements to dust: your name is blown on a tempest, you frighten the stars, you are ever-young, but old, and ignorant as some force of Nature.

O Man, your names are legion. And misery and defeat, anguish and rot, curl invisibly in the crib of the newborn beside the newborn, baby or hope or ambition.

O humanity, your heart is a serpent's nest, you call down the storming damnation of your arrogance, you laugh with pride to see the ruination of your ancestors' hopes, you confound all things by making illusions into substances, and substances into illusions.

This storm that rages, it rages by the will of humanity.

This evil that walks in the shape of a man and speaks with the whispering voice of a man and laughs and worries and speaks of dreams: lo, this evil is yours, humanity.

And these things that come, they come with cause, they come with our hearts' blessings, and they come clutching our hopes and our pride and our illusions fast, presenting our sorrows to us as a happy gift.

* * *

When he returned, dripping with rain that shimmered like clear blood, and reborn, glorying in the magnificence and the thunder and violence of the storm, Thameron found the troubled Eromedeus sitting by a small fire he had built near the mouth of the cave. Thameron stood by the fire and looked down at Eromedeus.

The undying one stared up at him with dark eyes.

"Now, I understand," Thameron told him. "I felt it, in the storm. The final—convulsion . . . I am evil."

"Yes . . ." Eromedeus averted his eyes. "You are necessary."

"Necessary . . ." Thameron crouched by the fire. He thrust his hands into the flames and held them there until they glowed red. He felt no pain. "Flame," he whispered. "Here is humanity's birth and death."

Eromedeus watched him critically.

Thameron smiled at him. "If I offered now to give up my life for you, your spirit would not answer."

"Shall I, Humanity, give up my long existence to you, Fear?"

"But if you will not give it up, Eromedeus, then I can take your spirit from you, and vanquish you."

"Evil can destroy Humanity, yes, if love is not present."

"This new prophet?" Thameron stood up.

Eromedeus nodded slowly. "We are the shadows of humanity, the imagination of humanity—you and I and him."

"Do you know what the storm told me?" Thameron asked Eromedeus.

"I am afraid to know."

"It told me this: that men for some reason think Evil to be ignorant, and that gaining knowledge will awaken men to strive for Good. Why do men assume that? They don't realize that Evil supersedes Good—that it encompasses all that Good comprehends, and goes beyond it. *Good* is ignorant! When one begins to *see* and *understand*—to *feel*—he sees and understands and feels that *all* is Evil! All! Because it is touched by Man! What then is Man to think of Evil? Good and Evil are not opposites!"

Trembling, Eromedeus stared at him.

"They are the same thing! They flow from the same well! They breathe with the same soul! Only Good is transitory, and Evil is All! Order cannot defeat disorder! Unity cannot control all its elements forever! Substance cannot prevail over dissolution! *This* is the Evil men fear! Not some superstition or god or shadow—but the end that began with the beginning! All things in the world

242

return only so that in some dark dusk, with the final tide, they will never return again!''

Eromedeus groaned and pulled his face to his hands. "It cannot be! I have lived so long," he groaned, "but I have lived only one life! Have I outlived my soul? Did my soul pass on one night or winter while I slept?"

Thameron's hands were still glowing hot. He walked around the fire, crouched beside Eromedeus. The undying one stared at the sorcerer's hands, terrified of them.

Thameron seemed to be only a curious boy. "So . . . you will not give up your spirit to me, Humanity. But I can take it from you."

"Has humanity suffered so much, for so long," Eromedeus asked him, staring at the hands, the heat of them bringing tears to his eyes, "that it comes to this—the greatest suffering, accomplished by all that it fears?"

"We are contained by the world, Eromedeus. Why should anything astonish us? Especially our eagerness to believe our own lies? Am I not . . . necessary . . . for humanity?"

He leaned forward. Eromedeus, choking, scrambled away from him but could not move quickly enough to escape. Thameron took hold of him and knocked him down, then plunged his hands into Eromedeus's chest, touched his heart and sent his fiery touch of pain all through the undying one.

Eromedeus shrieked and screamed, writhed terribly.

"Damn you!" Thameron yelled at him. "Don't you think that Evil can cry?"

Outside, the storm continued all through the night, booming and raining and thundering.

Eromedeus shrieked and screamed, a humanity trapped by the monster it had accepted and could not escape—as Thameron's hot hold tortured him all through the night . . . as the evil one's tears fell as heavily as the rain. . . .

2.

When he came into the port city of Hilum, Asawas found that his growing reputation had preceded him. Always, in his wanderings, he had warned his listeners to hear his words with their hearts; and he had explicitly told everyone that he was not Bithitu returned to

243

the earth. Yet a myth had grown up within the great body of believers, and it had been fostered to suit its own purposes by the Church: that Bithitu would, indeed, return some time in the future to redeem the humanity that had punished and crucified him. Asawas, when questioned about this, had always replied that this meant only that Bithitu would return in the hearts of men when all came to the awareness of the Light, and that this would be Bithitu's redemption of an erring humanity. Yet the Church had adhered to a literal interpretation of the Prophet's pledge; and so when the countryside of Athadia began to spread the word that a miraculous teacher and healer and prophet was within the empire, people assumed that Asawas was Bithitu recome.

The storm that had blown across the fields the night before Asawas's entry into Hilum had caused great distress within the city: for the rain that fell was not clear water but colored red like blood. Frightened people locked themselves inside their houses or in their shops; many took refuge within the Temple near the center of the city; and a large number of others began to gather in a throng outside the palace of Governor Abadon, calling him to stop plans for the mobilization of the Second and Third Red Legions. Abadon, alerted to the fact that starving Emarian troops on Omeria's northern border had begun sacking farms and villages there, had sent out word to his military commanders that they should prepare to contain this aggressive breach of international policy. The citizens of Mustala, only a few leagues outside Emaria's border, were already aware that the empire was engaged in conflict with the Emarians in the Lowlands and feared the outbreak of a full-scale war. The red rain that fell during the night seemed to the Mustalans the most ominous and portentous of signs.

So when Asawas came down the muddy road toward the gates of Hilum, many villagers and farmers who lived outside the city walls were anxious to speak with him and follow him, and have him clarify the meaning of the red rain.

Asawas led his growing throng into the center of Hilum, where he stepped up onto a great fountain located before the Temple of Bithitu, and faced the frightened and expectant people.

"You say to me," Asawas announced to them that morning, "that you fear the red rain is a portent of what will come? You fear violence, bloodshed, death and an evil storm loosed upon the world? I say to you, 'Where is your faith?' Where is your faith in

244

On, the one true god, that you cannot turn the bloody water into clear rain water?"

With that, Asawas drew back the sleeve of his tattered robe and plunged his right arm into the shimmering red water of the fountain. Within only a few moments the discoloration began to fade; and, as the people continued to watch, the water in the fountain became completely clear. Awed gasps and a few cheers met Asawas's miracle. The prophet lifted his arm high so that all in the square could see that the water on his arm was clear, not bloody red.

"Where is your faith?" he demanded of his crowd. "If you believe in a future of blood, then you shall have a future of blood! Where is your faith?"

Immediately many in the crowd surged forward, offering Asawas dishes, bowls and pitchers filled with red water. "*Ikbusa*! Prophet! Chosen One! Show us again! Prove to us that you have the faith! Lead us to the faith!"

Asawas dipped his hand into every dish, bowl and pitcher, to leave them full of clear, good, trustworthy water. With cupped hands he sipped some of the water he had just transformed, then raised his arms and showed his smiling, wet face to the people.

"Where is your faith? Where is your faith?"

Cheers and prayers answered him.

From the roof of the Temple behind Asawas, the Master, Anasiah, stood with several young priests, and saw and heard, and was not pleased. "This man," he muttered, "is extremely dangerous." Anasiah listened a while longer, then ordered one of his predicants: "Get you to Governor Abadon. Alert him to this."

In the street before the fountain, Asawas continued to speak to the ever-increasing numbers of people, and they were astonished at his doctrine, for his word was with power. Asawas told them of On, the one true god, who exists in men's hearts and not in temples. He told them that faith in On was within their own hearts but they could not listen to their own hearts if they listened to other things. And he told them of the days of tribulation to come.

"You will see the signs coming! Already we have seen the signs! You will hear of wars and rumors of wars! Do not be troubled in your hearts, for all these things must come to pass! But the end is not yet! Nation must rise against nation, kingdom against kingdom, and there will be famines and pestilences and earthquakes in many places! These are the beginnings of our sorrows! But you who endure until the end shall be saved! For there will come great tribulation, such as has not been since the beginning of the world to this time!''

The people in the street became terrified. Never had they heard of Asawas speaking in such a fashion.

"These things that come," he warned them, "mark the coming of On, who binds up the wounds of our hearts, who heals our flesh, who asks us to treat the stranger as though he were ourself! Where is your faith? Show me your faith! Is your faith in the Temple? Is your faith in the Church? Is your faith in gold? Is your faith in the glorification of your station? Then you have lifted yourselves above others, and you will be the first to fall!

"For I tell you that On will make the earth empty, he will make of it a waste, and he will scatter abroad all that live on the earth! The earth will mourn and fade away as it languishes, as the haughty people of the earth will languish! They defile the earth because they have transgressed the laws and broken their covenant with the earth! I say this to you in the name of On! Where is your faith? A curse will devour the earth and all who dwell on the earth will be made desolate!

"This is the voice of the one true god! And any of you who say that you do not wish this and do not deserve this, I ask you: Where is your faith? For you have hungered for this in your hearts and you have prepared yourselves for its coming! You have allowed the masters you worship to possess you! You have done what you have done to the earth and to your brothers and your sisters joyously, and with disregard! Now you will fear that which has grown from the seeds you planted! Who among you claims that he hasn't done this? You have done it! Where is your faith? Your faith is in the temples covered and filled with gold! Your faith is in the purses and coffers and wallets of rich men! Your faith is a prostitute, a harlot that can be bought and that does not believe in tomorrow! Which of you lifted your hands to the rain and believed that the rain was not blood? *Where is your faith?*"

As Asawas spoke to the trembling, haunted crowds, the young initiate returned from the governor's palace, bowed his head and told Anasiah: "Lord Abadon hears what this preacher is saying. He mistrusts him."

"Return to Lord Abadon and tell him that I and our Inquisitor would have words with this false prophet."

The young predicant bowed again, hurried down from the roof of the Temple and ran through the street toward the governor's palace.

246

"When the man of evil comes to you," Asawas warned the people, "the man of fear and intolerance, you will welcome him with your arms and your hearts, because he will not seem to you evil! He will promise you all the things that sound good! He is a man meant to be, as I am meant to bring you the word of On! But I, who come to warn you that the earth must die to be reborn—do you think I am a good man? Or do my words frighten you, so that you think I am evil? I speak the truth and I show you to yourselves, and you are frightened of me, and I am love! But the man who will not tell you the truth, the man who will reassure you and tell you what it is you want to hear—that man you will welcome, but he is to be feared!"

Then he said to them: "Listen and I will tell you of the signs that have come already and of the signs that are yet to come, marking the end of days! Here is the first sign, the sign that nature is upturned, that the earth rebels against the pain men have subjected it to: Birds fall into the seas to die and animals attack their masters—these are the signs of a rebellious earth! Last night you stared into the sky and saw a rain of blood—blood cleansed only by the power of God: That was the second sign! You will feel a great wind blow upon the earth, like the breath of On, delivering a storm upon the fields and cities and the seas: Know this to be the third sign! And know this to be the fourth sign: That I, the voice of the one true god that lives within men's hearts, will be taken by unclean men and made to face judgment in an earthly court! And the fifth sign is this: The earth will suffer a day and a night of plague that will strike the heathen and the believer, the clean and the unclean, the righteous and the condemned, for all are within the heart of god! Then know this as the sixth sign: That the Prophet of Light will meet the Master of Evil! And the old gods will fall away, the old ways will pass, and every man's crime will return upon him ten-fold and a hundred-fold, and the earth will grow angry, the skies will collapse and the seas rise up, as On grows angry and impatient to be done with the old days! For the seventh sign is the end of a beginning, and a beginning to an end!"

The citizens of Hilum, perplexed, frightened by the implications of these words, began to grow indignant. A few in the street picked up stones and bricks and flung them at Asawas, although none touched him.

"Where is your faith?" he called to them. *"Where is your faith?"*

The increasing temper of the crowd was suddenly arrested by a strident horn blast; immediately the throngs fell back in waves, and stragglers were rudely pushed back as a long double-file of Athadian foot soldiers imperiously advanced. The soldiers held the people far away from Asawas, clearing an area for the arrival of mounted troops. At their head rode a tall, darkly handsome man dressed in the garb of a state official. He brought his horse still before the prophet; from his saddle he sat at eye level with Asawas. The prophet said nothing as the official, regarding him sternly, finally explained:

"I am Governor Abadon, authority in Hilum by the gracious permission of King Elad the First, our emperor. Priest—your words have created civil unrest in my city, and that is against the law. You prophesy well. Consider yourself under arrest." To foot soldiers beside his horse: "Shackle him and bring him to the palace."

The office of Inquisitor, which once had commanded great power and respect within the Church, had become, with the Church's waning influence in a secular world, little more than a title. By tradition charged with investigating heresy, apostasy or other cardinal infractions within the Church body, Inquisitors in the past had ordered the wholesale torturings, mutilations, imprisonings and executions of entire communities deemed heretical in the sight of the Prophet—as the Prophet's Church on earth interpreted such matters. But Seraficos, before whom Asawas was brought, enjoyed no such extremes of authority. His duties were now reduced to a simple formula of inquiry into events contained within the jurisdiction of the Temple of Bithitu proper, in Hilum.

Seraficos was an intelligent man, learned in mundane matters as well as spiritual ones. If his office found itself looking after troubled young priests these days (and inquiring into the reasons for such personal distress) and investigating incidents for possible reform in the codes of conduct for Church brethren, nevertheless Seraficos was fully aware of how strictly he could apply the authority he held at his command. True, it was not within Seraficos's power to order the execution of entire villages, but the Inquisitor was more concerned in his later years with effecting more personally satisfying (and materially rewarding) objectives than he was in slaughtering the fallen and the lost. Seraficos, in his progress through the Church hierarchy, had spent several years studying administrative policies under the tutelage of Andoparas of Erusabad; and he had himself instituted several measures of reform within the Hilum Church since obtaining his post there. Seraficos was a man orthodox in his beliefs: belief in the Prophet meant adherence to the Church's regulations and proscriptions, and praise for Bithitu must necessarily translate itself into tangible offerings to the Church.

His reputation in Hilum was an enviable one. Regarded by the faithful as a stern administrator, and tireless in his work to improve people's souls, Seraficos was known to the government leaders as a singularly redoubtable politician of great influence and persuasion. It was upon the testimony of Seraficos, and none other, that Governor Abadon decreed which sections of the port city should receive government benefits, and which should not; which guilds of workingmen should receive certain contracts to perform government-authorized labor, and which should not; which young men should gain advancement within government offices, and which should not. Seraficos, although not yet the highest ranking official in the Hilum Church, was nevertheless invested with greater authority than his station actually obtained due to his powerful personality, his shrewdness, and his personal acquaintanceship with many important figures in both the secular and clerical offices of the empire.

After Asawas's arrest had been entered into the governor's ledgers at the palace, he was brought before this Seraficos, and the prophet understood instantly that with whatever crimes he might be charged, they would fall not under the jurisdiction of the civil authorities, but under that of the Church's. Perhaps it was simply as Governor Abadon had told him while he was being held in the palace: "As far as I'm concerned, you can get on a boat and begone from here. But our Church officials here want to ask you a few questions before we kick you out."

"Am I not under arrest, then?" he had asked Governor Abadon.

"Oh, you're under arrest, all right. But I'm not going to martyr you—not in this city. Haven't I got enough problems as it is?"

And so Asawas had been detained in a cell in the city government building until late in the afternoon when a young priest in the company of two city guards came for him and escorted him to the Temple.

"Am I to be brought, then, to the master of your Temple?" Asawas had asked.

"To Anasiah? Oh, no, he can't be bothered with you. We're taking you to Seraficos, our Inquisitor."

They led him by a back entrance into the Temple and down a dark stairwell into its underground. Here, where the damp walls of stone and the floors seemed to breathe with mist, the torches carried by the city guards almost suffocated in the rank humidity. Asawas, as he passed through the dank corridors, saw signs of the oppression of old: cells and bars and chains hanging on the walls, all rusted. It came to him that those who had enslaved the minds of men with their corruption no longer needed such gross methods: the work they had begun with torch and sword, poisons and handcuffs, was now accomplished, and the prisons men were held in, they had built themselves, in their own hearts.

He was taken into a wide stone room that stank of such things; and there, in the gloom relieved only by a whispering wall of torches and hanging oil lamps that smoked, Asawas was interviewed by Seraficos. The Inquisitor, an old man, tall and erect, with a seamed face and heavy brows, owned deep eyes that burned with an unquenchable inner fire. He nodded wordlessly to the young priest, and the two guards, once they had delivered Asawas, removed themselves, leaving the prophet and the Inquisitor alone with one another.

Seraficos did not ask Asawas to be seated although he himself sat in one of several high-backed wooden chairs placed around a long oak table. The old man kept his keen eyes on this prophet; he stood up slowly—a carnivore suspicious of its prey—approached Asawas and carefully walked around him, circling him twice, watching him, breathing but not yet speaking. Finally, with hands behind his back, head tilted forward so that he seemed a disembodied face atop a long, dull gray robe, Seraficos whispered:

"Is it truly you? Is it? Is it truly? Have you come back?" And then, before allowing Asawas any time to reply: "Don't answer . . . it doesn't matter. I don't know who you are and it doesn't matter. You spoke to them out there . . . they followed you like sheep. Is that your strength? Did you come here thinking that because they listen to you, you're as powerful as I am, as powerful as the empire? You're very wrong if you think that. I could draw up charges against you; I could have you executed tomorrow morning. Do you think any of them would care? You ask them to reach into their hearts, to listen to the truth. Do you think they care? Do you think they know what truth is? Do you know what truth is, *ikbusa*? Do you? Tell me. What is truth?"

Asawas only stared at him.

Seraficos grinned foully; the wrinkles of his face shifted in living patterns, the sweaty brightness of his face altering with the moving, creased shadows. "I've seen your kind before," he said to the prophet. "They come through here all the time. They all have messages; they all have something to preach. The crowds listen to them, then the crowds go away. They listen, but they don't listen. Do you know why? Do you know why the crowds listen to them, but stay with me? Who do you think you are, Asawas—'seeing one'—to tell people the truth? Do you want to know why the crowds will not follow you, but will stay with me? Why they worship within the Church? Why they serve this government? Do you want me to show you why?" Seraficos smiled, lifted an arm and showed Asawas his right hand; he wore a priceless ring upon each finger. Still smiling, the Inquisitor pointed to the stone blocks of the walls all around.

"I understand that you can create miracles," he said to Asawas. "Is this true?" Confidently, he walked to the stone wall nearest him; stones and bits of broken brick littered the corner. Seraficos stooped and picked up a small stone and carried it to Asawas. "The people have no work; they have no food," he said. "They are starving. If you can work miracles, do something for the people you preach to, Asawas. Here—turn this stone into bread. Is that asking too much of a prophet of the one god?"

He held out the stone. Asawas looked at it, eyed Seraficos, but refused to take the stone. "Shall the people live by bread alone?" he asked the Inquisitor.

Seraficos sneered at him, cast the stone aside and stepped back. "You're a poor man," he observed. "How long have you been traveling, preaching this word of the one god, claiming to be the new prophet? What do you receive for this? You command people's attention. But what do you do with that? How do you guide them? How do you tell them what to do? What is your reward for this authority of yours, this voice you speak with? Don't tell me that you're content just walking the roads and touching souls. The people like to hear that from us, but we all understand just how far that goes. Look you, Asawas, preacher, prophet—we own the world. From sea to sea, we own the world. Would you like me to give you my robe, give you my office, give you what I have? The people will understand. Would you like to own the world?"

"Should I serve On," Asawas replied, "but put everything else before him?"

Seraficos frowned with displeasure and said, "If you believe so greatly in this god of yours—if you truly believe what you say, that he is here, that he will do what he says he will do—then don't speak to me of signs and portents. Show me. Prove it. Look you: we will take ourselves up to the height of this Temple, you can call the people to you, they will watch you, and you can cast yourself from the height. If your belief in this one god is so strong, if he is truly all that you say he is, then surely his power is great enough, and you will not be crushed when you fall but will land as lightly as a bird."

"Why," Asawas replied, "for what benefit, should I test god? Have I not faith?"

Becoming angry, Seraficos turned his back to Asawas, sat down again in his chair and faced the prophet from across the table. "Who are you," he grunted, "to tell the people that they must free themselves so that they can love one another in the name of god? Who are you to ask them to reach into their hearts, disdain the authority they crave so greatly, and choose for themselves between the shadow and the light? When Bithitu came to redeem man from himself two thousand years ago, he sought to give men freedom, and to instill in them love—and see the result! And temples have been erected to him, he is made the greatest of all gods from the hearth to the battlefield, his statues stand taller than all other gods' statues—and men willingly bow down to us, his Church. Where is their freedom? Where is their brotherhood? Where are their hearts? Where is their faith?

"You come to give men freedom again, by allowing them to choose between the shadow and the light. So that they may with grace and love choose the light? Or live with the burden of the shadow? If men were meant to make that choice, they would have chosen already! And they *have* chosen! Do you come to warn men that an angry god seeks to heave the earth, to punish them? Do you come to warn humanity that what will come, they have themselves caused to come, through their generations of labor? They rejoice in this! They will rejoice in the punishing! They would rather have the *idol* and the statue, Asawas, than the true words of the Prophet! They would rather be punished, than take upon themselves responsibility for their lives! They would rather have you return to them so that they can speak with you, than believe in your words when you have gone! They would rather

252

have no gods, no prophets, than be forced to face the gods and the prophets in themselves! And you come to them offering them *truth*?"

Seraficos was very angry now. He rose to his feet, faced Asawas from across the table and pounded on it with both fists.

"You fool! The people do not want the *truth*! They *want* to believe in the authority over them! They do not want to take responsibility for their lives! They *want* answers given to them! And they will *find* their answers—in the Church, in their gold, in their businesses, in their wine and flesh! They want to be told what to think and what to believe! You ask people to open their hearts? They will *not*! You have shown them miracles! You have told them mysteries! You have come to them as an authority! And what will you do now? Ask them to believe in god?

"We already *have* our miracles, and the gods and the prophets have indeed given them to us! We earn *profit* with pieces of gold! We have *mysteries*! If a man will work, he will earn! If two will marry, they will come to love one another! If a man believes, he will make that belief become real! We have *authority*! We tell the people what to do, we tell them it is for their benefit in the name of the Prophet or in the name of the empire, and they concede us that right! And if they do not want our authority, then they'll find someone else to use as an authority! And you ask them to look into their *hearts* and *choose*? You ask them to *think*? You ask them to have *faith*? When anyone on earth would gladly turn a mountain into bread and feed the poor, and call it a miracle! When anyone on earth would gladly rule the world, and think it proper for himself to do it! When anyone on earth would jump from this building and expect the gods to rescue him? And you come to them, you ask them to have *faith* in themselves? They do not *need* to believe in themselves! *We* allow them to believe in *us*! Bithitu freed men to choose, and they have chosen, and we acknowledge their choice and support them! Why do you come now to harass them? They have faith in me! In gold! In everything *but* themselves! They *have* chosen!"

Asawas stood silent, listening only, and staring at Seraficos with sad eyes.

"What have you to say to this, you imposter?" the Inquisitor railed at him. "Explain yourself to me!"

For a long moment, Asawas merely met his stare. Seraficos, panting and sweating, leaned forward, balanced himself on the table and glared at the prophet with his sharp, penetrating eyes.

"Well?" he growled. "Explain yourself to me!"

"Where is your faith, Seraficos?" Asawas asked him in a very low voice. "Where is your belief? You command a church, you have allied yourself with a government, you make profit from your businesses—yet you believe in nothing. The thing you have not learned, Seraficos, is that Man *is* God. Have you not realized that yet? Do you not comprehend what these generations of toil yearn for?" And then, "What do you carry in your *ibi*, Seraficos? Where is your faith?"

The Inquisitor paled and began to tremble. This *ibi* was the small phylactery worn by all high officials and administrators of the Church; by tradition, it contained its wearer's own small relic or token of spiritual significance.

"I will have you arrested!" Seraficos hissed at the prophet. "*I* will not condemn you, imposter, and give you the benefit of martyrdom in the name of Bithitu! You shall not die in glory! But you will be taken to the imperial government and made to face the highest court in this land for your crimes! Inciting revolt, and calling on an end to our government! *I* will see that this is done! Guards!"

They appeared from the corridor outside and advanced toward Asawas.

"Imprison this . . . criminal! Detain him, hold him! He is under arrest! Governor Abadon will issue the necessary papers!"

The soldiers took hold of Asawas, knowing the power and influence that Seraficos had at his command. The prophet did not protest but walked between them, hands shackled. The three moved out the door and vanished into the shadows of the outer corridor.

The trembling, sweating Inquisitor, staring out the open door, tensely reached a hand to the small golden *ibi* he wore around his neck. Grasping it, Seraficos tore the locket from its chain. Shaking fingers twisted and fought with the metal until at last he managed to open it. The lid snapped off and dropped with a loud metallic sound on the table, as Seraficos stared inside his small *ibi* and saw—

Nothing.

3.

Neither Elad nor Salia slept the night before her departure for Erusabad. Unable to rest, Salia was excited by the prospect of her voyage and her meeting with the rulers of the eastern empire.

"But keep in mind," Elad warned her several times, "that these men of the east do not think highly of women. They hold them in low esteem; don't let their attitude harm you."

Salia was aware of this aspect of the east, but she was not much impressed with it. "I'm not just a woman," she smiled. "I'm the queen of Athadia. They'll treat me as such, won't they? Besides, our ambassadors will look after me."

"Yes . . . but I want you to bear in mind that—"

"Bear *this* in mind!" she grinned at him, and rolled into his arms and made love to him.

They made love several times that night. This was unusual for Elad, for although he was a man more than capable of expressing the ardor he felt for his wife, very often the duties of his office and the pressures he brought to bear upon himself would not allow him to enjoy his wife's attentions as often as both he and Salia desired. But tonight, and all night long, because she was to be away from him for two months, Elad found his passion for Salia, and his sense of possession of her, very much increased.

Still, he wanted her to take this voyage. He felt certain that it would mature her in many ways, and make her understand more fully how she should behave in her imperial role. More than that, Elad wished Salia and Ogodis to be separated, for he felt that this could only do them both good. The Imbur would rant and fume (he had already threatened to journey to Erusabad himself, in his own state vessel), but Elad suspected that Ogodis himself sensed the wisdom of his daughter's making this prolonged journey— even while, emotionally, he might find it compromising.

While Elad did not actually suffer any doubts about his decision, it seemed to him that only now, on the eve of Salia's departure, did he see just how purposefully he had insisted on her going—and he felt himself regretting some of that stubbornness. What was in him that made him do that? Did he, in some way, want Salia yet not want her? What selfish motive lay behind his apparently selfless act?

When he subtly and not completely broached these concerns to his wife, the queen laughed at him and dismissed Elad's confusions.

"But it's because you *do* love me," Salia reminded him, "that you want me to go, and at the same time want me to stay. Haven't you ever noticed that, between lovers? It's good for them to part, for some reason, and they want what's good, but they don't want to be away from one another. And it's *because* I'm queen, and at the same time a woman, that *I* want to go. Do you think I'll let them treat me like a woman when I should be treated like a queen? It's *better* that you send a woman to them, Elad! Such a thing will show them just what sort of people we are!"

"That's true."

"And I'll come back to you with so many things to show you and tell you about!" she promised him excitedly.

They passed the night talking worriedly and concernedly for a while, then lapsing into more lighthearted conversation until their ardor gripped them and they satisfied one another. Finally, they lay back and rested, yawned, sipped wine, and began once more to talk and imagine and share ideas.

It seemed to Elad that night that he had not been aware before of how deeply attached he had become to his young wife, of how dependent he was upon her for subtle things. The sound of her voice . . . the look of her eyes . . . the length of her fingers . . . the curving wrinkles of her nipples and the soft firmness of her belly . . . the light hair on her arms . . . the wisdom of her casual insights and the frustrations of her moods— all these things reappeared to him in a ribbon of experience and new wonder, and he found himself falling in love all over again with the Princess of Gaegosh: with her astonishing beauty that prevailed in any light, that became more wonderful the longer he gazed at her, with the depth of her eyes and with the whole of her—puzzling and alarming as she sometimes was, and yet always innocent and naturally seductive.

He wondered if all men felt this way about their wives, and he knew that they did not, for although many men in the world might be similar to him, there was surely no other woman in the world like Salia. He suspected that that was why he had fallen in love with her, and why in a portion of his heart he was somewhat apprehensive of her, and adored her, the way one adores a powerful thing. There were many women he might have married, but all of them seemed more similar to, than distinctive from, one another; and Salia was like no other woman. It was difficult to elaborate in words.

But she was his—as much as anything unique could be his. Did she understand that?

"And I'm going to learn their language during the trip there," she enthused. "What is it they speak? They call it *Hasni* or . . ."

Salia fell quiet when she looked at Elad; something in his eyes . . . He rolled beside her and moved partially atop her, slipped his arms under her shoulders and stared into her face, her beautiful face with the endless eyes and the shimmering lips, the hair that swept upon the pillows like—

"You *do* understand, don't you?" he breathed to her, in a needful voice that betrayed some cautious insecurity.

"Understand what, my heart? Oh, Elad . . ."

He moved his face to her throat, to her breasts, held his damp cheek to her smooth flesh, cupped one of her breasts in his hand and pressed it against his face so that his mouth and nose and closed eyes were covered by it, as though he might gladly suffocate himself there, or blindly seek nourishment.

Salia murmured to him and stretched her arms down his back; she understood. She understood how men, sometimes in their emotions, jumped like athletes from stone to stone, precariously balancing themselves at the same time in the world, while women, in their emotions, floated in a wide stream, all their emotions flowing at once.

"You . . . *do* understand?" he whispered moistly, lifting his face.

"I love you, Elad."

"Do you?"

"Don't you think I love you?"

He watched her lips move as she asked it. He swallowed, stared at her. "What is love," he wondered, "if it isn't what *we* have? What I need you for . . . when I have you . . ."

She kissed him and pressed him to her again, wanting the feel of him; and Elad, his head on her breasts, listened to her heart beating, beating, beating—

Beating, pulsing, moving, like the rhythmic beat of the earth and its tides, like the rhythmic beat of his own blood, the rhythmic beat and movement of—oars in the water, the beat of wings carrying her from him.

The pulsing beat of time moving on, unstoppable, inevitable in its tread . . .

On board the ship the following morning, Elad hovered expectantly in the hold as Salia and the Imbur made their good-byes in her cabin. The door was open, and from where he stood Elad could see their reflection in a mirror. They held each other, father and daughter, and spoke to one another quietly, with confident smiles, sorrowful gestures, brief kisses. Elad trusted Salia and knew that she must be warning her father not to follow her to the Holy City and not to wear himself down by worrying about her: the two months would pass quickly. Return to Sugat, now, Father; your daughter is the queen of Athadia. . . .

The dozen Khamars who guarded Elad, crowded as they were in the gallery and behind him in the storage hold, were silent and observant and kept their eyes on the sailors and dockhands who moved back and forth in the passageway carting the loads and bundles of Salia's clothes, jewelry and pets.

Elad was watching the mirror. He looked away—but his eyes were drawn back.

"As each human being has three selves, so do you have three enemies. Your first is a mirror, your second a blade, your third a foreign countenance. . . ."

When the Imbur exited, he glanced succinctly at Elad, said nothing but, holding his head high, moved toward the top deck.

Elad coughed slightly and entered Salia's cabin, closed the door.

"All is not what it seems; what things seem is not all. It is not the mirror's reflection that is real, but what it reflects. It is not the sword that slays, but the man behind it. It is not the wall that weakens, but those behind who do not repair it. Temper your sword, Prince Elad. Nourish your roots. See beneath your mirror."

They spoke of the many things they had discussed all during the previous night. Salia joked with Elad, saying that she meant to return with a shipful of rare and exotic eastern animals and birds; he would have to build her an entire new wing on the palace for her menagerie, or at least expand the animal garden he was constructing. Elad reminded her that all he wished was for Salia to bring herself back, sound and sure. She commented that she felt tired and light-headed; Elad grinned, nodded to the bed in the cabin and mildly suggested that they make their farewells on the cushions. Salia laughed at him, touched him and made reference to his "king's scepter," and told him to set up sixty candles in their bedchamber in the palace.

"Burn one every night, and let that flame stand for the love we share, Elad. And on the day I return, we'll light the last one together."

He was deeply moved by this sentimental idea and kissed Salia passionately.

From above came the shipmaster's call that the wind was up and the tide heading out, so the ship must move out.

Elad became nervous and impatient. "Count the stars every night," he whispered to Salia, holding her, "as you lie in your bed in Erusabad. Count the stars, and think of us, and the stars will put you to sleep. Dream of me."

"Always," she assured him, and answered his kisses with her own.

The shipmaster called out again, and Elad heard the Khamars in the gallery shuffling their boots restlessly. He held Salia's hands, kissed her right hand where her wedding band encircled one finger, looked into her eyes and held her head, felt her hair—then he turned quickly and moved to the door. When he looked back at her, he watched her, took in all of her.

Salia smiled at him.

Elad smiled back—it was a sad, melancholy smile—and then, like the king he was, he opened the door boldly and went out, hurried down the gallery and took the stairs quickly, as his Khamars followed.

Farther up the Sevulus, even as Elad was bidding Salia farewell, Prince Galvus was on the docks welcoming six visitors just disembarking from a merchanter. Adred was with him. As the six made their way onto the quay and retrieved their belongings, Galvus and Adred greeted them warmly and led them toward a large carriage decorated with the imperial seal.

"A royal coach?" the leader of the six, Bors, asked, as a dock attendant fastened his luggage to its roof. He seemed to find that suspect, for some reason.

The eight of them were somewhat cramped within the elegant interior of the coach, but that didn't interfere with their conversation.

"You've arrived just in time," Galvus told Bors and his companions. "I'm glad indeed that you could answer my summons so quickly."

Bors, still in his rough working clothes and smelling of the fields and of grain, answered him: "You've kept your word,

259

and so did Vardorian. I must admit, though . . . I was beginning to have my doubts."

"Don't," Galvus reassured him. "Count Adred"—a nod—"and I have been working diligently preparing our proposal. The High Council convenes today to begin its debate on the matter."

"The *sirots*, you mean."

"Yes. But, as I told you, I'm after a lot more than just the *sirots*. I've spoken with a few members of the Public Administration *Priton* and they're with us when we open inquiries into ideas much more far-reaching than merely establishing *sirots*. And Elad, so far at least, is amenable to my arguments. Today," Galvus told the workers, "or tomorrow—perhaps the following day—is when I'll ask you to appear and give your testimony."

"Are they even going to listen to us?" one of them asked.

"They'll listen; I'm sure of that." Galvus's voice had an even edge to it, now. "But keep in mind that the investigation was put into the hands of the patricians on the Nobility Council—the landowners, the businessmen. It sounds, from that, as though we're defeated before we even begin, but Elad wasn't wrong in approaching the matter this way. If nothing else, it's forced Rhin, Falen and the other four to at least open their eyes to what's happening."

"If not their hearts," Adred put in. "Or their wallets."

The Kendians didn't express much optimism to this.

"What I've got to make them aware of," Galvus remarked, "—and Count Adred, too, and you men, with your testimony—is simply this: That now is the time for a redistribution of wealth, and a pluralist economy. Time and events and crises occur at a more accelerated rate, and have a greater impact, outside the walls of Athad than these shielded aristocrats are aware of. But if we use force, then they'll answer with force—and they have the greater resources. And that means more of what happened in the Diruvian Valley, in Sulos, in Bessara. We can't regard that as an option. We must assure these aristocrats that our intention as revolutionaries is—"

"Our intention as revolutionaries," Bors broke in, "is to feed our familes, have roofs over our heads, wood for our stoves, oil for our lamps, and control over our own lives. Everything these aristocrats have kept for themselves for a very long time. I trust you, Galvus—I've trusted you so far. Just . . . don't become an aristocrat again, here, in the capital, when we *do* trust you."

The carriage rumbled. Perhaps the comment sounded harsher or

260

more aggressive than Bors had intended. Galvus felt somewhat threatened.

"I'm a man," he told the workers. "That's what you are; that's what these aristocrats are. There are certain things all men—all people—are entitled to, in society. I'm not going to compromise or cheat on things that are as much as a part of me as the air I breathe and the food I—"

"I didn't mean to . . . challenge your sincerity, Galvus," Bors told him. "But you must realize that we have much more at stake here than you do, yourself. That's a simple fact. If these lords start to push us—we'll push back. Talk is fine, time we can manage, if something's being accomplished. But if we're pushed, we'll push back. That's something else they've got to realize."

Galvus did not reply.

Adred, who'd been listening to all this with his arms folded across his chest, now spoke up. He told Bors, "All we're asking you to do, for the time being, is to treat these aristocrats as though they were your equals. For the time being."

Bors showed his teeth, chuckled and nodded his head slightly, then looked out the window.

As he faced his assembled Council, Elad thought, somewhat grimly, of how natural tendencies are manifest in political arenas. The first instinct, he recognized, of creatures in the wild or in men involved in politics, is toward their own self-interest and survival. But because all things are born to die and because everything exists at the expense of other things, all creatures will, when thwarted, take the path of least resistance when thrust into dangerous circumstances. And yet the irony with man is that these self-serving tendencies can be checked, or ignored, by the great difference that separates man from the animals—men, with their imaginations and wills, their thoughts and passions, can restrain their natural impulses for the sake of an idea, for dreams unproven and untried. Men will lay down their lives for rhetoric, or for a flag, or for a vision. No animal has ever done that.

The finest example of the clash between the two halves of the nature of man—the instinctive and the ideal, the brutal and the rational—was, for Elad, the Council Chamber in which the politics of the empire was accomplished. For in politics the basest of motives and arguments are, if tenuously, yet actually, allied to the highest of professed ideals and concepts. And Elad considered this, as well, as he listened to the noble Lord Rhin parley his findings on the possibility of workers' rights. For politics is the clash of authorities; politics is the planting of wedges; politics is the confrontation of possibilities with actualities. And politics is the baring of one's innermost heart and philosophy, for in politics the individual is brought face-to-face with his society, and his philosophy must actually be made to work—is challenged to work—in the world of men as they are, and not as they might be.

Elad watched, and listened. Torn, himself, among all those elements that sought to petition him, he had come to understand (the longer he sat on his throne) how weak power truly is, how shallow many passions are, and, consequently, how noble are the weak and striving, how defiant the honest and truthful.

Lord Rhin prattled on, occasionally making rude remarks about the impracticality of even considering the working people as capable of managing their own affairs, and summed up his discourse by appealing to a conservative heritage: the empire's long reliance upon men of rank and prominence for its leadership and guidance. "We have made this nation what it is today and I, for one, am proud of it!"

Sporadic applause, the majority of it from others in the Congress of Nobility, met this sentiment. Elad, head on hand, studied Rhin and saw through him. The king was himself allied to Rhin by self-interest and class; that much had been admitted in their conversation at the *Kirgo Amax*. And yet, because his position allowed him to be—insisted that he be—many things at once, Elad was reminded that, in moral or ethical issues (those which separate men from beasts), the greater one's feelings of guilt, the more fastidiously one is apt to proclaim one's innocence; and the higher one sits in the hierarchy of one's society, the more pervasive are the effects of that guilt, the more stridently self-serving the protests.

Elad moved his eyes from Lord Rhin to Prince Galvus and Count Adred, who were seated near the end of the Public Administration table. Galvus was fidgeting; Count Adred was listening with the look of a man long repulsed by such obvious hypocrisies.

With Galvus and Adred in the room—with their *attitude* in the Chamber—Elad seemed to see this shoddy prevarication by the aristocrats anew. And when the king opened the floor to debates on the issue of the *sirots*, he witnessed first hand the war between the ideals in men's hearts and the baseness.

Galvus's attitude was that of a man unquestionably in the right;

at times, his verbal attacks on Lord Rhin seemed almost light-hearted, so self-assured was he. "You're trying to defend an obsolete system!" he pointed out. "You're trying to buoy up a ship that's drowning in a storm, by punching more holes in it! I'm glad you're a High Councilor and not a sailor, Lord Rhin!"

Rhin, completely on the defensive and upset at having his values even questioned, lost his temper whenever Galvus spoke. "We have devised a system which will adequately—"

"*That*," Galvus proudly interrupted him, "is precisely the mentality that has brought our country to the brink of ruin! I don't believe in 'adequacy,' Lord Rhin—I believe in *competency*! And I don't believe in 'systems'—I believe in *people*! And *competent people* seem to be very much lacking in our hereditary class of—"

"This is outrageous! Are you a traitor, Prince Galvus? I *won't* retract that word, I use it for what it means! Are you prepared to—"

"Are *you* prepared, Lord Rhin, to trade places with a man in the field for a year? For one month? No! For one *day*? Because if you aren't—if you can't do that, and do the job that fieldman does—then you have *no right* to take from that man *anything* you aren't willing to give in return!"

"Our heritage has set down a system wherein each man does his part in a social order—"

"And I am not speaking of the *past*, Lord Rhin—although I'm sure you'd be happiest living when men were not only land-owners, but slaveholders, as well! I am—"

"This is absolutely—!"

"I am speaking of the *future*! I am speaking of *dignity*!"

Following a very necessary short recess, matters did not improve in the Council Chamber when Galvus took the opportunity to invite certain members of "Lord Rhin's esteemed human stable of cattle" into the proceedings.

Rhin was freshly outraged when Bors and the other farmers from the Diruvian Valley were escorted into the hall; but Elad quickly reminded the nobleman that it was the privilege of any Councilor or aristocrat sitting in the Chamber to introduce any visitor or evidence he wished, so long as that might shed insight into matters being debated.

When Galvus began soliciting testimony from Bors and the others relevant to the working conditions of the farmers in Sulos, their grievances, their ideas for reform and their opinions on the general inadequacy of the proposed *sirots*, Lords Rhin and Falen protested loudly. "These men are revolutionaries! Does our king now invite seditionists to take part in our government?" And, in a cruel moment: "Have they been checked for weapons? Are we certain that they don't mean to injure or assassinate any of us in this hall?"

Galvus answered this alarmist mentality with proud conviction. "If there is a revolution, then it is occurring because the ideas these men represent have been ignored for so long that their only recourse has been to *create* a revolution! A revolution in the streets, my lords, must be met—greeted!—with a corresponding revolution in *ideas* . . . values . . . our very identities as Athadians!—or else this so-called revolution will become exactly what all of us fear, and what none of us wants: an earthquake of violence and bloodshed, an ocean of inhumanity and destruction! Men turn to action, Lord Rhin, when their words fail—so *listen to these words*!"

Bors, controlling his temper and not at all intimidated by the Council Chamber or the aristocrats for whom it was a second home, made his points as succinctly as he could.

"It is, sir," Rhin reminded him midway through the session, "the destiny of some men to direct the destinies of other men!"

To which Bors replied: "Only, sir, if those 'other men' consent to it."

And to Lord Rhin's angry, "Impossible! *Impossible*! These men don't want an economy! They don't even want a revolution! I could respect a revolution, but these men are anarchists!" Bors replied:

"Of course it seems impossible to believe in something you don't understand. But if you were to work the way I do, Lord Rhin, and live the way I do, then what I'm saying wouldn't seem impossible at all. It would seem absolutely necessary."

Late in the afternoon, as Council began to weary of the passions and the appeals, the rhetoric and the posturing, Galvus made a final announcement—his plea for the redistribution of all goods and wealth—and boldly declared his own challenge:

"My friends, when a structure has become so wracked and ruined that it cannot fulfill its function any longer, do we continue to patch it up and pretend that it serves as well as it ever did? We do not. We face facts squarely and we tear it down, this useless structure, and we erect a new one, a better structure, a structure improved by what we have learned from the previous one. And that is what's happening in our nation today. For the structure that now constitutes our unfair economic system is collapsing; it has not grown or changed as our society has grown and changed. And while our economic structure has been collapsing, men have learned new things and they've studied how to build a better structure. Call this the act of revolutionaries if you will; but what is revolutionary to one generation becomes a commonplace to the next. I prefer to think of this 'revolution' as a challenge—not an attack—to those of us who, in our hearts, want to build good, new things! Those of us who are truly proud of this nation! Those of us who understand the reality of the situation and are bold and honest enough to face that situation, and not try to hide from it. Aristocratic private control of business has debased us; it has raped the unprotected, it has mismanaged what it claimed to direct, and it has created a situation so critical that if we do not act *now* to save ourselves from it, then not even those things we value will have value any longer! A cooperative society is not a sentiment; a nation of many kinds of ownership and economic strategies is a necessity! And believing in the best we have in us is not only a necessity—my lords, it is imperative!''

Galvus then told the collected Council of what he himself had done to help secure this vision, of how he had taken the first step in redistributing privately held property for public use: his purchase of large tracts of Diruvian fieldland which Bors and the other workers were managing for themselves.

This admission brought forth a vociferous tide of noise and confusion. Cries of ''subsidizing the revolution!'' clashed with outbursts of ''Galvus, we're with you! I'll leave half my estate to the people!''

And Elad, as he witnessed this from his imperial throne, reminded himself again of certain things apparent in the nature of man—self-preservation and paths of least resistance, and ideals, and thoughts, beliefs. . . .

Late in the evening, when Council had been adjourned for many hours, while the Chamber was yet redolent of arguments and loud voices and cries of revolution and calls for new beginnings, Elad sat alone on his dais and watched as the sunlight died outside the tall windows. When Abgarthis entered, Elad was so deeply involved in thought that he did not hear his minister until the old man was very nearly at the steps of the throne dais.

''Still here, my king? Are you not hungry?''

Elad showed a grave expression.

"Are you worried about Queen Salia?" Abgarthis asked, seating himself in a chair.

Elad shook his head; his voice was almost a whisper. "Am I," he asked, "going to bed with poisonous serpents? Or have I been in bed with those serpents all along?"

"Ah." Abgarthis tilted his head. "The Council—or the people. Do you ally with one at the expense of the other? Will the aristocracy show its fangs, as the workers have already?" He read Elad's stare. "You are king of both—of all. The only way to deal with these issues, is to deal with them collectively. They are not separate. What kind of nation," the minister asked him, "do you see in your mind, Elad?"

The king nodded quietly. "Am I the same man who ordered the massacre of hundreds in Sulos?"

Abgarthis watched him.

"Am I the same man who slew the Oracle? Who was nearly slain himself by one of the very revolutionaries I admitted into this Chamber today? Am I the same man who agreed with Lord Rhin, in fact, that we *must* control this nation—and agreed with Galvus, in my heart, that every citizen of this country already controls it?" He rose to his feet, stepped wearily down from the dais and paused, stared at the high windows where the light was fading. "It is difficult for me to do what other men do spontaneously. I seem to watch myself constantly, as though some part of me were a silent observer of the rest of me—where I go, whatever I do or think—as though I were my own audience. I play all these many scenes, as though this were a comedy or a play; I am the puppet inside the stage, but I also control the puppet." Elad shook his head. "It is too much for me. I deal with issues, one at a time, as though each were singular—but a strange thread connects them all. How can I condemn my own brother, and not myself? How can I ignore the working people, to favor this aristocracy and the business interests? How can I harm the many and not say that the few, after all, are also harmed by that? What do these nobles think they have gained? What do they fear they will lose? Money? Authority? Prestige? Is it wise to be hated, but to cling to one's gold? Is it wise to act like a god while one despises the gods? Can one claim that a goal, a good and honest goal, should be achieved by any means available? Or do foul means used to gain that goal dirty its achievement?"

He stared now at Abgarthis with pain-deep eyes.

"I sat here today and saw men act as brutally, and yet as nobly,

266

as they possibly can act—without weapons in their hands. I rejoiced one moment, I despaired the next. And . . . I had no control over it, Abgarthis. Not really. Do you understand that? I began to sense that . . . I do not control this empire, or the lives within it, nor the direction in which it moves. I wondered—and I wonder now—that it could easily fall apart. All of it—the pretense of order, of government, of authority—rests upon such an uncertain foundation. I watched these debates and asked myself again and again and again, *What holds all this together?* If tomorrow we decided to end the pretense, we could. And would anyone notice? It's all held together by only a thread, as if all of us, from noble to dockworker, concealed some great deep secret, and the whispering of the secret would suddenly bring it all to light and . . . release us. One real doubt—one voice loud enough—'It's all a lie, a *lie!*'—and . . . it's over." He shook his head. "And that's true; I know it is true. And, if that is true—because that is true, . . . then why, Abgarthis, hasn't it all ended already, fallen apart as it seems so eager to do?"

Abgarthis, intrigued by this train of thought, made no comment. Elad began to pace the vacant Council Chamber.

"Do you know what we are, Abgarthis? Humanity, I mean. Do you know what man is? Man is a fearful animal; he is an anxious animal, a doubtful animal. Man is an animal of fear, able to construct philosophies to which he cannot aspire. Able to harm himself in incredible ways, and unable to stop harming himself. It's as though all the creatures of a field or a forest somehow communicated their innermost thoughts to each other, but remained only what they were—coarse brutes—despite that. Is that all man is? Is that all our great dreams and philosophies and beliefs come to? Mere . . . useless fantasies? Mere excuses we use to apologize for our own criminal hearts? Because the ideals, once done, can always be undone. We do not have the courage, or the patience—the faith, perhaps?—to place ourselves securely in our own best beliefs. It's—yes, it is—the structure, the structure Galvus talked about. It's as if all that is best in us is composed into a structure, a tower—but the foundation is not secure. We live in the tower in comfort, in wisdom—so we think. But one doubt, one whisper . . . if one stone is removed . . . the awful truth returns. We could spend ten thousand years constructing the finest tower in testimony to ourselves, but one stone loosened—one angry voice, one doubt, one . . . animal—could bring it all crashing down. Man," Elad decided, "does not have the strength to be good. We appeal to what is best in us, only so that our attention is stolen from what we actually do to ourselves—revel in our baseness."

He walked to a chair and wearily sat down, some distance from Abgarthis. The dying light hid him in shadows—shadows he could not command.

"You're tired," Abgarthis told him. "Distraught. Too much emotion in too short a space of time. Revolutions . . . Salia leaving . . . the Imbur's temper tantrums . . ."

Elad smiled softly, rubbed his face with his hands. "When I was recuperating, Abgarthis, she was as solicitous to me as a nurse. Salia. But now I must wonder—how much of that care of hers reflected a wife's concern for her husband? Or a woman's concern for a man? How much of it was simply a queen ingratiating herself to the king upon whom she depended? She was like a child, a child acting as the parent to its actual parent."

Abgarthis swallowed and breathed deeply in the dusky hall.

"What holds it all together?" Elad asked, looking around, looking. "What holds it all together?"

4.

The last peaceful days came with the beginning of an early summer in Barl, the month of the Deer. And while the peace was not without tension or anxiety, and while the people did not realize that they lived in days of peace that foreshadowed a storm, the few weeks that marked the Athadian government's inquiries into economic redistribution, that saw Salia's royal barge make its way east across the Ursalion, and that witnessed Agors *mu-ko-Ghen* take power in Erusabad and become the true *ko-Ghen* were, indeed, days of peaceful suspension.

Some of them recognized it. A prophet imprisoned in Omeria knew. The second son of the dead chieftain of the east saw, and sensed, and knew. In Athad, Galvus and Orain and Count Adred and Lord Abgarthis would sit at the end of a day and look around them, look beyond themselves to see the events of the world and recognize the time of peaceful suspension, the balance in which they lived. And they wondered if the balance would hold. For they loved peace, even though they understood that peace is always suspenseful. For peace is in the beauty of a day's dawning, ephemeral, when we know that the day will be an inclement one. Peace is the silence of relaxation; it is the aching beauty of two lovers in a world that to them seems ordered and stable; peace is a routine of small duties done and accomplishments achieved; it is the companionship of friends, and memories; it is a sense of wholeness and harmony and completion. It is anger held in abeyance. It is promises sure to be fulfilled; it is the truth of the light. Peace exists when people anticipate an optimistic future; it is when the soul is governed by surety.

And it is a suspect thing.

Abgarthis, in one of his rare evenings free, as he sat with his friends, discussed this. For too many, he said, peace is an apathetic condition: they fear apathy and they mistakenly believe that peace can be achieved by action, when taking action ultimately serves only to unsettle the suspension and the balance, and mobilizes the world for further discord. "For it is humanity's damnation," he asserted, "that, even with our splendid imaginations, we forget that our grandparents' lives were as actual and real for them as our lives are for us today. And in forgetting that, we dismiss the lessons of the past as outworn and irrelevant, or we assume that they occurred within a different context and so can have no meaning for us now. But people today are no different than they were then; why then should the context be different? Yet we treat our difficulties as though they were occurring for the first time, immediately within our lifetimes. What good is the wisdom of the ages, if men believe that wisdom once pertinent, but no longer so? Thus we isolate ourselves, and our sensibilities, and our imaginations. The reasons why men harm themselves never change," Abgarthis said. "The joys that men relish never change. It's only the outer fabric of the world—done by man—that changes from one generation to the next, because of our activity; and so we tell ourselves that this transient changingness of impermanent things is actual change, or progress, or improvement."

Galvus, Adred, Orain all agreed with this. Nature does not change; nature is constant and cohesive. Only man's relation to nature changes, and thus his involvement with it, and his perception of it, and so his perception of himself. For nature does not judge man as man judges nature: neither does the spirit within man judge, as man judges his gods.

So it is in times of transition that those who embody new horizons come forward, some of them to be revered by the future, others of them to be damned. Persons who seem prepared, who seem to embody everything at once. Yet they are only men and women who, like prisms, break down the white light that surrounds us to show us all the colors, all the possibilities.

Some of them mean to build new towers.

Some mean to demolish them.

"Beware the man," Abgarthis stated (thinking of some of those in Council, and others in the world), "who sees the past in terms of himself and appeals to the people's emotions: he will do them injustice. But we must trust those who see the future in terms of all people, who appeal to our minds and our ideals. The first man is a shadow; the second, I think, is a light. Remember the parables of Bithitu? 'Is the shadow I see not that cast by myself? Why, then, should I fear it, or think it more than it is? But does not the light of life cause that shadow to be? The light will always return, to burn away the shadow. But we can only burn away our own shadows with the light that dwells within us.' That's what I mean. For if we misunderstand, in a moment of haste, where the shadow comes from—we will destroy the light."

In Hilum, where his ship docked for the day to unload passengers, take aboard new ones and replenish itself with supplies, Thytagoras took the time to visit the city, which he remembered from only a few short, previous stays. He learned that Governor Abadon, who had succeeded Governor Bothin, was sending forces north to the Emarian border in an attempt to contain acts of subterfuge and pillage by Emarian soldiers. This was enlightening. As he reboarded his ship late in the afternoon, Thytagoras noticed a royal barge make port farther up, and he wondered what the reason for it might be. Military advisers?

But as he watched it closely, Thytagoras's suspicions were confirmed: for he saw Queen Salia (whom he knew only by description) come up on deck to observe the city of Hilum from the larboard rail. The cautious guards surrounding her, and the many menials, confirmed Thytagoras's instantaneous impression that this was, indeed, the empire's new queen. Obviously, because Salia did not disembark, this stop in Hilum was but an interim. For where, then, was she bound?

A chill rose in his stomach and Thytagoras slowly shook his head as the most obvious possibility suggested itself to him. When other passengers bound west came aboard, he asked if they'd noticed the royal barge and if any knew its significance. At last a green belly having something to do with steerage told him: "Aye, that's the queen. Bound for Erusabad in that tub. Better hold to the coast in that one."

"Bound for Erusabad?" Thytagoras repeated. "Why?"

The sailor shrugged his shoulders. "You tell me, brother, why them people do whatever it is they do."

Thytagoras leaned on the rail as his galley moved out, keeping his eyes on the fading barge and piecing things together in his mind.

On the twelfth of Barl, Lord General Thomo in Erusabad received a messenger in his offices in the old Authority Building. The man was a courier dispatched a day and a half earlier from Abustad; the letter he carried was marked with the imperial seal. Thomo arranged for the messenger to have a bath, a meal and some sleep before returning to Abustad; and, once the man had left, he stared for several long moments at the roll on his desk.

It bore all the marks of something tremendously important. A single courier out of the last port city in the west bearing a message from the king meant that the dispatch had come by a complicated, speedy route: from boat to rider, from rider again to ship—a relay process the emperor used only for the most urgent of reasons.

Thomo settled his nerves with a cup of wine, then opened the scroll and read it.

It was not what he had expected. Dire expectation gave way to outright astonishment. But when at last Thomo had assured himself that the king meant what he had written (and that the message was not in code), he drank another full glass of wine and changed his clothes, went out of the Authority and took a civil carriage to the Salukadian palace.

He knew that the imperial family had only just returned a week earlier from the funeral service for Huagrim the Great, in Ilbukar; no doubt his intrusion was ill-timed. To his surprise, General Thomo found himself received after only a short wait by the estimable bin-Sutus. Once he was ushered into the *aihman*'s office and offered wine, Thomo pressed into the matter that had caused his unheralded visit.

"You will recall, sir," he said to bin-Sutus, "that I mentioned to you some time ago that I had alerted my lord, King Elad, as to the passing of your master, the most-honored Huagrim?" bin-Sutus nodded politely. "You recall that I suggested, then, to my lord

271

King Elad that it might be in the best interests of my people and your people to arrange a visit by high authorities of my empire, to meet with your new master, the honored Agors *mu-ko-Ghen*?"

"As I recall, my friend, I agreed with your wise decision."

"I have heard from my king and he, too, is in agreement."

"This is splendid."

"He has lately dispatched an imperial emissary from the Athadian court to greet the honored Agors *mu-ko-Ghen* as a friend."

bin-Sutus nodded. "And when may we expect his arrival?"

"Honored bin-Sutus, my lord King Elad sends his wife."

The *aihman* stared at him.

Thomo swallowed a deep breath. "I hope that neither you nor your esteemed Council nor the royal sons of the House of Huagrim will be in any way offended by my lord discharging this duty upon a woman."

bin-Sutus smiled slowly. "Your . . . King Elad . . . does not understand, I presume, that his gesture of goodwill could be interpreted in another way altogether by my master, Agors *ko-Ghen*?"

"I assure you implicitly that he does not. I give you my hands, honored sir, that he does not. And . . . if you would be good enough to do so, I hope you will make this matter quite clear to the *Ghen*."

"Of course, of course . . ." bin-Sutus's smile broadened, and he wiped his eyebrows. "Your people and mine—we have much to learn about one another!"

"I simply wanted to make clear to you that, by sending his queen to you, my lord King Elad means absolutely no disrespect. Please assure the honored *Ghen*, furthermore, that my lord King Elad loves his wife very deeply and looks upon her as his equal, and would in no way jeopardize her dignity by using her to offend your court."

"I am certain of that, yes," bin-Sutus agreed. "And I am certain that Agors will understand this, as well. But I thank you very much for alerting me to it."

Thomo nodded, rubbed his hands together. "I thought it might be best to do so—immediately."

"Very true. Very wise." bin-Sutus moved to allay his guest's anxiety. "I must tell you, now that any potential misunderstanding has been averted, not to worry about this any longer, Thomo-*su*. Please—put it out of your mind. Agors understands that these oversights occur. When may we expect your queen's arrival?"

"Next week; perhaps within a week and a half."

"Excellent; my heart leaps with joy. We will prepare ourselves to greet her with all honor. Thomo-*su*—please, have some more wine," bin-Sutus smiled.

"Thank you, my friend. I believe I'll have another cupful. . . ."

In Lasura one evening, a soldier who had come into the city alone sat drinking with six others; the solitary rider was in from the fieldlands; the six were personal guards to Nutatharis. They spoke quietly, although there were no others in the tavern save for the keeper, who was asleep in a chair at the other side of the room. The place was only partially lit. Outside, the silence of the summer night was complete, the streets desolate.

"More of them today," the rider told the others. "One of the villages halfway to Lake Kilham. Someone had tried to hide some meat and bread. A farmer. A whole mob of them cut him to pieces; killed his wife and children, too. Then, when they tried to get at the food—why, they started killing each other."

Silence, as pairs of eyes glanced at one another.

"What's he going to *do* about it?" the rider asked, desperation in his voice.

One of the palace guards shrugged. "He's doing nothing. He's hiding. Won't come out. He's afraid. Do you believe it?" He chortled grimly. "Nutatharis—afraid!"

"I spoke with Sir Jors earlier today," a second put in. "If anyone's still ruling in this country, it's him. But he swears he doesn't want any part of a plot to overthrow Nutatharis."

"Then he'll die with him," commented a third.

The first looked at the rider. "Have you heard anything from Captain Kurus?"

"He'll be coming. He's making sure that word-of-mouth gets around before he arrives here. It won't do to have him take the throne with half the army against him. Then everything falls apart."

"He'd better get some food in here before he does anything else, or *he* won't be king for very long, either."

A fourth man shook his head. "I don't trust him."

"Kurus?"

"I don't trust him. He knows the people can't do anything. The people of this country are nothing but serfs. Living year to year. They'll kill each other, or starve to death, before they'll move

273

against the government—any government. They don't have the spines for it. They don't know anything except planting and drinking and living day to day. We're the power in Emaria. The army.''

"And if we all side with Kurus, then—"

"Listen to me. After a week or two, enough of the men will become dissatisfied with Kurus and shove someone else onto the throne. Then in another week or two, it'll be someone else. Pretty soon we're just cutting each other's throats, like the peasants. Then what happens? Pretty soon Athadia or Omeria moves in, or Salukadia—"

"Salukadia," the first guard said, and heads turned. He faced the man beside him. "Tell them what you told me. About Nutatharis's letter to Salukadia."

The second man shrugged. "Their king died; the son's taking over. Nutatharis wrote him a letter. Remember that agreement they came to? You know what good it's done Nutatharis?" He gestured behind himself with his right hand, as if he were wiping himself clean.

A few heads bobbed; cups of ale were lifted.

The fourth man continued: "We need a leader, not a rabble-rouser. We need someone who can *do* something. And Kurus can't get food in here any more than Nutatharis can. And if he can't get food, the serfs starve or kill each other, or move off, and all of us starve or kill each other or move off—In a year or two—" He moved a hand across his throat.

One of them, shaking his head, reached for the pitcher of ale: "Just because of the spring floods!"

"No. There was more to it than that. As long as Nutatharis thought he could get away with it, he was giving away everything—he never kept anything in reserve. You know how much he was borrowing? He was borrowing money and promising to pay it back with crops three and four years from now! *I'm* not even *that* stupid! And you have any idea how much food and goods we lost last winter in the Lowlands? It'd all feed this country, right now! He traded food and gold for Athadian weapons, Bithiran weapons, Nisarian steel. . . . Do you have any idea how many merchants got wealthy off him, delivering Nutatharis all kinds of things every *day*? You ought to talk to Jors. Do you know how many *weapons* we have? Storehouses— buildings—full of arms! For who? For *us*? We have more weapons than we have food! Why? Because Nutatharis—hold on!—

because Nutatharis had to be *king*, that's why! It wasn't enough to have an army—he had to have more weapons than we could use in a century! And he kept nothing in reserve! Coffers are empty—always more where that came from! Gold . . . food . . . work . . . serfs—and one good flood, one military jab to your left nut, and it's gone!"

"Can an entire *nation*," one of them asked, "just crumble apart like this?"

Grim stares answered him, and a cold: "We're not crumbling apart; we're sinking under the weight of all those weapons and horses and—steel!"

"Did you ever think you'd see the day when soldiers'd think there were too many weapons?"

"Too many weapons, not enough food. Soldiers have to eat, too, to use those weapons."

Silence prevailed for a few moments. The seven slurped their ale, then listened to the sounds of footsteps in the street. They heard a hand on the tavern door, and mistrustful stares agreed: heavy hands dropped to weapons. If Nutatharis had gotten word of this meeting, of the rebellion—

The tavern door opened. The empty smells of the street blew in, and the newcomer stepped slowly into the room, his eyes lingering on the seven in the corner. He glanced to the proprietor asleep on the far side.

"I realize it's late," he apologized, "but could you possibly see about getting me something to drink?"

The keeper did not move. The stranger disregarded him and carefully approached the soldiers' table. As he came into the light of an oil lamp hanging from a ceiling beam, one of the guards gasped.

"Do you know who *he* is?" he whispered tensely to the man next to him.

"No. He's just a—"

"He's the one who brought *a full sack of grain* to Nutatharis!"

Three weeks of debate in the Council Chamber had made it apparent to Lord Rhin and the others on the investigating committee that, not only was King Elad absolutely sincere in his decision to set up workers' *sirots* throughout the country, but also Prince Galvus and Count Adred's preposterous plan for a gradual redistribution of some enterprises in the empire would actually proceed with the consent of the throne. Not that Elad had agreed to every proposal Galvus had raised: far from it. There were compromises to be reached and complex plans to be organized. But the king had agreed that, once the workers had instituted their *sirots* in the various cities, these new organizations could begin to work with the managers and owners of certain bankrupt and foreclosed businesses to take control of those businesses for themselves and operate them according to whatever guidelines and systems they might themselves set. Furthermore, Elad would set up an office so that the *sirots* would have a voice in the capital, and he would allocate certain funds and order commissions to study where additional funds, gained by taxes from the formal business interests, might best be put to use to encourage the working people's involvement in the economy.

It was, then, a King Elad very much changed by the experiences of his authority, who told Lords Rhin and Falen: "I think we should allow the productive citizens of this country the same benefits we have allowed our nobility, in their business pursuits—the opportunity to put their ideas to the test, and to fail or succeed on the merits of their ideas. Surely you would agree, Lord Rhin, that a simple one or two percent surcharge on your business investments, allocated by the throne to the working people's organizations, will not greatly limit your lifestyle, or your incentive to continue expanding your mercantile interests? I think it best, quite frankly, that Athadia investigate new methods—investigate them cautiously and proceed slowly and rationally—but, yes, investigate them. Is it not to our mutual benefit to have a strong economy? And thus, a strong empire?

Lord Rhin made as noble a protest as he could manage. "I must disagree that it is in the best interests of this nation, my lord, to disintegrate those businesses and that leadership which all of us have worked so long to centralize in these offices. A nation needs leadership, and many small leaders cannot have the force or persuasion or ability of one strong hand. I honestly believe that whatever ills may have been inadvertently created by our current mercantile system can be rectified within the limits of this same system. We have become a mighty empire by virtue of our central authority and the centralization of our businesses—not because we have allowed every man his wont."

The Council session was ended on that reminder—with the nobility against the diversification of businesses and the qualified redistribution of any interests, and with Galvus and Adred and the men from the Diruvian Valley confident that they had accomplished something originally dismissed as wholly impossible.

That evening, a group gathered on a verandah in the palace gardens. Galvus and Adred dictated ideas to Orain, who sat on a bench with pen and tablet and composed the initial draft of the open letter Galvus intended to publish and distribute to all the cities of the empire, augmenting the throne's imperial scheme for instituting the *sirots*.

Bors and the other Kendians all put in their opinions on what Galvus should say and how he should say it; even young Omos brought up a few fine points that Galvus and Adred had overlooked in their preliminary paperwork.

They were interrupted, in the comfortable cool of the evening, by the appearance of Lords Rhin, Falen and three others from the *Priton* Nobility. Immediately Galvus and Adred stood to confront them; Bors and the Kendians got to their feet and stood behind them.

Lord Rhin shook his head sadly, thoughtfully, at Galvus. "Very well," he sighed. "So . . . you have gained. We must deal with you a bit more seriously now."

"What the hell are you talking about?" Galvus growled.

"We will compromise with you," Rhin averred. "We'll allow you and the cattle you insist are citizens to purchase certain rights and certain businesses, to operate as you wish." To Galvus's transparent reaction: "Surely you don't believe that because the king agreed with you in principle, you can now do as you please? Be realistic, Prince Galvus. We'll allow you to buy certain tracts of land; we will allow you to purchase deeds from us; but we're going to need financial guarantees that—"

"You didn't understand a word I said in there, did you?" Galvus interrupted angrily. "For *three weeks*!—and you didn't understand a *word* I said, you lying hypocrite!"

"Of course I did. But you don't honestly expect me to believe that you and these"—a glance at the Kendians—"these workers are such altruists, do you? Let's face reality, gentlemen. None of us are naive; we all know how the world operates, so let's dispense with this charade of brotherhood and community and equality. Now . . . you can be heroes to your holy 'working class' by accepting our very generous terms—"

Bors grunted and pushed his way past Galvus and Adred; before anyone could stop him, he had his hands around Lord Rhin's throat. Rhin squealed once, grabbed Bors's wrists and tugged at them futilely, twisted and turned in the man's hold. Rhin was a stout man, but Bors had spent his life in the fields; he continued to squeeze. Lord Rhin's face quickly began to color.

"Let go of him!" Galvus cried, jumping forward and throwing his hands to the Kendian's shoulders. "Let go of him, Bors!"

"Son—of a—!"

"Not this way!" Galvus nearly yelled. "*Not this way!*"

Bors didn't look at him—he was staring evilly at Rhin—but the mad light in his eyes faded, and with the sticky sound of parting damp flesh, he released his hold on the aristocrat's throat and shoved him away. Lord Rhin, gasping and reeling, crumpled into the arms of Falen and the others.

"I—knew it!" he groaned, wiping frantically at his sore neck. "I knew it! You're just animals! Animals! You'll get nothing from us, *nothing*! See what happens to your precious workers now, you—*filth*! Filthy *animals*! *Nothing* Elad decrees can stop us from—*Nothing*! You filthy—"

Bors growled and fisted his hands threateningly. "Get out of here, you pig vomit, before I finish what I started!"

"You'll regret that you ever—!"

"*Get out of here, cockeater! Now! Now!*"

Still regaining his breath, Lord Rhin turned quickly and hastened from the garden. The others followed him—only Lord Falen paused long enough to warn Galvus and Bors: "That was very stupid. You have no idea who you're dealing with."

After they had gone, all of them sat staring at the ground, saying little. Bors was greatly upset—"I should have just strangled him, right here!"—and was convinced that their appeals in Council had come to naught. "We'll be back in the streets in a week or two," he said despondently. "Galvus . . . I don't blame you."

Adred made some remark about "half a revolution" and then said, "It's no good pretending that we're accomplishing anything when the same people are in control now as before."

But Galvus was impatient with this pessimism. "It'll work," he declared, "because it's the only choice the country has. The more tightly they try to hold it as it is, the faster it'll come apart. The only hope we *have* is the cooperatives and the workers. They'll fight us—but they've already lost. The nation has been sucked dry by these vampires; there's nothing for them to bleed anymore!"

* * *

When, two days later, Lord Rhin presented an unanticipated proposal in Council, he appeared resigned to the fact that, despite all his efforts, the Athadian economy would develop in a fashion counter to his own interests. Deferring to King Elad's decree, he announced:

"I disagree in principle, but in practice I must adhere to the policies our king dictates. However, to guarantee that the rights of all those involved be protected to the utmost, I submit that the institution of the workers' *sirots*, and their operation on a national scale, be overseen by a Coalition Ministry to be set up under the guidance of representatives from each of the assemblies involved—the aristocratic business concerns, the Public Administration Congress, and the workers' representatives. This Coalition Ministry will act as a board of final arbitration on any matters developing—"

Galvus was astonished; when he was recognized by Elad, he took to the floor and promised the Council that this proposal by Lord Rhin was a ruse and a subterfuge designed to check any real advances made by the institution of the *sirots*.

But Elad did not agree with his nephew; concurring with Lord Rhin and the Congress of Nobility that such a Coalition Ministry was a practical and resourceful concept, he had affixed his seal within the week to papers outlining its formation.

"They gave us what we wanted," Adred complained, "and now they're going to take it back, piece by piece."

"I should have strangled him when I had the chance," Bors growled.

When he and the other Kendians left, at the end of that week, on board a merchanter bound for Sulos, they took with them copies of the initial draft of Galvus's proposal for economic redistribution, as well as copies of documents explaining that the *sirots*, once organized, would be answerable to a tripartisan coalition in the capital, wherein any proposals, grievances and referendums would be endlessly debated by parties mutually antagonistic to one another. The Coalition Ministry—the *Khilu*—was obviously nothing more than another stratagem devised by the business interest to defraud the working people.

"Within a few weeks," Bors reminded Galvus, as he boarded ship, "they'll be back on the streets. You've done the best you can, but I'm afraid we've run out of time. You can't compromise principles. Adred was right; you can't have . . . half a revolution."

5.

Count Adred, because he was nervous and had nothing better with which to occupy himself, was sitting in a chair in Lord Abgarthis's office, cracking his knuckles and bouncing one leg on the knee of the other. Abgarthis glanced at him occasionally out of the corner of his eye as he sifted through the morning's box of dispatches.

"Why don't you go out to the games?" he suggested.

"No, . . . I don't feel like doing that. Fighting the crowds . . . nothing but noise and temperamental people . . ."

"Then go buy yourself a new pair of boots. Those are so old they're ready—"

"Well, these have a strong sentimental value for me."

"Or go to a bookstore. You're always good for browsing in bookstores."

"All the good books have been written . . ."

Abgarthis glared at him, friendly but exasperated.

"Am I making you nervous, Abgarthis?"

"Very. Why not go out into the gardens and count the leaves on the trees?" He returned his attention to the pile of documents and scrolls. "Invite Orain. She doesn't know what to do with herself these days, either."

Adred sighed. "Doesn't it affect you, Abgarthis? The Council, I mean. Elad's decision?"

"I've worked in government all my life—long enough to know that by the time men in office finally get around to accomplishing what needs to be done, the reason for it has long since—" He stopped abruptly, held up the letter he had just opened and examined it carefully.

"What is it?" Adred asked him.

The minister set down the sheet. "This is very strange. Very interesting, indeed. Remind me, Adred—what was the name of that *ikbusa* you told me had scared the wits out of Cyrodian? In Ithulia, wasn't it?"

"His name?" Adred dropped his feet to the floor and leaned forward in his chair. "I know Cyrodian told me . . . but I can't recall—"

"Asawas?"

Adred stared. "Yes." He glanced at the letter Abgarthis held. "Why?"

"If it's the same man, he's been arrested in Hilum by Governor Abadon. This letter is from the Church Inquisitor there, Seraficos."

"Why was he arrested?" Adred stood up and approached the desk, leaned over Abgarthis's shoulder and scanned the letter. "For *sedition*?"

The adviser nodded quietly and pursued his lips. "Isn't this intriguing?" he commented in a low voice.

"It's absurd." Adred took the letter from him and read it through. "He wants to send this priest here to stand trial before the government? This is ridiculous!"

"Of course it is, of course it is," Abgarthis agreed, tapping his index fingers on the edge of his desktop.

"Who the hell does Seraficos think he is?"

Abgarthis chuckled. "He thinks he's still living in the fourteenth century. That doesn't matter. He's a powerful Church politician and carries much weight in Hilum; he's a mosquito, a nag-fly. But he doesn't worry me; it's this priest."

"Surely you're not going to bring an *ikbusa* here to stand trial for civil disturbance?"

Abgarthis eyed Adred decisively. "Wouldn't you like to talk to the man who put such a fright into Cyrodian?"

Adred mulled it over. "Yes . . . it would be interesting. But how do we know it's even the same man?"

"With a name like 'Asawas'? I've never heard that name before in my life; obviously it's been made up by him. How many men by that name are there in that corner of the empire? No . . . if he's disturbed Seraficos this greatly"—Abgarthis nodded at the letter—"then this 'Asawas' must have a great deal going for him."

Adred studied the missive again. "'He claims that the world is going to be destroyed by the gods and that therefore men must revolt against their government and their Church. I myself witnessed him perform a sorcerous miracle. The people flock to him. He is a direct and immediate threat to the stability of the country, and I deem it a necessity of the first—'"

"More likely," Abgarthis interrupted, "this prophet is a direct threat to Seraficos himself. The Prophet help the man who tries to get people to think for themselves when Seraficos is around!" He chuckled grimly, set the letter aside.

An abrupt knock on the door brought him up. A Khamar stepped in, slapped his chest and bowed. "Lord Abgarthis—a

281

visitor wishing an audience with the king. He has just come here from Erusabad."

The minister lifted an eyebrow. "Show him in. . . ."

The Khamar backed out, held the door open. Abgarthis rose to his feet while Adred, curious, stepped away. Into the adviser's office came a strongly built man sporting beard and moustache and an intense expression and dressed in civilian clothes although his bearing and manner instantly gave the impression of long military training. Abgarthis recognized him on the moment.

"Lord Abgarthis." He came forward, arm extended; Abgarthis shook his hand, nodded, then, to the Khamar, who left and shut the door.

"Captain Thytagoras. You are out of uniform. Were you recalled here without my knowledge?"

"No, sir. I have resigned my commission and come back here as a citizen—and with a warning for King Elad."

Abgarthis's expression was grave. "Tell me—" Then he glanced at Adred.

Adred coughed slightly and bowed to the two men, politely excused himself and left the room.

As the door closed: "What has happened, Captain Thytagoras? Please . . . sit. There is wine . . . tea—help yourself."

Thytagoras, seating himself in the chair before Abgarthis's desk, leaned to unstopper a flask. He chose a decorated cup and, as he poured, told the minister:

"I have resigned my commission, Lord Abgarthis, because I feel I cannot serve the government if our king is determined not to answer the direct insults and diplomatic violations committed against Athadia by the Salukadian empire. I cannot with pride, sir, wear my uniform or discharge my duties if I feel that I can't uphold our throne's own policies and decisions."

Abgarthis slowly sat down, raised clasped hands to his chin and stared. "This is . . . a harsh verdict that you deliver upon us."

"I gave the matter much thought, my lord. A great deal of thought. But I love my country, and I cannot—as a matter of conscience—follow the dictates that seem to me only to harm the prestige and actual safety of our empire. I cannot do it." He swallowed some wine. "Were I to refuse to do this while in the imperial service, I would be liable for court-martialing; I did not wish that. Therefore—my resignation. And my journey here to alert my king of what I perceive to be profound dangers affecting our country from the east."

"I . . . see," Abgarthis replied quietly.

"May I request an audience with my lord King Elad as soon as possible?"

"Of course, of course," Abgarthis allowed, reaching into his desk and retrieving the book of schedules that he maintained for palace affairs.

As he wrote in it, Thytagoras told him: "I was given to understand by General Thomo that King Elad is sending an imperial representative to Erusabad, to meet with the Salukadian government."

"It is a diplomatic mission only," Abgarthis assured him. "There is nothing untoward in it."

"Has he not sent Queen Salia, Lord Abgarthis?"

Abgarthis set down his pen. "How did you come to know this, Thytagoras?"

"I beg your pardon. But in Hilum, during a layover, I chanced to notice a royal barge in port just as my ship was sailing out. I saw the queen and several attendants and a retinue of guards with her."

Abgarthis finished writing in his schedule, replaced it in his desk and locked the drawer. He stood up. "You would care to bathe and have a meal? Yes . . . Please—I'll show you to an apartment upstairs. Refresh yourself, while I mention your arrival to King Elad."

Galvus and Omos were sitting on the balcony of Galvus's room with despondent looks on their faces, while Adred, nervous and sitting in a chair, was absent-mindedly cracking his knuckles and bouncing one leg on the knee of the other. Galvus, who was becoming irritated, eyed Adred gloomily.

Adred misinterpreted his look. "So . . . is there really nothing we can do in the meantime, except wait? Just—wait to hear from the cities about how they're going to establish the *sirots*?"

"That's all we can do," Galvus replied.

"Did you tell Elad about that stunt Lord Rhin tried, in the gardens?"

Galvus made a sound. "That sort of thing doesn't concern him; Rhin was half-bluffing and half-afraid." He sighed. "It would be so much easier if all these wealthy businessmen and aristocrats were evil people . . . so much easier if the world were divided into black and white, good and evil. But it isn't. Those men are simply afraid—weak and afraid. Weak, because they're used to living at the height of society and have always had things done for them; afraid, because it's going to be taken away. The more successful they are, the more difficult it's going to be for them to adjust. And the harder they'll fight." His tone changed, then. "I'm worried about what will come of it, Adred. I'm afraid it may be out of our hands. We did the best we could, but—the time we need! Time!—for these old dogs to die, time for arguments to be listened to, concessions to be made . . . time for—just for changes to take place. Meanwhile, the people starve, and steal, and murder one another, and attack anyone wearing new clothes. Rhin and his lapdogs will ruin us before we can accomplish anything; that's what I'm afraid of. The *Khilu!*" he growled scornfully. "Do they want the people to go into the streets again? Do they *want* that? Is it just another trick for them to—continue murdering their own people?"

Omos said sadly: "If not in the streets, then . . . war."

That caught Adred's ear; he stopped bouncing his leg and asked Galvus: "War?"

"Didn't you hear? About Emaria?"

"Oh. That." He seemed to dismiss it as no threat.

"It's a very grim possibility," Galvus affirmed. "Elad's been getting a great many reports over the last two weeks from the border forts and from the governors of all the inland cities. The Emarians are serious. The spring floods totally destroyed their croplands; their army is in tatters because of that stupid war they started in the Lowlands; and their treasury is probably bankrupt, because all Nutatharis has been doing since he took the throne is spend money, borrowing against his expectations down the road. But he never expected this. He's just about borrowed all he can from anyone who'll loan to him; I don't even think he can meet his interest payments to Athadian banks, let alone anyone else. He's going to go into default. That certainly won't help the situation for anyone in this country."

Adred hadn't realized it was so serious. "What about our ambassadors there? What were they reporting about all this when it was happening?"

Galvus smiled cruelly. "They could only report what Nutatharis's men told them; they couldn't substantiate rumors, especially incredible rumors. Who believes that? But they all arrived home from Lasura two days ago—and they're not going back.

Elad is going to keep them here. What clearer signal do you want that we're going to start sending troops down the Ussal?"

"Hasn't Elad had any communications from Lasura?"

"Nutatharis replied to one charge: that he didn't actually order his field soldiers to attack Athadian villages and grain silos and steal Athadian grain. He claims his people are not responsible; he says it's some trick to discredit him."

"Hell, he's been a liar from the crib."

"Of course. But this is becoming critical. Abgarthis told me this morning that the latest word is a report of Emarian infantry wiping out a small village of ours just southeast of the border. Sixty-three people killed, the village burned, food and horses and cattle stolen. If anything's going to start a real war, that will. I spoke briefly with Captain Uvars—he confirms it. He's just waiting for the official signal."

Adred stood up and crossed the room, walked back to his chair and sat down with a disgusted look on his face. "So much for the revolution. Anyone caught in the streets will just have a uniform slapped on him and find himself in the front line infantry."

"Just watch and see how quickly it'll happen," Galvus sneered. "I'll tell you something else, too. I won't say who told me, but Rhin and some of his friends are selling weapons to Nutatharis—secretly."

Adred slapped a fist into the palm of his hand and cursed.

"Any money Nutatharis can scrape up—and he can do it, even if he has to steal it, because people will invest in war—he's using to buy all the weapons and supplies Rhin can send him. I think it's all lovely, just lovely. Our own money going into Emaria so that Emaria can use it to hurt us—Lord Rhin sucking the blood of his own country. And try to stop him. He's much too crafty. Did you know that he actually has bodyguards now?"

"I saw him in the street yesterday, yes," Adred nodded. "Two soldiers with him."

"They're mercenaries out of Pylar. The serpent . . ."

Galvus, thoroughly sickened by it all, looked out across the city and crossed his arms heavily over his chest.

Orain came into the room unannounced; at the sound of her footsteps, Galvus looked back across the room.

"Join us!" he called to his mother. "Omos . . . please." He picked up an empty goblet sitting on the table before him and passed it to his friend; Omos filled it from a flask on a nearby stand.

Adred walked over to Orain and took one of her hands; she looked very tired and upset. "What is it?" he asked her.

"Oh . . ." she said wearily, allowing him to lead her to a small couch. "That—Ogodis! He just makes me feel so—"

"He's leaving, isn't he?" Adred asked, sitting down beside her.

"No, no, not anymore, he isn't." To the expressions she received: "He was preparing to return to Sugat, yes. But this afternoon a Captain Thytagoras arrived from Erusabad with some bad news. Do you know him, Adred?"

"No. But I was with Abgarthis when he received him. I left—don't know why he's come back."

"Well . . . apparently he and Elad talked for quite a while. Thytagoras hates the Salukadians. Ogodis heard about his arriving here and so, of course, he had to interfere and drag Thytagoras off and talk to him in private. Idiot . . . So now the Imbur isn't leaving. He's just going to stay here and continue making our lives miserable."

Galvus lifted his head in Adred's direction. "How long, do you think, before Salia reaches Erusabad?"

"If she isn't there by today," he replied, considering it, "then she should be by tomorrow or the next day. That barge of hers wasn't built for speedy trips, though. And you've got to allow for the winds, and for a storm or two." He looked at Orain. "What exactly was Thytagoras complaining about? Do you know?"

She shook her head. "I just caught snatches of it in the hallway. Abgarthis is very upset. Thytagoras, I think, seems to feel that our policy toward the Salukadians is all wrong; he's hard-headed and he thinks we should be more forceful. Abgarthis said he's a bigot."

"More forceful!" Galvus chuckled darkly—and when Adred glanced at him, the young prince drummed his fingers on the edge of his table, mocking a war march.

"I don't know," Orain said quietly. "I don't know. I'm just . . . very frightened. I just feel very afraid that—that everything bad is going to happen."

PART VII

The Fall

1.

A swarming crowd of curious onlookers was waiting on the wharves as Salia disembarked from the royal barge. No announcement had been made to the people of Erusabad concerning her arrival: but the sight of the imperial ship from the western empire dropping anchor had sent waves of excitement through the streets. Lord General Thomo, who had been informed of the queen's arrival the moment the barge had been sighted, found that his coach was slowed and stalled by larger than usual crowds all the way from Himu Square to the Ibar Bridge. While he impatiently waited, fretting and concerned that the mobs might spontaneously lose control, Thomo ordered three of his escort retainers to hurry to the Salukadian palace and protest the situation and demand reinforcements from the city patrol.

Thomo's order had just been given when blaring trumpets and the clacking noise of hoofs stole his notice. Behind his coach, where the streets were clogged with swaying passersby, travelers and *shimari'i* ("people who lived in the open"), the lord general saw advancing standards waving atop erect poles. The horns continued to blare, and very quickly the packed masses parted in struggling waves, the people crushing each other in their hurry to clear the bricks. Many young boys and girls climbed onto walls or low roofs or statues to escape the city patrol's relentless advance.

Mounted Salukadian soldiers stood alongside Athadian guards, holding back the curious, while they, themselves, seemed eager to catch a glimpse of the western queen. Thomo stepped out of his coach and drew on his newly polished helmet, adjusted his belts and his vest and gloves. He glanced behind him, saw the other carriages lining up, and nodded to Lord Sirom, who was just stepping down. Thomo strode forward as a stiff double file of Khamars marched loudly down the barge plank and took their positions on the quay. He saluted them, then stood erect, arms at his sides, and waited for Queen Salia's appearance.

Two more Khamars appeared at the rail of the barge; then, with a prelude from an unseen trumpeter on deck, Salia appeared. She stepped up quickly behind the Khamars and followed them down the plank onto the stone. When she reached the quay, her Khamars moved aside, joining those others who had formed a double wall directing the queen toward Thomo, Lord Sirom and the carriages.

Thomo fairly gasped when he saw her. Salia was dressed in a beautiful simple blue and white gown studded with precious gems, her hair coiffed, her features delicately colored. Gilt sandals gleamed with sunlight where they showed beneath the hem of her gown; even her doeskin gloves, impractical in the hot eastern climate, were decorated with small diamonds. But it was the beauty of her, the total effect of her glamorous appearance, that stole Thomo's breath for a moment. He had never seen Queen Salia before, but he had heard it bruited about that his king had married the most beautiful woman in the west. As he looked upon her now, Thomo believed that to be the truth. The glow which Salia exuded, the delicacy, the pure wonder of her features—it was astonishing. Thomo had seen many attractive women, but this one, he thought in his fascination (recalling a scene from some old drama), was a beauty to divide houses, a woman to die for.

Queen Salia came forward in a spritely gait and eyed Thomo and Sirom frankly as she stepped before them and held out one gloved hand. Thomo cleared his throat as artfully as he could manage; he was aware of perspiration trickling down his forehead and face. He bowed formally, took his queen's hand and kissed her glove, straightened and met her eyes. Blue eyes, deep and sparkling as sapphires.

"Queen Salia. Welcome to Erusabad."

She smiled; it was a very feminine, a girlish or young woman's smile, guileless and genuine. "Lord General Thomo. Thank you for meeting me. Lord Sirom?"

Sirom bowed and took her hand. "My queen. Welcome, in the name of the gods."

Thomo, despite his still marveling at her, managed to inquire: "I trust your voyage was a safe one, Queen Salia?"

"Oh, yes, quite. And very speedy, too."

"With—your permission, I have a coach and an escort ready. Our men will see to your things."

"Thank you. Yes . . . it's very warm, isn't it?"

"I'm afraid so. It's always rather warm, here."

Sirom smiled in agreement, excused himself and moved to greet the ambassadors now exiting the barge.

Salia nodded to Thomo, indicating that she was ready to enter her coach. The lord general led the way and, offering his arm, helped her in.

A trumpet sounded and the coach rumbled forward, circled around and made its way back under the Ibar. Thomo, excusing himself before he did so, reached his head out the window and called to his driver: "Take Losun Boulevard, will you please?" He explained to Salia: "The streets were quite busy when we made our way here."

"Yes, I saw that."

"The people become excited. . . ." He was staring at her again.

Salia nodded, understanding, and pushed open the window on her side of the carriage to look out. "It's a very beautiful city, isn't it?" she remarked.

"Yes, it is. Very old. Probably the oldest city in the world, at least of any consequence. Some of these streets and buildings are over two thousand years old."

Salia shook her head as though incredulous.

"With . . . your permission," Thomo told her, "we'll stop first at the Central Authority Office where our government is located. Later today you'll be presented to the Salukadian court."

"That's fine. I've been trying to—" She stopped suddenly, seeing something in the street.

"What is it?" Thomo leaned closer to her to peer out her window.

The carriage, as it passed through a wide section of the boulevard, offered a view of a small mall just ahead. The coach slowed in traffic as it advanced toward the intersection with Losun Boulevard, which gave Salia time to see what was occurring in the mall.

A crowd of people were surrounding a stone platform. A man in Salukadian state colors was reading from a long scroll; behind him stood dozens of men and women, their ankles and wrists tied. As the official read from the scroll, Salukadian soldiers grabbed the persons in line and, one after another, walked them forward, forced them to kneel and variously placed a hand or foot upon a wooden chopping block. Without further preliminaries, a soldier wielding a decorated sword lopped off the victim's foot, or hand, or perhaps a few fingers. It was done mechanically and precisely; few of the prisoners cried out or showed any fear or even much expression. As they were mutilated, they were quickly pulled away and led down the stone platform to a clearing in the street where robed men were poking at fires with metal brands and working with bandages and tall jars of oils and ointments.

As their carriage moved onto Losun and the scene was hidden, Salia turned to Thomo. "What are they doing to those people?"

The lord general felt self-conscious. "They're criminals," he explained. "The Salukadians have a very strict form of punishment. If someone commits a crime and is caught, he's branded; if he commits another crime—well . . . if he steals, it means his hand; if he tries to escape, it means his foot. For lesser infringements—slander, let's suppose, or trying to bribe a city official, or even looking at another man's wife—a man is disfigured or—again . . . branded. . . ."

Salia remained quiet.

"It is barbaric," Thomo asserted. "Sometimes a quarter of the people you see on the street have been punished for petty offenses."

Salia asked softly, "I suppose, then, that they have fewer criminals than we have in the west."

"Actually, they don't. People won't stay honest because they're threatened with punishment; they commit crimes because for some reason they think they need to. And if they're hungry . . . Look at them all." He nodded out the window.

Salia didn't bother to glance at the teeming throngs. But she remarked, "You sound very bitter, Lord General. Do you dislike the easterners?"

He eyed her candidly. "No. Not entirely. In their own way, they are a very great people. What we have here in Erusabad are a thousand different tribes, more different kinds of people in one place than was ever the case in any of our major cities. All of them are ruled by Salukadia, but each comes from a different tribe or family. But—no, I don't dislike them. They have their ways, we have ours. I've tried to be patient; I've learned as much of them as I could, although I've only been here a short while. They are—" He seemed to search for a word, but settled for: "They are human beings, after all."

Salia smiled slightly.

"You'll meet bin-Sutus this afternoon. He is an *aihman*, a Salukadian courtier of high rank, a lord. If you're curious, he can explain them much better than I can."

"I would like that."

"Fine, fine. The peoples of Salukadia," he continued, "believe that each person leads not one life, but several—that the soul returns to earth following death. Time and history, for them, are a great wheel. I believe they call it *arka*, this law, this natural law. The Great Wheel of Return. Some such thing."

"It is fascinating," Salia allowed. And then, slyly: "Do you believe in any of it, Lord General?"

"With all honesty," Thomo replied, "the more I see of life, and the longer I live, the more sensible their beliefs seem to me."

Thomo had done the best he could in preparing an apartment for his queen. Although she would be staying at the Salukadian palace in Erusabad (which, Thomo explained to Salia, had once been the villa of an important Athadian family), still the lord general wished to impress her with whatever the refurbished Central Authority could provide for the queen's brief sojourn there. He had spent rather liberally from the government funds he controlled and had purchased new divans, cushions, draperies—a wide assortment of all sorts of furnishings.

Still, Thomo was somewhat apologetic as he escorted Salia into her room; but she allayed his disquiet with:

"No, no, Lord General, this is quite satisfactory. I thank you; you have gone to a great deal of trouble for me."

She was sincere. Thomo was impressed, for he had feared that Elad might have married a very spoiled and pampered young princess.

"Splendid," she told him as she walked about the room and examined a few things, then glided to an open window. "But this is the most enjoyable quality." She turned on her heels and grinned at him. "The nice, fresh breeze! It's so fragrant."

"I reminded myself of the palace in Athad," Thomo explained. "The gardens are just below your window."

"Do I smell hyacinth?"

"Oh, yes." Thomo clasped his hands behind his back and watched her, feeling pleased with himself. "I'll excuse myself, now, Queen Salia. Whenever you're ready—I've had a meal prepared for you. And then we can alert bin-Sutus. He will escort you to the Salukadian palace."

"Thank you." She smiled brightly from the window. "Thank you, Lord General."

Thomo left her, then, and sent in two woman-servants to attend her, while he himself made sure that the preparations for her meal were completed. The trays were just being done when one of the young servants came to him to tell him that Salia wished him to join her.

He entered Salia's chamber on the queen's cordial invitation and instructed the servants to place their dishes and trays on a small table across the room. Salia had changed her clothes: she was dressed now in a rather diaphanous pink gown, and she had let her hair down. Once the food and wine were set out and the servants gone, Salia thanked Thomo again and, alone with him, asked him to tell her more about these people of the east.

Their conversation was interrupted by a knock on the door. The lord general stood up and excused himself, crossed the room and greeted the Khamar who saluted him.

"Lord bin-Sutus of Salukadia, Lord General. Whenever you wish to receive him."

Thomo glanced across the room toward Salia; she had overheard.

Wiping her mouth with a cloth, she said: "Have him come up. I wish to see him, and it's much cooler up here, with the breeze."

Thomo nodded to the Khamar, who saluted, backed out and moved down the corridor. Thomo swung the door closed.

"He is a good man, this bin-Sutus?" Salia stood up and moved to a divan set before an open window.

"Yes," Thomo replied, without hesitation. "He is affable, intelligent—he understands our position, although he serves Agors *ko-Ghen*."

"I believe I will greet him in—"

A knock again on the door. Thomo answered it; in stepped two Khamars and, between them, the tall, long-robed and bald *aihman*. bin-Sutus did not smile, but his eyes were friendly as he stepped across the floor toward Salia. He bowed deeply, after the eastern fashion, with hands clasped, and greeted her:

"All the welcomings and best wishes to the Queen of the Athadians from my lord Agors *ko-Ghen* and our people. Queen Salia, I am bin-Sutus, your servant."

Salia smiled to him and held out her hand; bin-Sutus took it and pressed it to his forehed. Salia told him, "*Lo nosi nasin du padurru, see teh moru, sim aihman bin-Sutus-su.*"

General Thomo's eyes went wide in astonishment.

bin-Sutus, just as surprised, straightened himself and admitted, "I . . . was not told! You speak *iy Hasni*, Queen Salia?"

She was smiling with delight. "Only a little, *aihman-su.* I studied as much as I could during my voyage here."

"You seem to have learned a great deal. However . . . 'pad-dur-ru,' with your indulgence."

"What did I say? 'Pad-dur-*ru*'?"

"I'm afraid so."

Salia laughed out loud. "I have no wish at all to greet the Salukadian empire so unfairly!"

"I quite understand," bin-Sutus smiled. He seemed quite charmed by this young woman's natural beauty and graciousness.

Thomo, who had learned a small amount of the *Hasni* vocabulary, was yet unfamiliar with the error Queen Salia had committed. He coughed; Salia winked to bin-Sutus and explained to the lord general: "I meant to greet the Salukadian people with much respect and in friendship; unfortunately, I greeted them with respect and ox blood!"

"Ox blood!" Thomo exclaimed, finding it only grimly humorous. "Gods!"

bin-Sutus showed him a look of polite indulgence.

"Will you," Salia asked him, rising up, "share wine with me, *aihman-su*?"

"I would be much honored to do so, in the name of my *Ghen*."

"When my ambassadors are prepared, then we can visit your lord."

"I know that my lord Agors *ko-Ghen* looks forward to the moment."

"Thank you, bin-Sutus." Salia seemed touched. "Thank you. . . ."

Like all educated men, Agors was proud of those accomplishments of his that required the application of mental skill and an appreciation of life's subtler nuances. And, especially because he was a soldier and athlete, he thought very highly of himself for being a proficient poet. While many of his acquaintances in the military were able to play musical instruments, or paint wonderful landscapes on silk (as was worthy of a nobleman or dignitary associated with the court of the Son of the Gods), Agors considered poetry to be the highest art or form of expression one could attain, apart from the leadership of men and the authority of empire. He had, then, constructed many verses, which he kept in a golden box in his sleeping chamber, and which from time to time he reread with a mind to gaining inspiration to write further. One of his favorites was a fantasy (if, indeed, it truly was a fantasy) that he'd composed idly one afternoon while observing some of the beautiful young courtesans familiar to the nobility.

In former lives I know I've seen
You and these sights which I retell;
I was a warlock great and fell
Who loved you as a king his queen.
I captured you against your will
Through a spell known to a demon;
Against all laws made you my leman,
To salve your heart, my lust to still.
I gave you golden chalices,
Young girls and eunuchs for your own
And lutes of glad and subtle tone,
Lush gardens for your palaces.
There was no wish my warlock hands
Could not cull for your desire:
No ice-locked land or hell-pent fire
Prevailed against my dark commands.
My arrogance and quenchless pride,
Drowned my heart in deeps of lust,
And so it was, as all men must,
I, the peerless warlock, died.
My many lives have made me tame;
I suffered much to cleanse my sins;
With countless lives my magic thins;
I know you, but know not your name.
Through all Times each strains and strives;
This but the feeble art of men;
What gods, I dream, may once again,
Relight our love in future lives?

Agors had felt quite pleased with this poem. He was not a
romantic man—he had no wife, no true heart-love, and only
occasionally did he spend a night with a woman, when he felt that
he must to clear his mind for more important things; and yet, he
told himself that this verse of his had truly captured the simple
elegance, the drama and discord, of the Man and the Woman of
life, trapped on earth, uniting and reuniting, needing one another
but not understanding one another. He had discussed this work of
his with friends, and they had assured Agors that the poem
captured superbly the spirit of universal *arka'shi*. Even his brother
Nihim, upon reading the lines, had agreed that the verse had merit
but had seemed suspicious that such sentiments had issued from
his older brother's heart, and had commented: "What? Why so
truthful with your verse, O *Ghen-mu*?"

294

Agors was not, however, thinking specifically of this poem, or of any of his verses, the afternoon he prepared to greet the queen of Athadia and her retinue. The drama of Man and Woman was the farthest thing from his mind; how best to dominate these proud Athadian dogs was uppermost. Already today Nihim had cautioned Agors not to offend the westerners, not to gloat, not to bait them or treat them with contempt—not even with sly, veiled contempt.

But Agors thought so little of the western people, and so self-righteous was he in his own personal estimation, that it was asking much of him not to greet the Athadians as an eagle would a nest of mice.

Nevertheless, Agors did plan on restraining himself. By mid-afternoon, told that the carriage conveying the western queen and her ambassadors was making its way toward the palace, Agors felt that he had solaced his pride and suspicions enough to maintain composure as he took his throne in the Audience Hall. Nihim sat in a smaller throne to his left; and standing on both sides of him, stretching in wings, were his *aihman-sas*, his guards and the hundred ministers of the *Hulm*, his Council. The golden carpet had been rolled out; it stretched from the first steps of the throne dais all the way across the Audience Hall to the entranceway. Sunlight poured through the open roof; festooned banners and hanging draperies and clouds of flowers flapped and swayed in the breeze; birds fluttered high above, chirruping from the tall trees that reached through the ceiling; the great fountain at the other side of the Hall tinkled and splashed musically; and two hundred lamps and incense braziers filled the immense chamber with a wispy aroma of rose and sandalwood.

At the sound of gongs atop the palace roof, Agors settled himself in his throne, idly adjusted the rings he wore on his hands, straightened his mustache and awaited the appearance of the western dogs.

The great doors of cedar inlaid with gold and ivory were pushed inward.

Fifty Salukadian soldiers tramped in and lined up on both sides of the carpet.

Ten Khamars followed them, leading the imperial procession toward the *Ghen*.

Agors, curious, watched keenly; he could discern hints of Queen Salia's long blonde hair through the moving shoulders of

295

the armored Khamars. He was intrigued; he had heard of this young woman's uncommon beauty.

Like the sound of thunder falling silent, the Khamars marched to the foot of the dais stairs, parted and fell to both sides. And from behind them, dressed in white and rose and scarlet, attired with jewelry and ornaments, rings and torques and pendants—riches that could only enhance her beauty but not vie with it—came Queen Salia.

Agors leaned forward, stunned, and stared at the most beautiful woman of the west. His heart stopped. She was—

Trumpets announced her.

"Wise son of conquerors, *khilhat, domu ghen sa ko-ghen,* before you comes—"

Lines from that idle poem of his returned to his mind on the instant.

To salve your heart, my lust to still . . . My arrogance and quenchless pride . . . In former lives. . . .

Queen Salia looked up at him, said something in his own language, and smiled.

2.

To the prescient, history shows that it can be the simplest thing imaginable to assume power in a society that has fallen into desolation. And if one is boldly resolved and self-confident in taking that power, the process can be swiftly accomplished. Tyrants, though they are calculating and prudent, are loud. And it is that loud voice to which the people will listen, rather than to the whispering portents that issue from the ruins of their past.

In Lasura, where the powerless serfs had been reduced to savaging one another to keep their bellies full, the erosion of King Nutatharis's stability had been hastened by his own bad judgment. Unable to keep men loyal to him, with no money by which to pay them, without goods and crops in adequate amounts to trade with his neighbors, and in a position of military failure in the Lowlands, King Nutatharis—who but a scant year before had prided himself on his position, and who all his life had boasted that to live fully means to live dangerously—looked around him, saw the results of what he had done, and plotted to salvage what he could.

Sir Jors, his only remaining man of trust in a court that Nutatharis had deliberately kept exclusive, swore that he was still faithful to his lord, as were many of the palace guards and several legions of the army. But fully half that army—those men in the field who had been abandoned after the abortive spring engagements in the Lowlands—were swearing their allegiance to this upstart Captain Kurus, the rebel chief. Nutatharis remembered the man: Kurus had always been ambitious, jealous of the Athadian Cyrodian, and had often promised the king that should Nutatharis be in need of an ally to take command of the faltering troops, he was the man. Nutatharis had rejected him as dangerously arrogant and reckless. Here, then, was the result of that misjudgment: Kurus turned against him, organizing his own army and promising to form his own government once he had marched to Lasura and beheaded "the treacherous madman who sold his nation for his own benefit!"

Nutatharis looked around him, and knew that if he expected to live (dangerously or otherwise), then he must take refuge someplace, let these tempestuous events storm themselves into quiet, and meanwhile formulate his own plan for retaking his throne from the rebels. But when he had suggested this possibility to Sir Jors, that courtier had responded with the obvious:

"Where will you go for safety, my lord? To Athadia—where Cyrodian has been executed? To Salukadia—which refuses to answer your letters? Into the open territories? There you would live in a hut; and you would be forced to move far enough away so that no one—absolutely no one—would suspect who you were."

That was apparent; Nutatharis had come to the same conclusion. But . . . to *where* could he escape? It would be necessary for him to transport weapons with which to protect himself, to move a small army of men as guards, to take horses and clothes and—

That very evening, as he stood upon a balcony of his palace, looking out into a capital city that was quiet and dark, Sir Jors came to Nutatharis to explain that much of his soldiery, and all the peasants, had rallied behind a new rebel leader. No, he didn't mean Kurus; Kurus, so far as could be determined, was still to the east biding his time and collecting more and more of the dispossessed to him.

"Who, then?" Nutatharis asked his man.

"Do you recall the shaman who came here a month ago? The one with the sack of grain?"

Nutatharis went cold. "That . . . *sorcerer*? Thader— Thameron?"

Sir Jors nodded sharply. "I am given to understand that for the past few weeks he has been traveling the countryside in the company of our renegade troops. He has perhaps a legion with him."

"A *legion*? How—" Nutatharis was aghast. "How could he gather an entire legion of men to him in . . . two weeks? Three weeks?"

Sir Jors told him quietly: "They believe in him."

The king reddened. "Find him. Find this charlatan . . . I want to speak with him. Have him brought here, I want to—"

"He is here already, Nutatharis."

"What?" He rose from his seat and quickly approached Sir Jors, almost collared him in his anxiousness, his frenzy. "What are you saying, he is already here?"

"He's come here to see you. He—"

"*Here*? In this *palace*?"

Jors ducked his head.

"Show him— Bring him in here!"

"He is downstairs, my king. In the Throne Hall."

"What the hell is he—?"

"I couldn't stop him. But I think you'd better—"

"Jors, what is all this?" Nutatharis asked him, pained. "Why are you—"

"I think you'd better see him. He most assuredly wants to speak with you. He . . . can help you, my lord."

Nutatharis swallowed thickly. "*Help* me?"

"He is an extremely . . . powerful . . . charlatan, King Nutatharis."

Keeping his eyes on Sir Jors for some time, Nutatharis tried to see into his mind. But the king wasn't certain what to think. He wiped his sweating face, then moved past his minister and hastened through the door, hurried down the corridor and took the wide stairs leading to the ground floor of the palace.

The sorcerer was sitting comfortably in Nutatharis's throne chair, legs crossed; his right hand, resting upon the chair arm, held a drinking goblet. Thameron was dressed, not in the robes Nutatharis had last seen him in, but in armor: Emarian state armor, with all insignia removed.

Before the king could say a word, Thameron, betraying an odd

298

smile, lifted his left hand to indicate the wine jug and a second goblet on a table before him. "Drink with me, lord king."

"I want an explanation for this."

"Certainly. But do not pretend with me, Nutatharis: you and I must speak frankly. Come here; sit." He rose, vacating the throne. "Drink wine. I am here to—"

Nutatharis, taking the steps of the dais, came beside him; he placed a heavy hand on the sorcerer's shoulder, helping him away from the throne. "Do you think that this is just another chair?" he asked coldly, as he sat.

Thameron grinned and stepped part way down the dais, pointed to the wine goblet. It was filled.

Nutatharis told him, "I'll have no wine."

"You do not trust me?"

"You are foul; you are evil. You and that—Eromedeus . . . You're in a plot against me? Is it you two who've caused these crimes in my land?"

"So much simpler to place the blame on others, isn't it, Nutatharis? You have nothing to fear from me, nor from Eromedeus. Now take up your wine and listen to what I have to say to you."

"I'll have no wine." His stare was hot, his pose—as he sat— akin to a crouch.

Thameron frowned. He glanced at his own wine goblet, lifted it to sip, then approached the throne and handed it to Nutatharis. "Be done with this nonsense," he growled. "Here . . . sit, and drink, and listen to what I tell you, and your throne will be a throne again, and you king of the land, your dangers circumvented."

Nutatharis watched him for a long moment. Just as Thameron, exasperated, turned to set his goblet aside, Nutatharis reached for it; Thameron handed him the cup, then moved down to stand at the foot of the dais.

"You think I am evil?" he asked the king. "Not so. I am not capable of doing evil, Nutatharis, because the things that I do, I do for a higher purpose. I am much-learned; I have been to the place where good becomes evil, and evil good. You know nothing of evil: all you know are matters of pride and arrogance and vanity."

"You will explain to me why—"

"Drink your wine and listen to me, for I have come here to aid you. I am powerful. I know you are—"

Nutatharis watched him closely, lifted the goblet to his lips and sipped. The wine was warm.

"—you are in grievous circumstances. My journey to speak with the undying stranger proved fruitless; he could tell me nothing that I did not already know. I think it desirable for both of us to decide upon a mutual—"

"What are you doing?" Nutatharis broke in suddenly, an edge to his voice.

Thameron stared at him, not understanding. "King Nutatharis, I—"

"*What are you doing?*" he demanded again, his voice rising with a note of real fear. Nutatharis set his wine cup on the arm of his throne, grasped the seat strongly to lift himself up. His whole body was shivering. "You're . . .*changing!*" he gasped.

"King Nuta—"

"You're . . . *fading*, you're—"

"Nutatharis!"

The king gasped, struggled to hold himself up, then slumped weakly onto the cushions. "You are—!" And then, as his speech slurred, he realized. "You . . . *poisoned the wine!*"

Thameron stared at him.

"You . . . *poisoned* . . . the *wine*," Nutatharis whispered, feebly trying to move. "I—I can't *see* . . . I'm on *fire*. . . ."

Thameron told him quietly, "It is better this way, believe me. Emaria must survive."

"You . . . pppoissss—" Nutatharis jumped suddenly, his whole body quaking, hands and legs twitching; tears of pain poured down his face. "Not . . . like *this*. . . ." He coughed; he shook his head from side to side; the tears dripped down his cheeks and the king bared his teeth, bit his lower lip until he drew blood. "Not . . . like—"

"*You will yourself be slain by the heart of a child, and your own fear will encourage the slaying. You will not win, Nutatharis. A man may wish for more than he can endure.*"

The final convulsion seized him; as though a powerful force had grabbed his feet, he was drawn forward, and he slipped halfway from the cushion. Then he relaxed. A line of blood drooled from the teeth clamped in his lip; the blood seeped into his beard.

"It's . . . better this way," Thameron whispered.

A noise behind him. Thameron turned. Into the huge, empty Throne Hall came Sir Jors, armor clanking hollowly, the lights of the high-hanging lamps sliding upon breastplate and greaves.

Wordlessly he approached Thameron, looked at his dead king's body slumped upon the throne of state.

Thameron said to him, "Give me your sword."

Jors swallowed thickly. Gradually, he pulled his longsword from its sheath, handed it to the sorcerer. Thameron hefted it, then stepped up the stairs and with his free hand took hold of Nutatharis's warm corpse. He shoved the body back into the chair, draped the right arm over the throne so that the jeweled hand dangled. With a quick stroke, Thameron lifted and brought down the sword; Nutatharis's right hand jumped free of the wrist and a jet of blood arched and splashed onto the dais.

He bent and retrieved the hand; then Thameron turned and descended the steps to return Sir Jors's sword. The courtier took it, staring at the blood that streaked it. Thameron continued down the stairs; still holding Nutatharis's severed hand, he tore free a long hanging drapery that decorated one side of the dais's enclosure. He wrapped the hand in the cloth and carried it to Sir Jors.

Jors wiped his blade clean on another drape, sheathed the weapon, then took the sorcerer's bundle. Looking deeply into Thameron's eyes: "Was it . . . necessary?"

"You know that it was." And, more cruelly: "Why did you and your guards ask me to do it if you didn't think it necessary?"

Jors gave him no answer; he averted his gaze.

"Give this to the soldiers; see that they deliver it to Kurus. If they wish to speak with me, tell them to come here in the morning. For now, I would prefer to sleep."

Mutely, Sir Jors nodded.

"I have no ambition to rule this nation," Thameron warned him. "I do so only because you and the others have expressly asked me to do so."

"We understand that."

"Good." Thameron walked away, boots echoing in the large emptiness.

Jors called after him, "What of the grain?"

"Within seven days," the sorcerer replied, still walking away, "you can begin carting grain out into the villages."

'No one will dispute your rule," Jors told him, as if to convince himself, "if you give us grain."

At the door, Thameron turned and asked of him: "And after the grain? What then, Sir Jors? What then will you ask of me?" He shook his head and left the Throne Hall.

301

3.

Ostensibly, of course, the banquet was held to honor the visiting queen of Athadia and her ambassadors; privately, however, Agors assumed that much could be learned of the Athadian government's true aims and designs if he listened attentively enough to idle conversation. For this reason he drank little during his meal and even less during the entertainments that followed. What the *Ghen* had not anticipated, however, was that the presence of the beautiful Salia should so completely dominate the feasting. Agors beheld, more with amusement and intrigue than alarm, the pretentious antics of his court as they vied to gain the eye of the beautiful western queen.

During a presentation of white-robed dancers, accompanied by flocks of doves, Agors witnessed the elder bin-Hasses, in his day a womanizer of repute, order a sample of wine produced from his own vineyards presented to Queen Salia for her approval. And while a circus of jugglers and acrobats from Kudeshar filled the Feasting Hall with much applause and cheers, the unctuous Utto-sen-gar had one of his man-slaves deliver a priceless ring to Queen Salia as a token given in gratitude because, as Utto-sen-gar's slave explained to the surprised woman, "the richness and delight of your presence here makes the more material riches and delights of life seem pale and usual."

Salia accepted these gestures, and more, from the members of the Salukadian court with a graciousness and a self-effacing politeness that seemed, to Agors, curiously genuine. Despite his cynicism (he suspected King Elad for sending this beautiful wife to the east), he found himself drawn, as well, to the yellow flower of the western empire. But he refrained from displaying his mood with such obviousness that the entire hall might see and comment.

Yet the *Ghen*'s attraction to the young queen was not lost to some; indeed, it appeared very obvious to his brother Nihim, who was seated at a low table some cushions down, and to bin-Sutus, who relaxed alongside Nihim. Both men whispered carefully to one another from time to time, remarking on Agors's apparent fascination with the queen.

Nihim observed, "It does not seem that our court has quite accepted the Athadian queen as a diplomat. They appear to look upon her only as a woman elevated, as though she were pretentious, or unusual."

"Agors, I suspect," commented bin-Sutus, "apprehends some trick."

"Does he?"

Bin-Sutus nodded cautiously. "Although I explained to him that such is not the truth."

Nihim sighed. "Nevertheless . . . my brother is a crafty man. Of course he perceives that quality in others."

When the entertainments were finished, Agors ordered the late refreshments brought in; and, in accordance with the custom of the eastern court, he invited Queen Salia to join him at his table. She accepted graciously and rose from her chair to be guided by servants to the *Ghen*.

Lord General Thomo and Lord Sirom, who sat with Salia, moved to their feet as the queen did. Thomo, in a low voice, warned her: "Have a care, I beg you."

Salia faced him. "What do you mean, Lord General? Is there some problem?"

"The *Ghen* is—" He searched for words, uncertain how to phrase what he meant in the moments before Agors's servants reached them. "Be . . . honest with him. Confound him, my queen, with your honesty."

Salia smiled. "Do you mean to tell me that mere honesty and truth will perplex this man?"

"Yes. . . ."

Salia would have made some reply, but the court servants stepped before her and bowed low.

Thomo and Sirom watched as she was led to the *Ghen*'s dais. Sirom whispered: "Well . . . she is not a fool, at least."

"Perhaps our trust would be better consolidated," Thomo breathed, "if she *were* a little more foolish."

As Salia was taken to Agors, the entire court seated around the hall rose to their feet, attentive and properly respectful—although it annoyed many of the men to see this woman of the west treated as though she were the equal of any man of state. It was apparent, however, that Agors was proffering Queen Salia every benefit and assistance that a *Ghen* might allow a visiting potentate.

Salia smiled at Agors and thanked him as she was seated to his left. The *Ghen* made pleasant small talk as trays of fresh fruit and cool wines were brought around. The entire hall relaxed as new, lighter diversions were brought onto the floor. The first was a group of trainers with trick animals.

Salia watched as the dogs jumped through hoops of fire, as the chirping monkeys—dressed in miniature clothes—swung back and forth on trapezes and climbed up and down ladders.

Agors, fingering his wine goblet, commented: "I understand that you brought with you some animals of your own?"

Salia faced him, eyes bright. "Oh, yes. My pets."

"You enjoy animals?"

"Oh yes. Animals, King Agors, are like innocent children. And they're very pretty. They're . . . perfect. Haven't you ever noticed that?"

Agors didn't answer; he moved his eyes from Salia to the entertainments. But as the queen did likewise, the *Ghen* looked back at her and slyly studied her profile, and wondered about her. Why did she seem able to laugh so easily? The wine?

As the animals were taken away and the floor given over to a troupe of musicians, Salia's humor lessened and she began to ask Agors more pointed questions. "I don't mean to offend," she explained, "but you must understand that only open talk between our two thrones can eliminate any misunderstandings."

"I quite agree," Agors told her.

"Could you explain to me, then, why your father felt it important to dismantle our Temple here, in Erusabad?"

Agors was momentarily taken aback; he took a sip of his wine, then thoughtfully replied: "Are you religious, Queen Salia?"

"Religious enough to understand that your action has caused great concern in my empire."

"If I tell you that . . . we did not mean to offend you by that action, I would be untruthful. But we did it less to hurt you than to elevate ourselves. Remember that we took great care in relocating everyone living in the Temple, we moved the icons and religious tools to a new location, we did not loot it, and we kept the path open for all visitors and pilgrims."

"That still doesn't answer my question."

Agors was very interested in this woman. By way of further explanation, he reminded Salia of the Salukadian concept of the world's sympathetic relationship with human society: *sharu-n' ghen har nh owni*—"as the king, so the world."

"That is why you desecrated our Temple?"

"It was looked upon, this 'desecration' you speak of, simply as an ornamental thing, a symbolic act, done for its effect upon *our*

304

people. In this way, my late honored father could show the people of Erusabad that our claim upon this city was an actual one, and complete." He was surprised that Salia was not more upset with this conversation than she was; was it only an impartial inquiry for her?

"But then, with the death of your late honored father—"

"We made obeisance to his shade for a period of one month, yes," Agors finished for her. "Symbolic, if you will—but true in the way that symbols are true. And with my welcoming you here, you see, my people are very much aware of another aspect of the *sharu-n' ghen*—I accept the west and do not mean it any harm. In fact, my world accepts your world, and harmony can be maintained."

Salia smiled, gratified, and sipped her wine.

Agors asked her: "May I now speak frankly with you?"

"Yes, of course . . . by all means."

"Without intending any disrespect, may I tell you that I suspect your king sent you here to . . . well, perhaps 'ridicule' is too strong a word."

Salia was hurt by this; her eyes narrowed coldly. "Such was not the case, honored *Ghen.*"

There was no tone of apology in Agors's voice as he told her: "I would trust not. But regard this from our perspective, if you will. My people do not, as a rule, look upon your sex as being equal in political matters with our men; our men have traditionally dominated our way of life."

"Perhaps," Salia replied, obviously irritated by this slight, "you may begin to change your ways." She watched Agors as she said this, and it came to her that she should modify her intent. "I mean no disrespect, honored *Ghen*, but I assure you that my husband sent me here not to ridicule you, because I am a woman, but to impress upon you that as a woman, and as the queen of Athadia, I am as competent as any court minister or diplomat to accomplish what is needed."

"I understand this . . . I can understand that King Elad would mean for us to understand it in this way. But we must be honest with one another. I want to show you all graciousness, and I want to remove all doubts from my mind. You see, for Athadia to send a woman here as an official diplomat—such a thing may be accepted in the west in a certain kind of attitude, but it is accepted differently here. This must be taken into consideration."

"As true as that may be, *you* must take into consideration *our* intentions—just as we must allow for your customs."

Agors nodded politely. "I agree. To be frank . . . King Elad could have been aware that he was committing a possible offense, and deny it, yet still accomplish it. You understand? Two men, practicing with their arms, may declare that they do not wish or intend to wound one another, and yet realize that despite their denials quite obviously they *will* wound one another when they engage one another with their weapons."

"I understand," Salia replied slowly.

"To deny it is only to deny the obvious appeal of it, not the possibilities of the act. A man can be dishonest about his honesty—say no, but mean yes."

"But I, King Agors, can say yes, even if my husband says no."

Agors stared at her. He wondered if their conversation had suddenly slipped into another area; looking into Queen Salia's eyes—

She turned to watch the musicians.

—he decided that it was not entirely impossible.

"Please do not be offended by my honesty," he reiterated.

Salia swallowed a breath, eyed him once more. Her look softened. "I am not offended," she assured him.

"This puts my mind at ease."

Salia's look lingered. Agors was quite handsome, very proud and imperial, betraying none of the vacillating characteristics that sometimes marked Elad's own personality. She nodded at the *Ghen's* wine cup, saying to him: "Drink, honored *Ghen*. Why don't you smile? My father, too, is a king, and he taught me that to smile in a desperate situation, or an uncomfortable one, is to conquer it."

Agors's reaction was immediate; the insight of this, and the sincerity of Salia's trust in it, worked like a wine on him. He showed his teeth in an open grin and chuckled so loudly that his brother Nihim, bin-Sutus and others nearby glanced at him, wondering what Salia could possibly have said to so enliven the young *Ghen's* usually mirthless solemnity.

Salia returned her attention to the musicians—but she felt Agors's eyes upon her.

Agors *ko-Ghen* had expressly requested of Lord General Thomo that Khamar guards be placed in that wing of the Salukadian palace where the Athadian visitors were to reside—

306

this, to allay any suspicions, to allow the westerners the privilege of their own guardians in a foreign place. It was a gesture which Salia found comforting that evening, as she returned from the Feasting Hall to find four palace guards dressed in Athadian gold-and-scarlet and standing erect just outside her sleeping chamber door.

Agors, too, had ordered three servants to Queen Salia, and she found them waiting for her when she came into her spacious chamber. Two were menials, young women who hovered like nervous butterflies, ready to help Salia undress, eager to pour her tea or dim her lamps. The third was a middle-aged woman, educated, well-dressed in silks and jewels—one of the palace residents who in her younger years had serviced courtiers but had now graduated to a more responsible position. It was this woman who greeted the queen of Athadia as she entered and inquired as to what Salia might desire for the evening.

"A bath. And then, if you aren't too tired, perhaps you and I could converse for a while in *Hasni*?"

The elder servant-woman bowed her head, as the two younger ones hurried to prepare the small bathing chamber in an adjacent room.

Salia moved to a low table set against the wall beside her bed; on it she noticed a silver tray and on the tray a single yellow rose. These had not been here earlier in the evening before she had gone into the Feasting Hall. As she set upon the table the gifts that had been given to her by the Salukadian courtiers, Salia asked of her servant-woman:

"Why is this rose here?"

"Queen of Athadia, I believe that my lord the honored Agors *ko-Ghen* had it sent here for you."

"How very nice of him," Salia smiled, and began to undress.

"The yellow rose," the woman told her, approaching to help Salia undo her various pins and buttons, "is significant."

"Oh?"

"It is a symbol, to us, of strength-in-beauty . . . beautiful strength."

Salia smiled more fully—and reconsidered the lingering looks Agors had lent her all evening in the Feasting Hall. . . .

4.

Watching him in the early morning light, as he slept, was one of the great joys of Orain's life. This morning, as she lay beside Adred, she playfully blew on his face and watched as he twitched and blinked in his sleep. Looking at him, she was reminded of Dursoris—Dursoris, as he had looked asleep, gentle, with great good in him, full of hidden woes and truths, a man to face what others refused to recognize. A man like that, sleeping as comfortably and ignorantly as a child . . . Orain smiled, feeling complete and reassured in her love for Adred, in his for her.

But it was time for her to go. It had become a habit of hers every morning, whether she spent the night with Adred in his room or he slept in hers—in the morning, just at dawn, she would return to her own bed, or awaken him and remind him to return to his own chamber. He'd often made gentle fun of her for this, but Orain refused to compromise or apologize for her little virtuous quirk.

She threw back the covers, swung her feet to the floor, crossed to the chair where last night she'd deposited her robe and slippers. As she pulled them on, she heard Adred mutter from the bed:

"Lovely. Simply . . . lovely."

Orain grinned at him. "Shhh, you. Go back to sleep."

"Go back to sleep?"

"You need your rest."

"I do, do I?"

"You were tossing and turning all night."

"Was I?"

"You were," she told him. "You can't call that sleeping."

"How come you don't need your rest, then, if you were watching me toss and turn all night?" He smiled mischievously.

"Just roll over and close your eyes." Orain drew on her slippers and moved through the dimly lit room, heading for the antechamber that led to her apartment.

"Breakfast?" he called.

"When you get up."

"I am up."

"Oh, Adred . . ."

He listened to her open and close the door, then rolled over and dozed off again. When he awoke the second time it was to the sounds of birds outside and to bright sunlight patterning the thick glass squares of the lifted window.

Adred washed at his stand, dressed in his cool, loose-fitting trousers and a linen shirt, pulled on his boots and made his way out into the hall. When he knocked on Orain's door, one of the servants informed him that she was breakfasting with her son in his room. Adred continued down the hall; Galvus had his door open to take advantage of the breeze coming through the open balcony.

Adred was in a good mood, but faces were glum around the small table where Orain, Galvus and Omos were seated. Adred helped himself to the hot tea and a piece of freshly baked brown bread and honey before commenting:

"I see the sun rose again this morning. What do you think? You think that's a good reason not to be so grumpy this morning?"

But no one at the table smiled. Adred glanced at Orain, then faced Galvus as the young man told him:

"If you listen very carefully, you can hear the First, Second and Seventh West Legions marching down to the docks, getting ready to board ship and sail east."

Adred neglected his tea. "Emaria?"

Galvus nodded. "They're to meet the Twenty-sixth West in Galsia and join the other four legions already on the border. It's gotten very serious, very fast—just as we knew it would." When Adred didn't say anything: "King Nutatharis is dead."

"*What*?"

"It's not substantiated—but that's the report from the field. It could be a lie, or a scheme; it could be wishful thinking; then again—it could be true. But Elad's acting upon it, just to be certain."

"Dead?"

"Think of it," Galvus said grimly. "His whole country's starving, all that's left are peasants and the army. They're fighting one another for food, and the refugees are beginning to spill over into our territories in larger and larger numbers."

"Surely someone's on the throne. Some aristocrat or—"

"Emaria was a military state; any aristocracy or nobility were members of the army. Nutatharis kept them loyal with regular purges. We're talking about a country small in numbers, in its leadership: what fills one office, here, ran that entire nation. Power-mongers. If someone *is* in authority, we don't know yet

309

who it might be. And if there was a takeover—well, given the nature of the men of rank in Emaria . . ."

"Gods!"

Orain shook her head, reminded Adred sadly: "Your bread's going cold."

Galvus leaned to one side and pulled from his vest pocket a letter; he passed it over the table to Adred.

Adred took it, opened it, read it—and paled. "Not . . . Bors."

Galvus nodded. "Convenient, isn't it?"

"Galvus, you bought that land, you *own* it! Vardorian promised us that he'd protect everyone inv—"

"Vardorian has enough troubles of his own; keep reading. See what he says? Sulos," the prince said dully, tapping a fist on the table. "Sulos, Sulos, *Sulos*!"

"And—" Adred got a frightened look in his eyes. "And Elad? What's he done about it?"

"Believe it or not, he hasn't sent in the army. Yet. So far, he trusts Vardorian to continue mediating."

"Thank the gods!"

"I don't think the gods really care very much, Adred," Galvus smirked. He looked at his mother. He was thinking of a morning of terror and raw blood, and days and nights of hunger and cold and loneliness in wide fields, while people complained, while armor gleamed in torchlight, while human lives screamed as they died. . . .

In Lasura, mounted soldiers chosen by Sir Jors led thirty cartloads of grain out of the capital and down wide dusty roads into the countryside, where weak people unable to crawl waited, and waited, for the rumors of fresh grain and new bread to take life—grain and bread to be delivered by the king whose name they did not know, whose face they had never seen.

Thameron, humorless and humble, stood that morning on a balcony of his palace and looked down at the desolate streets. Memories surged. A knock on the door announced Sir Jors; the man entered with word of conditions to the east.

"Kurus approaches?"

Jors nodded curtly. "He must move quickly, with whatever men he has with him. The rumors are spreading that Nutatharis has been deposed and his throne usurped by a nobleman who is feeding the people."

"How soon will he reach Lasura?"

"Difficult to say. At last report he was tens of leagues to the east. At the pace he's been moving, it may be three or four weeks before we see his steel."

"Send word to him—" Thameron moved to a desk, took out a length of parchment, dipped a pen in an ink gourd and scribbled a message. He signed it with his name, titleless, but pressed both palms onto the empty margin beneath his scrawl: his palms left the imprint of his marks, the intertwined crescent moons and the inverted seven-pointed star, just as though Thameron had applied them with a heated metal seal. He rolled up the parchment, tied it quickly with a purple ribbon and approached Sir Jors.

"Your fastest rider," he commanded, "with a standard of truce."

Jors slapped his chest. "Done already."

"And if Kurus rejects this," Thameron continued, "and will not meet with me to discuss terms—have we an army large enough and loyal enough to confront his rebel forces?"

The minister smiled. "Enough," he assured the sorcerer. "Enough—and, I'm sure, enough men and women with filled bellies to help our soldiers."

"Perhaps. . ." Thameron allowed. "Now—find your rider."

Sir Jors saluted him again and hastened to the door, exited loudly. Thameron, alone again in the angled sunlight of the tall chamber, stood quietly; he lifted his hands and stared at his palms, while a thousand thoughts rode through his mind. He strode to a table whereon sat wine and fruit and bread and sweetmeats.

Deep in thought, he did not hear the movements behind him, nor sense the quick muffled sounds that breathed in the small archway across the room. Thameron sipped his wine—felt a vague presence behind him—then gasped as something suddenly punched him in the back.

Thrown forward, the sorcerer grasped the table, dropped his cup; blood shot from his chest, dripped from the bronze-tipped arrow that protruded from his leather jerkin.

Snarling, he turned, his fierce yellow eyes burning brightly, seeking out the archer. Footsteps shuffled, and a tall man dressed in wool and leather came forward; he lifted the bow he carried and dropped it to the floor. It clattered loudly.

Thameron held himself erect. He whispered: "Fool . . ."

"I had to attempt it."

311

"You know better than this, Eromedeus." Grunting, Thameron grasped the shaft where it pushed from his chest and snapped it; he threw the pointed end away from him, then reached behind with his right hand to yank free the feathered half. The splintered wood made a moist sucking sound as it was pulled, and fresh drops of blood erupted as it came out. Thameron held it before his eyes, frowning: runes had been carved into the shaft, ancient symbols of death. With a grunt he discarded it; the broken arrow skipped on the flags, making hollow noises.

"Stupid."

"I thought certainly that those signs would destroy you the moment the arrow pierced your heart," Eromedeus confessed.

"Use evil to slay evil? You are wiser than that."

"Nevertheless . . . I had to try."

Thameron shook his head, smeared the blood on the front of his jerkin; already the wound had stopped dripping. "I am now as deathless as you, undying one—until the hour of unmercy comes down upon us." His eyes glowed like smokey lamps. "Why did you come here?"

"Not to stay. I won't let you lay your hands on me again, evil one. Cursed I may be—but I won't allow myself to be damned. I will wander on, and warn the world what a king rules in fallen Emaria."

"The world will not listen to you, Eromedeus; they'll only ask if the rumors are true. They wait to be persuaded. 'Is there grain enough in Emaria to support the world?'"

"Is there, Thameron?"

"Be certain of it; evil always satisfies immediately. I create grain from dust; I make wine from water . . . from spittle."

"While men beg you for more. Always—more."

Thameron grinned. "They are only being men. I am Evil, spiritless one—I am the Evil. I am two spirits in one flesh. I understand what they wish, and why, and I supply it. You are vacant." He grunted with disgust. "Shall we discuss these things more? How will you warn men of my evil? They will not heed; they are hungry, they do not want honesty. Watch and see. For when their bellies are full of grain, and their minds with the glory of it all, they will become proud and vainglorious: they will ask me to give them the world."

Eromedeus turned away. "Time hastens. . . ."

"Begone from here!" Thameron warned him. "Begone from me, now. I'll excuse you one stupid, noble gesture, Eromedeus—

but go now, or I'll chain you down. Undying one, I'll torture you so foully you'll wish you had a screaming soul to comfort you."

"Aye . . ."

Thameron laughed. "The man in me is gone," he said simply, easily. "Who was that mortal child? Do we live by our decisions, Eromedeus, or by our associations?—our convictions, or our stations? Listen—you can hear them now. Yes, time hastens; it hastens with the pull of its own tidal end. There are not many dawns left for you to travel, wandering one. Do you feel the footsteps of humanity hurrying . . . hurrying?"

"I feel them. . . . They may yet pause in their tread, and step away from the chasm, step away from the abyss that lures them."

"Then go, and warn them if you can, for the things of man outstrip men themselves. They stare into the abyss . . . and that abyss glares back at them. Humanity will not listen to you, Eromedeus. Go—find the soul that will free you at last. And as you are freed, listen to the thunder of the night, as it comes down for man: for it will be the thunder of your birth and your death, all in one moment."

"Your death, too, Thameron."

"Thameron is dead already, and the thing that holds him—it is deathless. . . ."

In Hilum, a manacled Asawas was brought up from his cold lightless cell and led by his guards into the presence of Seraficos, the Inquisitor. As he stood before the prelate, the prophet's demeanor was relaxed, almost ambivalent. This seemed an irritant to the richly robed Seraficos—more arrogant than a defiant attitude might have been.

"I have received word from the government in Athad, rabble-rouser. The king's high minister wishes to question you and bring you before the Seat. I want you removed from my city as quickly as possible. Therefore, passage has been arranged on board a cattle ship leaving Hilum this morning."

Asawas looked at him.

"Have you anything to say to me, on your behalf, or in your own defense, before you're taken out of this city? Speak up, if you have a mind to; every paper will be forwarded to King Elad's court."

Asawas was silent for a moment; then he spoke simply, reminding the Inquisitor: "When at last you realize the Truth, Seraficos, it will terrify and astonish you with its completeness. You will not be damned, false one—you will be embraced."

313

The Inquisitor colored. "We shall see," he growled, "who is damned, and who is embraced, lawbreaker." To Asawas's guards: "Take him out. Lord Abadon waits with a coterie of troops to escort him to the docks."

The soldiers saluted and turned Asawas around, led him clanking and shuffling out the door, down the wide winding stairs of the Temple, and out into the brilliant hot sunshine.

Blinded by the brightness after his prolonged imprisonment in the cellars, Asawas blinked and bent his head to one side until he became accustomed to the day. Before the Temple he was turned over to Lord Abadon, who was seated on a tall white stallion. Abadon immediately dismissed the guards and, handing a thick bundle of papers to the captain in charge of the escort, saluted the dozen mounted soldiers and watched silently as they undid the heavy chains at Asawas's ankles and positioned him in the center of their horses. Then, six on each side of the prophet, they began walking him through the streets.

Abadon, evincing no emotion, watched the brown robe as it disappeared in the confusion of horseflesh and glittering armor.

Asawas, head bent, arms heavy, thought at first that he was ill or suffering because of his sudden expulsion from the cold damp into the warm day. But then he realized that he was not ill; he realized that the sounds he heard were not only his own beating heart, not only the dull steps of horses' hoofs biting the cobblestones and bricks.

They were the sounds of the earth.

Groaning . . . moving . . . breathing . . . changing . . .

Asawas drew in a gasp, listened, and heard. All around him, crowding the horses as the soldiers passed down the street, people began jeering and taunting the criminal. The people of the city . . . the people of the earth . . .

As the earth, to Asawas's senses, groaned and moved and breathed—changed . . .

5.

Early in the month of Isku the Fish, when Queen Salia had been in Erusabad for less than one week, the Athadian diplomats finalized certain terms and agreements with the Salukadian court regarding the general responsibilities to be shared by the two empires. Those mercantilists and others who, following the occupation of Erusabad, had initiated trade agreements and business rights, conferred with the queen's diplomats to reach comprehensive accords with the eastern government. Thus, as a hot summer filled the Holy City with bright sweltering days and humid nights, the lamps burned late, wine cups were emptied and replenished, lighthearted jests were traded, and two empires that had been divided, and had divided the world between them, came to mutually agreeable accommodations.

Queen Salia had done all that had been required of her, and bin-Sutus had assured her that her presence had been most welcome in the court. Still, when she sat alone in her chamber and stared at the vase of yellow roses—one for each day since her arrival—the queen felt her discomfort grow, and she did not feel relieved at the thought that soon, within a few days, she would take leave of the Holy City and the eastern *Ghen* who, almost wordlessly, almost invisibly, had come to dominate her thoughts.

Queen Salia was frightened.

Frightened by feelings strong within her, urges and curiosities that she did not quite wish to quell.

In an early hour of the afternoon, with her servants away and her chamber faintly incensed, dressed only in a light robe that allowed the transparent breezes to cool her, Salia of Athadia admitted Agors *ko-Ghen* into her apartment. He was all leather and bronze, and dark-eyed; his attitude anticipated her own inclinations.

"Perhaps," Agors told her, as he stared at her, "it would be necessary for you to remain in Erusabad a while longer, after your ministers and diplomats have gone."

"That would argue some pretext, honored *Ghen*."

"I am an emperor: what I command will be done."

"What purpose could there be in my remaining in Erusabad even a day longer than necessary?"

"That depends, does it not, on what one considers a necessity? My capital, Ilbukar, for instance, is a beautiful city, full of colors and noise. It is not old, like this city: it is new, fresh and alive. There is much trade there, much coming and going. Perhaps you would care to witness that—visit my world, before returning to yours."

"Perhaps . . ."

315

She was standing by a window, looking out—as though that window, with its view, might somehow be a mirror for her. The light of the window revealed her body beneath her robe. Agors noticed; he walked to Salia and stood beside her. She did not face him as he came; indeed, she seemed to tense, her figure tightening visibly as he stepped toward her. The *Ghen* noticed, too, her nervous hands; he remarked her coloring cheeks; he interpreted how intently she scrutinized the window sill.

"Why," Salia asked, still not facing Agors, "have you sent me roses every day?"

"I do so with respect. You are beatiful and strong; the yellow rose is beautiful and strong."

"Now you mock me."

In answer, Agors lifted a hand and touched her hair. Brushed her neck. Reached to stroke Salia's face . . .

She turned, then, alarmed, frightened—perhaps shamed. Her eyes flared, but her voice was bitter as she repulsed him.

"Do not touch me, honored *Ghen*!"

"How I misread you? Do I not understand what speaks between us?"

"There are many things between us."

"Forgive me." There was a note of disappointment in his voice, edged with that slight anger that was always a part of him.

Salia swallowed a shuddering breath. "I . . . should ask your forgiveness. But do not misread my confusions. . . ."

"Queen of Athadia . . ." Agors muttered darkly. "Yellow . . . rose. I salute you." He slapped his chest in a mockery of Athadian custom. "You have conquered this city and my court, Queen of Athadia. Surely you realize that? What an insult it was to learn that the west would send a woman as their representative to the endless empire! Yet you came, you have—"

"Do not presume, Agors—"

"Presume?" He grinned at her. "It is you who presume, beautiful woman. How many have been lost to you? How many have pledged their hearts to you? Yet I see in you an errant spirit; you are a prisoner of emotions, Salia, that you cannot express. Or will not express. What do you fear? Indiscretion only? Many emotions, perhaps? Aye . . . there are many things between us: but at this moment, not much more than a space of air."

"You do not see me as a queen, even less as a woman who—"

"Very much as a woman. You understand yourself as a woman, too. But let me tell you that here our women are as disciplined as

316

our men—as our animals are, as our society is. With discipline comes freedom, Queen Salia; but freedom itself will never create discipline. You of the west—what do you know of all this? What poetry do you have? How many hours do you spend staring at sunsets, or watching the flow of water or the lives of insects? What do you understand? For you, everything is obvious and apparent—and not mysterious.''

She stared at him, lips trembling, eyes wide, breath anxious. Was he lying? Or was it that truth, in the east, seemed to be a lie only to western eyes?

"I apologize for desiring you; you are very desirable. Return then to your cold west, where flesh and money are everyone's excuses. I apologize for not worshiping you, for looking upon you as a woman. Return to this king who claims to love you. Because I do not love you; I do not know what love is. But . . . you are very desirable.''

Salia tried to calm herself. "You are . . . very flattering.''

"Who is pretentious now?" Agors laughed at her. "You speak *Hasni* to me, you speak the words of my language to tell me how pretentious I am? You have no discipline; you have only illusions." He glanced at the vase of roses. "Were I to pluck but one petal from Athadia's rose," he commented, "would that diminish the beauty of the rose, or enhance it? Would it then lack, for losing one petal—or would it gain more than it lost?"

Still standing beside her, staring at her, his dark eyes filling her, Agors commanded Salia: "Tell me.''

Trembling, worried, confused but letting something inside her decide, she answered him: "Its beauty . . . would not be diminished. The flower that remained . . . would grow stronger . . . with the lack of one petal. . . .''

"What sorcery is this," Agors grinned at her, "that I command the queen of Athadia?"

"You do not command," she replied quietly, staring at him. "She commands you, by all that she is. Understand that, Agors. You are commanded by the thing you seek to possess. If one petal will not come loose, then you own the rose itself, entire.''

An early hour in the afternoon.

Just beneath the surface of her pale pink-white flesh he saw the bright coursings of blue veins, thin and fragile. It seemed to him wonderful that he could witness those veins beneath her skin: as though he were looking through sunlit water and spying on some

317

secret process just beneath its surface. Spying on some secret life within Salia that defined her, or had possessed her.

Yet when he made love to her, he began to wonder who and what she was, and who and what he had himself become.

Her aroma was that of wild ripe flowers combined with animal moisture: a thick field, fragrant, after a rainfall. The urgency of her made him tremble. The bestiality of her poses challenged him. With tightened muscles and flesh that moved in waves, she moaned like a small bird, thrashed, yelped like a puppy, was one moment trapped and clinging, the next freed and thrown. But her love did not reward him with himself: it swallowed him like some voracious new form of life. It was not her identity that did this, but her elemental spirit: as if her spirit, escaping through her body, had necessarily to create new forms of communication—savoring and exploring. Her spirit—a web, lost in its own tangles, sometimes burned by light, sometimes hidden by darkness. Even when she laughed, the laughter following moans or gasps or pulling suctions of breathless delight, her laugh was only nonsense. Her body's urgent demands and desires seemed more than she herself could withstand—palpitating, flowing, rubbing—and confused him; and her quick pauseless laughs, followed by arching moans before he had time to laugh in answer, vexed him. All bewildering and exciting, but—it was like trying to gauge the responses of animals, trained or untrained, that may suddenly revert to some instinctive snarl or snap.

Agors did not find this entirely pleasurable, having his curiosity and his pride compromised by a woman who had seemed pretentious and aloof, moody and yet playful, but who in his arms was transformed, her inner quarrels with herself undone by her passions. Was it not true that still water grows brackish, where flowing water is full of life and vibrant?

This woman of the west . . . what was she, inside?

Her beauty was enhanced in the afterglow of desire and release: her smile a thing in itself with smeared red lips and white diamonds . . . her eyes deep pools content and sated . . . glowing honey in a woman's shape lying still as though moulded, resonant and damp, moist . . . the rhythm of her breathing like some wafting incense—and the mystery of her was not cured by the passionate release, but only increased.

Agors, lying beside her, feared that he had not accomplished this miracle himself. He wondered, indeed, if he had commanded the thing he sought to possess. Or did not she, in her sudden freedom, in her sudden release, the flowing water, command—

He watched her.

Salia turned her head on her pillow and smiled at him, laughed. . . .

That evening, drawn back to her, Agors visited Salia again.

"*People don't take me seriously,*" she had told Elad. "*They don't think I'm the queen, or even a woman. They think I'm just— that I'm just here.*"

And again, the following morning, in the cool of dawn, he returned to her.

"*You've tried to make me into some other kind of you! You don't know me well enough to hurt me, Father!*"

She spent that day inside, in her chamber. Watching from the window . . . thinking . . . staring at yellow roses, thinking of candles burning . . .

"*I don't like spending all my time inside the palace, when I know the whole world is out there, and I want to do things, and be part of everything.*"

Again that night she and Agors made love. Their attitudes had changed. The challenges they had initially brought to one another had been overcome; love was not there between them, but there remained a kind of freedom—a defiant freedom, the freedom of denial: they did not speak of a future; they did not speak of being together.

"*I wonder if I'll ever love anybody that much,*" she had said to Orain. "*I never thought of myself that way. Loving someone that much . . .*"

Agors pronounced his feelings as though he were announcing a verdict: he delivered his thoughts as though commanding a trained animal. Salia issued her thoughts as if she were a child acting against her parents' counsel. And beyond all this, she told him:

"When we are tired of one another, Agors, I intend to leave. Not to return to Athadia as their queen, but simply to go into the streets as a woman."

He was shocked, but she was adamant. He suspected that her seriousness in the matter was a ploy and that it would pass, that it would be forgotten by dawn.

And even while her ministers and diplomats and mercantilists and lawyers prepared to take their leave from the Salukadian Holy City, Salia stayed by herself and refused to think of the past, did not dwell on the present and tried not to anticipate the future. But memories intruded, memories like swelling hungers assailing the starving man who must not think of food.

319

Sugat, her childhood, her father, a household with a thousand and five hundred servants, poets lauding her terrible beauty, aristocrats vying for her attention—yet, no one to speak to, no one to talk with, and no one with whom to experience things. Her own father, who did not know her, prostituting her to the Athadian throne for his own prestige. *Are you not happy, my daughter?* She had never been happy. *Why do you not laugh at life? Daughter, if you can laugh at a thing, you can control it.* Corpses smile, skulls smile, even as they corrode in the grave: all bones, all teeth and grinning, grinning, mirthful with some private glee known only to those dead and buried.

Freedom . . .

Freedom, to do with herself as she might wish. Even to hurt herself, as she might wish, the way distempered animals tend to hurt themselves, as though with great purpose, in answer to some great scheme.

When Agors visited her that evening, he found Salia sitting nude in the middle of the floor of her chamber very seriously and intently scratching herself, pressing her long sharp nails into her wrists and forearms. She was studying the discolorations, the slight bruises, that resulted. The *Ghen* was shocked.

"Why?" he asked her, kneeling down before her. "Why are you doing this?"

She looked him boldly in the eyes and laughed wildly at him, laughed loudly, and hurriedly helped him out of his clothes. Then, when they made love, Agors discovered that Salia moaned loudly, pleasurably, when he in his excitement happened to hurt her.

Later, she reprimanded him for this, rubbing her breasts and her hips and sides, pointing out to him: "Here . . . look . . . see what you did? You're like an animal. . . ."

A prisoner of emotions, he had told her, that she could not express . . .

The afternoon before the Athadians were scheduled to depart from Erusabad, Queen Salia made her way by carriage to the royal barge docked just outside the Holy City's walls. Lord General Thomo, who was aboard and standing alongside the captain and monitoring the loading of cargo, was surprised to see her arrive. Salia seemed troubled, preoccupied; she did not speak much with anyone and immediately went below into the hold, where her smaller and more precious pets were lodged. Thomo thought it best not to intrude and so allowed her to be by herself; but when

320

the queen came up to return to her carriage, Thomo reminded her that all would be in ready for the leaving in the morning.

Salia replied that that was fine, and requested that Thomo visit her that evening in her apartment in the palace before he retired.

That invitation was not in itself peculiar or inappropriate; yet it caused Thomo some concern for the remainder of the day, although he could not explain to himself why that was. He was, therefore, in an irritable frame of mind when, following a late supper taken alone, he was admitted into his queen's chamber, which was dimly lit and suffused with incense, and was confronted by a solitary Salia, who told him:

"I shall not return to Athad just yet, Lord General."

Thomo paled. "I don't . . . understand. . . ."

"Then I'll repeat myself. I am not returning to Athad tomorrow."

"Queen Salia, this is—" Thomo's astonishment was complete. "I fail to see— What has happened? My queen, have you been threatened? Made a prisoner, somehow? I promise that—"

"No." She did not even smile at the absurdity of that.

"Then . . . why have you decided not to—" He stared at her, confused, astounded. "—not to return—to Athad?"

Salia gave his question much thought and was silent for a long while. Thomo remained standing where he was. Thoughtful, the queen lifted a finger to her mouth; finally she told him, "If I try to explain, you would only misunderstand. As I'm sure everyone will misunderstand."

"But what am I to tell King *Elad* when we return without you?"

She seemed to ponder that. Decisively, then, she informed him: "I will—yes, I will—I will tell you the facts, Lord General, although the facts are not the apparent causes."

"Please . . . just—try to explain."

She nodded stiffly, in control of herself, cool in her demeanor. She had, Salia told Thomo—how would priests explain it?—she had committed a series of indiscretions with King Agors. Yes, Thomo could be shocked if he wished, but he was familiar enough with courtly life, and human habits and desires. And yet this willful romance had little in itself to do with her decision. She had come to feel—

"What of your *duty*?" Thomo interrupted her, becoming impatient, even beginning to anger now that he understood something about her reasons for staying. And he had liked this young woman. . . .

"Don't speak to me of duty, Lord General."

"You are the queen of the west! You have duties to your people—to your husband, to—"

"They are not my people. It seems to me, Thomo, that my duties have primarily been to appear beautiful and to act simpleminded."

"That is not true! You are mightily respected!"

"Am I? By whom? Elad? The people? The court? My father?"

"Don't use your attractiveness as an excuse! You are a woman! You are *queen*!"

"Call me a queen and I'll tell you that I am a woman; call me a woman, and I'll tell you that women have always been given their names by men—so what does the name matter, or the duty attached to it, or the person?"

Thomo was stunned. Was this some sort of protest? Was she trying to martyr herself?

"Whatever I have lost, or will lose," Salia told him, "Elad has gained. It's not that I don't love him; I do, in my own way, as much as I am able to love. But why should I trap myself further?"

"You exchange one trap for another."

"Perhaps. Perhaps the larger cage gives the illusion of freedom, where the small cage does not. In that case, the world is only a cage. But perhaps, General Thomo—and consider this—perhaps I am now truly free. As free as any man or woman can be in this world. Free to make a decision, because of my beauty and my station and my privileges, and all my other traps and cages. And free to live by that decision."

"This is absurd!" Thomo growled. He was shaking; to calm himself he moved to a table and poured himself wine, and as he poured he asked Salia: "Do you do this because the east flatters you? Do you think that somehow there is truth here that you can't find in Athadia? Truth? Freedom? What?—does Agors flatter you? Oh, yes, you say he doesn't matter! Well, my queen, men go to whores and men have relationships with bottles of ale—let me finish!—and they claim those things don't matter, yet they return, time and again! Queen Salia, this is an entirely different world! *Listen* to me, my queen! A week from now . . . a month from now, or a year from now . . . everything could be changed and you'll have only regrets if you make this decision! You can have memories, now. And you can make your decisions later. *Return* to Athad—yes!—and cast back, ponder all this more than you have, in your home climate, and *then* make your choice! But do your husband and your people the dignity of facing them with this!"

"It is not a choice, Lord General. I am not choosing between one thing and another. And I don't care to return to Athad. Why should I prolong this?"

"You're destroying everything you have!" he nearly yelled at her.

"That doesn't frighten me, Thomo, if I *am* destroying myself. But you're confusing who I am with what I am, again. Now, I ask you: if I have found something that gives me more than I have ever had before—and I don't mean Agors—even if that thing is destructive, should I not pursue it? Or should I reject it to live dull, long years and wait for my destruction to come from elsewhere? Shouldn't I grasp this wonderful thing and live brightly, even if for only a short time?"

"What is this 'thing' you wish to destroy yourself with?" Thomo asked her.

"It's . . . whatever it is that I feel," Salia replied. "And it may not truly be destructive, Lord General. It may only be . . . the intensity I have come to realize in myself. Have you never felt such things within you? No . . . of course not. It seems to me that I am less confused than our people of the west are; there, they believe that it is worthy to live long in confusion, rather than to live briefly in understanding. And where *is* the harm if I do this? The empire has managed to survive foreign wars and civil wars, rebellions and starvations, assaults from without and tempests from within. . . . I am first of all myself, and I cannot disown myelf; but I can disown all the pretense that others have heaped upon me. I suppose that if I could point to a 'thing' and tell you that that is why I am staying here, that would satisfy you. Or if I told you that I am staying because of greed, or hate, or something else that's as tangible as a 'thing.' But if I tell you that I am staying only because of myself? Do you really think, Lord General Thomo, that if I stay here, the Athadian empire will somehow be weakened? Or do you think that the empire will take it upon itself to come after me? I know what you're thinking; you need not say it—that this will lead to conflict, that this will lead to war. Well, it will not."

Thomo set down his wine cup. "You are wrong. You sit in a position where you cannot be the person you think you want to be. You cannot act, as queen, freely enough to renounce your queenship. If you desired this, you should not have married Elad."

"If I could change the past with a whisper, I would do it; if I could change what already has happened, though it cause me great pain, believe me, I would willingly allow myself to suffer. But I cannot. Therefore, I cannot make any excuses but only offer my reasons. And I remind you again, though you are threatened by the idea of returning to Athad without me, that I am only a woman, and one not much loved."

"There you are wrong."

"No, Thomo, no, . . . I am not wrong. I remind you, too, of this: that I have never had a home, not even in my own country, because there my father did not allow me to have a home, but only that prison we mentioned, where I was not myself. And I do not have a home in Athadia, but only another prison. Here—I am my own home, Lord General. Don't you think that I can be a queen, and great, alone and by myself without the robes and jewels? Or do you think that I can only be queen, and nothing else, because of what has been put upon me? I have no home, Thomo, other than myself; I have no heart, other than my own. If you try to threaten me by saying that what I do will cause harm to Athadia, then again I tell you that Athadia will only harm itself and use me as its excuse."

Thomo had nothing to say to this.

"I have never been loved, General Thomo: I do not even love myself. What will you say love is? Does Elad love his country? Does Agors love his people? I am not loved, but I can choose with my heart, and now I am doing that. I think that love is only another of those things men have devised, like politics and the gods, to coerce the mind and the body and the soul, to create ideals that fall short of reality. And reality is ideal enough. I have my own mind and soul and body, and I am free; do not speak to me of love or duty for Elad or Athadia." She smiled sadly, then, and looked at him.

The lord general had tears in his eyes.

"What?" she asked him. "You are weeping, Lord General. Do you cry for me?"

He shook his head. "No . . . not for you. Gods help me, Queen Salia, but I cannot cry for you!"

She nodded faintly and looked away. "How strange," she murmured. "Do you know?—I have never shed a tear in my life. . . ."

6.

Is this what the world had reduced itself to? A thousand anxieties and animosities, a thousand trade agreements and carefully phrased compromises, the balance so painfully preserved—and now all of it reduced again, dangerously, to the proud imbalance of two distrustful neighbors, because of a woman's whim? All this, done away with, over some thing as foolish as a woman's whim?

Scowling, Thomo glanced across the table to Lord Sirom. The old aristocrat was nearly asleep; his chin rested on his chest, and the seeping light of dawn coming through the windows grayed his face strangely, making him appear ill.

Thomo, himself, certainly felt ill.

Perhaps it had all been an illusion anyway. Perhaps the two empires were meant to charge one another headlong. Perhaps intransigent Salukadia and intractable Athadia were destined to clash; and if Queen Salia's damnable arrogance were to bring that crisis about, then it might as well be that as much as anything else.

Anything else . . . Thomo brooded. He was still, to this day, surprised that Elad had let the occupation of northern Erusabad, and the desecration of the Temple, go unpunished. Peace at any cost? For the mightiest nation on the face of the earth, with more weapons than it had citizens to use them—more weapons than it had food to eat—to continually barter for peace, when the world seemed so begging for slaughter? Peace, under those conditions?

Then again, perhaps Queen Salia was right. Why should her abdication and self-imposed ostracism lead to war any more than anything else? Surely the empire would not forfeit its safety and security over one madwoman.

But there are advantages to a war, thought Thomo to himself.

That old lie. But the balance was precarious, war had not been banished but only delayed, and always men had found that lie more comfortable before the fact than they did the results after it. Blood. Screams. Piles of the dead. Whole generations sent into red ditches; the faces of loved ones reduced by fire into smoking lumps of charred, knotted waste. Mutilations. Humanity's plunder, all red-dripping from gouged eye sockets. War. War . . .

325

Every man claims to be a man of peace, thought Thomo darkly, until the machinery of war presents itself in a profitable light. *There are advantages to a war.*

No. This did not necessarily mean a conflict. It could quickly become just another episode.

But Thomo feared that a trivial incident such as this could be just the lever to dislodge the fulcrum. Tempers would flare, demands would be issued, questions would be shoved aside and men would lift their swords while invoking justice and love and all the good things, and passions would drown out the heart and mind.

War.

Well, he himself would argue against it as best he could, when he got back to Athad.

But even now Thomo could hear the voices of outrage, he could envision the faces of the indignant and the proudly belligerent, he knew that—

Lord Sirom was staring at him.

Thomo shook his head. He reached for his cup of tea, found that he had emptied it already. He whispered: "I am . . . afraid . . . to return to Athad without the queen."

Sirom sighed. In a voice that sounded loud in the room's full silence, he answered his friend. "But there is nothing else to be done. You can't blame yourself."

"She was my charge, in a way. She was—"

"She was seduced by the—escape of this place. That is all. Look at her—she's a young woman, headstrong, attractive, perhaps a little—" He motioned toward his head with one hand, twirled a finger.

Thomo slapped the table. "Damned be Agors!"

"You can't blame him, either."

"Council will."

"You must present the facts to them."

Thomo abruptly pushed back his chair and stood up, began walking toward the door. But then he paused and faced Sirom. "I should try once more to speak with Agors."

"Why should the monarch of the entire eastern empire lose his sleep to speak with you, a general of the west, over the troubled delusions of a young woman?"

"Is that how you interpret all this?"

"It is. Sit down, Thomo. Sit." He waved a hand.

Gradually, the lord general found his chair again.

Sirom rubbed his face, stifled a yawn and glanced at the windows behind Thomo. "Dawn. Gods, aren't you tired?"

"I *am* tired," Thomo replied heavily, staring at the empty tea cup, "of passions and pride and people flinging challenges at the world, as if the world were there to answer them on their terms. I am *tired* of petulant, pretty young women raised to sit in thrones; I am *tired* of politicians fighting like spoiled children over things that are harmful and dangerous and stupid; and *I am tired*—"

"Restrain yourself, Thomo."

"*Restrain* myself?" he nearly yelled, slapping the table again. "This will bring us to *war*, Sirom! Don't you see that? And war is *useless*! Look at me—a military man!—and I tell you that war is useless! I know war better than anyone, and I can feel war coming the way farmers smell out a storm! Do *you* want war, Sirom? do you—"

"Don't be absurd."

"—want to see shiploads of young men brought into this harbor to be cut up like so much cattle and left in piles in the streets?"

"Don't be absurd; no one wants that."

"It will come to that!"

"I truly don't believe it."

"You don't?"

Sirom shook his head. "We've had wars to settle matters of pride, yes, and wars provoked by stupidities; but something this immense, just by its very size, frightens everyone. If our two empires were to clash—well, it would have happened by now. Long ago. I mean before the occupation and this business with the Temple. You would have sensed it coming; you would have felt it. But we're not involved in politics of war; we're involved in politics of trade. Now these politicians bluster and rant and threaten, but why in the name of the gods would they truly wish to jeopardize everything they now have? Salia, from what you've told me, has been suspect all along; no one seems to hold her in high regard. Her father and King Elad and Council will rant and rave, but after a while things will calm down. Abgarthis or someone will come up with some method of saving face for Elad; things will settle themselves, the west will remain west and the east east."

"You truly believe this, Sirom?"

He nodded sagely. "People in power are always looking for crises; that way, they feel they're accomplishing something. They get their hands dirty to prove something to themselves; then they wash themselves before the crisis actually gets dangerous, and then claim that some great progress has been made. Don't forget, I was here when the Salukadians occupied this city. We had skirmishes in the streets for one day. I'm not a hero; I'm not a general—I'm a politician, a diplomat; and I'd much rather spend my time collecting fine porcelain. And I have no interest whatsoever in getting my hands dirty just to wash them clean again. That didn't lead to war, and if anything might have led to war—name of the gods!—it was certainly *that*, a military occupation of our property! But things are too connected, now; there's too much in the world that *is* balanced, and sensible, for men to throw it all away and spend years fighting a war. Because any clash between Athadia and Salukadia, if it weren't somehow settled instantly, would continue forever."

"You believe men are rational, then?"

"Not always; not consistently; and not all of them. But enough of them, and enough of the time, not to allow an internecine conflict to occur. Mark me: If Council and Elad scream loudly enough, Agors will see to it that Salia is delivered directly back to Athad. Do you really think that the *Ghen*, of all men, is going to go to war over a woman?"

That comment brought a brief smile to Thomo's lips. "*That* sounds the right note, yes, Sirom."

The old man nodded. "I think you misread the reactions of the courtiers here. They don't care to discuss this with you, but that's not because they consider it a momentous event to be handled with caution; rather, this is something so trivial that they can't be bothered with it. A beautiful young woman, far from home, a child on her own for the first time, and doing something like this? A reason for *war*? You're being alarmist, my friend. I understand your reasons—but your fears are misplaced."

"I hope so." Seeing things in this light, Thomo calmed somewhat.

"The only problem with these monarchs and rich people," Sirom allowed, "is that their personal lives intrude upon our lives, just because of the positions they acquire. It's a nuisance. But storms always blow over. The benefit is that they're entertaining; they can act like fools—you and I excepted, of course!—and even though we know we're just as foolish, it's much more enjoyable to see someone who demands our respect—well, to see him thumping the table and calling out high-mindedly to the gods while everyone else chuckles at the hole in his pants."

Thomo was amused by the image.

"You're tired," Sirom assured him. "Go back to Athad," was his advice. "Don't try bothering Agors or bin-Sutus with all this; everyone here knows how absurd it is. By the time you get back to the capital and breathe some fresh air, you'll see all this for the nonsense it is. And by that time the queen will have thought it all out and decided to go home. Elad'll send a boat to fetch her, and we'll all have much to talk about this winter. Leave now; go on, go on. Take a galley and get to Athad before all these shocked businessmen create a fuss. You can't do anything more here, and now that I know the facts, I can manage."

Thomo sighed, leaned back in his chair, then stood up.

"Go on," Sirom insisted. "Get a boat and get away from this mad city. It's too hot here, and too crowded, and no one speaks a civilized language, and there's no fresh air. All these damned flowers and this incense and animal dung."

Thomo moved for the door. "Thank you, my friend."

"I'll forward a dispatch to you instantly, as soon as Queen Salia changes her mind. And don't be surprised if my letter reaches Athad before you do."

Thomo smiled and reached for the door. "I will come back to Erusabad," he promised Sirom, "to return Queen Salia to her husband."

"Then I'll see you shortly."

In his palace, Agors had not rested either, all night long. bin-Sutus was propped on a divan in a corner of the chamber, sleeping; but Nihim was at a window staring out at the lifting gray dawn. He was furious with his brother and angry with this turn-of-events. He had intended, himself, to speak with this queen of the west and make her aware of just what she was doing. But for now, Nihim could not argue more with his brother: his voice was hoarse, and there was no way of stopping the Athadians' return, nor of changing Salia's mind in the brief time remaining before those ships sailed out.

But Nihim, still not comprehending fully *why* his brother was allowing such a thing to occur, turned from the window and asked him again, as he had asked him a thousand times that night: "Why?"

Agors, irritated and defensive, proud and ambiguous, resolved his brother's persistent and deliberate thickheadedness by pointing to a table across the room. An *usto* board and playing pieces were set on the table.

"There," Agors growled.

"*Usto*?" Nihim did not understand.

"Yes. *Usto*. We are playing this game with the west, my brother. Think of it in those terms. And in playing this game with them—why, I have just . . . raped their queen."

The journey to Athad was misery for Lord Thomo. It was the middle of the summer and sweltering hot; and he was virtually alone on the galley aside from the crew (because of the great priority of his mission). Flies and gnats collected and buzzed incessantly; gulls and plovers circled the ship ceaselessly, raising their tireless chorus; and Thomo had nothing to do with his time save brood continually over the purpose of his sailing. Five days out, and he knew that the well-meaning Lord Sirom had been wrong—well-intentioned and rational, but wrong. The voyage was not clearing the lord general's mind of anxiety but, on the contrary, with every wave that bore him closer to home, Thomo found himself worrying more and more.

His irritability only increased when, upon making port ten days out, at Ovoros, Thomo was forced to accept another passenger bound for the capital on an imperial duty. The messenger was a young lieutenant who confided to Thomo that the scroll he carried contained very important news concerning the border war against Emaria. Thomo had heard that belligerencies had steadily escalated between the empire and Emaria in the past few weeks; it was the common gossip of the sailors managing his galley, and he had overheard such talk even in Erusabad. This young lieutenant, of course, could not speak in complete freedom of what he knew; but he went so far as to inform Lord General Thomo that rumors which had circulated concerning the assassination of King Nutatharis were true, and that the usurper was now upon the throne. More, a rebel army chief was preparing to confront the new king, and a starving Emaria seemed about to add a troublesome civil war to its list of woes.

Thomo suspected that his attitude in Erusabad had been the right one: the world was going to hell, and war between west and east was only a matter of time.

A day out from Ovoros, an unnatural wonder occurred—a mystery that, for a while, forestalled Thomo's endless worries over Queen Salia's defection. The lord general was upon the forward deck in the morning, alone as usual, when a wind blew up. That was uncommon enough, for the coastal stretch of the Ursalion was rarely reliable for sails in the middle of summer. But the wind came up nonetheless, out of the east, and blew strongly all day; and that evening, it was still blowing strongly. It was so singular an event that the captain of the galley, a robust man whose face had the seamed and weathered tan of a lifetime before the mast, remarked on it during supper.

"You live long enough," were his words, over stew, "and you see everything. Never had a wind like this before in Isku month. Never."

The young lieutenant, thinking the captain's words an exaggeration, said to him: "*Never*, sea master?"

"Is he deaf? What did I say? Never! I've sailed these deeps since I was this high." He slapped the rocking table at which they sat. "We never get eastern winds this strong, and never this time o' the year, never. No reason for it. The trades don't blow this way."

"Helping us along, then, is it?" Thomo half-smiled.

The captain nodded. "She keeps this up, my lord, I figure we've chopped off three days of our schedule. That's how strong a wind this is. That's how strange she is."

Thomo felt disturbed by this; it was too mightily peculiar, and foully timed.

Five days later, when the imperial galley made its second port of call in Suda in Gaegosh, the wind had still not let up, and the captain was utterly astounded. He made it a point to go ashore (even though time was precious) while his men carted stores and repair tackle on board; in a dockside tavern, he talked with a number of other seafarers. He returned in an hour; the galley oared out, then lifted sail, and Thomo asked him what men were talking about in Gaegosh.

"This wind's kept up steady for them as well, all along," he reported. "Hasn't let up, for them or us. Damned strange . . . very, very damned strange, my lord. Live long enough, I suppose . . . She's done damage inland, as well. Blowed the tops straight off some houses; kicked three boats bottoms-up last night. While they were sitting in harbor!"

"That's impossible," Thomo commented, feeling a coldness in his bowels.

"I'd always thought so, but Lart told me that; I know him since we were boys and Lart wouldn't lie to his friend. Should see the rubble in that town—bricks and stones and garbage everywhere, people being pushed along the street like they was kicked by somebody. Be glad you're out to sea, my lord. This damned wind's knocking houses off their sitting-stones, blowing the tops off everything."

Thomo walked away from him. . . .

When they made their way through the Straits of Ithser, plunging through the wide channel shouldered by the Gaegoshan coast on the north and distant Hea Isle to the south, the men of the imperial galley spotted an overturned merchanter out to the west. Two dozen men waved frantically; half the crew was still alive and clinging to waterlogged flotsam. Thomo ordered them retrieved; the galley circled wide and cast out lines, and during the afternoon those still breathing were hauled aboard. This made for a crowded galley, but the survivors of the wreck were grateful enough to have solid wood beneath them, and as glad as children to share in the portions of the lobscouse that the sailors dined on thrice a day.

As the galley tacked north that evening, the wind seemed to follow them.

This was confirmed early the next morning, and the captain, his crew and the rescued merchanter's men all remarked on it.

"Was blowing straight west yesterday this time," the captain commented to Lord General Thomo. "Soon as we make the bend, why, now it's following us and pushing us northward." He squinted at him.

Thomo refused to comment as to there being anything sinister about it; but inside, in his heart . . . "Believe me, Captain, if I could somehow manage this wind, I'd never have asked for it in the first place. Trust me; the longer we take to get to Athad, the happier a man I am. I'm not eager to deliver the news I know to King Elad."

"Uh-huh . . ."

And, just as strangely, when the galley made dock at the capital a scant two days later—and fully a week and one day ahead of schedule for a mid-summer sailing—the great wind died out, and within an hour all that was left of the tempest was a slight breeze, seasonal, weak, and wholly unsinister.

As Thomo took himself from the galley and walked down the heavy boards to shore, he was the recipient of many uneasy stares from those who'd journeyed with him.

"I hope," said the captain to his steersman, "that that gent don't want to be ferried back east again very soon. I don't think this little tub can stand another sailing like this last one. . . ."

7.

Lord General Thomo's arrival in Athad, and his delivery of the facts of Queen Salia's refusal to return to her throne, engendered exactly the consequences he had anticipated. The strange midsummer tempest that had left parts of the capital piled with litter and debris was yet nothing compared to the storm of outrage that followed Thomo's hesitant but honest portrayal of the queen's two-month sojourn in the Holy City.

Telling what he knew in one of King Elad's private offices, Thomo watched the anger build in his monarch. He presented the facts as carefully and cautiously as he could, and dispassionately; and when he had finished answering his king's questions, Thomo accepted Elad's offer to retire to the kitchens and take himself a meal.

The king had spoken in a restrained and very cold voice, and Thomo, as he stepped across the chamber, grieved to see Elad shivering with tension where he sat. The lord general offered a few last suggestions on how the situation might yet resolve itself without endangering the stability that existed between west and east.

Elad said nothing to this.

And when he closed the door to the chamber, Thomo paused a moment in the hallway to listen to the sounds of furniture splitting rawly, the bellowing cries of rage, the furious explosions of glass and pottery, the ripping of tapestries. . . .

"More wine?" Galvus asked him.

Momentarily startled, Thomo looked up. He wiped his mouth with his napkin and quietly nodded. Galvus reached across the table and poured.

He was just about to remark upon something when a slight tap on the office door was followed by the entrance of Lord Abgarthis.

Thomo watched him as the veteran courtier sat beside the prince and, with a wave of his hand, encouraged him to continue pouring into a second glass.

"Well?" Galvus asked.

Abgarthis told him, "He's calmed down . . . at least for the

333

moment. We . . . talked. He insists on treating this as though it were not a matter of national emergency."

"You mean," Thomo inquired, "he considers it a personal matter?"

"Yes."

The lord general appeared relieved.

"But it won't remain that way for very long," Galvus interjected. "Not when the Imbur discovers what's happened."

"That," Abgarthis informed him, "was the purpose of our discussion. How best to handle the Imbur."

Sneering, Galvus offered: "Allow me to make a few choice suggestions."

"We are civilized," reminded Abgarthis, trying to make light of a desperately dangerous situation. "Let us think before we act."

"I hope so," Thomo remarked, lifting his cup to his mouth. "That . . . we're civilized."

Abgarthis glanced at him meaningfully and saw Thomo's eyes, intense and hurting, above the rim of his decorated wine goblet.

"These people aren't going to listen to reason!" Ogodis shouted. "What makes you think they're going to listen to *reason*? They are *barbarians*!"

"No!" Elad yelled back at him, stopping as he paced and staring at the Imbur, then glancing around quickly for something to grab hold of or throw in his rage. "I refuse to think of them as barbar—"

"What are you afraid of?" Ogodis challenged him. "What are you afraid of, Elad? Tell me! You are king of the world! What do you fear from *barbarians* holding your wife *prisoner*?"

Elad stared at him, coloring, choking a response— "*Afraid* of?"

You will live to see the world die in anguish. . . .

He swallowed a deep breath, walked to the one window remaining closed and, despite the chilliness of the evening, yanked open its shutters and pushed up the thick-glassed sash.

"*You* may not have the courage to do what needs to be done, you young man," Ogodis growled, "but I assure you that every ship in my fleet, every sword in my army—"

"Vengeance," Elad reminded him, turning from the window, "has a way of burning like Arimu's torch."

"What are you talking about?"

"Isn't that true, Imbur? Do you remember reminding me of that?"

Ogodis's face settled into a mask of tightened anger, threatened pride.

"Vengeance lighting false doors, false—"

"I'm not speaking of vengeance, now, Elad! I am speaking of *justice*! My *daughter* is being held prisoner! Your *wife*—"

"General Thomo is under the impression—"

"General Thomo is spineless! General Thomo would sit and spin and talk until the sun fell to the earth, and nothing would be accomplished! 'General!' I'd like to know how he gained the rank of General!"

"Damn you! He gained his title for his intelligence—*not* because he pulls out his sword every time he is—"

"Enough!" The Imbur lifted his hands, shook his head, turned and prepared to leave. "Enough, *enough*! I will go in the morning, Elad. And the instant I return to Sugat, I am rousing my fleet and my army and sailing for Erusabad to retrieve my daughter!"

"Don't try to shame me, Ogodis. Don't *threaten* me!"

"*Threaten* you?" He laughed harshly. "By all the gods, King Elad, it appears to me that you, above all men, *cannot* be threatened, *or* shamed, *or* cajoled, *or* forced, or even inspired into doing *anything*! Where is your—" He caught himself as he saw a dark light enter Elad's eyes and quickly amended his words. "Damn you . . ." Ogodis said quietly. "Where is your . . . strong arm, Elad?"

"I used my strong arm once," was the chilly reply. "It brought me only pain."

Ogodis did not understand; huffing, he growled an obscenity, marched to the door and slammed it as he left. As he went down the hall, talking to himself in his hot anger, the Imbur did not see Thytagoras standing in a marbled doorwell, and did not hear him until, passing by, he heard a loud:

"Imbur!"

Ogodis turned, threw his arms behind his back. "Yes?"

Thytagoras motioned him forward.

Ogodis, suspicious, approached. "Well? I am extremely busy, and I—"

"I think, Imbur, that you and I, right now, ought to open a bottle of wine, and go sit in the fresh air for a few minutes, and discuss some things."

Ogodis watched him with a hawk's intensity. "Such as?"

"Such as . . . Have you ever visited the city of Erusabad, Imbur? Have you ever considered what it would be like, to approach the city of Erusabad with—oh, let's say, a heavily armed fleet of warships?"

Ogodis stared at him for a long heartbeat; then: "Get your wine, Thytagoras."

The quiet. The solitude. The ache . . .

Smashed candles . . .

When Abgarthis came to Elad's bedchamber, he entered without announcement to find the young king sitting before an open window staring out at the cool night. Here, too, were remnants of torn tapestries and thrown goblets. Abgarthis decided to ignore them.

"Elad . . ."

The king sighed, rubbed a hand through his hair, did not turn in his seat. "Do you realize, Abgarthis," he asked, "that once something happens, it is never again the same as it was? I mean"—he spoke very quietly—"a thing occurs, or you make a decision, and you think then that you understand it and have put it in perspective. But . . . you really haven't. Time passes . . . as more time passes, Abgarthis, that thing that happened, that decision you made . . . it changes. The perspective you had of it . . . it, too, changes. It never stays the same. Every year that passes puts a new perspective on that thing, and a new perpective on all the . . . perspectives . . . you had on it. It never ends. It's like some continuous, revolving wheel." Elad looked at his adviser then, showing Abgarthis his awfully pained, exhausted face.

Abgarthis coughed gently. "I came to tell you that Council has been summoned. Your lords and ministers await you in the Chamber."

Elad seemed not to hear him. "We live in a cemetery, Abgarthis. Look around. You think you see colors and life, beauty . . . life?" He shook his head. "It's all dead. We're trapped by it. It's all in a process of dying, and if you look carefully enough, you can see all the dead things beneath the living things. Everything is built upon the death of everything else. People . . . animals . . . cities . . . everything out there is dead. Death seems to be the natural thing; life is just . . . unnatural. Impermanent."

Abgarthis felt enormously uncomfortable. What was Elad doing to himself?

"I look out at that city and . . . it does not look nostalgic to me, adviser. It no longer conjures up images of pride, or heritage, or purpose. It all looks—dirty . . . worn . . . used up. My nation is—used up."

"Please, King Elad," Abgarthis reminded him carefully. "Council awaits."

He nodded. Elad had not been drinking; neither was he truly in despair. He was—thinking. . . .

He pushed himself up from his chair, straightened his shirt and breeches, looked Abgarthis in the eyes. "I apologize," he said. "But something very frightening has just happened to me, adviser. I must tell you that. I—Abgarthis . . . I am no longer afraid of the Oracle's words."

The old man felt a chill strike his heart.

"No longer . . . *afraid*. . . ?"

Elad slapped his hands together, lifted his head and made for the door, and the Council Chamber.

O mankind, born in a storm and wandering in a storm—these things that come, they come with cause. . . .

The special session of the two Congresses of the High Council came to order that night, just as the midnight gong sounded throughout the city. The ornate chandeliers that hung suspended from the tall ceiling cast their lambent oily glow upon the assembled tables far below. Servants, roused from their quarters, stood by yawning, filled water goblets and lit table lamps when they went low. Of the forty-two ranking nobles and aristocrats of both congresses, all save one were present: Count Vendasian had fallen ill and was abed in his estate outside the city and so had sent his eldest son, Vensador, in his stead.

Elad ordered a dozen scribes to commence the recording of the session, and after stating the reason for this specially arranged, hurried assembly (a cause known already to every face in the Chamber), he asked Lord General Thomo to take the floor and explain the issues as thoroughly as he could.

In as professional a voice as he could muster, Thomo delineated the facts. Emotions crept through, invariably, and his own opinions; and very often, when something pertinent caused the Councilors to break into abrupt, heated voices, the General paused, cleared his throat, and requested silence to rephrase what he had just said.

When he had finished, Thomo hurried to a table near the throne dais and quickly swallowed a cup of cold water.

King Elad opened the floor for general discussion.

Every hand in the room lifted immediately; every man in the hall wished to have his say instantly. Elad depended upon protocol and recognized members of the Nobility first, in the sequence of their years of service in the hall.

As the lords of the empire took their turns, some expressed outrage, and many were of the opinion that Queen Salia must certainly have been taken prisoner (contrary to Lord Thomo's explicit testimony) and swore that this act by the Salukadian empire must be regarded as the final arrogance hurled defiantly at the throne. Lords Rhin, Falen and Bumathis made high-sounding appeals for armed justice in the name of the empire.

Almost unanimously, every aristocrat there accepted the queen's defection—her "entrapment" in the conquered city of Erusabad— as an open invitation to conflict.

"Shall we offer them our king next?" was the thrust of these opinions. "Shall we offer them everything we have, piece by piece, and still declare that we can live as neighbors with such a people as this?"

And, in a startling reversal of attitude expressed only a few months earlier:

"I believe we must agree that King Elad so far has acted with the patience of a god in dealing with these savages. In the face of all that the Salukadians have done, our lord had sought to remain as responsible as anyone possibly could. I myself—and others in this Chamber—have argued with him over these matters; yet, I can understand why King Elad would argue for temperance over belligerence. I believe his heart has been right—but the circumstances have been wrong!—for this generous mentality. Gentlemen, . . . my friends, . . . how long can we afford to treat the Salukadians as though they are our equals? We give them every patience the empire can muster . . . we are as responsible as we can possibly be . . . and still they defy us and throw our goodness in our faces! Have we not had enough? We are a strong empire and a good people! Is it not time we showed these easterners that we have been patient this long only because we are the most powerful nation on the face of the earth? Hasn't the time come for even the most patient of us to run out of all patience?"

338

When Elad turned the floor over to members of the *Priton* Public Administration, their voices, though more concerned with the domestic effects of the situation, tended to echo the sentiments of the aristocracy.

Just as Elad was about to call for General Thomo to make a final statement, Khamars interrupted the proceedings to escort the Imbur Ogodis into the hall. All rose to their feet; Elad called for the Imbur to come forward, and spontaneous cheers lifted. Ogodis bowed before the throne and begged permission to speak to the assembly; more cheers and table-poundings met this request, and Elad allowed it.

Ogodis spoke quickly and forcefully. He made an appeal to sentiment because the queen held prisoner by the debased and animal-worshipping Salukadians was his own daughter. He made it known that he intended to sail in the morning for his own palace in Sugat, there to hurriedly arrange for his navy to embark for Port Erusabad—an armed navy prepared to make war, if war became necessary. Ogodis then declared that Thytagoras, late and erstwhile captain of the Athadian military forces in the Holy City, who had left the imperial service because of his uncertain feelings regarding King Elad's patient policies (as was well-known), had agreed to join the Gaegoshan forces in their sailing to Erusabad.

This announcement created a pandemonium in the Council Chamber.

Elad cried out for order several times as the Councilors rose to their feet and yelled, hurrahed and called for their king to reinstate Thytagoras and commit the Athadian fleet to just such an expedition.

Ogodis waved his hands wildly, crying out that he had absolutely no intention of shaming or denigrating the Athadian court, but that he had finally lost his patience and was only doing what he felt it had been necessary to do all along.

When at last some semblance of order was restored, an irritated Elad thanked the Imbur for his opinion and asked him to be seated with the nobility. He then proffered a proposal to his collected Council, not that they would decide the issue, but only so that Elad might have as clear an understanding as possible (and have it recorded) as to how the assembly felt regarding this breach of international trust and guardianship.

"My proposal is this," he announced. "That, in alliance with the armed forces of the throne of Gaegosh, the empire of Athadia will arm a flotilla of vessels and call upon her active legions to sail

339

immediately to the city of Erusabad within the empire of Salukadia, there to confront the *Ghen* of the Salukads, to make it known to him that unless the queen of this empire is returned to her people instantly, Athadia will regard this refusal as a declaration of war and will commence the use of military force against the empire of Salukadia and against the Holy City of Erusabad. My lords, may I have a show of hands?"

Arms shot into the air, Councilors rose to their feet, and a general confused babble, strident and emotional, again filled the hall.

Early the next morning, Orain awoke to the sounds of voices in the hallway just outside her chamber. She had not closed her door for the night, but had only pulled her curtain, to take advantage of the cool breezes. Now she heard what sounded like Galvus's voice, and Adred's. She sat up, listening, then moved out of bed and pulled on a dressing robe.

She was lacing the front of it when Adred came in carrying a small silver tray of warm bread, fruit slices, jam and tea.

"Well?" she asked him, as he set the tray down on a table.

"Well. . ." he sighed. He moved to a window, pushed the sash open the whole way and opened the shutters fully. New daylight struck him; Orain saw that Adred looked quite pale and very tired.

She remained standing where she was. "You've been up all night."

"Yes." He nodded stiffly and wiped his face. "Galvus has just gone to bed. I think young Omos cried himself to sleep. . . ."

"Oh, gods," Orain whispered. "Adred . . . Elad—the Council—they were up all night?"

"No; it didn't take them all night. Come, have some breakfast."

"Adred . . ."

He looked at her.

"Tell me, please, what they— Oh, Hea . . ."

He took a deep breath and walked toward her; he embraced her strongly and looked her in the eyes. "Oh, yes, Orain . . . oh, yes. And we can't really say that we're very surprised, can we?"

She was trembling.

"No . . . no . . . we can't really say that we're surprised. . . ."

War.

Came to him then those lines of verse that Abgarthis had shared with him, on the night before Cyrodian's execution:

The prisoning heart that suffocates love—
The sorrowing vengeance that love cannot placate.
Wars of anger, swords of hate:
We have the knowledge, but refuse to learn.
These things that come, they come with cause.

The Fall of the First World
The End of Book II:
Sorrowing Vengeance